Take Whit

The CANZUK At War Series
Book 1

Dedication:

To Grace

You get knocked down. You get back up. Period.

<u>Author's Note</u>: CANZUK is a political and military alliance comprised of Canada, Australia, New Zealand and the United Kingdom.

Prologue

In the near future...

"This is CBC news interrupting your regularly scheduled programming. It is exactly 5:10 p.m. eastern standard time.

"After two years of bitter partisan fighting throughout the eastern half of the former United States, the unthinkable has happened. Approximately one hour ago, the UCSA – the United Constitutional States of America - launched an unprovoked nuclear attack on what is understood to be nine different targets in territories held by the Federation of American States (FAS).

"Based on local reports and preliminary information coming from various sources, the CBC can confirm that five cities – New York, Boston, Chicago, Philadelphia, and Seattle – and four major military installations were subjected to an extensive nuclear bombardment.

"Though it's too early to have any accurate idea of the death toll, experts estimate that anywhere from two to five million citizens living in the cities in question would have died instantly.

"The federal government has issued a brief statement advising that the prime minister and key cabinet ministers have left Ottawa to undisclosed locations and that the Canadian Armed Forces have been placed on high alert."

———

Three Days Later

"Today marks another dreadful day in what could be the single most destructive week in the history of mankind. Only three days after the inconceivable attacks on several American cities by the UCSA or the Red Faction as it is commonly referred, the CBC has learned that the neutral states of Colorado, Wyoming, and North and South Dakota, known informally as the Colorado Alliance, have launched a pre-emptive nuclear strike on the UCSA military

3

installations responsible for the city-ending nuclear attacks that took place only three days ago.

"Sometime early this morning, the Air Force Base at Barksdale, Louisiana, and the naval base in Kings Bay, Georgia, were both subjected to multiple nuclear strikes from re-calibrated intercontinental ballistic missiles launched out of Colorado. Information is also emerging that the Pantex nuclear production plant outside Amarillo, Texas was also struck with conventional weapons.

"Details coming in from the targeted locations are minimal at this time. What we can tell you is that news of the strike came in conjunction with a message from the Governor of Colorado stating that her state had taken the difficult step of neutralizing the two Red Faction military bases for their role in the attack on Blue Faction cities and military bases only three days ago.

"The statement from the governor added that any reprisals from the UCSA or any other domestic or foreign actor toward Colorado would result in nuclear reprisals against the UCSA's twenty largest cities."

———

One year later, The British Broadcasting Corporation

"And our other top story this evening comes out of the former United States. The state of Missouri passed legislation today, authorizing that state's governor to begin formal negotiations for Missouri to join the UCSA.

"This development is seen with angst here in Britain and across the world as Missouri is in possession of one of the world's largest stockpiles of tactical nuclear weapons and the systems with which to deliver them, including the B-21 bomber.

"Military analysts suggest that in gaining access to these weapons, the Red Faction would once again have a strategic and tactical advantage over the Federation of American States, commonly referred to as the Blue Faction.

"It has now been just over one year since nuclear weapons were used in the former United States. Viewers will recall that the State of Colorado neutralized the two UCSA military bases that held the Red Faction's own stockpile of nuclear weapons in retaliation for the UCSA's own nuclear strikes.

The prime minister was said to be in consultation with leaders of the CANZUK alliance and others to discuss this most recent development, but as yet, there's been no official word from 10 Downing."

Chapter 1

Northern Ontario

By anyone's account, the place was a shithole. The bar's furniture was ragtag and duct-taped and if he had to guess, the window that looked out onto the town's main drag hadn't been cleaned in five years. It also had the hard-drinking smell of stale beer and too much bleach. It wasn't that the bartenders and waitresses who worked the place didn't make efforts to do some cleaning, but there was only so much you could do to wash away decades of hard men and their hard drinking.

Jackson Larocque wasn't sure if it was the fifth or sixth day he had been sitting on this same bar stool in this same bar. He hadn't intended to stay this long, but they hadn't cut him off yet, which had not been the case with the first four dives he had visited. He was on the second week of what was without a doubt the biggest bender of his life. Larocque had been on a few before, but never this long and never this dark. But that's the way it needed to be. Up north, alone, no responsibilities, no one to care for, and no one to care for you. It was a liberating feeling, depending on the moment.

This evening's bartender was a woman by the name of Erin. It was the third time she had worked while Larocque had been a paying customer. He guessed she was in her early thirties. Even with the severely hooked nose, she wasn't bad looking. Not in the least. Tall and lean, she walked the length of the bar with an air of competency and a look on her face that said to onlookers, *'Do not piss me off. Not one bloody iota.'*

Toward the end of the second shift that she had worked while he was at the bar, she'd tried to talk to him, but he had politely brushed her off. To his great relief, she hadn't made a second effort.

Larocque had started drinking over the noon hour. Checking his watch, it was just after 2100 hours and was now well on his way.

He'd finish off this third pitcher and a couple of shots of tequila and then he'd stumble back to the motel he'd been shacked up in since driving into town. Once there, he'd get into the rye, watch some hockey, and then begin to time how long it took him to start emptying out his guts.

For the past three mornings, his shit had been loose, black and smelled of the devil incarnate. Pancreatitis? Maybe. Larocque didn't care. He'd stopped giving a damn twelve months ago.

Elbows on the bar, he raised the glass of beer to his lips and took another swig as he heard the crack of billiard balls on one of the two tables in use. As he placed the half-finished pint of Rickard's Red down on the bar, the door opened and three men wearing brightly colored snowmachine gear walked in, talking loudly. It had been snowing steadily for the past two days. This far up north, it wasn't uncommon to see men and the occasional woman driving way-too-fast snowmachines alongside the 4x4 trucks that seemed to be the only type of vehicle being driven in this pissant town.

The three men walked up to the bar and the largest of the three loudly dropped his helmet on the well-worn bar top. "Well, if it isn't Ms. Erin Evans. How have you been, beautiful? And how is it that in this little town of ours we can go so long without seeing one another?" Larocque didn't know the men from Adam, but without a doubt, the speaker's tone was as smarmy as one could get.

Having seen the woman interact with a couple of difficult customers before, Larocque had expected the veteran server to verbally snap back at the man with something of a fiery rejoinder, but all she said was, "What would you like to drink, Grant?"

The man's face took on a scowl. "C'mon, Erin, you don't have to go straight into bitch mode. You don't like me. Fine. But that doesn't mean you can't offer up a smile and a *Hey, Grant, it's been a while, eh?*". It's no wonder all you're doing with your life is working in this place. Why don't you do yourself a favor and watch a couple of videos on customer service? Or maybe swing by one of the dealerships, and I'll see if I can't get one of the receptionists to give you a quick rundown on how not to be so goddamned bitter all the time."

"What part of 'What would you like to drink?' does not meet your definition of satisfactory customer service?" the tall brunette asked in a surprisingly pleasant-sounding voice.

"Whatever," the man said haughtily. "Continue with the cold-hearted bitch routine all night for all I care, but when you get a moment in your busy schedule, do you think maybe you can bring us a pitcher of Keith's? We'll be sitting over there," the man said, pointing in the direction of the booths that sat along the far wall of the tavern.

Arms crossed, she watched the back of the three men as they walked away and under her breath muttered, "Asshole."

Before she could get to work on the 'asshole's' order, Larocque said, "Hey, Erin."

Her head snapped in his direction, "Oh, so you do speak. Well, good for you. I'm busy, or didn't you hear my conversation with the local celebrity over there?"

Being sure to keep a neutral look on his face, Larocque slowly raised his hands in a signal of mock surrender. "Just a second of your time."

Uncrossing her arms, the bartender gave Larocque a hard glare but then started to walk to his end of the bar.

"Listen, I've been a dick for not introducing myself. My name's Jack."

"And would you like another drink, Jack?" she said in a low-toned growl that wouldn't carry over the ambient noise of the bar. "Because that's why I'm here, didn't you know? To serve drunks like you until you keel over, and to put up with assholes like Grant

Kominsky. Just because his daddy owns a couple of car lots, he walks around this town like a spoiled prince. He's a polack piece of shit and he can die from stage four dick cancer for all I care."

"Ouch. Dick cancer, eh," Larocque said hoping he sounded sympathetic. "Listen, you're right. I am a drunk, but you could do me a big fave all the same."

"Oh yeah, I'm all about favors tonight, my now chatty friend. What was your name again?"

"Jackson, but I like Jack."

"Well, Jack, how can I be of service to you?"

"Two things. I'll need a shot of tequila and a pitcher of Keith's with three glasses," he said.

Upon hearing the order, the woman's eyebrows furrowed while she proceeded to take a closer look at him. "Your nose," she said while her hand flicked in the direction of his face. "I dated a guy once who had a nose just like yours. Was a tough guy who played Junior 'B' and then when his hockey dreams went to shit, he moved down south and tried his luck at MMA. He was back here within the year, his face even less pretty. You a tough guy, Jack?"

Larocque stared at the woman standing across from him. "I'm not looking for trouble. I just thought maybe I could help with the customer service in this place. That's all."

The bartender looked in the direction where the three men were seated.

Over his shoulder, Larocque heard the man named Grant pipe up and call across the room, "Hey over there, less talking and more serving. Do I need to call the manager? Does this place even have a manager?" Kominsky said while laughing loudly. On cue, his two friends dutifully joined in on the merriment.

Her gaze moved back to Larocque and after a moment's hesitation, she said, "Listen. I'm gonna go on break. I'll be back in five minutes. Can you keep an eye on the place while I'm out?"

Larocque smiled and then replied, "Happy to."

She moved to grab her purse which was tucked away underneath the bar. She looked at him with her dark eyes and said, "Listen, if there's trouble and you get hurt, I didn't ask you to do anything. This guy is a huge loser, and I don't need to be saved by you or anyone else. I need this job, so if I'm asked, I went out to get some fresh air and I didn't see shit. Understand?"

"Perfectly," he replied.

Turning away from him, she exited from behind the bar and neatly slipped into the kitchen entrance.

In his forty years, Jackson Larocque had many jobs but never that of a bartender. Nevertheless, he got up from his stool, walked behind the bar like he owned the place, and then directed all of his inebriated attention to the task of trying to pour his first-ever pitcher of beer.

"Dude, what are you doing?" Larocque heard from the other side of the bar. Pushing back the draught handle, he looked up and saw the man named Kominsky was standing across from him.

"Hey, there you are. I'm getting you a pitcher of Keith's, just like you asked," he said while forcing a smile onto his face.

He gingerly placed the half-beer, half-foam pitcher on the bar in front of the other man. "Did you want me to bring it over with some glasses, or are you ok to make the trip? You seem like a strapping fella and could manage the load," Larocque said, injecting as much warmth into his voice as he could manage. "I'm having some issues with the keg. Just give me two secs, and I'll have it sorted. Are all three of you drinking?"

"Dude, who the hell are you? No, don't tell me. You're the manager who runs this hole. Look at you," Kominsky said, not making any attempt to hide the contempt on his face. "You look like shit. No wonder this place is a dive. You know what? I had heard that bartender of yours worked in this place and I thought it be fun to drop in and see if she was still a decent piece of ass. You know, I banged her in high school. Oh yeah, me and half the school. She loves to go, but I suspect you knew that already, eh, man?" he said, his chin rising slightly, no doubt looking to encourage Larocque to join him in the classless banter.

"Listen, on second thought, let me finish pouring this and then I'll walk this pitcher over to you and your friends. This one's on me. Go grab your seat. I'll be there in two shakes," said Larocque, inclining his head in the direction where Kominsky's two friends remained seated.

"No, man, I don't need you to pay for my beer. This place looks like it needs the money. Just give me the glasses. I just want to finish this so I can get out of this place. It fucking stinks."

A pleasant smile still forcibly slapped across his face, Larocque reached underneath the bar and retrieved three pint-sized glasses. "Here you go, friend. I'm sorry your experience this evening hasn't met your expectations. We'll try better next time."

"Whatever, dude. There's not gonna be a next time."

Kominsky reached for the glasses, his hand coming down on top of them in an attempt to claw-carry all three at the same time.

As the other man's hand made contact with the rims of the glassware, Larocque's left hand snapped forward and grabbed the collar of the unsuspecting man's jacket. As Kominsky's face transitioned from arrogant to surprised, Larocque slapped him so hard, he winced as his elbow joint wrenched in pain.

As Kominsky staggered back several paces, beer glasses flew off the bar and shattered, making a sound that easily pierced the music and conversations taking place throughout the tavern. If the ten or so customers weren't already zeroed in on what had been transpiring at the bar, they were now.

The smile on Larocque's face changed to a glower the moment his right hand connected with Kominsky's pudgy face. He glanced quickly at the stunned man's friends as he came out from behind the bar. The friends were smaller than Kominsky and were in the process of moving to help their mate. Like Kominsky, one had a rather doughy physique and a look of confusion plastered on his face, while the other was lean and rattish-looking. This second character appeared to have a clearer understanding of what had just happened, which signaled to Larocque that rat-face was the more dangerous of the two and by some measure.

In that instant, Kominsky came to his senses and began to square off with Larocque, his two friends now flanking him left and right. "Dude, are you crazy?" he exploded.

Larocque was now in front of the bar, directly across from the other man. Standing casually, he spoke to Kominsky in an equally casual tone, "Not crazy. Let's just say where I come from people don't shit on other people unless they're given a good reason. As best I can tell, you're being a douche for no reason at all. You don't get to do that. Not in my bar."

It had been a while, but this wasn't Larocque's first bar fight. Not by a long shot. Experience had informed him that it wasn't the one-on-one confrontation you had to worry about when you dropped the gloves in an informal setting. It was what was happening around you that you needed to be hyper-aware of.

To the left of Kominsky, Larocque watched the rat-faced man savagely grab a pool cue out of the hands of an onlooker. The wiry man quickly flanked Larocque to his left and choking up onto the thick-end of the stick, he brought the cue back over his shoulder as a prelude to what looked to be a competent-looking beer league softball swing.

Reaching across his body with his right hand, Larocque pivoted slightly, grabbing the half-filled pitcher of beer still on the bar and threw the golden liquid into the swinging man's face. As Rat-Face yelped, Larocque rotated his torso and raised his left arm in the air allowing the descending pool cue to make contact with his well-developed lat muscle.

Feeling the stinging contact of the wooden cylinder, Larocque's left arm came down and clenched the cue, savagely pulling the lighter, blinded man toward him. Too close for any type of punch, Larocque stepped forward and drove his right elbow into the side of the man's face. At the moment of contact, Larocque heard an audible *thwack* at which point the man's grip on the pool cue went limp and he collapsed to the floor in an unconscious heap.

Pool cue now in hand, Larocque turned back to Kominsky and his other friend. He did not need to rely on his skills as a fighter to see that the local standing to the right of Kominsky had zero interest in making a physical contribution to the melee. Reaching into the pocket of his snowmachine pants, the doughy man pulled out his phone and without missing a beat, hit the button on the screen that would no doubt connect him with emergency services.

As Larocque held the cue and projected a look of disdain at the two men, he listened to the man's conversation with 911. "Yeah, can you send someone to the Last Call Tavern on Main? This crazy asshole just knocked out my friend. He just came out of nowhere. He's a total psycho. I think he may have killed him. Okay, thanks. We'll wait here but hurry. He could do anything."

Larocque couldn't help but roll his eyes. "Your buddy's not dead," he said as he prowled toward the two men. "My bet is that the shifty little bastard has a broken jaw. It'll feel like he was hit by a Mac truck, but he'll come to in a minute or so."

As if on cue, the crumpled man groaned.

As Larocque moved forward, Kominsky and his friend backed up until they were both at the edge of the table at which they had originally been sitting. With nowhere else to go, the soft man who had called the police raised his phone and started to record

Larocque. "When the cops get here, man, you are in shit. So much shit, man! Our dad owns this town."

Lightning quick, Larocque rotated the pool stick clockwise and brought the slender end of the cue's shaft down on the same wrist that held the dough boy's phone. The cue shattered at around the sixteen-inch mark forcing the smaller man to issue a pained yelp just as his cell careened from his hand and made a cracking sound as it hit the bar's gritty floor.

"'Our dad.'" Larocque repeated the man's words out loud as he turned his glare at Kominsky. "You're brothers, then. Go figure.

"I bet you two have been terrors in this town for quite some time." Larocque focused his glare on the Kominsky who had kicked off this mess. "Junior here seems to think daddy's upstanding position in the community is gonna somehow hold weight with the local detachment, but from the look on your face, you're not quite as confident."

Kominsky said nothing and only stared back at him with bloodshot, hate-filled eyes.

Larocque was now less than two feet away and could smell the alcohol on the other man's breath. As he stared back into Kominsky's eyes, he brought the thick end of the pool cue up and under the silent man's chin and firmly pressed it into his jaw, forcing the other man to raise his booted heels off the ground. In that same moment, Larocque caught flashes of blue and red light coming in through the window that made up a large part of the bar's frontage.

"We don't have much time," Larocque said. "In the time that we do have, I'm going to give you some advice. In my professional life, I deal with dick swingers like you all the time, so as much as you will want to ignore what I'm about to tell you, I suggest you do your best to listen very carefully."

With his face now inches away from Kominsky's, Larocque increased the pressure on the now-vertical cue and in the process forced the local to elevate himself even higher on his toes. "Are you listening, Grant?"

"Yeah, man," Kominsky finally said through clenched teeth.

"Good, because whatever happens after tonight, I want you to know that should I hear from Ms. Evans that you so much as looked in her direction, I will come back to this town of yours with some men – some very bad men – and we'll settle whatever score needs to be settled. Do we understand each other?"

Kominsky hesitated and shifted his eyes in the direction of the bar entrance, where he too had picked up on the red-and-blue lights of an approaching police cruiser.

Larocque drove the cue into Kominsky's palate forcing him to grunt in pain, while at the same time delivering a firm cuff to the side of the man's face that he'd struck earlier. "Do we understand each other?" Larocque roared.

"Yes!" Kominsky replied, his voice nearly screeching.

Hearing the door of the bar open, Larocque slowly removed the cue from Kominsky's throat and stepped back. He turned in the direction of the bar entrance where he saw three Ontario Provincial Police officers standing abreast.

One of the officers, a female cop who had gold sergeant chevrons on the shoulders of her jacket had locked her eyes on Larocque, and in doing so placed her right hand on top of a holstered taser. "Sir," she said in a voice that suggested she was not at all happy with the scene laid out before her, "do me a quick favor, won't you, and drop that cue?"

———

Canadian Forces Base Petawawa, West of Ottawa

"Braz," the other man said, from across the small room he shared with several other junior officers. "You better pick up the phone, my friend. General Day is on the horn."

"Get bent, Singh. I gotta get through these here leave requests before the end of the day or the Sergeant Major is gonna have my ass. That man doesn't give one spec of shit I'm a company commander," Brazeau said in accented English, his eyes not coming off the stack of paperwork laid out before him.

"Dude, I am not joking. Day is on the phone, and he sounds pissed, man. Like, major pissed."

"If I pick up this phone and it's that douche bag Houle or Mustapha, I will beat your skinny Sikh ass. I swear on my mother's fucking grave."

Singh flipped him the middle finger. "Any time, Frenchie."

Captain Brazeau, commander of A Company of the Canadian Airborne Regiment looked at the standard-issue government phone that sat on his paper-strewn desk. It was just after 1400 hours Friday afternoon and there was no training scheduled for the weekend. He knew his fellow junior officers had paperwork to do, too. Why wasn't the Sergeant Major riding their asses? Goddamned slackers, he thought to himself as he reached for the phone.

"Captain Brazeau, bonjour," he said nonchalantly into the receiver.

"Captain, it's General Day. Where the hell is the commanding officer of your regiment?"

Brazeau shot a quick look at Singh and then sat up straight in his chair. Sure as shit, it *was* Major General Day, the Commanding officer of Canadian Special Operations Forces Command, CANSOFCOM. The man's voice sounded like gravel grinding on more gravel and was a virtual impossibility to impersonate.

"Ah... the colonel's on leave, sir," Brazeau said, more quickly than he wanted to. "I'm not sure where he's at. We got the impression he was... ah... heading up north. Me and the rest of the boys, well, ah, we've tried to give him a good amount of space over the past few months. You know, he's still working things out, so we don't ask too many questions when it comes to things outside of the job, eh."

"Brazeau, at this point, I don't give a rat's ass about your colonel's feelings." Day's words were at a near yell. "He's a goddamned senior officer and officers under my command don't go waltzing off without getting my say-so. As far as I'm concerned, he's AWOL.

"People tell me you have the closest relationship with him. Is that the case, Captain?"

"*Oui*, ahh, yes, I guess that's the case, sir," Brazeau said choppily.

"Perfect, then you have new orders, Captain Brazeau. You're going to track your CO down and get him back on base ASAP. I don't care if you pistol whip that son of a bitch, he's back on base in seventy-two hours, or it's the military police, a court-martial, and the end of his career and anyone who's been covering up for him – and that includes you, Captain. Shit is going down and I will not stand for it any longer. Do I make myself clear?"

"Crystal clear, sir," Brazeau replied. "Ah... sir, I wasn't making it up earlier when I said I have no idea where the colonel went. He could be anywhere."

"You know, Captain, I was dead set against bringing the Airborne back. Too much baggage, I said. A dumping ground for other units' head-cases, I advised anyone that was willing to listen. But did anyone heed me? Not a fucking soul. And now here you guys are and you're my problem. Jesus H. Christ," the piqued man said.

Holding the phone a couple of inches away from his ear, Brazeau said nothing, not having a clue how to respond to the two-star general.

"Take down this number, Captain. The guy will be expecting your call. Don't ask his name or make small talk, just give him whatever details you can. If your colonel has so much as gotten a parking ticket or opened his email, this guy will get a bead on him, and then it's up to you. And call his wife. She may have some idea of where he's gone off to."

Brazeau let the phone go silent for a moment. "Ahh, sir, the colonel will get seriously pissed if we contact Mrs. Larocque. She's ah... how do you say in English... she's definitely in the no-go zone."

The general's next words were made in a low and menacing tone. "Captain, listen to me very carefully. I don't give a fiddler's goddamn what your colonel wants or doesn't want. He's to be back on base and in command of his regiment within seventy-two hours, or there's gonna be hell to pay. That is a promise. Do I make myself clear, Captain Brazeau?

"Yes, sir. We'll make it happen, sir," Brazeau replied instantly.

"Good, then I suggest you hang up this phone and then dial up Mrs. Larocque and hope to whatever God you pray to that she or that other number I gave you helps you find your commanding officer."

On that statement, the line went dead.

After slowly hanging up the phone, Brazeau turned and looked at Singh, who was staring at him with a 'holy shit' look on his face. "So, Day found out that the boss is past due on his leave?"

"Yeah and he's pissed, man," Brazeau advised.

"Dude, that came through loud and clear. I could hear everything from here. So what does that mean?"

"I'm not sure. I've got to make a few calls. Whatever goes down though, our plans for the weekend have turned to shit. We have seventy-two hours to find the boss, or he's screwed as are the rest of us."

Chapter 2

Merielle Martel, Canada's Minister of Defence, walked into the second-floor federal cabinet chamber for the third time in a week.

She had been in the federal cabinet for three years now. Brought in at the halfway mark of the Conservative's first term as a result of a questionable decision by her predecessor, Merielle now felt she had a firm handle on her portfolio.

She had run for office six years ago during a by-election in her hometown of Montreal. Historically, Conservatives had fared poorly in that part of Quebec, but her campaign was boosted by some timely allegations of corruption involving her Liberal opponent.

Two short years later, her riding was swept up in the blue wave that resulted in Robert MacDonald becoming Canada's twenty-eighth prime minister. After this election win, it was another two years as a backbencher where Merielle learned the ropes of Canadian federal politics by serving dutifully on those committees to which she was assigned and by doing her best to serve her constituents in her home riding of Mount Royal.

As a twenty-three-year veteran of the RCMP, she enjoyed the constituency part of the job more than anything else. As a patrol officer and then a detective during the early part of her career, Merielle derived considerable satisfaction in solving people's problems, even when those problems were self-inflicted.

In many ways, being a Member of Parliament and being a street cop was similar, in that on any given day, you had no clue who was going to walk into your life. And more often than not, you couldn't make up the shit that people got caught up in.

As she sat down in her customary position three chairs down from where the PM normally sat, she wondered, not for the first time, how so many free-thinking, able-bodied adults struggled so mightily as they tried to move through life?

It was a question that had boggled her mind right up to the point where the United States had devolved into a full-scale civil war.

It all happened so quickly. Within a month of her being sworn into cabinet, the then-President of the United States had signed into law several highly controversial pieces of legislation, which in turn led to a cascading series of events that resulted in the first eight Red Faction states passing their own legislation to secede from the American union. Fast forward nearly three years later, the Red and Blue factions were stalemated, five major American cities had been incinerated, and something in the range of eighteen million people had died.

It had been a staggering cost and not just for the former United States. Here at home, the provinces of Ontario and Quebec were now home to over five million refugees and with Canada's largest trading partner mired in a horrific war, the domestic economy had stagnated. Economists hadn't started to use the word 'depression' yet, but estimates coming in from the Department of Finance suggested that the term would in fact be accurate within a year's time if things did not change radically.

In her estimation, matters abroad weren't any better. By the early part of the decade, world affairs had come to a reasonable understanding between the Americans and the Chinese. Détente was perhaps the word that best described it. But as it became clear that the US fracture was real and as American military and diplomatic assets were pulled into the civil conflict, the Chinese and other bad actors stepped into the colossal vacuum that had been created. International relations had become a free-for-all.

To Merielle and the rest of her cabinet colleagues, it was all madness of the highest order. Canada had tried its best to staunch the flow, both south of the 49th parallel and further abroad, but there had been more failures than successes, even with the formalization of the military alliance between Canada, Australia, New Zealand and the United Kingdom.

To their credit, the CANZUK nations had realized their collective commitment to invest 2.2 percent of their GDP on military spending several years before the American collapse.

In what was arguably the greatest bi-partisan undertaking in Canada in the past fifty years, three successive governments – two Liberal and one Conservative – had understood that the increasingly volatile situation in the United States meant that Canada would have to become less reliant on American might and would need to carve out its own hard power priorities. As a result, Canada's military was as large and as strong as it had been since the heady days of World War II when Canada had the world's fourth-largest navy and an army that had stormed the beaches of Normandy.

Merielle glanced at the door leading into the cabinet's chambers just in time to see the prime minister walk through the door along with several other officials, including two other cabinet ministers.

Five years Merielle's senior, Robert MacDonald was a striking figure. Tall, lean, and with features many would describe as severe, he generally looked about as approachable as a starving wolf. Once a crown attorney out of Saskatchewan, Bob had used his looks to great effect when prosecuting any of his cases that made it to trial. It was said that the man's glare alone won as many cases for him as did his legal skill and deft intellect.

Since becoming PM, the man had been required to put his glare and many other skills to full use. He was a second-term prime minister mostly because his fellow Canadians understood that they needed a competent if an entirely un-charming person to manage the country through what were unrivaled and perilous times.

The prime minister stopped at his usual seat at the head of the long table that sat in the center of the ornately furnished federal cabinet room. Standing behind his chair, he did a quick scan of the room looking to confirm that no one who was not to be in the room was, in fact, present.

"Folks, it's good to see everyone. Thanks for being here so late. Let's have a seat so we can get started. This could take some time," he said in his trademark voice that made it sound as though he had a never-ending throat infection.

As was customary, he sat with his hands overlapped in front of him on top of whatever briefing notes he had brought with him. In the years that Merielle had known the man, she had never seen him tired, and today was no exception. As was normal, his eyes had a keenness to them, and his demeanor was self-assured.

"Colleagues," the prime minister commenced. "This evening, it is my responsibility to convince you, Canada's most important leaders, that the political dominion that we all love, stands before what I believe is a dire political precipice.

"Since Archibald Cameron became President of the UCSA just over eleven months ago, we've known that the State of Missouri was at risk of joining the Reds. To be clear right from the top, this man Cameron is a monumental problem, starting with the likely consideration that he played a key role in the untimely death of his predecessor. President Fitzgerald may have been a war criminal for the ages and a religious zealot to boot, but one thing he was not was a messianic megalomaniac. I firmly believe that is what Archie Cameron is. We'll come back to this point momentarily.

"For good reasons of which you are all aware, we've remained neutral in this second American civil war. Personally, I will confess that it has been difficult not to advocate for a policy of intervention, but as the situation has developed, I have on many occasions silently thanked those of you who have counseled for our current position.

"Sadly, my friends, I believe developments out of the former United States require us to re-evaluate our policy concerning the civil war.

"What is this development, you ask? Put simply, it is Missouri. As you know, because of the actions of the Colorado Faction one year ago, the Reds' status as a nuclear power was taken off the table. All of the former United States' remaining nuclear weapons are being held in neutral states which have refused to join the war or have been shipped by the US Navy to trusted allies for reasons of safekeeping. As you will no doubt recall, with our government's permission the *USS Maryland* and her nuclear payload have been docked at the Halifax naval shipyard for the past eighteen months.

"Should a neutral Missouri become a Red Missouri, it would dramatically alter this nuclear equation.

"If Archie Cameron and the Reds get a hold of the nuclear weapons and the delivery systems at Whiteman Air Force Base in central Missouri, the Blue Faction's current military disadvantage becomes worse. Much worse, in fact.

"In this scenario, it is my calculation, and also that of our military, and our closest allies, that the nuclear weapons and the various delivery systems at Whiteman AFB will give the Reds an overwhelming tactical and psychological advantage over the Blues.

"Colleagues, I emphatically suggest to you that under no circumstances can Canada allow this to happen."

The prime minister paused, reached across the table in front of him and grabbed a pitcher of iced water. He then proceeded to fill the upturned glass in front of him. Taking a small sip, he continued.

"In response to the developing situation in Missouri, there are several highly classified developments that I'm going to apprise you of here in our country. In providing you with this information, you should be aware that it is classified with the highest level of protection within our system and within CANZUK."

The man went quiet and slowly looked at the men and women aligned in front of him around the table.

"Three months ago, a CANZUK special representative made contact with the Governor of Colorado. The name of this person is unimportant, but you should know that the prime ministers of the alliance were in agreement that this person would represent us.

"Upon meeting Governor Anders, they discussed the ways that CANZUK and the Colorado Faction could cooperate for the purpose of restraining the UCSA.

"Before getting into the specifics of any joint actions, let me run through the strategic considerations that are currently in play in the former United States and how these developments may impact the Canadian interest.

"We know that the Blues are weak and may not be able to stand long in the face of another all-out conventional war with the Reds. We calculate that any larger political entity that consolidates under Archie Cameron's leadership is unlikely to be satisfied with just the Blue territories. The neutral states and the four states of the Colorado Faction, nuclear weapons or not, will be hard pressed to resist Cameron, should the Blues capitulate. Neutral California, due to its size and location, may be the exception, but nothing is certain.

"Let me pause for a moment and ask you the following question: Based on everything we know of Archie Cameron and the broader political system that underpins his authority, is there anyone in this room who believes the Reds will be satisfied with only three-quarters of the former United States?"

MacDonald paused and looked searchingly at the individuals sitting around the long boardroom table that had faithfully served

Canadian political leaders for over one hundred years. No one said a word.

"Colleagues, it's not as though Cameron has been trying to hide the ball on the issue of manifest destiny. We know that as recently as two years ago as vice-president, he gave a speech at his alma mater, where he explicitly talked about leveraging all of North America's resources to rebuild the northeastern United States once the Blues were brought back into the fold.

"With five cities pulverized and with hundreds more in various states of ruin, there is little doubt in my mind that this man would look north and south in an effort to revitalize and rebuild that part of the United States that he controls.

"As an independent country that is unlikely to develop its own nuclear weapons, let me suggest to you that Canada and all of our vast resources now stand at a crossroads.

"If we maintain our neutrality and allow Archie Cameron to obtain a nuclear stockpile that enables him to win the war, it is my firm belief that we will be opening ourselves to the real danger of being forced to join the UCSA political system within two to three years."

The prime minister paused for a moment, giving this last statement the opportunity to sink in.

"My friends, I have had a candid conversation with the prime minister of the United Kingdom. As we faithfully did for Great Britain during the two great world wars, the UK is prepared to fully support any and all of our conventional efforts to resist the United Constitutional States of America. Like us, the UK abhors what the Red Faction represents. But, this support is conditional. It is conditional up and until the point where Archie Cameron has the weapons and the weapon systems that can turn the British Isles into an uninhabitable nuclear wasteland for the next thousand years.

"Colleagues, myself and the leaders of Great Britain, Australia and New Zealand are unanimous on the following opinion: we must not let the UCSA gain possession of the nuclear arsenal currently stockpiled at Missouri's Whiteman Air Force Base. Allowing such a development will tip the balance for the Reds, and as I have outlined for you, it will most likely result in a cascade of events that will lead to Canada being subjugated by a political body that has acted in ways that are anathema to all that is good and expected of those countries who continue to uphold the mantle of western civilization.

"So it is with this dire perspective that I am to outline the following proposal for your consideration and approval. The other CANZUK prime ministers are delivering this same proposal to their respective cabinets as we speak. Within the hour, we'll know whether or not the leading countries of the Commonwealth will be on board with the prospect of starting what is likely to be a full-blown fighting war with the Red Faction of the former United States of America."

After another moment of pause, Yvette Raymond, the wholly competent Minister of Infrastructure and Communities and the minister responsible for the Conservative's Quebec Caucus raised her hand to signal her desire to speak.

From Quebec City, Yvette had been the Prime Minister's right hand in all matters to counter the province's separatists. "Bob, before you go forward and outline the details of your proposal, I wonder if you might offer your thoughts on what this plan of action is going to mean politically in Quebec. You have to know Labelle and his ilk are going to make hay with the scenario you have just outlined."

"It's a great question, Yvette," the prime minister said to his senior Quebec lieutenant. "Of course, I've been wrestling with how this issue will play out politically in your province, and as you point out, we're in the most precarious position we've been in Quebec in over a generation. After considerable thought, here is the position I would propose that we take to counter Monsieur Labelle.

"First, it has been just over eighty years since the dark days of Maurice Duplessis. There are no Quebecers alive today who will have a direct memory of this man, but as you know better than I, Duplessis' dark legacy lives on in the hearts and minds of every Quebecer who came up through the province's education system.

"As desperate as Labelle is to see Quebec become its own country, it is my take that Quebecers are wholly unprepared to make nice with someone who so closely resembles the darkest days of their past. Consider the policies the Reds have implemented since coming to power. They're downright medieval.

"All of us in this room know that Quebec is Canada's most liberal province when it comes to social policy, so when it comes down to it, my clear sense is Quebecers will choose to stay with the devil they know."

MacDonald paused and looked to Yvette to see if his response would elicit some type of follow-up, but the minister appeared to be satisfied with the PM's explanation, so he continued on.

"As a second point for consideration, I would offer to the people of Quebec that we now have a reasonable understanding of how the Spanish language is faring in the Red Faction states since the start of the civil war. Though we haven't seen any overt persecution of Spanish-speaking UCSA citizens as yet, the Red's harsh immigration policies and the passage of their recent English-first legislation should be indication enough for any soft separatists that their lot is best cast in the direction of the status quo."

MacDonald paused and then said, "Here's an interesting piece of history. Did you know that in the late sixties over a million people spoke French in Louisiana? Would anyone care to guess what the number is now?"

Paul Blanchard, the Minister of Transport and a bear of a man from the Pontiac region of western Quebec offered the number of four hundred thousand.

"It's less than one hundred thousand, Paul. Much less. In Louisiana, the French language is all but dead. It might be that Monsieur Labelle thinks he could extract some type of special accommodation from the UCSA as Quebec has done with the rest of Canada, but I have my doubts. Quebecers will have serious doubts too."

Merielle watched as the prime minister and her political mentor slowly got up from his seat and moved behind his chair. His gaze moved across every cabinet minister sitting at the table and stopped on her.

"My friends, the Quebec question is an important one, but the challenge that faces us supersedes the matter of our country's unity. If Archie Cameron and the Red Faction get access to the nuclear weapons in Missouri, our right to survive as an independent and free state will be threatened and gravely so. The people of Quebec will understand this, as will the rest of Canada. To assure our survival, we cannot, we must not allow the UCSA to become a nuclear power again. And if that means that Canada must get involved in the American civil war, then that is exactly what we need to be prepared to do."

Chapter 3

Paris

"Good morning, Minister," the French intelligence officer greeted the diminutive and dour-looking man sitting next to a window overlooking an extensive courtyard garden well into its annual cycle of hibernation.

Coffee saucer in hand, Pascale Charron, France's Minister for the Interior looked up from the document he was reading and said to the still-standing man, "I trust you have been keeping a close eye on developments in North America?"

"Indeed, I have. It remains a terrible mess."

"Please, sit down, Monsieur Besson," the politician gestured to the table's only other chair. Would you like coffee? Perhaps something to eat?"

"A coffee would be nice, thank you, Minister," Besson replied as he moved to take the offered seat.

The smaller man took up the stainless-steel carafe with his own delicate hands and then leaned forward to fill the other man's cup.

"So, what is the latest from North America? I saw on the news last night that the Missouri state legislature is looking to throw in with the UCAS. What are your people telling us about that development?"

Coffee now in hand, Besson replied, "First, you should know that our intelligence on the ground could be better. We have people moving into Missouri as we speak, but it will take time for them to make the necessary connections."

"This is to be expected. Even now, the former United States is a big country, and the world is as complex as it has ever been. We can't be everywhere."

Charron paused to take a sip of his coffee and then enquired, "When will your people be in place such that they can start to give us a clearer picture?"

"Two weeks. Perhaps less if we're lucky," replied Besson.

"And what about this CANZUK endeavor I've been hearing so much about?"

"On the new Anglo alliance, our information is better. As you know, our assets in both Britain and Quebec are plentiful and while we don't have anyone placed on the inside of either government, the sheer quantity of the data that comes in from this many sources is telling in its own way."

"Then do tell, Director."

"As we speak, there's something interesting happening in western Canada. Together, the Canadians and the British have consolidated two divisions of mechanized forces across Canada's prairie provinces. And, we're aware that some number of Royal Air Force and Royal Australian Air Force F-35s and other CANZUK air assets have been sprinkled across Canada, no doubt in an effort to keep their total numbers indeterminate."

The senior intelligence officer continued, "And you'll find this interesting. Most recently, we received confirmation that Australia's 2nd Commando Regiment and elements of its Special Air Service recently set down in Alberta."

"Really?" Charron asked, raising an eyebrow. "That is interesting. If my memory is serving me correctly, that's not an insignificant force for the Australians to send halfway around the world."

"We think the same, Minister," Besson said as a matter of fact.

"Indeed," offered Charron. "The Australians wouldn't send their two premiere fighting units fourteen thousand kilometers away unless there was good reason to. If I remember correctly from a briefing not too long ago, China and the Australians are not getting along?"

"That's putting it mildly, sir. Things remain quite tense throughout the Far East since the communists took back Taiwan. The Australians and Japanese appear willing to check further Chinese ambitions but it is unclear whether the posturing of these two states alone will be enough to ward off the Chinese from further moves. Our current analysis is that the CPP has been temporarily satiated but our intelligence in this part of the world isn't what we would like it to be."

As was his way, the politician took in Besson for several moments without saying anything. If you did not know the man, it would be unnerving, but Besson had worked with Charron long enough to know that the pause was a prelude to what would be the critical part of their conversation. As he waited, he took another sip of his coffee. Only his second of the day, it tasted like magic.

"Monsieur Besson, I know you and your colleagues in the Directorate will agree that it is in France's best interest to ensure that the North American continent remains chaotic and ineffectual for as long as possible."

"Yes, Minister, the bulk of my colleagues and I would agree. The absence of America on the world stage has opened many doors for France. It has been a profitable time to be us."

"And there are still more doors to open, should the US remain on its knees. It is now clear to me and the president that the Missouri situation is untenable for the Canadians and by extension, their allies. Our ancient foes, the English, in particular, are keen to see the American situation resolved. They are planning something, Monsieur Besson."

"I concur, Minister. CANZUK is getting ready for something. What that something is, remains unclear"

"The time has come for us to act. What I'm about to tell you, I have discussed with the president. For your information and peace of mind, know that you have her full support. She is entirely on board."

Looking straight into the eyes of Besson, France's second most powerful politician said, "I know you, of all people, will appreciate the significance of having her making this type of overt commitment."

"I do understand, Minister, and you're correct. Knowing she is behind our efforts will make all the difference."

"Very good, because there are many difficult things that will need to be done in the coming months. We will all need nerves of steel if France is to maintain the advantages we have gained since the Americans started killing each other."

"We are ready to act, Minister," Besson replied. "You only need to direct."

"I know you are. It's why you are our man and it's why I'm entrusting to you what needs to happen next. In so long as we can manage it, the smoldering fire that is the former United States of America must continue to burn for as long and as hot as possible. A world without the United States is a world filled with uncertainty. It is this uncertainty more than anything else that has served to elevate France here in Europe and across the world."

The senior minister paused and again precisely raised his saucer to his lips, closed his eyes, and took a satisfying pull on the beverage. As the china left his lips, his eyes re-locked onto Besson. "Effective immediately, *les Division Action* is to make extraordinary efforts to fan the flames that are burning in the United States. And as your people make such efforts, you are to direct those flames toward the American's northern neighbor."

"My people do chaos as well as any, Minister. On the question of flames, just how hot are we talking?"

Smiles on the face of Pascale Charron were as rare as springs in the Algier's desert. Nevertheless, in that moment, the French President's go-to hatchetman wore one. That the man was so physically unassuming made the façade all the more malevolent.

"Hot, Monsieur Besson. Your people are to make North America so hot, I can see it's twinkle all the way from my office here in Paris."

Chapter 4

Colorado Springs

"Governor, the channel has opened up. We are free to join the call," Anders' chief of staff advised her from across the table.

"Let's connect then," she said.

With a quick nod, the man's eyes turned to the laptop on the table in front of him and undertook whatever magic was needed to make the technology work.

Governor Rachel Anders and those key staff she could trust were present in the secure teleconference room deep within Cheyenne Mountain, the military complex that had managed North America's air defense throughout most of the Cold War.

It was an extraordinary facility. Back in the 1960s, the US military had burrowed its way into the side of a granite mountain at fantastic expense to protect the country's ability to detect and respond to airspace incursions from flights of nuclear-armed Soviet bombers. However, due to dramatic changes in technology and the types of threats the country was facing, the US government had all but shut down the complex in the early 2000s. With the start of the civil war, Anders had ordered the structure re-commissioned.

The teleconference was taking place in a small, converted lecture hall. Anders and her officials were seated in three rows of fixed seating and together they looked to a large LCD that hung on the wall above a dais, which in other circumstances, would be used to elevate an instructor or briefing officer.

The LCD flashed to life and was instantly divided into four quadrants. There, on each of the four sections, she saw a different group of people, each in a different room. On the bottom right of each of the four portions, the name of a CANZUK-alliance nation was given. A woman who might have been in her late forties, and who had tight black curls and hints of mocha skin, was the first to speak.

"Good morning, Governor," she said in a voice that held the slightest hint of a French accent. "My name is Merielle Martel, and I am Canada's Minister of Defence. For much of our conversation, I'll be speaking for the Canada, Australia, New Zealand and United Kingdom alliance. It's a pleasure to meet with you and your officials."

"Good morning, Madame Minister. It's good to make your acquaintance, especially under these difficult circumstances. As you know, I'm the Governor of Colorado and I have the authority to speak for my state and those whom the media have dubbed the Colorado Faction. We appreciate the time and consideration that all four of your governments bring to this virtual table."

"Governor, I believe you were provided with an agenda that outlined the items that we have agreed to cover during this conversation."

"I was," Anders said. "Shall we jump into item number one, then? As it pertains to the politicians on the call, I believe it's the more important matter."

"Then why don't you start us off, Governor," the Canadian Defence Minister indicated.

"Very well. Let me start by being blunt. We are not your friends, but nor are we your enemies. As Colorado sees it, the action we are proposing to undertake together is a relationship of pragmatism and necessity. Outside of Whiteman Air Force Base and more specifically, the weapons that are housed on that base, my state, and the faction which I represent, have no interest in any broader or longer-term relationship with the CANZUK alliance. Long term, we are interested in one thing and one thing only. A reconstituted United States of America that is not under the leadership of the UCSA, but also a country that is not beholden to any foreign power, be it CANZUK, the Chinese, or any other foreign actor.

"The civil war my country is presently fighting is an American war being fought by Americans. What you and your alliance want to do outside of our interim relationship is entirely up to you. Win or lose, we will owe you nothing when our proposed collaboration is over. This is a partnership of equals who bring equal value to the table. Is this position clear to you, Madame Minister?"

If the Canadian representative was taken aback or concerned by the directness of Anders' initial foray, the woman gave no outward appearance of it.

"Speaking on behalf of CANZUK, let me say that I appreciate your candor, Governor. Further, let me offer to you that we are entirely comfortable with the position you have just set out. As you say, there will be no quid pro quos contained within whatever relationship we may or may not come to terms on today."

"This is encouraging," Anders replied. "Then let me proceed to what is our second expectation. As we made exceedingly clear to your envoy, the weapons at Whiteman are American weapons and under no circumstances can they stay in the possession of CANZUK any longer than is necessary. I understand for reasons of capacity that it is CANZUK who will have to secure Whiteman, but assuming the successful extrication of those weapons, it is imperative that each and every one of them is placed in the care of the Colorado Faction as soon as possible.

"If this is not done, you will be placing myself and those I am representing in an untenable political position. Under no circumstances, can we be seen to be providing American nuclear weapons to another country, even ones such as Canada and the United Kingdom. All weapons must be delivered into our possession, with no exceptions. I trust this is an understandable and reasonable outcome that CANZUK is amenable to?"

The Canadian politician replied without hesitation. "We do not want any American nuclear weapons, nor do we desire any of the delivery systems at Whiteman. We have quite enough already with the *USS Maryland* docked in Halifax. I can assure you that, in all of our conversations as an alliance, we have not discussed, nor contemplated the idea of the weapons at Whiteman going anywhere other than Colorado."

"I am glad to hear it," offered Anders. "We have a third and final requirement."

The Canadian immediately nodded her head and said, "Please proceed, Governor."

"Minister, I take it you have not met Archibald Cameron?"

"I have not had that pleasure," said Martel

"Well, I have not had similar good fortune. In an earlier life, I was a political staffer for a short period and worked in Washington. In that time, the senator I worked for partnered with then-Senator Cameron on a legislative project. Through that relationship, I got to see firsthand the man that Archie Cameron is, and I can tell you that his people have done an admirable job of hiding what this man is capable of.

"Under no circumstances, and I mean none, is Colorado prepared to permit Archibald Cameron to obtain the weapons at Whiteman Air Force Base. Madame Minister, and to the other political representatives on this call, if your militaries fail in their effort to take that base, we are prepared to do to Whiteman AFB what we did with Barksdale and Kings Bay."

Anders paused, allowing the gravity of her position to sink in.

"And I will give this order regardless of whether or not there is one CANZUK soldier or twenty thousand within the blast range of that installation. Understandably, this is a harsh calculation, but in the analysis that confronts me, your people will mean no more to me than the thousands of American military personnel and civilians who died in the strikes I ordered just over one year ago. I would take no pleasure in making such a decision, but I can assure all of you on this call I will order a strike on that base if I see that it's going to be taken by the Red Faction."

Finishing her statement, Anders remained silent, allowing her eyes to burrow into the divided screen that held the four member states of the CANZUK alliance. Anders was not surprised to see that the Canadian Minister of Defence maintained an admirable poker face. Her briefing on the woman had advised her that she had been a high-ranking police officer in the RCMP, and in that role, the woman would have been no doubt confronted by unexpected situations, though nothing as daunting as what Anders had just laid out.

Eventually, Martel broke the silence. "Governor, I want to thank you for sharing this information. As you can appreciate, this is a position that each of us will have to bring back to our governments for discussion."

"That is fine Minister. It's to be expected."

"I do have a question, however."

"Ask away," Anders offered.

"Governor, you have set out for us that you are prepared to do to Whiteman AFB as you did to Barksdale and Kings Bay. I do not want to seem insensitive or crass, but why should we sacrifice thousands of our soldiers and potentially the wrath of the UCSA, when you've just admitted to us that you're prepared to destroy that location in the event CANZUK is not successful? I mean, why not give Missouri two hours notice and then nuke the base and be done with it? With all due respect, Governor, why are we even having this conversation?"

"It is a reasonable question, Minister, and if I were in your position, I would be asking the same things.

"At the moment, the Colorado Faction has just under fifteen hundred nuclear warheads under our control. After the Red Faction's strikes and then our own, we estimate there are another twenty-five hundred nuclear weapons that remain within the broader US inventory. Thankfully, as it stands for the moment, all of these weapons are in the possession of neutral states except Missouri.

"Despite reasons that would have them do otherwise, these states have chosen neutrality because they understand the world-ending power they have in their possession. Until President Fitzgerald and the UCSA attacked the Blues, Colorado had made the same determination – that as painful as it was to sit on the side-lines and see our country torn apart, it would be infinitely more painful and irresponsible for us to engage in the fighting where we might be tempted to do as the Red Faction had done.

"I can now tell you from personal experience that nuclear weapons are an awesome responsibility. If they are to be used, it must be for reasons so compelling that you are prepared to sacrifice millions, and perhaps all of humanity. In my mind, the Reds' destruction of New York and the other cities was a compelling enough reason for me to do what I did in ordering the destruction of Barksdale and Kings Bay.

"But let me answer your question directly, Ms. Martel. If we were to strike Whiteman pre-emptively, what message would we be sending to the rest of the world? More specifically, what message would we be sending to the likes of North Korea, Iran, Pakistan – even Israel? In my view, we'd be setting a dangerous precedent.

"In the case of the strikes I ordered a year ago, they came three days after the destruction of five great American cities. If this wasn't justification enough for my actions, then I don't know why a country would have nuclear weapons.

"For these reasons, but more so for reasons we cannot foresee, we must first try and resolve the Missouri problem through conventional means. Right now, the nuclear genie is back in its bottle, but I'm afraid that should I order a strike of Whiteman without having made the effort that we are on this call to discuss, we're giving permission for every petty tyrant that has a nuclear bomb to do as you would have me do. This is why I reached out to your governments.

"As I've said, I am prepared to issue the order to destroy Whiteman, but before I go down this road, Colorado owes the people of this state and I dare say the rest of the world, an effort that does not begin with Missouri being turned into a nuclear wasteland.

"Colorado cannot gain access to those weapons on its own. Whether they realize it or not, the rest of the world needs a champion who is prepared to do all that it can to keep Missouri's nuclear weapons out of the hands of the UCSA and Archie Cameron. Minister Martel, it is my view that CANZUK must be that champion."

———

Ottawa

Lying in the hotel bed, Brazeau looked at the back of the woman he had just finished making love to for the second time in as many hours. Her back was taut with well-defined muscles, which served to broaden her figure ever so slightly. That she was so fit was one of the things that he found alluring about her.

He wasn't sure if he was in love with the woman. That was a complicated question. He had a wife that was not the woman who was lying naked beside him, and it was not two years ago that he had told himself that his wife was his soulmate and that he would grow old with her. The birth of his daughter had no doubt contributed to this sentiment, but at the time, he was sure the feeling was real and abiding. He had tried to make the relationship work. He had wanted it to work, but here he was in this hotel, working as hard as he had ever worked to win the affection of this other stunning woman.

The woman with long, perfectly black tresses turned over in the bed and looked at him with tiger-green eyes. In combination with her well-toned physique, the woman's intense gaze gave her an exotic quality. Had she been taller, Brazeau surmised that she could have had a career as a model. As it was, the twenty-eight-year-old beauty was a corporate lawyer working out of Montreal, where she had used her father's substantial political connections and her own fierce intelligence to carve out a career that would someday place her at the highest echelon of Quebec society. As the only daughter of the leader of Quebec's separatist party, Josee Labelle's name and image were well known within the province they both called home.

"Well, Captain, now that we've been satisfactorily re-acquainted, why don't you tell me what's brought you to Canada's capital on short notice," Labelle said.

"Just satisfactory? That's not how I remember it," Brazeau jibed.

"Ah, yes," she said. "The male species. Even the self-assured ones need validation when it comes to how they perform with their dicks.

"Well, if it makes you feel any better, soldier, I can confirm that it was the right decision to cancel all of my meetings today. The part of my brain that's responsible for my career thinks I'm a fool, but the other parts are cheering me on. Is your ego okay with that assessment?"

Reaching out his arm, Brazeau placed his calloused hand on the small of the woman's back and roughly pulled her much lighter frame against his body.

"It's a perfectly satisfactory assessment," he said while smiling at her. "But to answer your question, I'm here because of the colonel. As you know, he's a bit of a mess. Singh and I had to drive all the way up to goddamned Cochrane a few days ago and pull him out of jail."

Josee gave the well-muscled man a quizzical look. "Cochrane? Where the hell is that?"

"Exactly. Unless you're from there, you don't know the place exists. It's a shitty little town ten hours north of Toronto – about an hour north of Timmins if you even know where that is. And cold like you would not believe."

"I've never heard of either place. What was he doing up there?" asked Josee.

"As best I can tell, he was in the midst of a suicidal bender that had him trying to drink dry all of the small-town taverns from Petawawa all the way to Vancouver. He got as far as Cochrane before some local made the mistake of saying something he didn't like to a bartender I guess he'd taken a shine to. After all was said and done, the cops locked him up pending an appearance in court."

"So, was he charged?" Josee asked. "Cause that's not going to be great for his career or the Regiment."

Brazeau looked at her with a grin. "The charges were dropped. Turns out the guys he roughed up got to the bar on their snowmachines and were way over the limit on their booze consumption. When the cops eventually found out what set the boss off, they worked a deal to drop the locals' DUI charges in exchange for the assault charges going out the door."

"This colonel of yours, he's a lucky guy," Josee said. "So how is it you had to drive up to Cochrane?"

"There's an interesting story there, but one I can't tell. At least not much of it. Suffice it to say, we got information that the boss was in jail and it was pure coincidence that Singh and I walked into the local detachment just as he was getting processed for release. You should have seen the look on his face. Perfectly neutral to thunderhead in an instant. We didn't know it at the time, but the colonel had refused to give them any information outside of his driver's license. So until we got there, they had no idea who he was. That was two days ago. As to why we're now here in Ottawa, he was called in on short notice to see the general."

"The general?"

"General Day. He's the overall commander for all Canadian special forces, including the Airborne," Brazeau explained.

"Have you spoken with him?" Josee asked.

"With who? The boss or the general?"

"Larocque, you dope."

"The boss, yeah, briefly. We're off to Edmonton in a week, which is the reason I wanted to see you. It sounds like we could be out there for a while."

"Edmonton?"

"Yeah, something about us conducting a major ex with the Brits. We'll be out there at least six weeks."

"Well, I guess that means we won't be seeing each other for a time," Josee said with a frown. "Will you get time off while you're out there? Maybe I'll come out for a visit. I've never been to Edmonton."

Brazeau smiled at the beautiful woman lying beside him. "I'm that good, eh?"

"Let's just say I know how difficult it would be for a handsome officer such as yourself to be on his own in a cold place like Edmonton for any extended period of time."

"Listen, Josee, I'm not twenty anymore. And there are enough complications in my life already with you and Monique." Saying his wife's name aloud delivered an instant pang of guilt. In the hours leading up to this rendezvous, Brazeau's conscience had been delivering a steady stream of reminders screaming that he needed to sort his love life out sooner versus later.

Locking her green eyes with Brazeau's brown, she leaned in to give the man a kiss and to signal that a third bout of vigorous love-making was in the offing. "Complicated is the right word. But I knew we were going to be complicated the moment you and I met. You'll figure this out, Marcel. And while you do, I'm happy to wait. Just not forever, mind you."

———

CFB Petawawa

Hall and Wallace sat in separate chairs in front of a large desk. Both had said nothing to each other since being seated by the army corporal who had her own seat outside the office. Hall could hear the woman's fingers mercilessly pounding out some document on her keyboard.

The office they had been seated in was nondescript. The walls were painted an off-putting shade of green and on those walls, nary a photo, book, certificate, or piece of art was present. The resulting impression provided Hall with zero insight into the type of person that occupied the space.

Hall heard heavy booted footsteps approaching and then heard a deep and raspy male voice address the corporal-admin guarding the office, "Good morning, Corporal. How's the little one?"

"Tickity boo, sir. The base doctor told us to keep feeding him Advil."

"Glad to hear it. I see the two candidates await me?"

"They do. Their files are on your desk."

"Perfect as per the norm. Thanks, Angie."

Hall's chair had been set at ninety degrees to the desk in front of her, so her back was to the conversation between the unknown officer and the corporal. Four years at the Royal Military College had drilled enough discipline and decorum into her to know the last thing a junior officer did in this situation was to crane their neck as though they were one of the gossip-loving civies she had encountered during her first posting to National Defence Headquarters. Unsurprisingly, Wallace, also a Royal Military College grad, was eyes front as well.

The moment they heard the officer enter the room, Hall barked the word, "room" and she and Wallace both snapped to their feet and came to attention.

Arriving at the desk, the officer looked at both of them in turn and said, "Rest easy and have a seat."

Hall took in the middle-aged man. He was as tall as Wallace, but that's where the similarities between the two men in the room ended. His complexion was olive in tone, while his eyes were a dark brown and had a kindness to them. Ethnically, he was most certainly Mediterranean in origin. But that wasn't the man's most standout feature – not by a long shot. The full colonel standing in front of them had the largest barrel chest she had ever seen on a human being. Where Wallace had the physique of a wiry prizefighter, the man across from them looked as though he had spent the last fifteen years competing in the world's strongest man competition.

Taking a seat, the colonel proceeded to open the files sitting on the center of his well-organized desk. Moving his eyes from the folders to the two young officers sitting in front of him, he said, "Lieutenants Sarah Hall and Maxwell Wallace. Do I have that correct?"

"You do, sir," Hall said on behalf of the duo.

"Good. Nice to meet you both. My name is Colonel Azim and I have the overall responsibility for the program that the two of you have been participating in for the past two months. I want to start our conversation by commending you both for the commitment and determination you have brought to the small but important endeavor you've been involved in."

"Thank you, sir," said Hall, while Wallace uttered his own words of appreciation.

"It's worth noting that you have exhibited these efforts in the absence of a lot of information. By design, we've told you almost nothing about the program you've been participating in. Perseverance in the absence of information - in my estimation, that's no small thing in today's day and age. I trust you've both been keeping an eye on world events in the former United States?"

Both Hall and Wallace nodded their heads and replied, "Yes, sir."

"Good," Azim said. "Then you'll both have at least some context that will help you better understand what I'm about to tell you."

He paused briefly, and the kind eyes that Hall had noted moments ago took on a degree of hardness. "Until advised otherwise, the information I'm about to share with you is not to be discussed outside of this room. Not between yourselves, not with other candidates, and most certainly not with anyone outside of this program. If it is found that you've violated this directive, you will be dropped from the program immediately, and depending on the circumstances, you will be court-martialed. Is that understood?"

"Yes, sir," they both replied, their voices resolute.

"Lieutenants, there is an increasing chance that our country is going to start a war, and it looks like the two of you are going to play a key role in helping to get that war started."

————

Somewhere east of Ottawa

The highway rest stop was busy. It had been an hour since she had parted ways with Brazeau. True to form, he'd offered enough information so that their relationship would need to continue. The details about the Airborne's colonel were both juicy and politically helpful, though it was a shame the charges had been dropped. With no formal charges in the system, there was no hard proof to leak to her media contacts. For sure there was a story there – the commanding officer of one of the country's most infamous army regiments getting into a drunken brawl in some shit-hole town over a barmaid. That type of behavior had minor scandal written all over it, but more importantly, it would once again raise questions in Ottawa about the wisdom of bringing the Airborne back.

To say that the Regiment's re-constitution had been a divisive political conversation was an understatement. The country's ever-growing army of wokeists had done overtime whinging over the message the government was sending Canada's equity community by bringing back a unit that had been disbanded for, among other reasons, the torture and killing of a Somali teen during a peacemaking operation all the way back in 1993.

Perhaps the personal trials of the noble colonel could be used at some opportune moment, but now was not that time. The more important information Josee had gleaned from her afternoon tryst was the movement of the Airborne out west. That was strategic and actionable information that her contact at the DGSE would appreciate.

Josee paid for her Starbucks and then walked over to a table occupied by a lone man who looked like he had ten years on her. He had taken off his winter coat and she could see that the man was neither fit nor soft. Unremarkable enough, she thought.

"Excuse me," she said in accented English to the seated man. "I'm having trouble finding a place to drink my coffee. I wonder if I might sit with you?"

The man, who up until that point had been concentrating on his smartphone, looked up to see who had addressed him. He looked around the rest stop, confirming that the place was indeed busy. Looking back to Josee, he smiled and said in French, "Of course. Please have a seat."

Josee moved to take a seat across from him. "I see you speak French. Where are you from?"

"I am from a small town just east of Lyon," the man said.

"Ah, Lyon, that's a wonderful area. I was there not two summers ago. The cheese in that region is incredible. I was particularly fond of the Comté."

The man smiled. "I'm partial to the Vacherin du Haut-Doubs myself."

"Just so," Josee offered in reply. "It, too, is wonderful in its own way."

The man paused and waited until Josee had fully seated herself. "So, Ms. Labelle, I've driven out to meet you at your request. And urgently I might add. Why don't you tell me about your visit to Ottawa and what about it was so important?"

Chapter 5

Ottawa

Merielle stood alone in her office in the Centre Block of Parliament Hill looking out her window to Wellington Street, the main thoroughfare that ran parallel to the country's legislative home. It had been snowing in Canada's capital, so everything was covered in a growing blanket of white. If she had to guess, this particular snowfall was approaching the fifteen-centimeter mark. Well beyond the point of a dusting, it did not faze the people and vehicles going about their business in the least. Though the city of Ottawa struggled with a lot of things, snow removal was not one of them. As this rare appreciation of local government crossed her mind, one of the city's massive plows came into her vision from the east, its blade driving and scraping the snow and ice off the road.

The conversation in cabinet about Colorado's conditions had gone as she had expected. The group the prime minister brought in to discuss the Missouri question reaffirmed their commitment to the policy. Intentionally or not, the Governor of Colorado had caught Canada and the rest of CANZUK in a classic Catch-22 moment. If they chose not to intervene, cabinet felt it was a certainty that the Colorado Faction would decimate Whiteman. It was clear that Anders had the will to pre-emptively strike Missouri, should that state formally throw in with the Reds as it now looked like it would. What a pre-emptive strike would do to the politics of the US civil war and to the international political climate was incalculable. Yes, Cameron and the UCSA would be denied Missouri's nuclear stockpile, but who could say what would come next? It was not a door Canada wanted to open. Not with them being so close to the action.

If they continued down the path of intervention and their efforts were stymied and Governor Anders leveled Whiteman with

CANZUK soldiers in the vicinity, the loss to Canada and her allies would be devastating. The casualties they'd see in Missouri, in such an eventuality, could rival those suffered in Canada's darkest moments during the first and second world wars. That Canada had suffered so mightily in the distant past would be of no comfort to the families whose sons and daughters fell south of the border. The hurt would be particularly acute if these same families came to the understanding that the spilling of Canadian blood could have been avoided altogether. If the Americans wanted to incinerate swaths of their own country periodically, who the hell was Canada to get involved?

On its surface, it was a compelling position to take. It was the Americans' war after all, so why should one drop of Canadian blood be shed for it? That position had worked well for the country during the Americans' first bout of internecine warfare.

The harsh answer to that question was that the path leading from non-intervention had outcomes that were far worse for Canada and the rest of the world than the prospect of losing several thousand CANZUK soldiers. It was a hard reality that was now official government policy, and it was her job to make sure that whatever sacrifices were made prevented the Red Faction from obtaining another batch of nuclear weapons. This was now the bottom line for the four countries that made up the CANZUK alliance.

The phone in Merielle's hand vibrated, forcing her to pull her eyes from the still trundling snowplow. Looking at the display, she saw it was, as expected, her ex-husband. She activated the connection.

Merielle remained on good terms with her ex. They had met some twenty years earlier at a detachment in Moncton, New Brunswick. She was in the midst of transferring from the patrol division to investigations when he had transferred in from out west. Both coming off bad relationships and looking for new starts, serendipity found them married one year later.

In the first ten years, the relationship had worked well. Both good at their jobs and career-driven, they agreed early on in their relationship that kids would not be part of their marital equation. But as time passed and various assignments required them to spend less and less time together their relationship had inexorably moved in a new direction. To his credit, her ex had had the courage to call it off before moving on to a new partner. It had been kids. He had come to want them and she had not. It had taken several years, but in time, she had come to respect him for his forthrightness. It was for this reason, and because she had come to realize that the male species was chock-full of assholes, that she continued to be close with and even adore her first and only husband.

"Hello, Stephane," she said. "All is well with Anik and the boys, I trust?"

"All is well, so long as I don't think about the money I'm shoveling out the door for the boys to play hockey. They're both playing Triple-A this year. Anik had to drop hours to manage it all and I'm going to need to stay enlisted for five more years, at least. The cost of playing minor hockey in this country should be a national scandal. Maybe there's something you can do about it?"

Merielle offered a genuine chuckle. "If memory serves me correctly, I believe we re-introduced the old recreation tax credit in our budget two years ago. Surely, the five hundred dollars offered per child is a windfall for clan Martel?"

Stephane scoffed. "I'm glad to see politics hasn't served to dull that cheeky wit I was so fond of. For the record, I voted Liberal in the last election."

"You did not," Merielle said quickly.

"Alas, Madame Minister, it is so. But rest assured, my affection for you remains steadfast and always will."

"What can I say to that, my love?" said Merielle. "I am forever thankful for your resolute emotional support."

"Shall we talk about the separatists?" Stephane offered.

"Yes, what were your friends at CSIS able to tell you about everyone's favorite separatist leader, Monsieur Labelle?"

"Well, first off, you should know that the information I'm about to provide you with is all off-the-record. No formal ask was made and no meetings were held. It was all one-off conversations with people I know I can trust. Not that I think the good folks at CSIS can't be trusted, but you and I both know questions would be raised if a formal request came into them from your office. Better to back-channel things for the time being."

"You won't get any argument from me," Merielle said. "If I had asked for this briefing formally, the Prime Minister's Office would have felt the need to get involved, and while I think the world of Bob, there are one or two operators on his staff that I would like to avoid for the time being. They may be on our side, but they're some of the worst political operators I know. So until you tell me I need to be concerned, we'll keep the CSIS angle on the down-low."

"Works for me," Stephane said. "As things pertain to Labelle, I think we're good. Certainly, there's no need to hit the panic button. He's a crafty politician as you know and he's well connected, both in Quebec and internationally, but based on all of the available information, he's shown little to no interest in what's happening south of the border. And that's not just our folks' analysis. After I made the initial inquiry, my guy connected with the Brits. Not hindered by domestic legislation like we are, they did their own review of our guy."

"And?"

"And, MI6 says as best they can surmise, he's neither interested in nor connected with anything that has anything to do with the UCSA or Archie Cameron."

"Well, that's encouraging."

"Indeed it is," the senior RCMP man said, "but there's an interesting *but*."

"And that is?"

"Labelle's daughter."

"Josee Labelle," Merielle said.

"Do you know her?"

"Not personally, no, but I know a little of her through a few indirect connections. You know, three degrees of separation and all that. I think she might live in my riding. I definitely know that she works for one of the bigger law firms in Montreal. If memory serves, she's also not tough on the eyes."

"You're right on all counts. She does have an apartment in your riding, she's going into her third year as an associate at Garneau and Langlois LLP, and I can confirm based on my own personal research efforts that she is, in fact, a looker."

"Jesus, Steph, you're almost old enough to be her father."

"No tut-tutting please Madame Minister. Getting the full and complete picture of a potential suspect is one of the hallmarks of a policing professional. I'll brook no thoughts whatsoever of lechery when it comes to my efforts to serve our country."

"You're too much. What's the deal with our separatist princess?"

"It would appear that Ms. Labelle has an interesting side-hustle working as an informant for the DGSE."

"Get outta here! French Intelligence? That is interesting," Merielle exclaimed. "Are we sure about that, and does that mean Labelle senior is involved somehow?"

"The Brits are pretty sure she's working for the French and are equally confident she's operating on her own. My guy at CSIS supports that view. It turns out that in her third year of university, Ms. Labelle did an exchange in Paris. We have no idea what she got up to while she was there, but it's not unreasonable to think that the DGSE got to her while she was in-country and that they've been working her ever since. As the daughter of a high-ranking separatist politician, they would have every reason to believe that she could develop into an important asset for them. Smart, beautiful, connected. She's an intelligence service's wet dream."

"Geez, you're really hot and bothered about this woman, aren't you?"

"Wait for it, Mer," he advised using the shortened version of her name that only he and a few others got to use.

"Okay, now I'm intrigued. Tell me why it is the Defence Minister of Canada should be concerned with this *femme fatale* you seem to be so interested in?"

"Femme fatale, eh. I like that. That might not be too far off, but I'll let you decide once you hear who she's been sleeping with."

The moment the words 'sleeping with' registered, alarm bells fired off in Merielle's head. If this Labelle woman was working for the DGSE and was sleeping with someone from cabinet, or the right bureaucrat, the country's burgeoning plans concerning the former United States would be dead in the water, never mind the political damage that would occur to the relatively new alliance that Canada was now a part of with her three Commonwealth allies.

Merielle shut down her running thoughts; she could not reveal her inner distress to her ex. Stephane had no idea about the government's recent decision concerning the UCSA, so it was imperative that she ask the next question in a manner that suited the rest of their conversation. "Alright, Stephane. Let's hear it. Who has this separatist tart been screwing?"

———

Upstate New York

Altov stood by and watched as the three men on his team loaded their gear and several large containers into the navy blue cargo van idling in the west end of the casino parking lot. As he had come to find out in recent days, upstate New York could get bitterly cold. Not Moscow cold, mind you, but uncomfortable nonetheless. While his career as an independent contractor had most often brought him to the warmer regions of the world, as a product of the Russian military, he had endured his fair share of brutally cold weather. He would survive the New York cold as would the men of his team.

The tall man with raven-black hair that had met them inside the casino lobby walked over to him from where he had been watching Altov's team load their gear. "I take it you didn't have any trouble getting here? I know in some other parts of the state things aren't good. Bandits and gangs are everywhere. It was like something out of a goddamned movie. Had you have told me five years ago that New York would end up as a Mad Max spin-off, I would have told you to check into a hospital, but here we are, eh."

Altov listened but didn't want to talk to the man. His experience told him the less talking the better, but the man had come highly recommended, and saying nothing at all would make him and this team more memorable than engaging in some superficial chit chat. "There were no problems on the way here. Should we expect any with the crossing?" Altov offered.

"There won't be any problems when we cross. 'Cause of the war, the Americans are no longer patrolling the border. They've left it to the Canadians entirely and they're spread way too thin. Even in those rare times where we do run into a patrol, they half-ass it. At least with us. These lands are Mohawk lands, my friend. Ain't no piece of shit bureaucrat – even one with a gun on his hip – is gonna tell me where we can or can't go. Nevertheless, seeing as you've paid for our 'VIP package', we've taken some additional precautions to make sure everything goes off without a hitch."

"Good to hear," Altov said.

The consummate professional, when he found out that he and his men would be taking this route to get across the border he had done some research on these Mohawks. Turns out the Canadians weren't that nice after all. The discovery of Canada's dark history as it related to the country's indigenous people had delighted him. Altov didn't know all of the intricacies and didn't want to, but that didn't mean he couldn't accept the small pleasure of being able to contribute to this enterprising man sticking his finger in the eye of the country that had done so much to screw over its natives. One could only guess how thrilled the man would be if he were let in on the nature of Altov's mission. When all was said and done, the man standing in front of him would put two and two together. He seemed to be a smart enough fellow.

"Okay, my friend," the Mohawk said and pointed at the van. "You can ride in the front with me. Your boys will have to ride in the back with their kit. We won't be long. When we get to the river, we'll load your stuff onto snowmachines and then we'll make the dash across the river. As requested, one van and one car will be waiting for you on the other side. You're on your own from there."

"Perfect," Altov said. "This is quite the service."

"Glad to hear it," the other man replied. "Nowadays, we know you have options when it comes to getting across the 49th parallel, so unofficially, on behalf of my people, let me just say that we appreciate the business."

Chapter 6

Ottawa

For perhaps the tenth time, Merielle asked herself the question that had been dominating her thoughts since the morning's conversation with her ex-husband. 'Why would France and its intelligence service be interested in a captain in the Airborne Regiment?'

While it wasn't great news that a foreign power of France's stature was using a Canadian citizen to target an officer who was a part of the country's special operations community, it had been a monumental relief to Merielle to find out that Josee Labelle wasn't bedding someone with more political value.

When she asked Stephane what CSIS thought about the matter, he advised that the best his contact in Canada's intelligence service could come up with was some far distant play where this Captain Brazeau would be used to foment notions of defection, or more likely, that he would be used to generate sympathy for the notion of a separate Quebec among the French-speaking soldiers within Canada's special forces community.

Merielle and Stephane had agreed the theory was plausible, but not particularly strong. Once CSIS completed their deep dive on Brazeau, they'd get back to her ex with their updated thoughts and he would get in touch with her.

When Stephane had asked Merielle for her thoughts about the honey trap, she resisted. Her many years of police work had taught her that her subconscious mind needed time to bring things together. To be sure, she had made a handful of on-the-spot deductions over the course of her policing career, but her mind was more effective when it was given time to knit unrelated data points together.

The Brazeau-Labelle matter and how it connected with the DGSE was fascinating and certainly appealed to the skills Merielle had developed in her former career. She immediately discounted the notion that Labelle was somehow homing in on the Missouri issue. Those senior officers who were in the know about the nascent CANZUK mission had been under explicit direction to not discuss the operation widely. That the preliminary details of the proposed invasion had filtered down to an officer at Brazeau's level was highly unlikely.

She knew the French kept an eye on Quebec and there were some indications that their involvement in the American civil war had been growing on the side of the Reds. From Canada's perspective, French engagement with Quebec was to be expected in one form or another. That had been happening for generations, though the use of informants such as Labelle had not been common. French involvement with the Red Faction was also hardly unexpected. The strongly nationalist government in Paris believed in many of the same things that the UCSA did. Less immigration, less diversity, more protectionism, and foreign policies that made nice with strongmen and dictators if those states' interests aligned with France's.

It wasn't clear how a junior officer in Canada's military fit into this picture. Why would the DGSE look to risk a valuable asset on such a low-grade target? If she were handling Josee Labelle, Merielle would have her working political staffers in Ottawa. She was in that age group and God only knows what confidential information she could get her hands on from some love-struck minister's chief of staff.

For now, the Labelle-Brazeau file was a mystery and that was okay. Stephane and his contacts in CSIS would do their thing and with more information, Merielle hoped the DGSE angle would become clear. Until then, the political princess from Quebec could continue to have fun playing spy with her officer from the Airborne.

Edmonton

In combat fatigues and wearing the Airborne's maroon beret, Larocque walked down the corridor of the hospital with a sober look on his face. As he progressed down the hallway of the emergency ward, Captains Brazeau and Singh loped on his flanks like a pair of wolves.

"So his parents drove in and they're in the room now?"

"That's my understanding, sir," said Singh.

"And this Brit Colonel will be there as well?"

"That's what Corporal Glenn's friends advised me of not twenty minutes ago. Apparently, he saw most of what went down and wanted to check in to see how the corporal is doing."

"Aces, he'll give us the best understanding of what happened. Goodness knows whatever we get from Glenn's buddies ain't gonna do shit for us. It'll be a 'he said, they said' and we all know where that goes," Larocque said to the lean Sikh-Canadian company commander on his right.

The threesome turned a corner and then took in a small group of men standing outside one of the rooms. Though in civie attire, Larocque instantly recognized them as men from Singh's B Company.

Larocque stopped in front of the four men and delivered a withering stare that advised the young soldiers they shouldn't say a word.

"Quite the mess we have here, gentlemen," Larocque said with a hard edge to his voice.

"Sir," one of the men began to say.

"Check that shit, Robbins," Larocque barked, cutting off the young man. "I don't want to hear a goddamned word from any of you. There'll be time enough for that when you're back on base, which is where all of you are going right now. Until you hear otherwise, you're all confined to barracks."

"But, sir," another one of the soldiers said in a pleading voice.

This time it was Singh who cut him off. Stepping forward, the four NCOs' commanding officer towered over them with a combination of height and the Sikh's maroon turban. "Shut your pie hole, Bell. If so much as one more word comes out of any of your mouths, this situation gets way worse for each of you than it already is. Not one goddamned word."

On that, the four men elected to take on a temporary vow of silence.

His voice still low and unhappy, Larocque spoke again to Singh's soldiers. "I want you four out of here now. It's back to your rooms until we get this sorted. There's a truck out front waiting for you. We have someone coming in to liaise with Donny's parents, so I don't want to hear anything more on that front or anything else for that matter."

Larocque turned to Singh. "Captain, take this gaggle of yours out front and get them on their way, and then see yourself back here."

"Yes, sir," Singh said while staring daggers at his four bedraggled young NCOs. "With me, you four."

With Brazeau still at his side, Larocque made his way into the room. It had four beds, though only one was occupied. In that bed, Larocque's eyes took in the unmoving form of Corporal Donald Glenn. The young man's eyes were closed and his head was bandaged. Oxygen tubes trailed from his nose, while several other medical sensors were affixed to other parts of his body. The soldier's chest was slowly moving up and down.

To the right of the bed, Larocque took in a couple who looked to be in their mid-fifties. Without hesitation, he walked up to them. Donny Glenn's parents got to their feet as Larocque arrived and each, in turn, offered the Airborne's commanding officer a firm handshake. The pair looked like the dairy farmers Larocque knew them to be. By chance, they lived two hours south of Edmonton and when the hospital found out that they were so close, they had made the call asking them to come see their son. Together, they looked tired and grim.

"How's he doing?" Larocque asked

"Not good," Donny's mother said with a trembling voice.

The father, Gary Glenn, placed his arm around his wife's shoulder and pulled her in close. "They've done a scan. He's got a nasty fracture of the skull and there's some swelling of the brain, but the doctors think he's gonna pull through. We'll know in the next twenty-four hours whether we need to get more worried than we already are."

"I'm sorry this has happened," Larocque said, the tone of his voice offering compassion.

As he said the words, his ears caught the sound of someone entering the room behind them. Singh, he thought. That had been quick. But when Larocque turned, he saw a short and thick man who was sporting a perfectly kept handlebar mustache. He was carrying a tray containing four Tim Horton's coffees. Though he was in civies, there was no doubt the man was military.

"Colonel Larocque, I take it," the short man said in a sing-song British accent that Larocque couldn't place. The man placed the coffees down on a table and walked over to him and thrust out his hand and said, "Colonel Simon Costen. I'm in command of the Royal Tank Regiment. I'm surprised we haven't met yet."

"Good to meet you," said Larocque.

Larocque cocked his head sideways in the direction of the unconscious paratrooper. "So I hear you might be able to shed some light on what happened?"

"Aye, I was front and center for the whole mess. I was on my way back from a pub when I came across your lads jawing back and forth with a few of those newly arrived Aussie blokes. I'm sorry to report that your lad there was severely outclassed by the Digger who put him down. Apparently, he's an MMA phenom of some sort. Sure, they drew up on one another, but it was hardly a fair fight. The Aussie had hands like bloody lightning. After seeing what I did, I figured I best come to the hospital to let the right people know what transpired, seeing that everyone else involved in the mess was thoroughly plastered."

On hearing the man's unvarnished explanation, dread began to fill Larocque. He quickly moved his eyes back to Donny's parents.

Reading Larocque's face, Corporal Glenn's father promptly said, "It's all good, Colonel. Colonel Costen has been kind with us and was very helpful in helping us manage Donny's friends. As he mentioned, there was no shortage of alcohol in their systems. We know our Donny and he's no angel, but by the sounds of it, this Australian fellow shouldn't be going around looking to get into random street fights. You might want to speak with the Colonel in more detail. I think you'll find out what's happened to our Donny is neither right nor fair, even if he did square up with this fella."

"Fair enough," Larocque said. "Colonel, why don't you and I and Captain Brazeau step out for a bit, so we can hear exactly what happened to one of my boys."

———

Lexington

Standing off stage, Archie Cameron, the President of the UC-SA, listened to the Governor of Kentucky as he addressed the at-capacity theatre. To the governor's left and flanked by two hulking bodyguards, Cameron could still command a partial view of the crowd who had come to listen to the speech he had been crafting for the past week.

While the attendees were predominately white older citizens of the state, here and there, he saw some black and brown faces. Since the start of the war, he had been concerned with how the UCSA's political messaging was playing out with the faction's various minority populations. It was always a lift to his confidence to see some degree of diversity in the crowds that he addressed.

Regardless of skin color, religion or gender, everyone was critical to their efforts in so far as those groups understood that Cameron and the USCA would not go back to the days where some groups were more equal than others. Of the many issues that led to the breakup of the United States, equity, or to be more accurate, the increasing lack thereof, had been the most insidious.

Undoubtedly, it had been the Democrats' dual efforts to repeal the Second Amendment and open federally mandated abortion clinics in several Red states that had ultimately broken the country in two, but the fracture would not have been possible in the absence of the vicious and unremitting political fight that had been raging in the country around the issue of equity.

In his opinion and that of the political elites that were the backbone of the Red Faction, diversity had never been the problem. The UCSA, just as the United States before it, welcomed and celebrated people's differences. Even the gays. As he had said to many gatherings over the past year, and as he would say to this one, he looked forward to the day when the UCSA could once again open its borders to those looking to pursue the American dream. Like Jesus Christ, the UCSA loved all of God's children. And just like God, the UCSA loved all of its children and citizens equally.

Equity. Orwell had it right and put it out there for all to see in his powerful parable *Animal Farm*. The Democrats – or more precisely, the progressive wing of the Democratic party – had become the pigs, just as the average citizen of the United States had become Boxer the horse.

Cameron liked to think that the former United States was one of many real-world applications of Orwell's cherished story. In *Animal Farm*, you did not get to see how the pigs' oppression was eventually overcome by the other animals. But overcome the farm's self-appointed porcine betters would be. History, not fiction, had validated that inevitable outcome time and time again.

And it was history that was on the UCSA's side in its struggle with the Blues. At the core of the political fight that had brought the United States to its knees was the question of equity and how it was set out by the country's founding fathers. For the Reds and for the people in this room, equity of opportunity was a philosophical keystone. No, it was *the* keystone. Everyone, regardless of circumstances, had the God-given right to achieve success and personal victory. In another time, he would have called it the American Dream.

Yes, he knew and he agreed with the notion that some people and some groups started further down the ladder of life than others. He was not stupid, nor without empathy, and to the full credit of the United States, it had implemented many programs over the years to compensate for those who had different starting points. To be sure, there was a greater good in trying to address such barriers as poverty and access to education. But what had become untenable in the right-left dialogue in the years leading up to the war was the unceasing effort of the progressives to systematically denigrate and then replace the principle of equal opportunity and its children – merit and hard work – with the morally bankrupt principle of equality of outcome and its own loathsome spawn – mediocrity and quotas.

Cameron turned his attention back to the governor who remained at the podium in the middle of the stage. Wrapping up his remarks, the governor announced, "Friends, please join me in giving a warm Kentucky welcome to the President of the United Constitutional States of America."

Taking the cue, Cameron strode toward the governor and upon reaching the taller man, they shook hands vigorously while being buffeted by rapturous applause. Releasing the handshake, Cameron turned to the podium and, as he had thousands of times before, he squared himself on the lectern and then closed his eyes and said a brief, silent prayer.

Opening them once more, he took in the capacity crowd that remained standing and cheering. Letting it go on for several more seconds, Cameron eventually raised his arms and gestured for the crowd to find their seats.

"Ladies and gentlemen, it is an honor and privilege to be with you on this fine January day. Find your seats as you can. The good Governor's people only scheduled twenty minutes for us and I have so much to share with you." His face beamed with the warmest smile he could muster.

"There we go. Are we all comfortable? Once again, thank you so much for taking time out of your day to make your way to lovely downtown Lexington. I feel blessed by God being able to stand before you in this wonderful theater, located in the heart of this most hospitable and honorable state."

Briefly, he paused and allowed his focus to take up the words of his speech on the teleprompter. Turning his attention back to the audience, he saw a youngish-looking man in the central bank of seats still standing. For security reasons, the audience area was well lit, so Cameron could see the man as clear as day.

Without warning, the man roared in the direction of the stage, "Archie Cameron is a war criminal, a racist, and hates women and transpeople! Resign Archie! Resign Archie! Resign Archie!"

As the man's chanting continued, several people in other locations in the theatre leaped to their feet and joined the protest.

In the same instant, men from his security detail appeared from nowhere and placed themselves at the front of the stage while local police began to pour into the theatre via the entrances located behind the last row of seats. While no weapons had been drawn, Cameron could see that a number of the bodyguards standing below him at the foot of the stage had hands underneath their suit jackets.

While his security agents intently watched the protesters and scanned the rest of the audience, the local cops were in the process of laying their hands on the still-yelling protesters. The initial rabble-rouser had been several seats in from the aisle, so it had taken a bit of time to get to him as no small number of elderly audience members had to be pulled out of their seats so as to clear a path. Getting their hands on the protester, two fit-looking officers efficiently dragged the man kicking and screaming to the aisle.

Cameron watched it all with a well-practiced disdain. It was all Kabuki theatre and had happened so many times over the past year that he had developed a stable of ready responses with which to reengage his audience.

On this occasion, the miscreant who had kicked off the bruha-ha had the pathetic look of a too-old barista who might have had a writing career that had never really taken off. Placing a grin on his face, Cameron stepped back to the podium.

"Do be gentle with them, officers," Cameron said into the mic. "No doubt they're misguided souls, bitter about the fact that this new country of ours is doing important and necessary things, while they brood in their parents' basements wondering exactly at what point their pitiable leftist lives went so wrong."

"Fuck you, Cameron!" a shrill female voice cried out.

In response to the curse, someone to Cameron's right started a new chant, "U.C.S.A, U.C.S.A, U.C.S.A!" In short order, the new chant had drowned out the protesters' clamoring. Cameron

watched the unified and now fired-up crowd as they worked to collectively smother the protesters through a combination of volume,
pitying head shakes, and no small number of rude hand gestures.

Raising his voice so that his words would carry over the boisterous discord, Cameron said, "That's it, officers. Let's move them
along. Their parents will wonder where they've been."

After another minute, the police and some portion of his security detail had the last of the protesters out the doors at the back of
the theatre.

In response to soothing verbal ministrations from Cameron,
members of the audience slowly turned their attention back to the
stage.

"Well, thank you, everyone, for being tolerant of that sad spectacle. Ladies and gentlemen, I love free speech and I love the people
of Kentucky. Even the ones that do not love me back. I ask you, my
fellow citizens, is this not what a vibrant democracy looks like?"

The crowd hooted and cheered in response to the question.
Beaming at them, Cameron carried on.

"As you may know, my friends, I write all of my speeches, and
tonight's address is no exception. There's a funny thing that speech-
writers do. Whether it's done for reasons of posterity, or because we
have an overinflated sense of ourselves, many of us like to give ti-
tles to the speeches we write. For myself, I brand a title on all of my
speeches because I need a north star. A north star that will inspire
and guide the message that I need to deliver. A north star that will
fill me with emotion and purpose, and should the teleprompter go
down, some indication of what the heck I should be saying to the
people who are sitting in front of me, just as you are now."

Cameron paused as a smattering of laughter rolled through the
crowd.

"My fellow citizens, it is my privilege to be your president during these dark times. And it is my honor to be with you tonight.

Friends, the title of my address is 'Progressivism and Why the American Constitution Shall Remain Unbowed.'

"America and the values that did and will once again unite us as Americans cannot and must not change. And for those of you that are in the audience tonight or for those of you that are watching online, but who are not yet convinced of this reality – to you I say, with the greatest respect, stay with me for the next twenty minutes or so. It may just be that you hear something that allows our once united and mighty country to turn the page on this wholly unnecessary war. Whether you are from a Red state, a Blue state, or a neutral state, as a people under God, our founding fathers endowed to us an indelible pathway that we must reclaim. That pathway is lined with the American constitution. It is who we are. It is who we must always be."

Chapter 7

San Antonio, 5th Army HQ

"To be perfectly honest with you, I don't care a drop of piss whether or not your squadron is fully operational, and I could care even less about what the Chinese will think. What part of 'fly your planes over Jefferson City in two days' do you not understand Colonel?"

"Sir, I don't want to put this on the record, but I will if I have to. The men and women who we've asked to fly these planes are not yet qualified. They need another five to six weeks at least."

General Mitchell Spector, commander of UCSA's 5th Army group slowly got up from his chair and stepped away from the speakerphone sitting on his desk. Turning, he looked across his second-floor office to the window that opened up on a trimmed lawn with a small copse of still hibernating trees at its center.

"Chet, are you goddamned serious? What are you going to put on the record? That I asked you to have your people fly the very same planes they've been flying for the past two months, only a few hundred miles north of your present location? Is that an accurate assessment? Personally, I'm surprised by your hesitation. Are you not the same man with seven kills to his credit?"

"Sir, are you calling into question my integrity, bravery, or both?"

"Neither," Spector snapped back. "I'm simply asking you to follow orders. The calculation on this little airshow I'm asking you to do is straightforward. The president looks to me to get things done. You may not agree with the direction he has provided, but in the name of everything that's right in this crazy world, in so long as his orders have some strategic and political sense to them, I will do everything in my power to carry out those orders."

Spector turned back from the window to face the phone.

"Chet, you're a great pilot, but you're also just a colonel. It is not your job to see the big picture. It's mine and it's the president's. And while I have heard your concerns about the readiness of your pilots and that our Chinese friends might not want us to show off their tech, I can assure you there are larger things at play.

"That being the case, here's the bottom line: you fulfill the order I just gave you without complaint, or I'll find someone else who's prepared to turn loose those slick-looking fighters of yours over Missouri's state capital."

Upon issuing the ultimatum, Spector let the squadron commander stew for several seconds.

Finally, the man on the other line spoke. As the words came out from the phone's speaker, they were flat. "We'll be ready."

On hearing the words, Spector leaned the frame of his body forward and placed his left hand on his desk to stabilize his top-heavy bulk. The index finger on his right hand hung over his phone as it readied to press the end-call function.

"I'm so glad to hear that. I'll be sure to pass word of your enthusiasm to the president the next time we speak, because I know that's what I just heard in your voice. Enjoy Missouri's blue skies Colonel Montrell."

———

Ottawa

National Defence Headquarters, NDHQ, in Ottawa had several operations rooms, but this one was the largest and had the most modern equipment. Upwards of a dozen large screens hung at various points along the walls. While most were inoperative, several were streaming in news feeds from various networks. At the moment, the news cycle was concentrating most of its energy on the images coming out of Jefferson City, Missouri.

No doubt given a heads up that UCSA air power would be put on display above the state's capital, camera crews had been able to score plenty of high-quality footage. While there was no sound on the display, Merielle's eyes took in the sight of half a dozen Chinese J-31 sixth-generation fighters tearing across the skyline of the American city in tight formation.

Merielle shifted her focus from the wall-hanging screen to the display embedded in the thirty-seat conference table, showing a map of the American Midwest. In several locations, she saw indicators marking off where various UCSA army units were undertaking a series of combined-arms maneuvers. Approximately fourteen thousand soldiers, she had been told.

She turned her head slightly and looked at the Canadian Chief of Defence Staff, CDS, standing immediately to her left. "So you're convinced this is all a show to put pressure on Missouri and its decision to join the UCSA."

"Yes, Minister," the older man said, employing the formal address that all public servants used in the Commonwealth when they were speaking to a Minister of the Crown.

Upon first assuming the role of defense minister, Merielle had tried to get the officials who worked with her most frequently to drop the honorific, but three hundred years of Westminster tradition would not be denied.

"Setting aside the signals and human intelligence that we have on this, the satellite imagery further confirms this is for show. The force the UCSA has put in the field couldn't be sustained for the amount of time it would need to invade Missouri. Without a doubt, this is Cameron sending a message," Canada's most senior general said in a confident tone.

"I take it from the way the talking heads are squawking in the news that these Chinese fighters are a big deal?" Merielle inquired.

"They're a big deal to be sure. How big, depends on how many of them the Reds have."

"And how many do they have, General?" As the question left her lips, it parted with an edge to it.

A long-time operator of Ottawa's political scene, the CDS easily picked up on Merielle's tone. "Madame Minister, I'm sorry to report that we were caught with our pants down on this one. To their full credit, the UCSA military has done a hell of a job of keeping this deal with the CCP quiet. Based on the intel we've managed to collect over the last few hours, we think the Red Faction could have as many as thirty of the planes. By this time tomorrow, we'll have a solid number for you."

Merielle didn't reply to the general's commitment immediately. It didn't take a seasoned psychologist to pick up that the CDS and the other officers in the room were not happy with the current state of affairs. In their defense, the revelation of the J-31s was more of an intelligence failure than a military one, but the planes had been missed, and this was no small thing.

With her vexation made clear, Merielle elected to move the conversation forward. "I shudder to think of the deal Cameron had to make to get these jets. Even if it's only thirty, the price would have been steep."

"Indeed Madame Minister," said the CDS. "The sight of those planes being flown by UCSA has kicked up a panic in the Pacific. The question everyone is asking is who's next after Taiwan. Because that's what Cameron would have given up to get those planes. My bet is the Philippines. It's the country that makes the most sense."

"I'm hearing the same thing. Tokyo and Canberra are apoplectic," Merielle said while her eyes moved back to the display playing the footage of the Chinese fighters. "And we're sure American pilots are flying these things?"

"On that at least, we have new and solid intel. We know that UCSA pilots are in the cockpits of those planes. We've also found out that Chinese techs are servicing them on the ground. Apparently, the Sinos trust the Americans to fly their tech but not enough to let them play inside their guts."

"Interesting," Merielle noted. "So they don't trust each other entirely. That can work for us."

"It's something we're thinking about Minister. In the interim, there is a silver lining to this development."

Merielle's eyes turned from the display and delivered a frosty look she had pattened early in her police career. "I'm not a big fan of silver linings General. In my experience, they are a cop-out for folks who are okay with losing. The path you and I and the rest of the people in this room are walking – we can't be okay with cock-ups like this one. We need to win every day moving forward. The stakes are too high, General. Is this clear?"

In a testament to the man's professionalism, the CDS weathered the rebuke like a statue. After a moment's pause, he offered, "None of us in this room got to where we are because we like losing. But I take your point Minister. You've made yourself very clear."

"Outstanding," said Merielle in a calm tone that perfectly matched the delivery of the general. "Now what is it about today's events that help our plans?"

"The Reds don't know it Minister, but they've made a significant tactical error today. By playing their hand with the J-31s, we now know they have these planes in their inventory and we can game-plan accordingly. This will help immensely should we move forward with the operation."

The CDS moved his eyes from Merielle to the British Major-General who was standing on the other side of the conference table.

"General McEwan is better placed than I to speak to the J-31's capabilities and what it means for our own plans. As you know, the United Kingdom has the Tempest, its own sixth-gen fighter, and based on that airframe, he can give us a sense of what this development means for us tactically speaking."

The distinguished-looking Englishman with hair that was more grey than black reached forward and tapped a large square on the table-embedded monitor and said, "Bring up file thirteen." Immediately, two similar-looking fighter jets appeared side-by-side. They were facing Merielle and below each jet, there was a list of technical specifications, though in several rows under the jet labeled J-31 the word "unknown" was indicated.

"Marvelous looking, aren't they?" General McEwan said. "Because of cost overruns, I can tell you that the UK only has twenty-nine Tempests in service and only eight of them are here in North America. The rest remain in the UK, staring down the continent."

His eyes came up from the screen and he looked at Merielle. "I can also tell you that in hundreds of direct engagements with our F-35s, Typhoons and the Swedish Gripen, the Tempest is the superior machine in every way. As any pilot will be able to tell you, fighting success in the modern age comes down to visibility. The longer you can stay undetected, the more effective you are going to be. The moment you manage to put one of these two fighters on radar, the opposing flyers' odds ramp up significantly. It's getting them on radar that's the challenge."

Merielle interjected. "What was the win-loss ratio of the planes you just mentioned versus the Tempest?"

Pausing, McEwan's eyes moved to the Canadian CDS and then back to Merielle. "It's eighteen to one."

"And what about the J-31? How does it stack up to the Tempest?"

"As you can see from the information on the display, we don't have a full picture of the Chinese fighter. Having said that, all the evidence that we do have suggests that the J-31 belongs in the Tempest's peer group. Which is to suggest to you, Madame Minister, that we best hope the planes we saw today is the entirety of what the Reds have in their inventory."

"Thank you, General." Turning back to the CDS, Merielle said, "So, General, what does all of this mean for the big picture?"

"Well, I'm convinced it's not as bad as it looks. Here's what we know. The governor of Missouri met with Cameron two weeks ago and our intelligence informs us the governor came out of this meeting with an interest toward accelerating the state's timeline to join the UCSA. We have confidence that the show of force over the past twenty-four hours is a pressure tactic to help the governor win over those legislators that are dragging their feet.

"Satellite imagery and other intelligence have confirmed that the Reds have shifted forces into both Texas and Kentucky, but as mentioned, they've undertaken the ongoing maneuvers without the ability to sustain them. It will be important to determine if their build-up continues further than today's exercise. We guess it'll depend on what Missouri does in the next few days."

"We're still working through our analysis on what the added ground forces and J-31s mean for our own plans, but there's an emerging consensus."

"And what would that be, General?" Merielle asked.

"We don't take our foot off the gas. While it's true the Reds have positioned assets closer to Missouri, that they've done so in the manner that they have suggests that this was a show of force for Missouri and not us."

"Alright. Let's assume they're not onto our plans, how do the J-31s play out? Are they a game-changer for us or not?

The CDS replied, "We need to find out how many are in theatre. General McEwan has confirmed that Whitehall is prepared to fly over more Tempests depending on what that number is. Madame Minister, we still have the element of surprise working for us, so for the time being, it's our recommendation we keep up the current pace of our preparations. In fact, if we do anything, we should speed up our efforts."

Merielle looked at the four-star general. The man's eyes were searching. Of course the CDS and his fellow generals wanted to continue with their plans. Getting into wars is what military folk did, even the bloody female ones. On the other hand, the aggressive moves by the Reds to pressure Missouri only served to reinforce the notion that Archie Cameron was a bully and was prepared to employ force to achieve his political aims. To think that what was now happening in Missouri could not happen to Canada in the next two to three years, was a calculation of Chamberlain-like proportions.

"I agree, General. Keep moving forward with our plans. I'm meeting with the PM tomorrow morning and will brief him then. In the interim, get a call set up with the CANZUK political liaison group. They'll be anxious to discuss today's developments."

Merielle pointed at the display that once again was showing the images of the Chinese J-31s flying across the skyline of Missouri's state capital. "And for that meeting, we'd best have the total number of those planes and what we're going to do if it is the case we take the Reds on."

Chapter 8

North Carolina

There were many things the UCSA presidency had not been able to replicate satisfactorily from its antecedent government in Washington. Getting the same armored car – the famous Beast, as it had been dubbed by the news media – was but one example.

The war and the politics that had come with it had made getting one or more of the fifteen thousand pound hulks impossible. So like many things, the Fitzgerald administration and now Cameron's had been required to compromise or make do. And so, as it was, Archie Cameron was being driven down a rural moonlit North Carolina state highway in an up-armored Tahoe. Looking out the vehicle's window, he could see that the trees were still bare. Being from the south, he was no fan of cold weather. By way of his southern upbringing, the blood that flowed through his veins required more external warmth than the average person. Perhaps that was the reason he had been drinking as much as he had recently. Or perhaps that was him making excuses for a habit he really should be looking to curb. Like the rest of his body, his liver was not getting any younger.

Feeling his chest vibrate, Cameron reached for the phone tucked away in the interior of his suit jacket.

Bringing the phone to his ear, he said, "General Spector, good to hear from you."

"Good evening, Mr. President," the three-star general in charge of the UCSA's 5th Army said. "All is well, I trust?"

"All things considered, I think it's been a good day. Listen, Mitch, thanks for making time for me. I know you have a lot on the go. As it turns out, I'm on my way to an important meeting and we're almost there, so I'm a bit pressed for time."

"No problem, Mr. President. I'm all ears. How can I help?" Spector said.

"First, I want to commend you for your efforts to get our men and women into all the right places around Missouri. I don't think that could have gone better. I haven't heard from Governor Powers yet, but information coming out of the state would seem to indicate that today's spectacle had the desired effect. Intel says that the good governor has called for a meeting with key legislators for tomorrow morning. I expect we'll get a formal update on their intentions shortly thereafter."

"That's good news, sir."

"It is, and my fingers are crossed that hedging jackass of a governor has the wherewithal to take advantage of the political offering we've so generously given to him. If he can't bring his hold-outs to see reason after the display you've put on over the past twenty-four hours, then he and the rest of his people will get what they deserve.

"In less encouraging news, I had what I would categorize as a discouraging call with our charge d'affaires in China. It would seem our big reveal of those magnificent planes over Jefferson City was not appreciated by some of the higher-ups in the Chinese Communist Party.

"Now, this is outrageous, of course. Those fighters were provided to us with no preconditions and is it not a delicious irony that, after decades of stealing our technology, these Chinese sons of bitches are now telling us how and when we can use their planes. It's all a bit too much if you ask me."

"I believe we talked about the possibility that our Chinese friends would not be pleased with our decision," Spector interjected.

"Indeed we did, but I would not change a thing, General. The politics work in our favor. If using these planes forces Missouri's hand and primes the Blues for the upcoming peace talks, then I could care less what those cagey bastards think. We need to win this war on our terms. When we are once again a united country, the Chinese will come to collect and we'll make it up to them."

"But we're not there yet Mr. President and if the Chinese make those planes inoperable, it changes the calculus for us and not in a good way," said Spector.

"It's a fair point, Mitch, and it brings me to the reason why I wanted you to give me a call. I wanted to plant the idea that we may need to come up with a workaround regarding these planes. While it looks like we were able to smooth things with our CCP friends on this occasion, I don't trust the little bastards as far as I can throw them."

"Mr. President, the Chinese have always been a slippery lot. As you may recall, I did some time at our Chinese embassy as a military attache in my younger days. I wasn't involved in most of what went through that building, but from what I did see, the communists are as crafty as a starv'n raccoon. Knowing this, we've been working on a possible solution."

A grin leaped to Cameron's face. "General, this is why you are my man. Tell me more."

"As you know, the Chinese won't let us touch the inside of the planes. They have a team of technicians that live on base and if there's work that needs to be done on the fighters, it's these guys who do it.

"About a month ago, one of their senior techs approached us suggesting he would be willing to defect for the right price. We brought the right people in from intelligence and it's my understanding he's ready to come over to us on two conditions."

"And what would those be?" Cameron asked.

"The first is easy. He wants a one-time payment of $10 million and what would be the equivalent of his military pension."

"Interesting," Cameron said. "He wants $10 million but he still wants his pension?"

"He's an interesting fellow, sir," advised Spector. "The cash is payment for any future services rendered, while the pension represents his time served in the Chinese military. It's owed to him whether he's working for the communists or us. Apparently, he's 'entitled to his entitlements', or some horse shit like that."

"Aren't we all?" Cameron said with a bemused tone. "What's the second condition?"

"As I said, it's the tougher of the two, by far. He has a daughter back in China. Somehow we need to get her out of the country in and around the moment the Chinese find out he's come to our side."

"That is a challenge. Even when we were a united country, China was a struggle to operate in. And as you know, a majority of the intelligence establishment threw in with the Blues."

Cameron paused and saw the lead SUV apply its brakes and begin to make a turn onto a tree-enclosed gravel road that inclined steeply. "Mitch, do you still have your fingers on this defection operation?" he asked.

"I do, Mr. President."

"Good. Be sure to stay involved. Our people in intelligence are capable, but in their current state, this file may be beyond them. I'll leave it with you. You have my full support to get this done, though it's my hope we won't need to outmaneuver the Chinese in the manner you've suggested. It would be a shame to lose their support.

"Listen, Mitch, I've arrived at the meeting I mentioned so I'm going to have to let you go. I trust you'll keep me posted."

"Count on it, Mr. President," said Spector.

"Very good. We'll talk again soon," Cameron said, ending the call.

―――

Montreal

Josee had been given a new handler. For the first time, the French had sent a female foreign service officer to liaise with her. And one close to her own age no less. An interesting choice, she thought. Sitting across from each other in a café in Old Montreal, the two of them had the look of fast friends who might be talking about their latest shopping engagement or maybe their latest drama with the opposite sex. Which in Josee's case, wasn't that far from the truth.

Had she been someone who loved her country, not loathed it, perhaps the other woman's career would have been her own path. Sharp-witted, beautiful and a speaker of three languages, Josee would have been a highly sought-after recruit for the Canadian Security Intelligence Service, even with her last name.

She did not hate Canada or Canadians. By all accounts, they were a tolerable people and country, even with the smug air of superiority its politicians tended to project internationally. But Canada, for all of its benefits and advances, had forgotten where it had come from. At its birth, Canada had been a forced relationship of two very different peoples - the English in Upper Canada and the French in Lower Canada. It was subsequent generations of federal politicians and their unending willingness to engage in an immigrative cycle of acceptance, amalgamation and growth that had eventually ruined one of the world's most successful, if wholly unexciting, political marriages.

Of course, it had been this way since the heady days of Pax Britannica. The British, their language, and their way of doing civilization had been predominant. The English, through their many regional proxies, had always known that their success and dominance depended as much or more on their ability to play the policy long game as it did on their willingness to project their military strength.

Britain had survived and thrived as long as it had because it was one of a few countries in all of history that had an innate ability to see political outcomes fifty, even a hundred, years down the road. And while Canada had always lacked the willingness to effect its policy priorities through physical projections of any kind, the country most certainly had the genetic disposition of its political forebear when it came to making policy decisions that would serve it long into the future.

Canada was now a country of forty-one million people. And for nearly fifty years running, it had been one of the fastest-growing countries in the western world.

But what was a boon to Canada and a validation of the British long view, had been a growing disaster for Quebec. While Canada's population had grown rapidly and become increasingly diverse, Quebec's population remained stagnant. But more important than population, during this same period, Quebec's culture and way of life had been under siege. The Canadian model of growth, the feckless malleability of its culture, and the willingness of the country's elites to unceasingly thrust their views of diversity and multiculturalism on the province of her birth had resulted in what was the political equivalent of stage four cancer.

That Quebec was dying and was almost too far gone to save was a concept lost on Josee's father. Eric Labelle loved Quebec – of that there was no doubt. But like any elite, her father had neither the impetus nor the courage to do what needed to be done. Elites by their nature were conservative and comfortable. No, Josee thought, if Quebec was going to survive on a continent of pandering multiculturalists and woke idiots, her province did not need another referendum on sovereignty.

If Quebec was to be saved, Josee knew in her heart and mind that her province would have to ally itself with governments and political entities that understood the true peril of the French-speaking world. And if that meant that Quebec needed to be force-fully torn from the political fabric that it had been a part of for the past two hundred years, then that's exactly how far Josee and her allies in the province were willing to take things.

"We want you to go out to Edmonton," the female DGSE officer said, pulling Josee back to the matter at hand.

"I had a feeling you were going to ask that," Josee replied. "Outside of a few quick trips I've needed to take to Quebec City, I've been putting extra time in at the firm. I should be okay to take some time away. When do you want me out there and what do you want done?"

"We need you to liaise with the captain. There's something going on in western Canada and we need some on-the-ground resources to help us fill in the blanks. By our count, it's been six weeks since your last meeting with him."

A too-hungry grin surfaced on the intel officer's face. "We presume he'll be over the moon to see you."

The smirk on the other woman's face, and that's what it was, annoyed Josee to no end. She took a brief moment to look around the café and reconfirmed that everyone else was engaged in their own conversations or was far enough away that they wouldn't be able to hear what Josee was about to say to the twenty-something woman sitting across from her.

She leaned her head forward and gestured for the DGSE handler to do the same.

"Listen carefully you *chatte*, if you think we're playing a game or that the work that I do is the basis for some trite romance novel, let me remind you that you have a serious fucking job to do. I don't give a damn if you frig yourself day and night thinking about

Brazeau or anyone else that I might have to work with. If you're gonna work with me, you're going to treat me like the professional I am, or at the very least, you're going to convincingly fake the respect I deserve. It would be the greatest mistake of your young career to think that I don't have the means to have you sorting through inconsequential embassy dispatches from people half as talented as you think you are for the next five years."

Pausing, Josee leaned back from the table. She had delivered the whispered tirade with a face of complete contentment. The French handler however was no longer smiling.

In a tone and volume that matched the initial part of their conversation, Josee said, "Now, why don't you tell me about Edmonton?"

Chapter 9

Edmonton

By Larocque's count, there were twenty-three senior officers in the room, excluding the planning staff attached to the three-star general who had overall command for the outrageous mission that had just been described to the attendees. No one under the rank of full colonel was present. They were all sitting or standing on one side of an elongated conference table and were collectively focused on an oversized map of the United States splayed across the table's well-polished surface.

On the other side of the table stood a Canadian lieutenant general by the name of Alain Gagnon. With graying hair and of medium height, he was flanked by a taller two-star general from the UK on his right and a shorter three-star from Australia on his left. There was a Kiwi three-star sitting directly in front of Larocque on his side of the expansive table.

Standing in the second row of officers, Larocque examined the various yellow squares that represented the battlegroup-sized units that Gagnon had just proposed would invade the former United States. Invade the US, he thought. It was an outrageous proposition in every way.

He was still struggling to bring himself to understand how the prime minister had signed off on the plan, never mind that the man had come up with the concept in the first place. He genuinely liked Bob MacDonald. He voted for him in the past two elections. He had always considered him to be intelligent and serious. How the hell had the man come up with such an absurd plan?

As Larocque understood it, the eleven hundred men of the Canadian Airborne Regiment, plus another two hundred ancillary soldiers of various trades, were to do a mass jump along the eastern boundary of the air force base located at Whiteman, Missouri.

Once said jump had been executed, the Airborne, his unit, would storm the base, overwhelm its defenses, and then for a period of thirty-six hours, hold the base until mechanized elements from Colorado or North Dakota arrived, at which point he and his men would load up the base's two-hundred-plus tactical nuclear weapons and ship them west.

A walk in the park, he thought.

Larocque's mind flashed back to a particular slide from the presentation Gagnon had given. Seventeen thousand fighting soldiers, three thousand vehicles, and well over two hundred frontline fighter jets. It was a coordination challenge of nightmarish proportions, and he and his men would be at the center of it. It would be insanity if not for the plan's combination of surprise and audacity. Granting those two elements, his informal risk assessment of the mission rose from batshit crazy to balls-to-the-wall stupid.

As though the man had been reading his mind, at the mid-way point of the presentation, Gagnon surprised the group by streaming the prime minister and the minister of defence into the room via secure video feed, at which point the Canadian PM himself made the argument as to why the country needed to stand outside of itself and its history since 1945.

As Larocque listened to his country's leader, he'd found the rationale underpinning the mission compelling, but after the two politicians had signed off and his mind churned through the factors in play, he had become less sure. Whatever his final deliberations turned out to be, in the current moment, there was one thing he knew to be true. General Day had been right. Despite his own bullshit, he loved his regiment and the men and women he commanded. If his people were going to survive the meat grinder that had just been presented to him, he was the best person alive to make it happen.

"So, as you can see on the map, we'll have eight mechanized battlegroups in total," General Gagnon said. Four Canadian, three British and one Australian. As the battlegroups drive from their launch points along the southern border of North Dakota, we want to employ multiple routes to avoid any log jams. As I have mentioned, this mission will only achieve success through a combination of surprise and speed. For any history buffs in the room, this mission is the first half of Operation Barbarossa. With the exception of some quick-on-their-feet National Guard units in Nebraska and Iowa, there shouldn't be any opposition on our way to the objective until we get to Missouri proper.

"As the battlegroups move south, they will have continuous airborne coverage. If we do this right and if luck favors us only slightly, our opposition in the air should be minimal. The UCSA capacity in the air is not what it was – not by a long shot. When we do kick this off, every Red airfield that is within a thousand klicks of the main theatre will be put out of commission and if we have it our way, they'll stay out of commission for the duration of the conflict. Royal Navy assets in the Atlantic and the Gulf will be responsible for whatever targets the CANZUK fighter-bombers can't get to from the forward operating airfields we will have in Colorado and the Dakotas.

"Now, to those commanders who will be driving their ground units toward Missouri, let me be very clear. You need to move quickly, but this is not a race to see who can get to the objective the quickest. We need to move expeditiously but in a disciplined manner so that when we do get to Whiteman, we have the forces necessary to manage whatever resistance the Reds put on the field and hold the base such that we can load up the nukes."

The three-star general's eyes then homed in on Larocque from across the table.

"And mark my words, ladies and gents, when the Reds find out what we're about, you can bet they will fight like crazy to take that base from Jack and his boys."

"Boys and girls, sir," Larocque interjected. "At present, the Regiment has nine tougher-than-leather gals that will jump if this party does happen."

"An important clarification, Colonel," Gagnon said. "Men and women, badasses one and all, to be sure."

Larocque nodded his acknowledgment.

"Indeed, it will be a party," the general said, resuming his overview for the assembled group. "Fort Campbell in Kentucky is only eight hundred klicks away from our objective. Campbell is home to what remains of the 101st Airborne. Fort Hood in Texas is the other concern. It's home to what remains of the 3rd Cavalry Division and is about a thousand kilometers south.

"Unfortunately, our intelligence is not as good as we would like it to be as it pertains to these units and their garrison strength. We estimate at least forty percent of all UCSA units are in the field in opposition to the Blues along the fighting corridor that stretches across the northeast.

"So, taking into account that the Reds have recently moved soldiers into Kentucky and Texas for the purposes of pressuring Missouri, our estimates are that something in the range of thirty thousand fighting soldiers will be within a two-day ride of the Airborne once they drop.

"And that doesn't include the tens of thousands of regional militia they could send our way with a single broadcast. It's our best guess that within twenty-four hours of your people's arrival, Jack, central Missouri is going to become a beehive of action, so it is imperative that each of the battlegroups move quickly, but not so quickly that they get strung out and become vulnerable."

Gagnon paused and surveyed the officers arrayed opposite him on the other side of the conference table. "Battlegroup commanders, are we all crystal clear on this key point?"

In various accents, Colonel Costen and the other seven officers that would lead the fifteen hundred-strong fighting units replied with some variation of "understood," "aye," or "yes, sir."

"Excellent," Gagnon replied. "Which brings me back to the Airborne.

"Jack, this mission is a paratrooper's wet dream. It's the reason why this country brought back the Regiment. Everyone at this table has a role to play, but it's you and the men and women of your unit that will be in the crucible. We've walked through the plan. You'll have air support on standby, special operations will be in the vicinity, and we have other undisclosed assets that will be in play. But when the shit starts to fly, you and your soldiers will be the tip of the spear of this operation for what could be thirty-six or more hours.

"Everyone from the PM on down believes the Airborne can do this, but it's not him and it's not me who is going to be in this fire. It's you and the Regiment."

Larocque's gaze remained locked in on the general. It was only a few months ago, he was on the path to killing himself. Larocque did not believe in God, but there was most certainly a part of him that believed in things like fate and having a purpose greater than yourself. Something somewhere was giving him a purpose and a reason to keep living. If he signed on to this mission, he had little doubt that soldiers under his command would die. But he as much as anyone knew what loss felt like, and it was he more than anyone else who could give his Regiment and the men and women who served in it the very best chance to survive the storm coming their way. His soldiers' partners, kids, and parents needed him to do his job and to do it well. If he could minimize the type of suffering that he had endured over the past year, then he was all in for what was being proposed, even if it was madness.

Larocque gestured in the direction of the map. "Sir, with respect, this whole thing... Well, it's one of the craziest things I've ever heard of. But, as I see it, crazy is the only way we're gonna pull this off. So, I'm in. And when it comes time to let the rest of the Regiment know what they need to do, I know they'll be in too. Every last one of them. You just tell us when we drop, and we'll take and hold that base for as long as we need to."

———

Brazeau felt his phone vibrate in his pocket. Grabbing it he looked at the number. It was Josee. He hadn't talked to her in almost four weeks. Their relationship was like that. When they could be together, they chatted like the infatuated lovers they were, but if there was to be separation, they had at some point agreed that interactions should be minimal. He liked it that way. There was no sense getting hot and bothered if there was no way to blow off steam. And as they weren't married, there was no need to get all domestic and talk on the regular. Josee was a young lawyer trying to make her own way in Montreal's dog-eat-dog legal profession. Brazeau was certain she didn't have the time, nor the desire to take time away from her busy schedule to check in with him. It was a flighty notion and Josee Labelle was not a flighty woman. Not in the slightest.

"Allo," he said as he put the phone to his ear.

"Marcel, my chum, I have a surprise for you."

"I love surprises. Do tell."

"I'm in Edmonton."

Brazeau didn't offer an immediate reply. On the one hand, having Josee in town would be wonderful. They could get together for however long he could afford and they could reacquaint. On the other hand, the Airborne and other units stationed in Edmonton were ramping up their readiness. Something was going down. He didn't know what it was yet, but you could feel it in the air. Senior officers, including Larocque, had been meeting hours on end, and when outside of those meetings, orders were being issued fast and furious.

Picking up on his hesitation, Josee interjected. "Listen, I know you must be busy with your training, and I don't want to impose, but my firm asked if I could meet with a client in Calgary, so I agreed. I took a couple of days off in advance of the meeting on Friday, so I'm here for two full days and my calendar is wide open. Do you think you can squeeze me in at some point, Captain? I figure it's been over a month since you've had some of that forbidden fruit you claim to love so much. That's unless you've found some other way to satisfy those urges I know all men your age struggle with?"

Brazeau smiled. This gal. She was all vixen. A dynamite-looking and brilliant woman, who knew how to pull all the right strings.

"It's all good," Brazeau said. "I can make it work but only after 1700 hours. Where are you staying?"

"I'm at the Marriott. Can you make it there for six?"

"I have something at ten this evening that I can't miss, but until that time, I'm all yours, beautiful. Come to think of it, the event I need to be at is open to the public. Why don't you come?"

"Maybe," Josee offered coyly.

"I'll take maybe. I'll give you deets when we meet. To say that it will be an interesting time, would be one hell of an understatement."

Chapter 10

Edmonton

As the door to the arena dressing room opened, Corporal Kettle heard a banshee-like scream echo down the hallway. "This guy really is a first-rate douche bag, eh?" he said to the other soldiers who were in the room with him.

One of the other paratroopers, one Kenny Bitternose, a First Nations kid from southern Saskatchewan piped up. "That Dune bastard, man. He thinks he's the next coming of McGregor."

"Yeah, well that Aussie pretty boy is gonna pay for what he did to Donny," Kettle said.

"You da man, Kets!" Mac Okafor, a sinewy, lightweight boxer out of Scarborough belted out to the collection of paratroopers that had gathered in the dressing room to prime their friend for what would be his toughest fight of the tournament.

"And it's not just us who wants you to lay this guy out," Okafor continued. "I heard he wrecked a couple of guys from the Patricia's just the other day outside of the Bower. He's a mean bastard and from what I've seen, he's got good hands and a solid ground game. Kets, man, you gotta keep an eye out for his left hook. He's nasty business, my man. Just nasty."

"Which means you're gonna have to be careful out there," Sergeant Castellanos said, jumping into the adrenaline-fuelled conversation. He was the Airborne's senior hand-to-hand combat instructor. With a black belt in Tae Kwon Do and his own respectable amateur MMA career, the man knew his stuff and had been helping Kettle tighten up his striking and wrestling skills. "We all saw what he did to that Brit earlier today. As soon as you can, you get him on the floor, and you take it to him there. You've got good hands, kid, and Mac's right, that jaw of yours is like granite, but this golden boy is one hell of a striker. You can beat him standing up, but I want to see you implement Plan A – get him on the ground, use your bear-like strength, and dominate him. You hear me?"

"Clear as a bell, sarge," Kettle said.

Before any other advice could be thrown Kettle's way, they heard another unhinged-sounding howl come into their room from the hallway. "You ain't gonna make it one round, you Canadian pussy! This country is too soft. Way too soft. Why don't you come out here now and we'll finish it here, so I don't have to own you and your pussy Regiment in front of your mates!"

With a look of murder on his face, Kettle took a step to the door but then felt several hands grab him from behind. "Ease up, eh," Castellanos said. "He's just trying to goad you into fighting the fight he wants. You know that's exactly what he's doing. Save it. You'll be in the ring soon enough and then you'll have your chance to wipe that pretty grin off that piece of shit's face. Remember - you fight your own fight, not his."

As the taunting outside the door began to subside, the door to the dressing room swung open. Captain Brazeau walked in and barked, "Room." Kettle and all of the non-commissioned soldiers snapped to attention and set their eyes straight on the entrance.

Facing the door, Kettle watched as a man wearing the Army's standard-issue parka with its hood drawn tight stepped into the room. The stranger was promptly followed by the Airborne's Regimental Sergeant Major, RSM, and disciplinarian-in-chief, Mario St. Pierre, the Regiment's second-in-command, Lieutenant Colonel Levar Delgado, and the three other captains that led each of the Airborne's fighting companies, Singh, Geddes and Horth.

All of the officers and the RSM were wearing their dress uniforms and, as a result, they looked as sharp as they did serious. Of all the men, Singh looked the most resplendent. A Sikh, the captain wore a turban, and like the berets of all the other men in the room, the headdress that signified the man's religion was maroon with the Regiment's cap badge right where it should be. The collection of strapping and diverse-looking officers was a resplendent sight.

Surrounded by the senior cadre of the unit, the hooded man who had been doing his best to keep his eyes to the floor stepped forward and placed himself in front of the well-muscled corporal. Looking up, the figure pulled back the parka's hood and revealed himself. Kettle recognized the face instantly.

"Corporal, on behalf of every soldier in the Regiment and the whole damn country, I commend and thank you for what you were about to do today. My money would have been on you. But I need you to stand down. I'd like to find out for myself just how fast and tough this Lance Corporal Dune is."

———

It had been several weeks since Colonel Costen of the Royal Tank Regiment had been at the Edmonton hospital and suggested to Larocque the idea of an activity to keep the growing number of lads in Alberta busy. That the Olympic-style CANZUK Games had been the outcome of the suggestion delighted him to no end.

Costen knew that tonight's MMA card – the culminating event of the Games – would be the highlight for each of the involved countries' soldiers. As he watched the spectacle around him, he realized he had failed to appreciate how engaged the two-thousand-strong audience would become. Those soldiers that managed to get a ticket for the evening's final set of bouts were on overdrive. And that excitement had been playing out in various unit-to-unit interactions throughout the evening across the arena floor.

As it was, the units who had been competing against each other for the past three days in the various team and individual events had been hollering at each other from their assigned sections, and but for a couple of exceptions, it had been all in good fun.

For those scuffles that did break out, squads of military police from all four militaries were stationed around the arena. Where they stood, they watched their fellow soldiers like wary but wholly determined herding dogs ready to engage their flock.

He had arrived in the middle of the card and had seen seven fights of various weight classes, including a single Kiwi entrant who ended up choking out his Canadian opponent. The participating soldiers had represented their respective countries with honor and at times, quite a bit of skill.

Having been to a few MMA events over the years, Costen could attest that this evening's event setup was standard. The elevated octagon ring at the center of the covered ice surface was surrounded by hundreds of metal chairs. With few exceptions, the seats were now filled with men and women wearing different shades of green and beige. As he took in the scene, the sea of camouflage undulated symbiotically with the action taking place in the ring.

Senior officers and several high-profile locals occupied the first two front rows of seats around the ring. More than a few of the officers had had a pint or two by the looks of it and in some cases were cheering as hard as the soldiers sitting behind them. But a few exceptions – himself included – managed to keep their attention divided between what was taking place in the ring and what was happening in the seats behind him, where a couple of hundred soldiers of the British Army were seated. Thus far, he had only been required to turn around and deliver a blast on one occasion. The offending junior soldiers were immediately set upon by the senior enlisted men sitting around them and that had solved the problem.

Costen had been keeping a seat open beside him at the request of Captain Brazeau. He had come to know the handsome paratroop officer in the few weeks since they met in the recovery room of poor Donny Glen.

The affable Quebecer had called him out of the blue and asked if he could save a seat for a friend who might be attending the event later on in the evening. He'd heard rumors that the man was a bit of a player, despite the ring he wore on his left hand.

Costen himself had been married twenty-four years and was as chaste as they came. But he was also no prude and knew how hard the military life could be on relationships. He did not judge, or at least he did so rarely. He didn't know why the French Canadian thought *he* was the best person to play chaperone to whoever would be attending this testosterone-fueled affair, but like the generations of British officers who preceded him, he was a gentleman and would act that way should the occasion require it.

The final minute bell of the final round between an evenly matched pair of super lightweights sounded. The pair of fighters were once again back on their feet. It was clear both men were exhausted, but at the crowd's renewed urging, the heavily tattooed Scottish airman and the hatchet-faced Canadian tanker endeavored to finish the fight with one of them lying on the canvas.

As the two rejoined at the center of the ring, it was clear the Canadian was the more labored. The entire arena was now on its feet. No matter the military, unit, or rank, everyone in attendance was urging the two warriors on with a collective roar.

Directly in front of Costen, the Canadian soldier was forced against the barrier by his British opponent. Hands up, he was doing his very best to protect his head and face from a storm of punches from the seemingly possessed Scotsman.

In the flurry, the Scot landed a jab that firmly caught the right side of his opponent's face. As the Canadian stumbled backward, the British airman was on him in a flash. Now frenzied, the Scotsman delivered a series of blows to which the Canadian's only hope was that none would land solid. But one blow did connect, and from his front-row seat, Costen watched as the Canuck's legs wobbled and then gave out from under him.

As the soldier crashed into the octagon's mat, Canadian soldiers in the crowd groaned in agony, just as the British and Australian soldiers roared in unified conquest.

Like everyone else in the venue, Costen was on his feet cheering in support of the young airman's gritty and oh-so-British performance. As the referee rushed to call the fight, Costen caught the movement of a figure walking the length of his row. As the pandemonium from the soldiers sitting behind him began to wane, he shifted his eyes from the scene in the ring and took in what was easily one of the most stunning women he had ever seen. Attired in a navy-blue pantsuit, the woman walked toward him imperiously. She was taller than him but only because she was sporting a pair of stylish stilettos. But the most alluring part of the approaching woman was her eyes. Framed in by shimmering jet-black hair, her irises were so green they were almost glowing.

She stopped in front of him. "Colonel Costen?" the woman asked in a lovely sounding, French-accented voice.

"Yes, my dear," he replied, without missing a beat. "How can I be of service to you?"

"My name is Josee Labelle. I'm a friend of Captain Brazeau's. He said you might have a seat for me?"

"Indeed, I do," he said and flourished a gesture toward the seat on his left. "It would be my honor and that of the King himself if you were to join me. Please have a seat, Ms. Labelle."

"Please, Colonel, you can call me Josee," the young woman said as she moved to take her seat.

"Very good." Still standing, he reached out his hand and collected hers for a formal handshake. "And you, my dear, should feel free to call me Simon. On behalf of the Royal Armoured Corps, it is an honor to have you join us for what remains of this evening,"

Costen said as he moved to sit in the chair beside the spectacular young woman.

———

Captain Benji Chen sat in the end seat in the first row of the section where the 2nd Commando Regiment and other Australian Diggers had been assigned. It had been several weeks since Lance Corporal Dune's bust-up with the Canadian paratrooper. Thank God the man had survived and was on the mend.

Like the Australians, the Canadians were a proud bunch and as he had come to understand it, the Airborne Regiment was a bit more sensitive than most outfits due to its infamous legacy. The unit had only been recommissioned five years earlier and he'd heard that the current commanding officer had been brought in because in the short time the Regiment had been operational, there had already been performance issues.

Setting aside the notion that he expected the men of his company and the whole of 2nd Commando to be professional and stand-up soldiers, Chen knew full well that one of the worst things one could do within a larger military family was to cast aspersions on another unit's honor. In the case of Dune, the brash Lance Corporal had made the cardinal mistake of using his well-honed fighting skills to publicly shame the soldier of a tight-knit and proud military outfit from another country. That the fight had been determined a fair one was hardly the point.

So it was to his tremendous relief that when he sought Colonel Larocque to apologize for Dune's actions that the Airborne CO had assured him not to worry. According to Larocque, he too had no shortage of jackasses on his payroll. "Don't worry about it," the square-jawed Canadian officer had said to him. "I've already had words with my guys, and they've advised their boys in no uncertain terms that there is to be no more bullshit with 2nd Commando, including your Lance Corporal. I won't tolerate it. Full stop."

When he had been advised that an MMA card would be a part of the three-day competition the Canadians had organized, Chen had initially resisted the idea of Dune joining the tournament but thought better of it. If the Canadians were ever going to get past whatever resentment they had toward the corporal, he thought it best that they be given the chance to get it out of their system. Whoever took a run at Dune would get their ass handed to them, but at least they'd have their chance.

But that was his thinking two weeks ago. As he watched and listened to the bedlam reverberating through the arena as Dune strutted and crowed his way into the octagon, Chen called into question the wisdom of his decision.

As Dune bounced into the octagon and climbed atop the caged wall to scream and taunt the section of the crowd where the paratroopers of the Canadian Airborne Regiment were raging, Chen wondered if the better call wouldn't have been to put the testosterone-fueled bogan on a transport heading back to Oz.

But what was done, was done. He didn't relish the idea of further bruising the Airborne's collective ego, but the idea of telling Dune to lay off the gas in the name of whatever dynamic was playing out between the two elite units was not in the cards. Chen and 2nd Commando didn't lay off on anything. Outside of the SAS, it's what made them Australia's most elite fighting unit. The Airborne and the rest of the too-sensitive Canadian Army would learn to take their licks whether they liked it or not. This being the land of ice hockey and all that, he reckoned these blokes would have had a bigger set on them. Well, he thought, there was no bloody help for it now.

———

"Ladies and gentlemen," the ring announcer's voice boomed over the PA system. "I have just been advised there has been a change to this evening's card. Due to injury, the Canadian entry for this match, Corporal Kettle, has had to withdraw."

Costen heard an audible groan rush from the mouths of the one-thousand-strong Canadian contingent. His eyes darted diagonally to that section of the seating where the Airborne Regiment was located. Dismayed and shocked looks dominated the sea of faces where only moments before it had been nothing but bravado and unbowed confidence. Shifting back to the ring, he saw a look of supreme smugness on the face of the young Australian fighter. Surprisingly, however, the Canadian soldier who had been announcing the matches was sporting his own elated expression. Interesting, Costen thought. The Canadian's best fighter had gone lame, yet the hometown announcer appeared to be as giddy as a kid about to open his presents on Christmas morning. Something was in the offing.

With a flourish, the announcer brought his microphone to his mouth. "With the endorsement of the organizers of this tournament, Corporal Kettle is to be replaced by another man of the same weight class from the same unit."

Another flourish and the man held up a white cue card.

"Ladies and gentlemen. Let me direct your attention to the south end of the arena."

Two thousand faces and necks strained to the area of the arena where the ice-cleaning Zamboni would drive onto the rink's ice surface. There, standing four abreast, was a parade of Canadian bagpipers and drummers dressed in full military splendor. In front of the band were three soldiers in their parade uniforms, each with a flagpole harnessed onto their waists. At the center was the country's red maple leaf, right, the flag of the Canadian Armed Forces, while on the left was the maroon and sky-blue flag of the Canadian Airborne.

"Hailing from just south of Winnipeg, the soldier representing the Canadian Airborne Regiment has an amateur record of forty-seven wins and seven losses. At nineteen years of age, he represented Canada at the 2019 Pan American Games in Lima, Peru, where he won a silver medal on decision. At the 2021 Olympic Games in Tokyo, this unsung Canadian boxing legend lost the bronze medal bout, once again by decision. Wearing the all-black trunks and fighting out of the United Boxing Club of Winnipeg, this leader of men has weighed in with a fighting trim of 182 pounds."

The elated announcer turned to face the section of soldiers wearing maroon berets and chopped the proffered white cue card in their direction. In that moment, it seemed to Costen that the penny had dropped for the two-hundred-plus paratroopers. The entire section surged to their feet and as one larger organism men and women were clutching each other's uniforms and howling as they waited for confirmation of who their champion might be.

"Airborne," the announcer roared. "Stomach in, shoulders back, chin up, chest out, look proud, and give your full-throated appreciation for none other than the former Canadian amateur middleweight champion, the Red River Demon, the one, the only, Colonel Jackson Larocque!"

No sooner had the announcer bellowed Larocque's name than Costen's ears were waylaid by the blare of bagpipes and the martial rattle of drums as the band made its best effort to blow the roof off the jam-packed hockey arena.

Taking his eyes from the marching band that was now in stride, Costen turned his attention to the young woman standing beside him. Her face was lit up by a million-watt smile. Sensing Costen's gaze, her eyes met his. "I take it this was a surprise?" the woman asked.

"Yes," he replied. "And a lesson."

"Oh, and what lesson would that be, Colonel?"

"That it is always a risky proposition – even in today's day and age – to slight the honor of an officer and his regiment."

Chapter 11

Ottawa

Merielle glanced at the watch on her wrist. She was maintaining her normal pace. She had been a long-distance runner since high school, having competed in city-wide and provincial competitions. Maintaining her running habit had been harder as her career progressed, but she'd proudly kept the three-times-a-week habit going even as a Member of Parliament and now Minister of Defence.

When in Ottawa, she lived at her rented condo which was a ten-minute walk from the Hill. Living there, she had easy access to several lovely pedestrian routes that hugged the Ottawa River. For the most part, the City of Ottawa and Gatineau, its sister city across the river, had done a fine job of not allowing their urban environments to encroach upon the riverfront. The combination of being a national capital and the foresight of long-dead politicians had produced long uninterrupted boulevards, pathways, and good-sized parks for the region's citizens to enjoy.

She had taken her normal route running east from her apartment toward Ottawa's historic and tony neighborhood of Rockcliffe Park and in the process had powered by the prime minister's official residence at 24 Sussex. A kilometer past the gated Victorian-era estate, her earbuds signaled to her that a call was coming in. Pounding the pavement hard, she hesitated a look at her watch and saw that it was Stephane.

She tapped her wrist to make the connection. "Steph, it's a bit late for you, no?" she said.

"Hey, Mer. Did I catch you at a bad time? Sounds like you're doing a lot of heavy breathing there. I can call back if you're busy."

"For God's sake," she said. "Your species. Is it never not about sex?"

"Almost never. And don't let any hot-blooded man tell you otherwise. Even today."

"Well, thanks for that tip. I'll keep it in mind whenever I undertake my next failed leap into this city's inglorious dating scene. What's up?"

"CSIS finished their deep dive on Brazeau."

"And?" Merielle prompted.

"There's nothing there. As best as they can tell, he's not a separatist or sympathizer of the cause. He grew up in the Eastern Townships, played competitive hockey growing up, and then at twenty-one, he joined the army. Four years in, he got his commission and since then, he's been a soldier's soldier. His personnel file glows with positive feedback from his commanding officers and all indications are that the soldiers working under him think he's a fantastic officer. His performance ratings are off the chart.

"On the personal side, he's a bit of a mess, but that's no different than half the military or the RCMP for that matter. After getting a warrant, CSIS ripped into his social media accounts and personal emails. He has a wife of two years who's living on base with him in Petawawa and they have a baby daughter. Based on what we're seeing in his emails, he's juggling her and Ms. Labelle, and as best we can tell, Ms. Brazeau is in the dark about our DGSE operative."

Merielle picked up her run again.

"You know, Stephane, in my experience, where there is a secret lover in the picture, it's often the case that it is not as secret as you might have thought. Let's send some people out to Petawawa to speak with Ms. Brazeau. Maybe she's clueless about the affair or maybe she's not. My gut is telling me something is going on here. If getting a lead means that I have to shatter whatever notion of fidelity this woman might have toward our handsome captain, well, I'm prepared to do that."

She paused and gave careful thought before uttering her next words.

"There are other things at play on this file, Stephane. Things I can't share with you at the moment. The bottom line is that we need to find out what Josee Labelle is up to, and we need this intel sooner rather than later."

————

Gatineau

Finally, things were happening. The time that had passed since they had crossed into Quebec had been interminable. But a week earlier, Altov had received an encrypted packet activating him and his team. Since the order had come in, they had spent every early morning for the past four days in the densely forested park directly across the river from the downtown core of Canada's capital city.

During the day the park was a delightful location for families and nature lovers. A well-worn collection of paths ran under an emerald canopy for what was the equivalent of several city blocks on the Quebec side of the Ottawa River.

In pairs, or on their own, Altov and his team members had walked or run the urban green space, and in that short time, they had identified three areas where they could operate. Due to their two previous early morning jaunts, they knew that few people came into the park after sunset. Mostly, it was teenagers looking for a secluded place to do what kids can't do when at home.

On this morning, Altov had brought all five members of the team. One was with the van in the parking lot that served as the launching point for the recreation area's daily visitors. He would advise Altov and the rest of the team if anyone arrived and whether or not that person or persons was going for a late-night stroll.

Two other members of the team were deep into the park proper. Experts in wilderness fieldcraft, they would observe the trails, and if necessary, they would distract or delay any late-night travelers who wandered into the area from some other direction. That left himself and Heng set up near the end of one of the park's trails, half a dozen meters back from the dark water that separated the provinces of Ontario and Quebec.

They had chosen the morning in question due to the cycle of the moon. The timing would be such that there would be little in the way of celestial glow to be cast against the drones Heng was about to launch. Not that moonlight would have made much of a difference. Impressively quiet, the four-fanned unit hovering in front of them had a diameter that was a smidge larger than a standard frisbee.

Altov nodded his head to the other man at which point the mercenary slipped a pair of goggles over his eyes, while both of his hands began to manipulate what looked like a video game console controller. As the delicate-looking drone began to rise upwards, he noted with interest that the underbelly of the machine appeared to be shifting as it took on various dark hues.

Five minutes later, Heng said, "I'm in position, two thousand feet above the target."

Altov looked across the river in the direction of the Canadian prime minister's residence. In the air above the property, he could see nothing. He brought a pair of small binoculars to his eyes and looked to where the drone should have been, but again, he couldn't see a thing.

"Do it," Altov said.

Knowing what would happen next was well beyond anything his binoculars could see, he turned to watch Heng. The man stood erect as his thumbs and fingers manipulated the controller that rested along his pelvis.

"All sixteen units have successfully released and are moving to their pre-designated locations," said Heng

Some minutes later, Heng's hands stopped moving and his body tensed. "Shit," the mercenary said under his breath.

Altov, knowing how the other man worked, said nothing and waited.

"There's a dude standing right below where unit eleven is to position itself. What kind of loser smokes anymore?" Heng's tone was more annoyed than panicked. "Ahh, there we go. That's right. Finish up your cancer stick, you idiot."

Seconds later, he piped up again. "He's done. Looks like he's going back to the guard barracks. The unit is now moving into place."

After what seemed like an eternity, the drone operator said, "Done." Pulling off his goggles, Heng handed them to Altov. "Have a look."

The Russian took the goggles and slipped them on. Immediately, his vision was filled with the crystal-clear image of the main entrance of a 19th-Century chateau that once belonged to a long-dead lumber baron.

"That's unit six," Heng advised. "It's about thirty feet high in a tree on the other side of the driveway."

Altov whistled. "Nice. These things have really come a long way, haven't they?" He had no problem making out that the iron-wrought handle on the single door entrance had an intricate, likely one-of-a-kind design.

Without any warning from Heng, the image shifted. He was now looking at what was the beautifully landscaped backyard of the residence. Well lit, he could see the perfectly manicured lawn stretching from the residence to the tree-lined edge of the two-hundred-foot cliff face that dropped into the fast-flowing Ottawa River. Beyond the swaying tops of the trees, it was the urban glow from the Quebec side of the border.

He pulled off the goggles and tossed them to the other man. "That's some good work, my friend. If we get the call, these will serve us well. Very well."

———

Edmonton

As Josee watched the referee in the ring give instructions to the Airborne's commanding officer and the handsome Australian soldier, she was concentrating on a conversation taking place between two female soldiers in the women's washroom via the micro-earpiece that she had had surgically installed during her last trip to France.

Before searching out the British colonel, she had used one of the arena's washrooms and in so doing, had carefully placed a tiny listening device on top of one of her stall's privacy panels.

Until the present conversation, all Josee had heard were banalities and the occasional bowel movement. The current conversation offered what she thought was her first morsel of real intelligence.

The two women had been friends who had been posted together a half dozen years ago but had drifted apart once the first of the pair had been shipped out to her next assignment.

After catching up on what Josee thought were two entirely unremarkable lives, one of the two women mentioned that she and part of her unit were getting ready to post out to a small airfield in North Dakota. Orders had come down that afternoon. They'd ship out next week and the woman had no idea when they'd be back. The other woman had asked if she knew what they were going to North Dakota for, but the woman who had offered the information about the highly unusual posting had not given any hint as to what she or her unit might be doing.

It hadn't been much, but it was more than Josee had been able to glean from her frisky lover earlier in the evening.

She would see what other tidbits she could pick up by listening to the conversations taking place around her. If she was patient and had a bit of luck, perhaps she would be able to give the DGSE something they could make sense of. And, of course, whatever information she provided to the French was just as likely to help her own plans.

———

The referee bade the two men to come together at the center of the ring.

Larocque and the younger Australian locked eyes. As Larocque stood still and said nothing, the Aussie seemed to be on the verge of vibrating as he shifted his weight from one foot to the other. As the referee gave his instructions, Dune raised his voice and with one of the thicker accents Larocque had heard since the Australians' arrival, the younger man said, "Oi, old man. You're no colonel in this here octagon. You're just a sad old fella who's gonna get rolled and hard, mate. On behalf of all the 2nd and the rest of the ADF, it's gonna be a pleasure thrashing you. You got that, ol' man?"

Larocque said nothing in return. He'd been in this situation too many times before and had heard it all. As the referee stepped back from instructing them, he slowly issued his right fist toward Dune in the universal gesture of sportsmanship. With what had become the man's signature smug look, the Aussie lance corporal looked at his proffered hand with disgust and without reciprocation, thrust his arms straight into the air and howled like a banshee. The slight was met with a deep wave of boos that rolled in from Canadian soldiers that dominated the capacity crowd.

Larocque turned and walked to his corner and waited for the bell. Making it there, he looked at the section where the soldiers from his regiment were standing and cheering him on. The past year had been the worst year of his life. It had got so bad that he had walked out on some of Canada's best sons and daughters. He knew that had been a mistake. Without these soldiers and the purpose of command, he would be dead, or near it. With what was to come, Larocque now had a north star. He would lead these soldiers through what was to come and if he survived, he'd figure things out with his wife, Madison.

Hearing the bell, he turned and let his body assume its well-honed fighting stance. Gloved fists raised to the sides of his face, his body, led by his feet, began to weave rhythmically.

His opponent assumed a similar stance, and the two men began circling one another. Larocque cleared his mind and allowed his eyes and fighting instincts to assess Dune. Larocque's video work and intel from other sources had suggested that the other man would look to dominate the fight immediately with his first-rate striking skills. But it was also the case that the cocky showman had a penchant for putting on flashy displays that would wow the crowd.

Larocque watched and waited.

And then it came. Dune stepped forward and unleashed a combination that seemed impossibly fast, and a firm jab caught Larocque just below his occipital bone. Stumbling backward, Dune was on Larocque like human lightning, delivering a flying knee straight at his chin. With decades of ring experience, he let any feelings of panic flow past him. Pressed against the caged barrier, he allowed his hands to meet Dune's knee, while in the same instant he pivoted right and slipped away from an elbow that came the moment Dune's feet made contact with the mat.

Shakily moving to the center of the ring, Larocque looked to give himself time to recover. This had happened before and on instinct, he knew what to do. He would make the lithe Australian chase him for as long as needed so that he could pull himself back together.

But instead of pursuing him, the Aussie commando circled Larocque at a distance and in a display of arrogance suited to the young or the mad, the man tilted his head upwards and howled savagely.

Finishing his war cry, Dune locked his ocean-blue eyes onto Larocque. "You're pathetic and old. What did you reckon, mate – that I was gonna take it easy on you because you're an officer? Or maybe you thought I'd ease up because of your sad story? I don't give a shit about your kiddie, mate. I don't give a shit about any of it. You thought you'd come in this ring and embarrass me in front of my mates. Oi, you're fucking with a top dog, old man. It's me who's gonna give the lesson."

The moment Larocque heard the words 'your kiddie' and 'I don't give a shit,' whatever dust had been swirling in his head settled. A vision of Lauren's pale face and hanging body flashed in front of his eyes. A controlled rage flowed into his veins and sloshed around with the already-present cocktail of hormones. He gave the Australian his own hard stare and waited.

Dune offered Larocque a mocking smile and then like a viper closed the distance, his fighting posture ready to once again lay down a flurry of blows on his older Canadian opponent.

Larocque let the onslaught happen. Interpreting a series of almost imperceptible movements, his now fully sharpened mind anticipated a fast but wildly executed left hook. Instinctively, he took a half-step back and leaned his body to the right allowing his opponent to overcommit. With twenty-five years of fighting experience urging him on, he shifted his weight forward and snapped the six-ounce glove on his right hand straight into the Australian soldier's jaw. *Crack.*

Sidestepping, Larocque watched the younger man's legs give way, allowing the Aussie's now-limp body to career uncontrolled into the canvas.

He did not pursue the fallen man to the ground as most MMA fighters are taught to do. He had been in too many fights and knew the moment his gloved hand connected, the fight was over. Satisfyingly, he had felt the hinge of the younger man's jaw give way. It had been the perfect strike. There was no getting up from that kind of injury.

Larocque slowly walked over to his corner, where Brazeau and the other officers of the Regiment were starting to pour into the ring, their faces elated and relieved. Allowing his senses to expand beyond the ring, he processed the explosion of noise echoing within the arena's structure. It was chaos.

One of the soldiers from his corner handed him the maroon and sky-blue flag of the Regiment. Grabbing it, he held it aloft as Brazeau, Singh, and his Second in Command, 2IC, the hulking Delgado grabbed him by the thighs and powered him into the air.

Surveying the crowd of mostly elated faces, he forgave Dune for his transgression. He had been a young man once too and knew full well that men of that age had little appreciation for how much of a man's soul could get wrapped up into that of his children's or to what lengths an officer might go to restore his soldiers' honor. The honor of the Regiment now pulled back from the rocky shore it had been listing toward, Larocque could turn his full attention to the task his country had thrust upon him. It was time to lead Canada to war.

Chapter 12

Whiteman Air Force Base

As Havez left the base, his hands were shaking. He had never been a frontline soldier. With a graduate degree in computer science from the University of Florida, he cut his teeth in the US military by working up the ranks of the Air Force's various electronic and cyber warfare outfits. In addition to being a talented programmer, Havez had been gifted with administrative abilities all too often lacking in those who could code. It was his ability to run large organizations combined with his technical skills that had allowed him to move through the ranks as quickly as he had.

Giving what he thought was a casual salute to the soldier manning the reinforced security post that managed the flow of people and vehicles entering and leaving the base, Havez took a left onto the lightly trafficked state highway that ran parallel to Whiteman's north-south orientation.

It was the prospect of getting back onto the base that had his heart going at a steady clip within his chest.

As the civil war went, it had been an easy decision not to join the Constitutionalists. As a Baptist who went to church every Sunday, Havez understood and even sympathized with the Reds. He too had been upset when the Democratic-dominated Congress had passed legislation to fund and then build dozens of federally-run abortion clinics on the borders of half a dozen Red Faction states. And this was but one of several egregious constitutional end-arounds the Democrats had pulled in the years leading up to the war.

But when push came to actual shove, Havez couldn't bring himself to support a division of the country. While the former United States had its problems, it was and remained his sense that with the passage of time the country would right itself.

So when the Reds proclaimed their collective secession three years ago and Missouri had declared itself a neutral state, he and his wife had packed their things in Virginia and made their way to Kansas City. From there, he had a front-row seat from which to watch the country tear itself apart.

In throwing in with a neutral state, Havez had been in the minority. The vast majority of officers and soldiers felt the country was worth fighting for, and as the fighting broke out between the factions, there was a rush of military personnel moving to and fro as they declared their politics and picked a side.

It was following the incineration of the Blue's major cities and neutral Colorado's subsequent atomic strike that Havez knew his decision to throw in with Missouri had been the right call. That he had been tapped to play a key role in helping to manage and protect the state's inherited nuclear stockpile had been the ultimate vindication of his decision.

Rounding a bend in the two-lane highway, he saw the roadside diner he had been looking for. As he approached the still-functioning business, Havez saw signage indicating that the four pumps in front of the restaurant were operational and were for the moment selling gas. That was no small thing, he thought.

Havez had chosen this location because in all of his conversations on base, he had never heard anyone mention the tiny town that this roadside establishment was supposedly a part of. While he had not taken the time to perform a formal probability analysis, he assumed that if in the past three years no one mentioned this backwater location, there stood a decent chance he wouldn't run into someone he knew when he visited the way station to pick up his new charges.

The drive had served to calm his nerves, but as he pulled into the diner's parking area, his heart was once again jackhammering. Sitting in the seat of his car, he proceeded to take several deep breaths while counting to sixty. At forty, his heart rate began to subside to the point where the irrational part of his brain was no longer screaming 'heart attack'.

At sixty seconds, Havez took a final deep breath and opened the door of his base-owned sedan. Getting out of the car and standing, he took in the frontage of the eatery and gas station. It was as ordinary and unremarkable-looking as he hoped. He took his first step in the direction of the entrance and to his relief, he kept moving. With every step, his confidence grew. In his soul, he knew he was doing the right thing, even if that thing meant that many or most of his fellow Americans would gladly see him shot as a traitor to his country.

———

Missouri

"He's here," Hall said to the square-jawed young man sitting across from her. Wallace's brush cut was still fresh and made him look as though he was either an athlete or an active serving member of the military.

Both were true. From her days as a cadet at the Royal Military College, Hall had watched him lead the RMC's volleyball team in their struggles against the stronger programs in the division they played. Not unlike the United States' own military varsity programs, RMC had neither the student numbers nor the resources to field top-tier sports teams.

She too was fresh-faced. With sandy brown hair, hazel eyes more brown than green, and an athletic build that had been achieved with years of distance running, Hall confidently projected the look that Wallace had dubbed "sun-kissed sorority girl." Which was good, because that was the very image she was trying to exude.

The colonel, looking exactly like the pictures they had been shown, walked hesitantly as he entered the restaurant. Stopping in front of the 'seat yourself' sign, he surveyed the interior of the diner. In all, there were ten other people seated at various tables, and in Hall's estimation, all were locals.

Searching the room, the colonel's face lit up with a smile when he finally made eye contact with their table. Reciprocating the warmth on his face, Hall waved the man over. Arriving at their booth, he exclaimed in a voice that carried well beyond their table, "Well there she is. Another newly minted and proud University of Florida graduate. Jenna, you look wonderful."

Following the man's boisterous lead, Hall got up from her seat and allowed the older and surprisingly short man to gather her up into an embrace she hoped had the look of an uncle and a niece.

Separating from one another, she turned and looked at Wallace. "Uncle Vic, I want you to meet my fiancé, Blake."

Havez then turned to Wallace, who had gotten out of his seat while the colonel and Hall had their initial exchange, and thrust out his hand, greeting the younger man with what looked to be a vigorous handshake.

"Good to finally meet you, son. I'm sorry it couldn't have been sooner. My wife is excited to meet you. She's heard so much about you from Jenna's mom. Though I'll confess in all that I've heard, she failed to mention that you would be so damn tall."

Wallace offered the older man a smile and a shrug of his shoulders and replied, "Good to meet you, sir. A long time coming."

The two fake lovers had agreed that Hall would do as much of the talking as possible, while Wallace would play the nervous and doting romantic partner.

Havez turned his attention back to Hall, a smile still holding fast on his face. "Well, I guess congratulations are in order. I'm excited for you both. Not only because the commitment of marriage is one of the most important things that two people can do in the eyes of our Lord, but also because I hope you'll be producing lots of little Gators in the not-so-distant future."

Hall manufactured a giggle, looked at Wallace with what she hoped passed as fondness, and then offered a response to the colonel's improvisation. "I told you, my love. It's all Gators all the time with this guy."

Looking at the mugs of coffee on their table, Havez thumbed over his shoulder to where the kitchen was and asked, "It looks like you haven't eaten. Do we want to order something, or shall we hit the road? It's up to you."

"We're fine," Hall said immediately. "We had a big breakfast before we left Nashville and I'm anxious to see Aunt Beth."

According to intelligence reports, Elizabeth Havez had suffered from a second bout of breast cancer and had had a full mastectomy four months before. That same intelligence reported that the colonel's wife did in fact have a lone niece who lived in Florida and had gone to the University of Florida, but three years earlier.

It was this family connection that had resulted in CANZUK's mission planners choosing the two fresh lieutenants for this assignment.

Based on a pilfering of the real Jenna's hacked social media accounts, Hall knew that she shared some physical characteristics with the other woman. It wasn't an uncanny resemblance, but it was ballpark, and if no one became too interested in her or her story, she was confident the cover would hold.

"Well, if you're fed and watered, let's settle up your bill and get on the road. As I said, your aunt is whipped up to see you and I'm under strict orders to get you home ASAP." Havez reached into his pocket, pulled out a thin wallet, and proceeded to put old US currency on the table paying for the pair's coffee.

Still wearing an expression of mock happiness, Havez took in the two large wheeled suitcases sitting on the tiled floor at the end of the booth's benched seating. Realizing what must be contained in each of the cases, his smile faded. Pointing at the two suitcases, he said "Grab your things and follow me."

Hall and Wallace moved promptly to comply. Grabbing the luggage, the two Canadian officers formed a line behind the commanding officer of Whiteman Air Force Base and followed him out the door.

———

North Dakota

In the moonlit darkness, Costen watched as the train came to a final screeching stop. This was the second fully loaded Canada Pacific delivery this week. Each train was over two kilometers long with somewhere in the range of one hundred and thirty cars, each carrying one to three British military vehicles, or a shipping container filled with supplies. With one more train due to arrive next week, the entirety of the four battlegroups that had been formed in Shilo, Manitoba would be unloaded and gathered at designated starting points across this part of North Dakota.

Once offloaded, individual vehicle crews would start up their machines and move to a predetermined location somewhere along the southern border of the state. Three British and a lone Australian battlegroup would drive out of the southeast corner of North Dakota, while the four Canadian battlegroups would set out from the southwest part of the state, having arrived from Alberta via the Burlington Northern Santa Fe line. Altogether, it had taken two weeks of trains and hundreds of road convoys to position seventeen thousand soldiers and their equipment.

For the CANZUK militaries, the movement of this many soldiers and their vehicles had been no small feat. It also hadn't been subtle and had strained the alliance's now-combined intelligence corps and their efforts to hide and misdirect why so many foreign soldiers were gathering in this part of the United States.

It started with the North Dakota National Guard undertaking communications with local governments and even individual farmers across the impacted parts of the state. They had been advised that small groups of Canadian and British military units would be arriving along the southern edge of the state to participate in a series of military exercises that would culminate in the expansive badlands that made up a large part of the western half of South Dakota.

The exercises with the Canadians and British had been agreed to by both state governments because neither state's National Guard had been able to engage in meaningful multi-unit operations since the start of the civil war. Though small in size, the locals had been advised that both state's National Guards needed practice to keep their operational edge.

Communities, farmers and ranchers were asked to be patient and would be offered generous compensation for any damage that might be done to their property by any of the vehicles moving across their land.

Limiting social media chatter about troop movements had been another challenge. Having spent the entirety of his life in a world dominated by social media, Costen was familiar enough with how information traveled and gained currency such that the wrong people or governments might take notice of the fact that nearly twenty thousand troops had suddenly appeared in part of North America where they had never been before.

On this front, CANZUK had taken several precautions.

They had made every effort to disembark the alliance's loaded trains after dark and once off-loaded, units only moved to their designated staging areas between the hours of midnight and five in the morning. Where possible, vehicles were positioned out of sight from roadways where curious onlookers might gawk or take video.

Where such low-tech evasive tactics came up short – which of course they would – each of CANZUK's cyber warfare units would step in. If anyone had asked, Costen would have had to confess he didn't understand most of what these outfits did, but as it pertained to the growing military presence across North Dakota, he and the rest of the battlegroup commanders had received an almost fully comprehensible briefing that suggested the alliance's cyber warriors had the matter in hand.

The moment CANZUK soldiers began to arrive in-theatre, a combined cyber unit from all four countries had released a near-AI software package onto the web that would identify any and all social media users in the general vicinity of the eight battlegroups. That same program would monitor these individuals' posts and other communications for any mention of the CANZUK military buildup. If they did post about what they saw, the software would first embargo the output and then insert malware into the person's device that would make it inoperable for whatever amount of time CANZUK's shadow warriors desired.

According to the brigadier who gave the cyber briefing, the near-AI that would drive the suppression program would be able to co-opt and manipulate ninety percent of all phones. For the remaining ten percent, the four nations' cyberwarfare units had tricks up each of their electronic sleeves to make up the difference.

If the alliance's preporatory efforts had a weakness, Costen knew it was satellite imagery. Quality space-based imaging was not the exclusive domain of nation-states anymore. In addition to the few remaining satellites that the UCSA had access to, for a small fee, anyone from that government could go to half-a-dozen companies and within a few hours could have every square meter of North Dakota painted by high-resolution images.

The tactic to employ on this front was not to give the UCSA a reason to look at this part of the continent. If CANZUK had done its job effectively, and Costen thought they had, there was no reason for the Reds to train their sights on the Dakotas. The latest intel suggested that the Red Faction and Cameron were engrossed in the question of Missouri joining the UCSA and its upcoming peace talks with the Blues. So long as CANZUK continued to do a good job of staging their forces quietly and kicked off the operation on time, Costen was convinced they would be able to maintain a strategic advantage over the Reds.

After walking several hundred meters down the length of the train, he arrived at the car carrying the Challenger 3 tank that would bear him and his crew across three states and nine hundred kilometers. Costen was convinced they had a solid plan for what they needed to do, but it was also true that the best-laid plans went to shit the moment your vehicle moved off its starting line.

Whatever happened, come hell or high water, Costen and his battlegroup would make it to that airbase, and they would make it in time. The plan called for the expeditionary force rolling out of Colorado to relieve Larocque and the Airborne within thirty hours of the mission's kick-off, but Costen and the other battle-group commanders were hedging their bets that the Colorado National Guard wouldn't be able to make it across Kansas that quickly. They weren't reg force soldiers and lacked the heavy armor and training that the Brits, Aussies and Canadians had.

As a collective, and over pints in a secluded corner of the officer's mess at CFB Edmonton, all eight of the colonels leading the CANZUK battlegroups agreed that if things did go to shit, they would do what they needed to do to get to the Airborne in time.

The generals had been clear. They wanted coordinated and orderly. And, to be sure, that was all well and good if Larocque and his soldiers were sitting pretty. But if the Airborne was pressed to the point where it looked like they might buckle, all eight commanders had agreed that caution would be thrown to the wind, and these Red bastards and whoever else got in their way would find out just how hard, fast, and – if need be – nasty, each of the three country's armored regiments could fight. And consequences be damned.

———

Paris

Minister Charron pulled his eyes from the satellite images laid in front of him and looked at the senior intelligence officer from the DGSE.

"These are compelling," the bespectacled man said. "Tell me again why we shouldn't tell Archie Cameron that the British and Canadians appear to be up to something?"

"Chaos, sir," advised Besson. "Our best analysis tells us that France is best served by a United States that remains divided. As it stands at the moment, the Reds hold the upper hand over the Blues. We don't yet know exactly what CANZUK is planning. Our recommendation is that we hold off on passing this information along to Cameron until we know what their plan is. And even then, I suggest we only inform the Reds at the last minute. If France holds back on the intel and allows CANZUK to give a boost to the Blues, yet we still aid the Reds when the time is right, we might be able to extend the American conflict for some time. Perhaps indefinitely."

Charron grunted. "This is quite the needle you're proposing we thread. And how is it we're going to find out what CANZUK's actual objective is? If they're saying it's an exercise, for all we know that might be exactly what it is."

"The Quebec-based asset I briefed you on," Besson advised.

"Labelle, the separatist's daughter. Yes, I remember her. You had mentioned she's quite talented. Ambitious, too. Is she in the know?"

"She is both of those things, to be sure. She had a contact in one of the fighting units that we think will be at the center of whatever CANZUK is planning. The asset is of the junior variety, but as soon as he knows what the plan is, Labelle will know and that will be passed along to us. We may know weeks in advance, or we may only get hours of warning."

The politician sat back in the expensive leather chair behind the ancient oak desk that dominated his office and contemplated the other man's assessment.

"This plan you're proposing is not without risks to us. What happens if this CANZUK outfit throws in with the Blue Faction and they overcome the Reds? There's little doubt that the UCSA better aligns with us politically. Goodness knows the world doesn't need more of the woke nonsense that Blues continue to proselytize. One would have thought this civil war of theirs would have taught them a lesson, but it seems they've only doubled down in their rhetoric. And you're no doubt aware that our president loathes the poison pill that is American progressivism. In fact, if you told her that the outcome of the conflict was starting to lean in the direction of the Blues, you might be able to convince her to formally throw in with this Cameron fellow, war criminal or no."

"With the approach I'm proposing, we can always pivot in the direction of the Reds if we need to, but if our objective is to keep the whole of the American political enterprise on its knees for as long as possible, then I believe we have to walk this line."

Charron stared at the spymaster with hard, dark eyes and per his practice said nothing for several moments. Waiting for a reply, Besson patiently listened to the hands of the Bonaparte-era gilt bronze clock on the minister's desk march forward.

Finally, the minister steepled his fingers together. "As I see it, the proposed course of action is sound. Proceed as you feel is best within the parameters that you have just set out. I'll brief the president and if she has any direction to give, I will let you know."

Chapter 13

Edmonton

Captain Chen of 2nd Commando, 3 Company had listened carefully to the major who had presented the operation to secure the American airbase. The CANZUK planners had done well. They'd committed to a straightforward approach. As it must be with any airborne operation, success would come from the element of surprise.

After a series of airstrikes and the execution of several diversionary tactics, the Canadian Airborne Regiment would drop along the eastern perimeter of Whiteman at which point they would move west to secure the base's airfield and key buildings. Once secured, various elements of the eleven-hundred-strong unit plus two hundred other soldiers would transition into tasks ranging from readying the base's two-hundred-plus nuclear weapons to building a slew of defensive positions to help hold off any Red Faction counterattack.

If all went well, the Canadians would only need to hold the base for thirty-six hours and perhaps less. Mechanized forces originating from Colorado were to race across Kansas, and upon arriving at Whiteman, they would load up the nukes and the Airborne and then drive everyone out of the state under the protective watch of CANZUK air units that would be operating out of the Dakotas and Colorado. If for whatever reason, the Colorado National Guard was held up or was somehow prevented from reaching Whiteman, the Airborne would have to hold the base until one or more of eight CANZUK battlegroups reached them from their own starting points in North Dakota.

Though disappointing, 2nd Commando's role in the mission was understandable. Its three companies would be held in reserve in Edmonton, where if things went poorly at the airfield or there was some other task to be done, Chen and his fellow commandos would load up on another flight of Hercs and would fly south.

As the husky Major Landry finished up her overview, Chen watched as several senior officers joined her at the front of the room. Larocque was there.

It had been several weeks since they had last spoken. That conversation had been on the night the Airborne CO had put down Dune in the octagon. At the time, Larocque had assured him that the grudge between the two units had been buried.

Chen wanted to believe that. After what the colonel had done to make that fight happen and then to win in such a memorable fashion, he couldn't help but respect the man, even if Dune was one of his lads.

To be sure, the Canadian paratrooper was an unorthodox leader and most certainly there was an unhinged element to him, but there was no denying the loyalty that Larocque's soldiers had for their commanding officer. Chen had seen nothing like it.

All of which made the current dynamic between 2nd Commando and the Airborne interesting, if not concerning. How would the two units operate if 2nd Commando got the call and they waded into the shit with the Canadians down south? In Chen's mind, it was an unanswered question.

It was not as though he wished ill on the paratroopers. The Airborne and the soldiers within it were like first cousins you didn't get to see very often. It just so happened that on the occasion of this most recent gathering things hadn't gone particularly well.

So, in the name of finding a final peace between the two elite units, 2nd Commando's CO had stepped in and offered words to his officers suggesting that Dune had had it coming, and though he wasn't happy with how things went down in the lead-up to the match, he had given direction to his officers to let the matter go.

In the end, the inherent pragmatism of the Australian Army won the day and Chen and his fellow junior officers agreed to bury the hatchet. But no matter how you sliced it, in Chen's mind, he and his company had something to prove. If they got the call to fly to Missouri, Chen promised himself that he and his lads would show these too-proud Canadians just how martial and badass 2nd Commando really was.

———

Quebec, east of Montreal

It was a glorious day and Josee couldn't help but smile as she took in the vista laid out before her. The undulating gold-and-green farmland that rolled along the shores of the St. Lawrence River was spectacular, while the farmhouses and oversized churches that dotted this same geography were a quaint reminder that the province of her birth had a soul that was both unique and abiding. In that moment, Josee promised herself that she would never get tired of the drive from Montreal to Quebec City.

Looking down the stretch of highway that lay before her, Josee's eyes caught a glint of sunlight refracting off something high on the horizon. No doubt it was one of those new drones the provincial police were using to nail unsuspecting drivers for speeding. The self-driving software now in control of her vehicle had been upgraded with an off-market navigation package. A combination of radar detection and enhanced optics, the software dutifully scanned the road ahead to identify anything that might lead to the vehicle's driver receiving an infraction.

Taking her eyes off the sky, Josee quickly advised the car's driving software to reduce her speed. The radar-invisible drones had been the latest high-tech attempt on the part of the *Sûreté du*

Québec to disabuse the province's many time-efficient citizens of their need for speed.

As her Tesla Model Q began to decelerate, the vehicle's interface advised her that she had an incoming call. Looking at the console, she saw that it was an unlisted number. Under normal circumstances, Josee wouldn't take a call from a number she didn't recognize, but these were far from normal times.

Canada, like most countries, had passed laws banning the use of software that encrypted the phone conversations of average citizens. And understandably so. When such tech was used, it was impossible to intercept and listen to the communication between the involved parties. The technology was a dream come true for organized crime and to its credit, Canada had done more than most countries to make sure the illegal software stayed out of the country.

Josee had considered making arrangements to get the software herself but had thought better of it. If the authorities found you in possession of such a program and you couldn't provide a good reason as to why you had it, it was the clearest indication possible to the feds that you were someone they should be taking a close look at. Josee didn't need that kind of attention.

"Accept the call," she advised the car. "Allo."

"We need to talk," a male voice said.

Upon hearing the voice, Josee's body tensed up while her hands thrust forward and unnecessarily grasped the steering wheel. "This is unexpected," she said.

"Do you have access to a secure portal?" the voice asked.

"No. I'm on the road. I can be available in two hours."

"That will have to do. There have been developments. Call as soon as you can. I'll be waiting."

The connection ended.

The call was a major breach in operational protocol. Her contact was under explicit direction not to connect with her through her cell unless it was a matter of the greatest urgency. In their three years working together, he had never reached out to her in this way before.

With the sun further into its decline, Josee could now clearly see the traffic enforcement drone languishing high in the sky above the highway.

There was no help for it, she thought. Taking her hands off the wheel, Josee commanded, "Increase speed to one hundred and eighty-five." Any more than that and Josee risked the drone taking the step of flagging her for an actual bored-to-tears cop who would no doubt do their utmost to pull her over.

As Josee felt her car flex its battery-infused muscle and begin to pass the first set of vehicles that lay in front of her, she scoffed at the notion that a fine was going to delay her from obtaining information she suspected would be crucial to her efforts to free the province she so dearly loved.

———

Ottawa

"With the exception of two people I don't trust with this kind of information, I've spoken individually with every cabinet minister. They all understand what's being proposed and what's at stake. As you would expect, in a few cases there was hesitation, but the holdouts came around. With the exception of those mentioned, cabinet is on board," Canada's prime minister said to Merielle and General Kaplan, the country's Chief of Defence Staff.

"Prime Minister, we're as ready as we're going to be," the CDS said. "The longer we wait, the more time we give to the UCSA to find out what we're up to. Time truly is of the essence."

The three of them were alone in the PM's office on the second floor of the Centre Block of Parliament Hill. MacDonald sat in a leather-backed armchair while Merielle and the general shared a couch that framed in the small seating area that took up about a third of the wainscot-dominated room.

Though Merielle knew the PM had heard Kaplan's question, he was staring intently at the Tom Thomson on the wall behind her. To be sure, he was working through something.

Finally, he dropped his eyes from the painting and looked in Merielle's direction. "Tomorrow, I'll be announcing a cabinet shuffle. Merielle, you'll keep the defence portfolio, but you're also to become deputy prime minister. The public will need to see that you have my full confidence. There will be a few other moves, but your appointment will be the standout."

He shifted his always-hard gaze to the CDS. "An hour ago, I got off the phone with the other CANZUK leaders. We're still convinced this has to move forward. We agreed that you should go ahead and launch the operation. Everything will be ready on my end the moment you walk out of my office."

He slowly rose from his chair and walked toward the oak desk that dominated that side of the office. Arriving there, he turned to face his seated subordinates.

"I want you two to know I trust you implicitly. Whatever happens, know that this was my decision. And whatever comes our way, it will be my cross to bear. Is that understood?"

Kaplan was first to answer. "We're all in this together, sir, but I appreciate the unique risk you'll be taking. The CAF are ready for this mission. We won't let you or the country down."

When it was her turn to speak, Merielle looked into the eyes of the man who had been her mentor for the past four years. Without any doubt, he was the only person in the country who had the skill and political capital to steer Canada through the storm that was about to erupt. "Bob, I trust you too, and I support this decision with every fiber in my body. I'm glad you'll be the one out front, but whatever happens, I'll be with you every step of the way. No matter what."

Upon hearing her words, the PM's face took on a rare look of kindness and warmth. "Alright then," he said. "Then let's get to work and show this SOB Archie Cameron and the rest of the damned world, what this CANZUK outfit can do."

———

Edmonton

Larocque sat in the windowless office they had assigned to him at CFB Edmonton. The past day and a bit had been madness. Somewhere in that time, he had forced himself to try and get some sleep, but the effort had mostly come up short. As he lay on the cot someone had set up for him in his office, he had pulled up info about the Dieppe Raid in 1942.

Without question, it was Canada's single worst military disaster during World War II. When all was said and done on that fateful day, over three thousand men had been killed or captured, and the nation's honor lay in tatters for the world to see. The country would have to wait two long years before it could find redemption on the beaches of Normandy and in the ferocious fighting that followed.

It was tough not to make comparisons with that now-ancient action. In the case of Missouri, it would once again be Canadian soldiers who led the way, and like the young men who stormed that French port all those years ago, he and his boys would be on their own for what could be too long a period. But there were significant differences too. If all went according to plan, they would have a genuine surprise, the air support that would be in play would be far superior to anything the RAF could have brought to bear all those years ago, and unlike the Canadian raiders who hit the beaches of that seaside town, they wouldn't be facing the reinforced steel glove that was the German army.

As he sat there by himself and brooded, Larocque mused that in short order, he and his soldiers would soon find out just how capable the remnants of the US military remained.

The phone on his desk rang. Looking at the extension on the phone's display, he realized the call must be coming from off base.

It wasn't a number Larocque recognized, but seeing that it started with the Ottawa 613 area code, he thought it best to pick up. It was too much to hope that it was Madison. What kind of serendipity would that have been? He still needed to write something to her before things kicked off, but he was struggling mightily with what to say. Their last words had been both unpleasant and unequivocal. He needed to find the words to make things right. Jesus, he knew how to forgive just as she did. So why did reaching out have to be so hard?

He picked up the phone. "Colonel Larocque speaking."

"Excellent. I was told that you were at your desk," a woman's voice said.

The voice sounded familiar to Larocque. Somewhere in the nether regions of his subconscious, a collection of synapses was firing off like a cannon in an effort to place the voice. As his fatigued brain tried to place the voice, some other part of his grey matter forced him to sit up straight.

"Colonel, it's Merielle Martel calling. We need to talk."

The moment he heard the name, the chugging part of his brain trying to confirm the voice screamed its confirmation that he was indeed hearing the voice of the Minister of Defence.

"Of course, Minister. I'm all yours," Larocque replied, his mind now fully engaged.

"First, on behalf of the prime minister, myself, and the rest of the cabinet, I wanted to reach out to you to wish you and your soldiers good luck. The mission you're being asked to undertake – it's not lost on us how dangerous it is. We're behind you all the way. And when the country finds out, everyone will be behind you, too."

"Thank you, Minister," he replied. "If the final call comes and we're in the air, I'll be sure to let the men and women of the Regiment know you reached out to me personally. They'll consider it an honor, as do I."

"Yes, well, a phone call is the least I can do. I'd like to be there in person, but we don't want to draw any media attention to your final preparations, nor take resources away from what I suspect is a busy time. I hope you understand."

"We understand completely."

"Good. I knew you would. There is another reason for my call and truth be told, I'm a bit hesitant to bring it up, considering all that's on your plate. But the cop in me is screaming that I follow it up, and since I've never been one to ignore my gut, I'd like to ask you a few questions about one of your officers."

"And which officer might that be?" Larocque said, keeping his tone neutral.

"Marcel Brazeau."

His brain now firing on all cylinders, Larocque's head quickly landed on what this was likely to be about. She was concerned about the separatist. For all that's right in the world, he thought, surely to goodness a minister of the crown had more important things to worry about than who one of his officers was sleeping with. The prospect of it raised Larocque's temperature, but only slightly. Best to let Martel ask her question first before he took to breathing fire at a senior cabinet minister for what he felt in that moment was unwarranted salaciousness.

To his own credit, Larocque had been on top of the Josee Labelle matter from the get-go. On the very day he found out that Brazeau had taken to having an affair with the daughter of the country's most powerful separatist leader, he had called Brazeau into his office and read the captain the riot act. And not just because he was not-so-secretly sleeping with separatist royalty. Not a year earlier, he had had a baby with his young and beautiful wife. 'What the hell are you thinking?' had been one of several pointed questions he had put to his best company commander.

"I'm at your full disposal, Minister. Please feel free to ask any questions about the good captain or any other member of my unit. We're an open book," Larocque said.

"Did you know that Josee Labelle is working for the Direction Générale de la Sécurité Extérieure?" said the minister.

"French intelligence?" Larocque said.

"Yes, French intelligence. We suspect Ms. Labelle is feeding them everything she knows about your regiment."

Jesus take a shit, Larocque thought, Labelle had been here in Edmonton recently. He had seen her on the night of the fight with the Australian.

The defence minister's voice broke into Larocque's thoughts. "Listen, Colonel, I might as well tell you. You'll be getting word within the hour that each of the CANZUK cabinets has signed off on the mission. Operation Vandal is a go. By this time tomorrow, you'll be at war."

The minister paused to let her words sink in.

"Now that you know what's at stake, Colonel, it's important that you tell me everything and anything you know about Captain Brazeau and his relationship with Josee Labelle. And then together, we can decide just how bad this development might be for our country."

––––

San Antonio

Spector heard his phone go off. Angrily lifting his head from the pillow he'd been sleeping on moments before, he reached across the body of the much-younger woman who was in bed next to him.

She groaned as the full bulk of his body fell across her. Grabbing the phone, he placed it to his ear and readied a blast for whoever was calling him at this hour. He had given his staff explicit direction – unless the Blues restarted the war, he didn't want to hear anything from anyone for any goddamned reason.

"Whoever this is, you had best have one hell of a good reason for calling this number," Spector spat into the phone, caring not a fig for the now-complaining woman lying beside him.

"General Spector," a French-accented voice said. "I do apologize for the early morning call. I hope I've not interrupted anything?"

On hearing a voice that wasn't American, his annoyance with the intrusion started to veer in the direction of unmitigated fury.

"Listen, what I'm doing and what you may or may not have interrupted is none of your goddamned business. That you know my name and that you got this number is the only reason I'm not telling you to fuck off and hanging up this phone. If you've got something to say, you have twenty seconds. So get to it."

"General, I appreciate your directness," the man said courteously. "I will aim not to waste your time. I have reached out to you because I know you work very closely with President Cameron. In fact, as it pertains to the Red Faction military, I understand you are his right hand."

"Ten seconds, *mon ami*," Spector said, the words almost a snarl.

After a pause, the voice said, "I have it on good authority, General, that Canada and the CANZUK alliance are coming for your nuclear weapons in Missouri. I wonder if this is something you and your president might have an interest in?"

Chapter 14

North Carolina

"It's good to hear your voice again, Mr. President. Your call is unexpected, but your timing is good. How do things fare in the United Constitutional States of America?" Reginald Powers, the Governor for the neutral state of Missouri, said through the speakerphone that sat on his desk.

"Governor, I'm relieved to speak with you. Unfortunately, I must dispense with the small talk. I'm calling with a concern of the utmost urgency," Cameron advised.

"Mr. President, I know that we've exceeded the deadline that you set out for us, but there is good news on that front.

"As of this evening, enough of my legislative colleagues have agreed to accelerate the passage of the UCSA Act. It'll take us another three weeks or so to make it official, mind you, but as promised, I got the job done. Now, I know it's not as quickly as you would like, but trust me when I say that this is the very best deal I could get. I..."

"Reg. Stop talking," Cameron cut off the other man. "You're out of time. More accurately, *we* are out of time. The time for Missouri to join the worthy enterprise that is the UCSA was months ago, but you lacked the political courage and the vision to make this so. While I long ago grew tired of you trying to hedge your political position, I have allowed it to happen because of my deep and abiding commitment to the democratic process. Well, Governor, events beyond my control have forced my hand."

Cameron paused for a moment and got up from his chair and leaned over the speakerphone. "Are you still with me, Reginald?"

"Yes, Mr. President. You have my full attention."

"Well, that is good for both of us, because the information I'm about to provide to you is of critical importance.

"Within the past hour, I have been advised that a sizeable military force is coming east from Colorado and south from Canada, and we have every reason to believe that these forces are headed for your state, and in particular, the nuclear weapons at Whiteman Air Force Base. At this time, I do not have all the particulars, such as the exact timing of the operation or how many soldiers will be involved, but I am convinced, as are my generals, that an operation of this nature is imminent.

"Governor, in the interest of the future United States and whatever form it takes, I am asking you – no, I am imploring you, to allow UCSA forces to enter Missouri immediately so that preparations can be made to defend your state, and if necessary, to remove those weapons from Whiteman for their security."

"The Canadians, Mr. President?" the governor said. "I mean, really – the Canadians? Isn't that out of character for them? Do they even have an army?"

"I can most certainly assure you that they do. I can also assure you that it's not just the Canadians. The British are somehow involved, as are the Australians. Christ, man, even that pissant New Zealand is involved if you can believe it. Governor, if you have access to a computer, I would suggest you search the term CANZUK. It's a very real alliance and I have been led to believe it is going to invade your state."

The connection went silent for several long seconds.

"Mr. President, with all due respect, the information you've just shared with me seems almost too fantastic to be believed. I'm looking at this CANZUK thing now online. Now, I'm the furthest thing from a military expert, but wouldn't it be the case that we would have days, if not weeks of notice if these folks were going to make their way down to us? Missouri's in the heartland of America. How many states would they have to get through before they got to us? Surely that would give us enough time to get ready for them?"

Cameron let out an exasperated sigh.

"Governor, I've grown tired of your prevarications and quite frankly, your density. Nevertheless, I will lay it out for you as best I can. The Canadians and their allies are somehow aligned with the Colorado Neutral Faction. The Canadians will not have to drive from their border, because as we speak, they're already somewhere in the Dakotas. Perhaps they are even further south. We're looking into it now. For all we know, columns of foreign soldiers could be crossing your state's border as we have this conversation."

"Come now, Archie," the governor said. "Let's not be alarmist. I've just told you you've won. Missouri is going to pass legislation to join the UCSA. In three weeks, we'll be part of your commonwealth. There's no more need to saber-rattle or intimidate. There's been quite enough of that, wouldn't you say?"

Cameron raised his voice. "Mr. Governor, if you do not issue an executive order that allows General Spector and his 5th Army to enter your state in the next twenty-four hours, I will have no choice but to issue an executive order telling him to occupy your state. And to hell with the people in your legislature who call me a tyrant. My reputation is secondary to the safety of the good people of your state, even if their politicians are too dim-witted to help themselves."

The connection went quiet as Powers wrestled with the idea that the sitting president of the Red Faction had just called him an idiot. "Mr. President, I do say that your choice of words is not helping win me over to the idea that I should let your soldiers into my state. I..."

Cameron again cut off the other man. "Governor, in the next twenty minutes, you will receive a file of all the satellite images we have been provided of the Colorado and CANZUK militaries and their current positioning. These images are from the past twenty-four hours, and I can assure you they are very real. I would suggest you get together some of your people and have a look at them. If I can't convince you your state is in trouble, maybe one of your generals can."

Finally, the governor spoke. "Evidence would be helpful, Mr. President. I can assure you I won't be the only skeptical person."

"When we press send on those images, you have three hours to decide if you're going to issue that executive order. If I haven't heard from you by eight this evening, I will give the order for General Spector to roll into your state. Am I making myself perfectly clear, Governor Powers?"

"Perfectly clear. One way or the other, you'll hear from me, Mr. President."

"See that I do, Reg."

On that warning, Cameron severed the connection.

"You heard all of it?" Cameron asked.

"Yes," Spector replied. "I can see why you don't like him. The man sounds clueless. And I can tell you they've done nothing, and I mean absolutely nothing, to harden Whiteman or any other assets they might want to protect. If this CANZUK outfit *is* coming and they beat us to that base, there's nothing Missouri can do to stop them."

"Well, that's encouraging," said Cameron. "What assets can we get to Whiteman and when can we get them there? You know as well as I do how important those weapons are to us."

"Well, the saber-rattling from several weeks back was a hell of a thing for us. Between Campbell and Hood, we have two underweight divisions that we can send into Missouri faster than would have been the case two months ago.

"But we'll have to divide our forces. We got some intel out of Colorado that's an hour old. They're definitely planning something. And unlike your friend in Missouri, Colorado's Guard units are in good shape."

"So where does that leave us?" said Cameron.

"Well, the two brigades out of Texas will look to head off whatever Colorado is going to send east. Depending on when this whole thing kicks off, they're likely to make contact somewhere in the eastern half of Kansas.

"The two brigades out of Kentucky will drive straight across the northern part of Missouri to Whiteman and will aim to head off whatever CANZUK is sending from the Dakotas. If they really push, they can be at Whiteman in two days."

"Can we not fly something in? Why can't we be there first thing tomorrow?"

"At the beginning of the war we could have, but we've lost almost all of our rapid-reaction capabilities. What we do have is in the northeast and it might take them as long to get organized as it takes for the units in Kentucky to drive across Missouri."

"So, the soonest we can be at that base is forty-eight hours?" asked Cameron

"If we pushed things and everything went our way, we might be able to get it down to thirty-six. Any quicker than that and it becomes rag-tag. We still have our pride, Mr. President so running around like chickens without heads is not something my soldiers are going to do."

"Fair enough. Then let's aim for two days," Cameron said. "I expect by eight this evening we'll get consent from the none-too-bright governor, so at the very least, this won't have to be an invasion. Goodness knows that the politics around this are going to be difficult enough."

"Speaking of politics, Mr. President, what are your plans to bring in the Joint Chiefs? You know how they feel about you coming to me directly. If they want to, they can make everything I need to do more difficult than it needs to be."

"Don't worry about the Chiefs, Mitch. Leave them to me. You just worry about that base and my nukes."

———

Whiteman AFB

It was perhaps an hour before sunset on their fifth day staying with Havez, and Lt. Hall was on her third extended run around the base.

As was the case for most American military facilities, Whiteman took the form of a fair-sized town. It had everything its stationed soldiers needed – restaurants, medical facilities, shopping, schools, and lots of housing.

If you were to run the entire circumference of it, Hall's best guess was that it would be a twenty-five-kilometer run. She could do that distance easily, but she didn't need to see the perimeter of the property. She needed to see the guts of the place and so she wove up and down streets to identify key installations while waving greetings to the many active soldiers and families who were enjoying the day's final few hours of sunshine.

As her feet rhythmically pounded the pavement, Hall's mind played through the conversation with Havez as he drove them from their pick up location at the rural diner to Whiteman.

The man had been clear on several things. He wasn't helping because he was a traitor to his country. The way he saw it, if there was anyone that had betrayed the United States, it was Archie Cameron and the rest of the mad constitutional purists who surrounded him. Havez had granted that the United States' political system had not been working for many years, but in the colonel's mind, meaningful political compromise had always been the answer, not civil war.

From the safety of neutral Missouri, Havez and his wife had watched with horror as the two sides began to tear themselves apart.

Hall and Wallace knew the details, but they had let him tell the story all the same. It had begun with a great political purge, savage bloodlettings, and massive relocations with millions of people forced to uproot themselves and move either north or south, depending on what their political leanings were. Hall recalled the images of Americans struggling to transport whatever possessions they could fit into a vehicle or, in many cases, on their backs as hordes of refugees looked to run from the growing carnage.

Conventional war had quickly followed, and the fighting had been as brutal as anything seen in the past hundred years. Frontline cities like Cinncinati, Richmond, and Pittsburgh became meat grinders reminiscent of Stalingrad or Hue, while urban centers in the hinterlands were turned into horrific conflagrations courtesy of the war's competing air campaigns. Within a year, large swaths of Philadelphia and Atlanta had become modern-day replicas of Chechnya's Grozny or Syria's Aleppo. All of it had been appalling.

But worse than the conventional war, Havez had been most disturbed by the vicious low-grade fighting that had broken out in hundreds of towns and cities, where Blue and Red factionalists had refused to leave to join those of their tribe that had consolidated somewhere north or south. The myriad of competing groups had undertaken atrocities that would have made even the most brutal of Mexican drug cartels blanch.

It was the Reds who had been the worst offenders, according to Havez. And as the war churned into its third year and the Blues seemed to be gaining the upper hand on the conventional side of the conflict, the Red's low-level persecutions, pogroms, and insurgencies grew more frequent and desperate.

But for Havez, it was the incineration of the five Blue cities that had brought him to the conclusion that the Reds could not be allowed to win the war.

On the day that word had come down through the chain of command that Missouri was entering into discussions with the Reds on the matter of joining the UCSA, Havez had reached out to a former colleague with the Colorado Neutrals to see if there was any information or even assistance he could offer to help steer his adopted state away from the searching arms of Cameron and his lot.

Several weeks later, someone from the Neutral Faction had asked him if he could help, and without any thought to the risk to himself and his wife, he had agreed.

As Hall turned onto the colonel's tree-lined street, she pulled up from her run and started walking. As she breathed rhythmically, she transitioned her thoughts to the operation that was to come. This would be her last run through the base. Earlier in the evening, an encrypted message had arrived on her laptop. "Vandal to proceed. Commence op 0420 hours."

The colonel's home would be perfect for their part of what was to come. Located at the end of a cul de sac with a backyard fenced in by several acres of mature middle-America forest, Wallace would be able to dispatch two dozen targeting drones from the window in the bedroom he was now occupying. Barring something unforeseen, Hall was sure this part of the mission would go off without a hitch.

It was the second and much riskier part of the operation that was now dominating her thoughts. Earlier, when she had described what needed to be done to the base commander, Havez had raised his eyebrows and with a concerned look on his face said, "But there's only the two of you."

"Agreed," Hall had responded, "but with your help and a bit of luck, we'll make it happen. We have to."

Hall looked to the west and took in the setting sun. It was a glorious vista saturated with a wonderful collage of pinks, oranges, and blues. It was serene and she drank it in. Whatever happened in the coming hours, Hall's conscience was clear. Their conversations with the colonel had swept away any remaining hesitations she had about the mission. The Reds could not gain access to the weapons on this base and if that meant there had to be sacrifices, she could live with whatever was to come. This was on the Reds, not Havez, not CANZUK, and certainly not her or Wallace.

––––

Ottawa

While Merielle prided herself on her ability to push herself for long periods, there was no getting past it – she was on her way to exhaustion. Further to her conversation with Larocque on the Labelle matter, she made the call not to delay the timing of the mission. She and Larocque had agreed that Brazeau would not be a threat in the field, but that Josee Labelle was most certainly a problem. They had no idea what she knew, nor what she had passed along to the DGSE. Had Merielle not had such a close relationship with the PM, she would have had to put the whole thing on hold, but her mentor had been clear. If she needed to make a call and she felt there wasn't time to check in on any particular issue, she could make the decision and he would support her. His trust in her was implicit.

So when she got a call from Stephane asking for her to meet with him at his place, she had leaped at the offer. She needed a break from the rush of planning taking place at NDHQ, even if it was only for a few moments.

News had just come in from his contacts at CSIS. Stephane had details about Labelle that he needed to share ASAP, but he didn't want to discuss it over the phone.

Fortunately, her ex lived close by and upon arriving at his well-kept suburban home, Merielle could see there were several lights on. She looked at her driver, an officer from the RCMP's VIP Protection division and said, "I'll be fifteen, tops."

As she walked to the front of the unimaginative two-story, two-door garage domicile, Merielle was comforted by the scene that lay about her. While suburban Ottawa had many qualities, architectural bravery did not make the list of adjectives that could be used to describe the city's many well-kept suburban neighborhoods. But the scene was comforting and in its own way strengthened her resolve. It was this life and the people who lived in this cosseted world that needed to be protected from what was happening in the south. She was confident Canadians would understand this when they were advised in a few short hours of what their government and its CANZUK allies had done.

Stephane was waiting for her when she arrived at the door to his home. His kids and wife were no doubt asleep.

"C'mon in," he said. "Jesus, Mer, you look terrible. Can I get you a coffee?

"Still the charmer, I see," Merielle said with a smile. "No. I'm good. I've been drinking the stuff all night. You've got news for me on Labelle?"

Seeing that Merielle had cut straight to the chase and knowing a spent person when he saw one, the RCMP Inspector and CSIS senior liaison said, "You got it, but first, why don't you have a seat before you fall on your ass." He guided her to a chair that sat along the wall of his small office and then took his own seat.

"At about one this morning, this file officially went beyond my pay grade. I suspect CSIS will be giving a full briefing to the PM later today, so you're likely to get more details soon. And Mer, the Director of CSIS is not happy that you've been operating in the background on this. You'll want to think through some type of reason as to why you didn't flag your suspicions through the appropriate channels when Labelle's DGSE connection first came to light."

"Honestly, Steph, I don't give a shit what questions the Director of CSIS may or may not have for me. The man's people should have been on this, so it's him who's going to have to answer the tough questions. Tell me what's going on with Ms. Labelle. I don't have a lot of time."

To the man's credit, he didn't flinch at the boss-woman vibe rolling off her. He knew her too well, but more than that, he was too much the professional to allow a female superior's no-nonsense approach chip at his ego. It was but one of several things that made him an exceptional cop.

"As you suggested, my contact at CSIS sent some people to Petawawa to speak with Brazeau's wife and you were right. She had a lot to say. Brazeau may have thought he was seeing Labelle on the sly, but he wasn't fooling this young lady. Turns out she had her own suspicions and hired a private investigator to follow Brazeau. And as luck would have it, the PI was first-rate. According to the agents that spoke with him, he'd been monitoring Brazeau and Labelle off and on for the past three months."

"Well, that's a stroke of luck if there ever was one. What's the story?" Merielle said.

"The story is that Labelle wasn't only seeing Brazeau. On a lark, the PI stayed with Labelle on one of her visits to Petawawa and saw her meet with another man-hours after she had connected with Brazeau. Being good at his job and curious, from then on, the PI made efforts to surveil Labelle whenever she and Brazeau parted ways. Eventually, he was able to identify the other man."

Pausing, the senior RCMP officer rolled his chair toward Merielle and spoke. "Does the name Pierre-Paul Geoffroy ring any bells for you?"

The moment Merielle heard the name, something deep in the back of her mind began to tickle. Her eyes left Stephane and stared at nothing in particular as she struggled to recall where she had heard the name before. And then she had it.

"Got it. He was a bombmaker for the FLQ back in the late '60s. He was charged with multiple counts of setting off an explosive device with the intent to kill. The bastard blew up the Montreal Stock Exchange, among other locations."

Merielle's eyes once again met those of her ex-husband. "But Geoffroy is long dead, as is the FLQ. What do either have to do with Labelle?"

"The man Labelle was seen with on multiple occasions after seeing Brazeau is one Lieutenant Curtis Gauthier. He commands one of the four platoons in Brazeau's company. He's twenty-four years of age and is from the Eastern Townships. As you would expect, as soon as they got the name, CSIS pulled everything they had on him."

Pausing, he turned around in his seat and grabbed a piece of paper off his desk, handing it to Merielle. There were two pictures on the page. On the left was a soldier wearing the standard-issue fatigues of the Canadian Army. On the right-hand side of the man's chest, she could clearly read the name tag, 'Gauthier'. He looked non-descript. He was neither homely nor handsome. He looked to be in good physical shape, as you would expect from someone who commanded soldiers in a unit like the Airborne.

The other picture – clearly candid – featured a shirtless man who was covered in a swirl of tattoos. Across the man's athletic-looking chest, she could see there were several names written in a stylized font – Villeneuve, Hudon, Rose, Lortie, among others.

The man's face was covered in thick facial hair and he wore a pair of fashionable dark-rimmed glasses, that by coincidence or by purpose, looked as though they had been pulled out of the same era that the Front had terrorized Canada.

"The names. I recognized some of them," Merielle said. "They're FLQ. Are these pics both of this Gauthier fellow?"

"They are and they aren't," Stephane replied.

Merielle gave the man a quizzical look.

"Three years before joining the army, Curtis Gauthier had another name. The man with the tattoos is, or was, Guy-Michel Geoffroy. You're looking at the great-grandson of Pierre-Paul Geoffroy, and as best we can surmise he's one of the founding members of the new FLQ and one of Josee Labelle's right hands."

"Jesus," Merielle muttered, before going quiet as she worked through the bombshell she had just been it with.

"How the hell do the Forces not know about this guy, and how in hell was he allowed to join the army?"

Despite her fatigue, Merielle's mind moved quickly as she tried to sort through the events of the past few days, including her recent conversation with Larocque.

"Labelle's been playing us the whole time," Merielle said as she sprang from her seat and began to pace the small office.

"Brazeau was a ruse." She stopped her pacing and once again made eye contact with Stephane. "I called Brazeau's commanding officer yesterday evening."

"Mer," Stephane interjected, "are you crazy? You can't be involved in this directly. You're the country's bloody Minister of Defence. You're not a cop anymore. You have to let the right people do their jobs. Jesus, if this blows up, your resignation is in this mess somewhere. And Christ knows what it'll mean for me."

"Stephane, listen to me. There is shit going down that is bigger than me. Way bigger and it's moving fast. So fast, I had to call the

Airborne's CO yesterday. He knows Brazeau as well as anyone and I had to hear from him directly whether or not he thought Brazeau was a risk."

"And what did he say?" the RCMP man asked.

"He said there's no way Brazeau is feeding intel to Labelle."

"And how does he know that for certain?"

"Because Brazeau himself knew that Labelle was trying to pump him for information. As far back as a year ago, the CO and Brazeau had talked about it, and they agreed that so long as Brazeau never gave more than crumbs, they felt it was something they could manage."

"I take it the CO and Brazeau didn't know she was working for the DGSE, then?"

"No. He was floored when I told him that. Of everything he knows about Labelle, the thing he was most concerned about was that she made an impromptu 'business' trip to Edmonton a few weeks ago. At the time, Larocque – that's the CO – brought together a small group of officers to manage her in the time that she was there, but they couldn't keep an eye on her the whole time, so he couldn't say for sure that she didn't leave the city without some type of actionable intelligence."

"And why didn't he report this concern to CAF intelligence or CSIS? Surely, that must have crossed the man's mind at some point?"

"They did think about it, but then dismissed the idea for the very same reason we didn't make a formal report on the woman. Like us, they grossly underestimated what Josee Labelle is capable of. You've heard me call her a princess."

"And a silver-spooned tart, if I remember correctly," he added quickly.

"Well, shame on me, Stephane. It turns out that Josee Labelle is no vapid, well-to-do elite. She has manipulated this situation masterfully. Brazeau was never her target. He was a distraction, a sleight of hand that allowed her to engage in-person with Geoffroy or Gauthier, or whoever the hell this guy is. And if it wasn't for Brazeau's wife and her PI, we'd know jack about it."

"Well, whatever damage has been done, we're gonna have some or all of the details soon," advised Stephane. "As of early this morning, CSIS has made a formal request of the CAF to have the military police in Edmonton detain Gauthier. CSIS is also done pussy-footing with Labelle. Separatist scion or no, they got a security certificate issued for her about an hour ago. The RCMP will be kicking down the door of her apartment sometime in the next few hours."

Stephane paused as he took in the look of alarm that crossed his ex-wife's face. "What's wrong, Mer?"

"They're not going to find Gauthier in Edmonton, Steph, and I'll be shocked if they find Labelle in her apartment."

"Ok, if he's not in Edmonton, where is he?"

Merielle glanced at her watch. She had to get back to NDHQ. If it wasn't already too late, the generals had to be warned. The damage this Gauthier fellow could do, Merielle thought. And what if this separatist bastard wasn't alone. What if there was a dozen or more of them in the Airborne?

"I have to go," she said abruptly. "The PM will be speaking to the entire country at 1100 hours. Watch the statement. Things will become clear then."

She walked over to the man she was still very fond of and gave him a quick kiss on his cheek. "You've done good, Steph. Real good."

Hurriedly, she turned and left the office and made for the car that would take her back to Canada's defense headquarters and what she hoped wouldn't be an unfurling disaster.

Chapter 15

Hall watched as the seventeenth palm-sized drone gently flew out the second-story window on the backside of the Havez residence. Almost there, she thought.

Still in the early phase of summer, there remained a touch of coolness in the night air that filled the room. She had every confidence in the man's ability to pilot the small targeting units. Over the months they had been unknowingly training for this mission, both of them had been required to develop such skills, but of the two of them, Wallace had been the natural. He swore he hadn't played a lot of video games growing up, but as he sat there on the edge of the bed with the VR goggles and control unit, Wallace looked every little bit the esports enthusiast that he claimed not to be.

The stillness of the night air was also working in their favor. The result had been that Wallace was ahead of schedule in placing the unobtrusive flying machines in the various places they needed to be.

Hall's eyes turned back to the laptop on the desk where she was currently sitting. An hour earlier, they'd launched a larger drone that would independently hover above the base allowing Hall to observe the areas where each of the targeting drones were to be placed or whatever other part of the expansive property she deemed necessary.

The unit had a near-AI processor, so it did not need to be piloted. At four thousand feet, the battery-operated unit was high enough that whatever noise it did produce would be washed away by the ambient sounds of Whiteman. As she quickly panned the drone's camera across several key locations, everything appeared to be normal.

"We're looking steady," Hall said. "The perimeter looks as it should and activity around the base's ops center doesn't look any different than what we've seen in the past two nights."

"Number seventeen is in position," Wallace advised. "Activating numbers eighteen through twenty."

As he uttered the words, three of the drones laid out on the floor started to quietly whir and slowly began to rise into the air. Hall watched as each of the small targeting devices flew through the open window and into the early morning darkness.

"These units will be set on the fence that forms the eastern perimeter of the base. It's about four klicks away, so this is gonna take about ten or so minutes. After that, it's one more flight and then we'll be golden."

"Aces, Max. Keep it going."

As she offered the encouragement, Hall heard a soft knock on the door to the room. Havez, she thought. Though she was as taut as a highwire, she didn't let interruption throw her off. Through the eyes of the larger surveillance drone, Hall had kept a constant eye on the Havez residence. In the past hour, only one car had come onto the street where the base commander and his wife resided, and that person had got out of a truck and walked straight into a house six doors down.

Hall, along with Wallace, had finalized plans for Havez and his wife earlier in the evening. In under thirty minutes, the colonel would be turning onto US Highway Fifty heading west on the premise that Ms. Havez wasn't feeling well and that she needed to check-in at the regional cancer clinic in Kansas City. From KC, they had agreed that they would drive to a location in South Dakota and from there they would be moved by CANZUK agents to either California or Canada.

On finalizing the plan, they had all said their goodbyes and had agreed that they wouldn't speak again. That Havez was now knocking on their door most certainly meant something important was up. Hall got up from her seat, moved to the door, and opened it just wide enough that she could slip her frame into the hallway.

Havez was wearing civies. Blue jeans, a green-dominated plaid shirt that played well with his brown eyes, and a pair of well-used hiking shoes. He had a look on his face that she hadn't seen before. It was some combination of angst, alarm, and fear. Not good.

"We have a problem," the colonel said.

"What's up," Hall replied.

"The Reds know something is up. I just got a call from my commander who just got off the phone with someone from Missouri's National Guard. He didn't have a lot of details, but the word from the governor's office is to elevate the security level of all military installations in the state with particular emphasis being given to Whiteman. Effective immediately, I'm to order the base to its second-highest readiness level."

Hall cursed. Her mind was now revving with the implications. She looked at her watch: 0241. The Airborne had just taken off and in just over three hours, they'd be lobbing into the sky along the eastern edge of the base.

"What does that mean? What's the second-highest level of readiness?"

"Well, it's several things. We lock down the base to the public. We double the number of guards at entrances. We ramp up patrols in and around the base. The number of pilots that are on standby increases. We have six F-16s on base - two of them go airborne AS-AP while two more stay ready on the deck. The B-21s are also put on the tarmac and made ready to lift off in less than five, with other air assets set to move as needed. Finally, the Guard garrisons in Kansas City, St. Louis, and Jefferson City would start making call-outs to their respective units. If directed to, these garrisons would look to provide a company-sized force to Whiteman for added security, but as best I can tell, no one's made that call yet."

"And this is all on you to make happen? Is anyone else on the base advised? Your 2IC or the commander who's responsible for base security?"

"Here on the base, the order would go through me, but the same order is going out across the state. If I don't push the order out ASAP, within the hour one or more of the garrison commanders will be calling their contacts here on base to see whether or not they should be getting ready to roll out their soldiers. If I don't pass on the order, it's going to put me in a difficult spot. Even if Beth and I leave right now, there's a chance security will have the base on lockdown by the time we reach the gates and security will want to know why I'm leaving."

"Your wife's sick. You're taking her to the hospital. Surely they'll let you go."

"Maybe," Havez said. "But it's also possible that they'll call in one of the orderlies from the base clinic and have them take her while I stay back. I am the base commander, after all."

Hall took it all in. Someone knew they were coming, but they didn't know when, how, or how many. If they did have that intel, they would be moving to their highest level of readiness, and the order would have come in for base personnel to start digging in. There was none of that. Up-and-ready F-16s weren't great, but they shouldn't offer much of a problem for what was about to bear down on this part of the state.

The intel Havez just provided was crucial as it pertained to Missouri, but it didn't tell her much about the UCSA. What did the Reds know? How would they be reacting? As much as Missouri or more? Thinking it through, she came to the conclusion that it didn't matter. She was a bloody lieutenant. The right call was for Hall to advise mission command and they could decide on next steps. For all she knew, once she got back on her laptop, there would be orders telling them to stand down.

Hall looked up and saw that the colonel's wife had joined him in the hallway. She, too, had a worried look on her face. Hall met their eyes. "Listen, I need to report this up the line. Hang tight for ten. I'm not sure if this is going to change anything, but it may mean we're going to have to implement a secondary plan for the two of you."

She took her eyes off the pair and opened the door to the bedroom. She sat in front of her laptop and after a quick review of her drone's camera feeds, she concluded that the activity level on the base remained unchanged. A good thing. She closed down that program, opened another, and placed her Battlefield Asset Management system, BAM earbud into her ear. After several clicks on the laptop's screen, she heard a crystal clear voice through the unit.

"Tiller One, verify."

Hall provided the validation code confirming her identity.

"ID confirmed. Hold," the signals officer replied.

Seconds later, another voice was coming through her earbud.

"Tiller One, this is Rider Eight. Go ahead." It was the voice of Colonel Azim, the special forces officer who had overseen their training for this mission. He was somewhere in the bowels of ND-HQ, in the mission control center. It was Azim who would be the person coordinating their mission and no doubt several other covert elements of the operation. It would be his job to vet Hall's intel and then decide where it went.

As efficiently as she could manage, she relayed the information that Havez had just provided.

The colonel listened and then offered a short reply. "Hold, Tiller. Back in two."

In just over two minutes, Azim was back. "Tiller, you are now on the line with Joint Ops Delta. Rider Actual is on the line. Please repeat your update."

Joint Ops Delta had overall command for Operation Vandal. Hall, a lieutenant, barely one year out of the Royal Military College, was being asked to brief what was likely a room full of staff officers from four different countries.

Focusing like a laser, she repeated the information she had given to Azim, and then she waded into the deep end of the pool by offering her own analysis of the new developments. As she walked through the details, Wallace had pulled off his piloting goggles and gave her a thumbs up to confirm his work was done. They had finished the first half of their mission.

A voice that was not Azim's came through her earbud. "Tiller One, hold for five. Rider Eight out."

———

Ottawa, NDHQ

"Well, it looks like the cat is out the bag. At least partially," said General Gagnon, the Canadian three-star general who had overall command of Operation Vandal.

Wicked sharp, he was Canada's most experienced staff officer, having been the deputy commander of NATO forces in the Baltics during the recent Sebezhsky Crisis. During that ill-advised Russian adventure, it had been said that the General's calming influence and ability to see the bigger picture had enabled a US-absent NATO to outfox a much larger force and achieve a mutually acceptable stand down with the Russians.

"Folks, we have the Airborne en route and our combined air and naval assets will be unleashing hell in ninety minutes and counting," Gagnon said. "She may be a green lieutenant, but I think she has the right of it. If they do know something, they've only just got the intel. As I see it, we maintain the advantage and will do so for a period of time, but less than we anticipated. We built room and redundancies into the plan to account for this type of thing."

Gagnon turned to that part of the operations room responsible for coordinating CANZUK's air assets. "Are we picking up any increased activity on radar or satellite that would tell us their air defenses are ramping up?"

General Campbell, the British major general charged with the responsibility of overseeing the alliance's air campaign, replied, "Nothing has come up to say the Reds are on to us, but as you know, our AWACS and other air assets have a range of about four hundred kilometers. The Red's air bases are well out of range. It could be that whole flights of enemy fighters are waiting just beyond our sensors."

Gagnon then turned back to Azim. "Colonel, what are your assets telling you on the ground?"

Canada's tier-one special forces unit, Joint Task Force 2, had drawn two chief responsibilities for Vandal. Rapid response to any UCSA reprisals that might happen within Canada and intel gathering and target acquisitions of key military installations in both the Red and Blue states.

Setting aside regional accents, Canadians and Americans sounded just like one another, and if you weren't being pedantic about it, the two countries' cultures were as similar as any two other countries in the world. As a result, it had required very little in the way of training to prep several dozen JTF-2 soldiers to infiltrate the former United States and have them meld into the communities adjacent to military installations that CANZUK wanted to keep a close eye on.

Azim was standing behind a pair of seated officers who were looking at a bank of screens. One of the officer's eyes came up from one of the displays and locked on to Gagnon. "We're beginning to see the signs of activity on those air force bases where we have assets. We're getting reports of fighters in Texas and Alabama being loaded out with drop tanks for extended operations. And it looks like at least two air refueling tankers are being prepped in Florida. Upwards of a dozen fighters will be in the air within twenty minutes."

"And what about the J-31s?" Gagnon asked.

"No activity as yet."

Gagnon's face was pensive and, without looking at anyone in particular, he said, "They won't commit their Chinese hardware until they know for sure they're in the shit. If they had any idea of what was coming, they'd have those things up in the air, if only to keep them safe."

For several moments, the Canadian general said nothing. As the seconds passed, the tension in the ops room ratcheted up exponentially.

"Okay, people," Gagnon finally said in a clear voice. "Here's my analysis and recommendation. The Reds know something is up and they've passed some intel along to Missouri, but they clearly don't have a sense of our timing.

"As our young lieutenant at Whiteman pointed out for us, if they did know our timeline, that base would look like a pissed-off hornet's nest. As I see it, surprise remains with us. And based on what Azim is telling us, we still have far superior numbers in the air.

"We've always known that within an hour of our first strikes, the Reds would know who kicked them in the teeth. As I said, our mission parameters allow for adjustments to be made. To be sure, things are now going to be tighter and more costly, but my confidence in the plan and the soldiers who are about to undertake it remains resolute in every way. My recommendation is that we push on and push hard."

Gagnon looked around the room searchingly. He had been charged with directing the overall operation, but this was a multinational effort and there was no way he would move the operation forward if he didn't have the support of the liaising generals who had been given the authority to make operational decisions on behalf of their respective countries.

The British liaison, a lieutenant-general, was the first to speak, "I wouldn't say it's an inconsequential development, but I'm with you, Mike. It's not enough of a setback to take us off course. It's a top-drawer plan and it's clear we still have initiative. It's steady on for Britain."

The Australian liaison, also a three-star flag officer, went next. "We all know the cliché. After first contact, your best-laid plans go to piss. The way I see it, it's a huge bloody win that we've got those two soldiers on that base and that we've come into this information. The Reds may know that we're coming, but I can't see how they would know we're on to them. It's our job to find a way to use this to our advantage. There's too much on the line for all of us. You have Australia's full support, General."

Finally, all eyes in the room turned to the female three-star admiral from New Zealand. "Right. It all makes sense. We all know what's on the line if we don't make this happen. It may start here in North America, but New Zealand remains convinced as ever that we need things to shakedown in the US in the right way. Vandal is our best chance. We stay the course."

"Then we proceed," announced Gagnon. "Someone find out where Minister Martel is at. She needs to be briefed."

———

Whiteman AFB

While the time on Hall's laptop advised that fourteen minutes had passed since she last heard Azim's voice, it felt like an eternity. She had given Wallace a brief run down and when the ten-minute mark passed, she asked him to duck into the hallway and update Havez. Like Hall, the colonel had every reason to be anxious, if not terrified. Best to give him an update even if there was nothing to say.

Just as she was about to check her laptop's satellite connection for what must have been the tenth time, Azim's voice came through clearly in her earbud.

"Tiller One, you still there?"

"I'm still here, Rider Eight."

"All elements of mission are to proceed as planned. The information provided was critical and considered. Use your operational judgment and adjust efforts as necessary but you are to move forward. Your efforts remain critical. Any questions or further updates?"

"Rider Eight, I have no questions, and there are no new developments on this end," Hall replied.

"Good to know. Then I'll let you go. Winch Actual and company will be there soon. Good luck to you both. Rider Eight out."

Hall closed down the program that had allowed her to speak directly with Ottawa and stared at the screen. They were still a go. Wallace had successfully tagged each of the targets they had carefully confirmed in their time on the base. While this element of the mission had been the least dangerous for them personally, it was by far the most important part of the op for the soldiers who were about to take the base. And they would take the base – of that, Hall's confidence held. But holding it had just become a more difficult challenge. Would the Red Faction come sooner, come harder, come in even larger numbers? These were the critical questions that Azim and others would be hashing over.

Rising from her seat, she walked out of the room and took in Wallace, Havez, and the colonel's wife. Each was looking at her expectedly.

"We proceed as planned," she said soberly. "Colonel, you're going to have to make some decisions quickly."

"I'm not leaving the base," Havez said, as though he didn't trust himself not to change his mind. "It's now too risky. Even if we get off base, there's a good chance we'll encounter police or military on the roads, and it won't take them long to figure out who I am. And if I am caught, they'll have some hard questions for me. We were counting on at least two hours of lead time and then several more hours of confusion. That would have got us well into Nebraska and almost to South Dakota. Now, I doubt that we'll make it past Kansas City. Beth and I have discussed it. We'll hunker down here and if things go as I hope they do, we'll catch a ride with you on the way out."

Havez looked at Hall with determined eyes. "I'm an officer with twenty-four years of experience. If my time in has taught me anything, it's that plans change. Perhaps it's for the best, anyway. If this thing goes pear-shaped, it might be that you'll need my help in some way."

He looked at his wife. The woman was frail. Hall had seen her grandfather die of cancer. Her mother had brought her and her brother to see him regularly right until the end. Hall knew what close to the end looked like. The woman reached out and gently touched her husband's face. "Don't worry about me. You're doing the right thing. God will see us through this one way or the other, my love."

Havez looked back into his wife's eyes. The love shared between the two was obvious. After a few seconds of silence, he turned in the direction of the two Canadian soldiers. "Give me five minutes. I need to change."

"Change into what?" Hall asked.

"I'm coming with you. I'm pretty sure I know where you're going. You may need help."

"You know what the Reds will do to you if this doesn't go as we hope, and you're exposed?" Hall said with genuine concern in her voice.

Havez looked her in the eyes.

"I know exactly what those bastards will do to me," he said. The man's face looked resolute. "And it's the reason I'm coming with you. We need to make this work. I'll be ready to go and waiting downstairs in five minutes."

Turning, Havez moved in the direction of his room.

Watching him go, Hall then turned her eyes on the older woman who remained with them. Havez's wife walked forward to Hall and Wallace and reached out to take one of their hands into each of hers. Her hand was warm and had an unexpected strength to it. "He's a good man and he'll be as brave as he needs to be.

"You are not of my blood. You're not even soldiers from my country, but seeing you two together and knowing what you're prepared to do... Well, it gives me hope that there is a path forward for my country. May the Lord guide both of you on this day."

She released their hands, turned, and then followed after her husband.

After the woman turned the corner, Hall turned to Wallace. "You ready?"

The lanky soldier sported his usual look of quiet determination. "A hundred percent. This is gonna be one hell of a show, and I, for one, am glad we're going to have a front-row seat. History in the making, or some shit like that," the young man said cavalierly.

She was buoyed by Wallace's stalwart take. Her own confidence had been moving in the direction of shaky in the moments after hearing Havez's news, but with the trust of Azim, and now Wallace, it was like a rod of steel being driven into the length of her spine.

"Well, I'm game, too. Let's gear up and make history or some shit like that."

Somewhere over Montana

"Questions?" General Gagnon asked. "No, sir," Larocque replied via his BAM.

"Alright, then. Good luck to you and your people, Jack. Rider Actual out."

Several weeks ago, he'd been pleased beyond measure when he'd been advised that a pair of human assets would be operating on the base and that they would be working to ensure the Airborne's drop would be as routine as an exercise. He knew nothing about them – he only had their call signs – Tiller One and Two - and the alpha-numeric codes they would proffer when it came time for them to identify themselves. Whoever they were, they had balls of steel and he'd owe them a couple of beers on the condition they survived the next seventy-two hours.

He was at the front end of the Herc. He closed his eyes and listened to the engines of the venerable machine thrum. With all that stood before them, the sound was a tremendous comfort. When they arrived in Missouri, eighteen Hercules and six of the behemoth C-17 Globemasters would disgorge the entirety of the Airborne Regiment, dozens of vehicles and supply pallets, and several support units, including a surgical team and platoon of military police. All together, nearly thirteen hundred men and nine women would be lobbing out over the flat and wide-open agricultural land just east of Whiteman AFB. Warned or not, the cascade of floating soldiers in the early morning sky would be one hell of an impressive sight for whatever soldiers were up and about when the jump commenced.

As it should be, the plan to take the base was straightforward. Dozens of CANZUK fighter-bombers would fly out of bases in either Canada or the Dakotas and using a combination of GPS and locally designated targets, they would hit Whiteman with a series of devastating strikes. Radars, runways, and roadways, among many other targets, would be taken offline or would be out-and-out pulverized. These strikes, in combination with hundreds of others across the central and southeast United States, would target those UCSA military assets most likely to be used in a counter-punch to take back Whiteman.

Larocque stood up and surveyed the full length of the plane's hold. They had packed this particular Herc to the gills with seventy-five men and women. That their faces were cammed up with various shades of green, black, and brown did not prevent him from recognizing individual soldiers. Being Airborne was not easy and to the last, each of the men and women on this plane had earned the right to wear the maroon beret.

Today, and for however long they needed to be in Missouri, Larocque knew that these soldiers would finally get the chance to fully repair the legacy of the Canadian Airborne Regiment. But in restoring their unit's honor, it might be that some or many of these same soldiers would have to die. If his soldiers were going to go into the shit, they needed someone who could walk with them in their darkest moments. He, as much as anyone, knew darkness. He'd walk with them every step of the way and when it was all said and done, the Airborne would be whole again. Perhaps he would, too.

Chapter 16

Gulf of Mexico

The British submarine captain looked at the display and saw the position of his boat relative to the continent of North America. They were where they needed to be - seventy kilometers off the coast of Alabama. The *HMS Audacious*'s fin was just below the calm waters of the Gulf. He checked the time and saw that it was 0435 hours.

The captain walked over to the comms station, reached around the petty officer who was manning the position and took up the mic.

"Bryant, be a good lad and open a channel to the entire boat," the captain said.

"Aye, sir. Channel is open."

"Right then," the captain said, before thumbing the button on the mic that would allow him to transmit his voice to the entirety of his crew. "This is the captain. As you now know, our government, along with those of Canada, Australia and New Zealand have elected to interject themselves into the American civil war. In moments, those of us on this proud fighting vessel will do our part to execute what will be a continent-wide operation."

He paused, giving himself and the listening men and women of his vessel a moment to digest what was a monumental statement, even if the crew had been briefed already.

"Make no mistake, people, the moment the first of our weapons hit the air, we will be at war with one of the most powerful countries on the planet. In total, we will be launching all twenty-two of our TLAMs. Once done, we will then prosecute any and all targets of opportunity that come into open waters here in the Gulf.

"And mark my words, ladies and gentlemen. For the remainder of our mission's duration, we will be in real peril. You have all trained and prepared for this and I have supreme confidence in your abilities. For King and country, be your best, and together, we will all see our families again. I will do my best, and that is my commitment to you, as it has always been. God save us all. Callahan out."

The captain handed the mic back to the petty officer and turned in the direction of the weapons officer. "Lieutenant, you may fire the first salvo when ready. Be sure to mark the exact time of the first launch. Historians will want to know, to the *exact* moment, when Britain started its third war with the United States of America."

He paused and moved his gaze to look at a few of the other officers and NCOs who were working the ops room. Not speaking to anyone in particular, the twenty-year veteran of His Majesty's Royal Submarine Service said aloud, "And this time around, let us pray that it is us who are on the winning side."

———

Somewhere over Nebraska

Major Harry Khan, call sign Pony, was cruising at thirty-one thousand feet somewhere in the sky over Nebraska. He looked to his left and saw his wingman but couldn't make out the other three members of his flight. To be sure, the 6th gen fighters were there but the Tempest's paint and materials scheme made the three fighters indiscernible from the ink-black sky in which they were presently flying.

All five fighters were cruising absent their powerful radars. They were being fed data from one of the two Boeing 737 Wedgetails that Australia had committed to Operation Vandal. At thirty-three thousand feet, the Airborne Early Warning and Control System aircraft could identify airborne targets at a distance of up to six hundred kilometers.

Prior to their launch from their base in southern Saskatchewan, Khan and the rest of his squadron had received a final briefing suggesting that the Reds were in the know that CANZUK was up to something and that there was now a high probability that they would find hostiles in the air in and around the central United States.

He and the lads in his squadron had one objective over the next seventy-two hours – to dominate the airspace over Missouri so that CANZUK air and ground units could operate with impunity. Nebraska, the current state they were flying over, had neither fighters nor air defense systems. If UCSA fighters were going to be sortied to meet whatever CANZUK force they thought might be coming, their assets would come from the direction of Texas or Alabama, where the Reds had reconsolidated large parts of what remained of their air force.

The latest intelligence confirmed the Reds still had something approaching two hundred serviceable fighter jets. Over the course of two years of ferocious fighting in the skies across the eastern United States, the vast majority of each side's premier fighting machines had either been destroyed or had been cannibalized for parts. In the case of the Red Faction, the situation had become so desperate that they had taken to the extraordinary measure of flying the on-loan Chinese fighters.

Khan and the other pilots of the squadron had blown their tops when they saw the footage of the sixth-gen Chinese fighters screaming over the skyline of Missouri's state capital all those weeks back. For Khan and the rest of his mates, the idea of getting into a scrap with one of those exotic machines was the equivalent of shagging the hottest bird you had ever laid your eyes on – when you were eighteen and still a virgin.

Airborne radars like the Wedgetail AWACS presently shadowing them were not proficient at picking up stealth fighters, so it was most often the case that a machine like the J-31 would need to reveal itself before it could be targeted.

In all likelihood, some other CANZUK pilot – flying a Canadian Super Hornet or a now aging RAF Typhoon – would need to be sacrificed before Khan and the rest of his flight could identify and then engage with one of the Chinese fighters.

Of course, the very same thing could happen but in the opposite direction. The next few hours would be a fascinating game of cat and mouse between the world's two most sophisticated fighter jets as the pilots from the two air forces felt each other out and found out just how well the Tempest and the J-31 matched up.

"Knife One. This is Ares Three, we have incoming from the southeast. You should have the data. Undertake a course to intercept and eliminate all designated targets," the Aussie female radar tech instructed.

"Ares Three this is Knife One," Khan said. "I can confirm the data is streaming. I confirm four contacts. It looks like we have two F-15s and two F-16s cruising at twenty-four thousand feet. Moving to engage now. Knife One out."

Looking at data being fed to his fighter from the Wedgetail, Khan could see the four hostiles south of his current position. North and east, another group of pings began to appear on the radar. Within a few seconds, a flight of twelve planes had been flagged by the Aussie AWACS. It was one part of the first wave of CANZUK fighter-bombers heading to high-priority targets across the UCSA. The Red bastards were in for one hell of a night, Khan thought.

Opening the encrypted comms channel that would allow him to speak freely with his pilots, Khan said, "Dodger, you're with me. We'll accelerate to five hundred knots and drop down to twenty-six thousand - at forty klicks out we begin to prosecute this little war of ours.

"The rest of you – keep on your toes. I'll be right chuffed if this is all the Reds have put into the air, but they know we're coming, so best get ready for anything. Pony out."

___

Whiteman AFB

Havez had gone ahead of them on his own piece of business. Hall and Wallace got out of Ms. Havez's car in a parking lot that had a helipad at the center of it. Standing in front of the vehicle, the two young officers looked at each other. They were dressed as Air Force Security Police and in Hall's opinion, they looked the part.

The plan was straightforward. Havez would attend the base's operations center and would update his soldiers on the orders that had come down. They had agreed that Missouri's National Guard had only partial information about what was coming and that the state's command structure was responding conservatively. Putting the base at the second-highest level of readiness was not going to delay or prevent what was coming, and if it meant that more Canadian soldiers got hurt or even killed in the initial assault, Hall and Wallace had agreed that the intelligence Havez could feed them would be worth the trade-off. It was a harsh calculation, but there was no help for it.

The air traffic control tower loomed high over them. Several banks of clouds were slowly sliding by in the night sky with the result being that the lights in and around the tall structure had to work extra hard to keep the blackness at bay.

As they stood in front of the tower's only entrance, Wallace removed the backpack he was carrying and pulled out a green box about the size of a child's pencil case, handing it to Hall. Accepting it, she placed the unit into the large pocket on her right thigh. "Are you ready?" she asked.

Wearing his standard easy-going smile, Wallace's reply was immediate. "Aces, Lieutenant."

"Then let's do this." She reached into her pocket and pulled out the access card that CANZUK intelligence had provided to them. Holding it in front of her, she tapped the face of the access point to the right of the entrance and then, in a moment of relief, heard the door's locking mechanism click. Quickly, she moved to open it and let Wallace walk into the first floor of the structure.

The interior of the room was well lit and as she walked through the door, Hall's eyes locked onto the lone soldier sitting at a duty desk in the middle of the square room. The eyes of the airman moved between the two security soldiers now standing in front of him.

"Can I help you?" he asked.

"We're looking for Sgt. Williams. We understand he's working," Hall said without any hesitation.

"He sure is," the young man said. "You just missed him. I'll call him back down."

"That won't be necessary. We'll go up and get him," Hall said, applying a hint of firmness into her voice.

"Sorry," the duty soldier advised. "Unauthorized folks don't get to go into the tower and that includes MPs. That's protocol and if you didn't know that, you do now. I'll give him a call. He'll be down in two minutes. You can grab a seat if you'd like?"

The soldier moved to grab the phone and as his hand made contact with the receiver, Wallace moved like a cat. He was around the desk in an instant, and in the time that it had taken him to move that distance, he grabbed a hand-sized incapacitation unit from somewhere on his person and driven it into the shoulder of the still-seated man. Contact made, Hall heard the unit's signature electrical crackle and watched the young man's body become rigid and then start to spasm as Wallace continued to apply the high-voltage charge.

At last satisfied that the soldier's nervous system had taken a temporary hiatus, Wallace pulled back the device and watched the airman slouch back into his chair. As the soldier moaned, Wallace reached into his backpack and pulled out a roll of heavy-duty duct tape and zip ties, and tossed them to Hall. With the full strength of his athletic six-foot-three-inch frame, Wallace hauled the airman out of his seat and roughly put him on the ground. Hall was there in an instant. With practiced hands, she applied strips of the duct tape to the airman's mouth, and then with Wallace's help, the still-groggy soldier was flipped so that his hands and feet could be tied off with the plastic restraints.

Together, they grabbed the soldier by his arms and dragged him in the direction of the floor's lone restroom. Hall opened the door and watched as Wallace efficiently placed their new charge in the corner of the small room. The airman's faculties now returned, he looked at Wallace and Hall with panic in his eyes and began trying to say something. In one quick movement, Hall drew the pistol from the holster on her hip. With her other hand, she accepted a suppressor that Wallace deftly produced. As she locked eyes with the bound soldier, she began to thread the black cylinder onto the muzzle of the weapon.

As she did this, Wallace stepped in front of her and affixed the small black object to the wall to the right of the soldier's head.

As he stepped back, Hall leveled her suppressed pistol in the direction of the airman's now-terrified face. "That's a microphone," Hall said, canting her head to the black box. "If I so much as hear one *peep* out of you, I'll come back here and it's lights out – no questions asked. Nod your head if you understand."

The soldier nodded vigorously.

"Smart man," said Hall.

Pulling the pistol back from the airman's face, she looked at Wallace. "Let's go."

As they closed the door to the bathroom, Hall looked at the BAM wrist unit that she was now wearing. They were good for time. She then tapped the display and listened intently to the earbud in her right ear. Inside the bathroom, she could hear the bound soldier's regularized breathing but no other sounds. She looked at Wallace. "Looks like he got the message. We're good to go."

Hall moved to the door that led to the tower's stairs and opened it. Together they began to climb. In top physical condition, they easily chewed up the four flights and arrived at the secured doorway that led into the glass panel room where the base's air traffic controllers were plying their trade.

She felt a slight vibration on her wrist and then looked to see the message that had arrived. It was Havez. He had just advised the command center's morning watch of the increased readiness order. In moments, the men on the other side of the door would get that same message and their activity level would pick up considerably as they began the process of getting Whiteman's standby aircraft ready for take-off.

Preventing those aircraft from getting in the air was now their number one priority. Hall pulled the slender green box out of her pants pocket. On its side, she depressed a black button and held it for three full seconds at which point a green dot beside the button began to flash.

In exactly thirty seconds, the device would begin to emit aerosolized carfentanil. It was the British who had suggested its use and provided the device.

Back in 2002, Russian special forces had used carfentanil - an opioid derivative - to knock out an entire theatre of eight hundred concert goers and their Chechen hostage-takers. The gas had worked to magnificent effect, but Spetsnaz operators had botched the job by not telling emergency workers what substance had been used, and more importantly, how it could be medically neutralized.

The result had been dozens of incapacitated hostages being killed unnecessarily.

With gas masks on and several doses of the neutralizing agent on both their persons, Hall tapped her card on the access point, while Wallace carefully pushed the door inwards. With the entrance no more than six inches wide, Hall placed the green box on the floor just beyond the door's threshold. Wallace closed the door and they waited.

At forty seconds, Hall heard the rumble of moving furniture and then felt the vibration of what might have been the full weight of an uncontrolled body slamming onto the floor somewhere close to the door. At ninety seconds, she double-tapped Wallace on the shoulder and he again tapped the access point to the right to the door.

Hearing the locking mechanism click, she said, "Three, two, one, go."

On 'go', Wallace pushed open the door allowing Hall to gain an unobstructed view of the room. Her suppressed weapon at the ready, she stepped into the room and immediately took in the body of the man who had made his way to the observation deck's entrance. She could see that the large man's lungs were heaving. Further into the room, she watched Wallace as he checked three other soldiers laid out on the floor beside the tower's bank of control panels.

"They're alive," he said through his mask.

"Good. That stuff worked as advertised," Hall said. "Let's get them tied up and then we'll give them the naloxone."

Looking at her wrist unit, Hall again took in the time – 0552 hours. Still on schedule. She walked to the bank of windows on the east side of the room. From that vantage point, she took in the horizon. Instead of blackness, she could see several shades of somber grey and touches of blue that had formed a thin pane low on the horizon. As it must, dawn had arrived. The Airborne were coming.

———

It was official. Major 'Baja' Alverez was now supremely pissed off.

"What the hell is going on with those guys," he said, pointing to the control tower.

"I don't know, maybe they ran out of coffee," said his co-pilot.

As was standard operating procedure, two B-21 crews had been on standby in the aircrew lounge. The call to scramble two of the ten stealth bombers on base had come in from the ops center fifteen minutes ago. As per standard operating procedures, he and the captain sitting beside him had been fully suited and strapped into their machine in under five minutes and had taxied to the northern end of the air field's tarmac in another five. His bomber, a second B-21 Raider, and four F-16s were now impatiently waiting on permission from the tower to go wheels up.

"Someone is gonna catch hell for this - we are now officially three minutes beyond expected take off," Alverez said.

His co-pilot, Captain Steyer, glanced up from the display he'd been looking at and turned his gaze in the direction of the tower. "This happened to me three years ago. Someone in the ATC had a heart attack right in the middle of a scramble, but don't you know it, they still managed to get us off in under fifteen. Whatever is going on up there, someone is gonna get a strip torn off them for sure."

As flight lead, it had been Alverez's responsibility to cajole the techs in the tower to move things along. He toggled the bomber's comm system, "Control, this is Wraith One, what is your status?"

Once again, there was no reply.

"Alright, enough is enough," Alverez said. "Let the record show that we made best efforts to contact those clowns."

"Roger that. Let the record show," Steyer said, the tone of his voice nonplussed.

He toggled the comms a second time and opened a channel to the other planes laid out in front and behind him. "Wraith Flight Echo-Charlie, we're going to execute an independent tactical take-off and hope our friends in the tower get their priorities figured out sometime before we get back. If we stay on the ground any longer, we'll be as screwed as they are."

"Copy that, Baja. We are on your six," the commanding pilot of the second B-21 said.

"Nickle One, what say you?" Alverez addressed the officer who was commanding the flight of F-16s.

Before a reply could be delivered, the interior of Alverez's plane was lit up by a huge flash and less than a second later he felt the structure of his aircraft sway and shake as it was struck by one or more concussive waves. Confined as he was behind the steel and thick glass of the cockpit, his ears easily picked up the crack and roar of multiple explosions. Looking out to the north, he could now see several pillars of fire and smoke beginning to plume at various points along the length of Whiteman's only runway.

"Holy shit!" he yelled. "What the hell was that?"

Alverez quickly toggled the plane's comms, "Control, Control, Control, this is Wraith One, I need a status report now! What the hell is going on?"

"Wraith One, this is Control, we are back online," said a female voice. "We had a comms problem. Jamming of some kind we think. We're still figuring things out. Hold your position."

Alverez again saw the still night sky light up clear as day but this time the explosions were further away in the east. With the benefit of distance and time, his brain was able to process what he was hearing. "Jesus Christ, Reds are hitting us. There's no way they're this stupid. The Blues will walk from the negotiations for sure, never mind what we might do. This is crazy."

"Jim."

Upon hearing Steyer call his first name, he turned his eyes in the direction of the man sitting to his right. Steyer was pointing out the cockpit window.

The sun had just broken on the horizon. The lower portion of the sky was layered with a spectacular collection of red and orange hues, while the upper reaches of the panorama were an assortment of softening blues.

In front of the early morning canvas, Alverez took in the scene of at least a dozen low flying transport planes, and from each of them, he could see a growing stream of black silhouetted blobs falling downwards. "Fuck me ragged. There are hundreds of them."

As the paratroopers began to fall to the ground behind buildings and a treeline east of the base, his brain undertook a quick calculation. Wherever those soldiers had come from, they were only about a mile out from the base.

His eyes shifted back to the runway. He counted ten different impacts and around each of the smoking craters, chunks of debris were strewn in every which direction. Whiteman's one and only runway was now off the board.

He toggled open the frequency to the tower. "Control, this is Wraith One. I think it's a safe bet that we're not going anywhere."

―――――

Missouri

The pilot's voice came alive in Larocque's earbud. "Winch Actual, we are at altitude and on course. You will begin your drop in ninety seconds. Good luck, Colonel."

Larocque and the jumpmaster assigned to his Herc locked eyes, and he gave the man a thumbs up.

Encumbered by a heavily laden rucksack affixed underneath his secondary chute, Larocque half walked, half waddled to the front of the line that flowed away from the starboard door that he and the other members of his HQ would jump out of. On the other side of the fuselage, the Airborne's Regimental Sergeant Major, St. Pierre, stood ready to lead the other half of the plane's contingent.

Stepping into the space controlled by the jumpmaster, he looked at the men and women in the two formed lines flowing to the back of the plane. Loaded like pack animals, their faces painted green and black, to the last, they looked like the determined soldiers that they were. They were a magnificent sight.

All eyes on the plane were now looking at him. He raised his fist in the air and then bellowed, "Airborne ready?" As one, the fighting soldiers roared back, "Ready!" As he pulled his fist down in response to the confirmation, he heard the two doors of the Hercules open and felt the cool rush of the Missouri morning air. The noise was loud, familiar and welcome.

At the top of his lungs, the jumpmaster yelled, "thirty seconds!"

The notification was loudly repeated by Larocque and the line of soldiers that flowed down the length of the plane.

Larocque affixed the nylon static line that would pull his chute the moment he stepped out the door.

As he had done for every previous jump, his mind focused on his family. Though broken, and a part of it lost forever, they nevertheless remained the center of his universe. In his mind's eye, he saw Madison holding a much-younger Lauren after a particularly bad fall off a bicycle. Tears now gone, his wife stroked the soft brown hair of their only child as she rocked slowly in a well-used nursing chair. He would make it right between them. He had to. But at this moment and for the next few days, it was the soldiers of his regiment who would be his family. He needed to focus on them and their survival. He hadn't done that well enough for his daughter or his marriage. Redemption, at least some form of it, was but two strides away.

The jumpmaster's voice bellowed. "In five, four, three, two, one."

Larocque saw the bulbous green light above the open door turn on and without hesitation, he stepped into the morning light and fell.

Chapter 17

Outside Atlanta

Major General Mitchell Spector listened to the Air Force colonel as she listed a growing number of targets that CANZUK air and naval assets had struck. As he took in the growing list, he brimmed with righteous anger. The UCSA general staff had been warned, but by all accounts, the fools had done almost nothing with the intel. Granted, the four-nation alliance had unleashed their assault sooner than even Spector anticipated, but still, the men in the room had been warned.

Objectively, Spector was prepared to admit to himself that the planners of the CANZUK operation had done their jobs well. With their limited resources, they had prioritized targets that would effectively limit and perhaps delay UCSA's ability to re-take Whiteman.

In the Atlantic, Royal Navy F-35s launching from the aircraft carrier, *HMS Queen Elizabeth*, had savaged various targets in the southeast. The airfield at Pensacola and several of its airborne fuel tankers had seen the worst of it.

Out of the Gulf, coastal radar had identified four launch points, where it was presumed British and Australian submarines had launched a combined salvo of just over one hundred Tomahawks. With a range of one thousand miles, the cruise missiles had struck military targets throughout UCSA-held territory. Particular attention had been given to elements of Spector's own 5th Army at both Fort Hood in Texas and Fort Campbell in Kentucky.

The moment he had gotten off the phone with the anonymous Frenchman and before even speaking with Cameron, he had made calls to key commanders to give orders to disperse vehicle concentrations and to camouflage or hide key pieces of hardware. The quick action had no doubt served to reduce their losses, but damage, and there had been a lot of it, had still been done.

The most spectacular of the strikes had been the destruction of a temporary ammunition depot at Fort Hood. The resulting explosion had been god-like, and of all the alarming images being shown by the media, it was the mushroom cloud looming over Foot Hood and that part of Texas that was getting the most airplay. And rightly so, Spector thought. Mushroom clouds – even small ones – made the citizens of the UCSA extremely nervous.

"Look at the image, General," Cameron said in an elevated tone, pointing to one of the many screens affixed to the walls of the large operations room. The UCSA Joint Chief of Staff, General Colin Evans turned to look at the newsfeed streaming the still-exploding inferno.

Cameron walked to the front of the room and stood to the left of the display. The man's grey eyes contrasted harshly with the flushed tone of his face.

"This image and the dozens like it are now playing on every television and on every phone on this planet. This is on you, General. It's on you and the men in this room who share in your incompetence," Cameron said.

"I have spoken to the Secretary of Defense and we are in full agreement. The entirety of the Joint Chiefs is to resign, effective immediately. Every last one of you that is in this room can get out of my sight. I expect your letters of resignation to the Secretary within the hour."

Evans did not move. Instead, he glared in the direction of Cameron. "Mr. President, this is not the move our country needs. Now more than ever, we need to be united. You are right to be upset, but I can assure you, we would have been in a much worse position had we not made the moves we did in response to the warning provided by General Spector. I understand why you are upset, but in two to three days..."

Cameron cut the man off. "Two to three days!"

Cameron jabbed his finger at another screen. "Do you not see what is happening in Missouri? Are you telling me you did not see the images of soldiers falling out of the sky? Take a look. They're right there on that screen. Take one damned close look at it, General."

"I'm quite aware of what's happening in Missouri, Mr. President."

"Are you? Because I'm not sure you appreciate the gravity of what's transpired. At this very moment, a foreign country is in possession of a military base on the continental United States, and on top of that, that same force now controls nearly three hundred tactical nuclear weapons and the means to deliver them. Tell me, General, do you have any appreciation of what this means for us politically, never mind the strategic implications?"

"Mr. President, I appreciate the importance of Missouri, but we are so close to finalizing terms with the Blues. This obsession you have with the weapons at Whiteman – it has compromised our position. The Blues are weak, sir. It is our conventional strength along the demilitarized zone that is going to secure favorable terms at the negotiation table, not more nuclear weapons."

Cameron slammed the palm of his hand onto the large conference table in front of him with a crack that made several of the political staffers and even a few of the present military officers jump.

"Well now, there we have it. We finally have an admission. And in front of an audience, no less. Just to be clear, General, the words I just heard come out of your mouth were that I have an 'obsession' and that the weapons at Whiteman AFB will not impact the negotiations with the Blues. Those were your words, General, and they are now on the record."

Cameron left the front of the room and walked in the direction of Evans. The men could have been brothers. They were of similar height, they both had lean builds, and both men had full crops of hair, each with more grey than black. Cameron stopped, leaving several feet between himself and the uniformed man.

"You and the other members of the Joint Chiefs have fought me long enough. Winning over Missouri has been my government's policy since I became President, but you have fought me every step of the way. This charade that is your fickle loyalty ends today. We live in a democracy, General, not a military dictatorship. You do what I tell you. It doesn't go in the other direction."

The entrance to the operations room swung open and several men wearing black-and-grey mottled battle fatigues and balaclavas quickly took up positions on both sides of the room. Each had an automatic weapon at the ready.

"General Colin Evans, the people of the United Constitutional States of America, will not tolerate a military insubordination, incompetence, nor a military coup." As Cameron made the pronouncement, his voice became brassy in its fury.

Evans' eyes shot from the masked soldiers and once again took up Cameron. "Coup? Are you insane? You can't do this."

The look on Cameron's face hardened. Spector wondered if the man would physically explode. "General Evans, our country has been invaded by a foreign power. On the record, you have just admitted to undermining the policy of a democratically elected president and commander-in-chief. If that's not a coup, I don't know what is."

Not moving his eyes from Evans', Cameron said, "Major, please remove Generals Evans, Singleton, Stevenson, and Baumgartner from the premises. They have just resigned their commissions. They are to be driven to their respective residences where they will remain until I or the Secretary of Defense advise otherwise."

"Yes, Mr. President."

As the words came out of the mouth of the impressively thick soldier, several of the other men moved quickly, and in seconds, the four named generals had two black-clad soldiers standing at each of their shoulders.

"You can walk out with your dignity intact General, or you can be dragged out. You have failed your country, so I don't have a particular care which it is," Cameron said in a tone that was almost a growl.

After several seconds of silence during which Evans kept his eyes on Cameron, he finally said, "We'll see ourselves out."

"See that you do," Cameron said.

Spector watched the four men and their accompanying guards leave the room. Once the door closed, the remaining staff and officers moved their eyes in the direction of Cameron.

"As per the power of my office, I am appointing General Spector to the position of Supreme Commander of UCSA and Allied Forces effective immediately. Appointments to all other staff positions will be filled by the end of the day.

"Ladies and gentlemen, I take no satisfaction in making the decision you have just witnessed, and I regret that it had to be done in such a public fashion, but the situation we face as a country is dire. As this great country's democratically elected president, it is my burden and my burden alone to set policy as it pertains to our struggle to reunite the United States of America. This is the struggle of our lives, and you are wholly with me in this endeavor, or you are not. If you have any doubts about the importance of Missouri and what we need to do in that state over the next forty-eight hours, then you can walk out that door and no questions will be asked. But if you stay in this room, it means you are resolute in your commitment to our country and its duly elected leadership."

Cameron looked around the room. Not a person moved.

"Good then. General Spector, the floor is yours. Tell us about your plan to send these CANZUK bastards packing."

———

Whiteman AFB

From the moment Larocque's boots hit the ground, it took the Airborne fifty-two minutes to secure the base. It had been a textbook assault.

As he was floating to the ground, he had the opportunity to briefly survey the damage wrought by the CANZUK airstrikes. It had been impressive. Columns of smoke were located in dozens of locations across the base. The runway alone sported several gaping holes that were still oozing grey, dust-laden smoke, while another set of strikes had precisely torn through various parts of the chain-link fence that formed the eastern boundary of the property. The resulting gaps had provided Larocque and his soldiers with multiple points of entry to the expansive property.

Once on the ground, each of the Regiment's four companies quickly consolidated and efficiently readied the up-armored four-man Polaris RZR's that had been dropped. The small four-wheeled units gave the Airborne instant mobility, and the ability to move and concentrate heavy weapons as they were needed. Carrying soldiers and towing supplies, the vehicles pushed west toward the base's airfield and were followed by lead elements from each of the Regiment's four fighting companies. It was an imposing sight as hundreds of heavily armed soldiers advanced menacingly across the farmers' fields in which they had just landed.

Via constant communication over the BAM system, he listened, watched, and directed his company commanders and other key units as they moved along what was a kilometer-wide front. Within twenty minutes, they had secured the airfield. In another twenty, designated platoons had secured the requisite number of choke points on the base proper, while other units backed up by

RZRs carrying a variety of heavy weapons, secured the base's three main entry points.

It was only at the main entrance where they encountered armed resistance. As a pair of RZRs and two sections of paratroopers approached the brown-bricked building that managed the main flow of traffic onto the base, soldiers armed with the US military's standard assault rifles opened up on the approaching Canadians.

The RZRs, one equipped with a fifty cal and the other with the Canadian Army's standard C-6 heavy machine gun, unleashed on the defenders, and within seconds, two men were dead while several others were wounded.

Larocque had jumped into the BAM video feed of the lieutenant leading the attack and saw for the first time the damage that could be wreaked on the human body when it was exposed to company-level fighting weapons.

One of the defending soldiers – a military police officer – had been subjected to a fifty-cal round that had skimmed across the hood of the old-model Humvee he had been standing behind. The round had hit him at the base of his neck, shearing away most of the man's throat. Through the streaming video on his BAM tactical pad, he observed the sinews of gore keeping the soldier's head attached to his body, but only just.

The other man had made the classic folly of overestimating the strength of the material behind which he had been taking cover. The electric patrol car that he had been standing behind lacked the solid engine block of the gas-driven vehicles that still made up the majority of the US military's motor pool. The bullets of the RZR's mounted C-6 machine gun had cut through the chassis of the patrol car like it was tissue paper. Unlike the nearly decapitated soldier, this man had been worked on by his mates as several blood-soaked staunching kits were affixed to the now dead man's body.

Larocque closed down the feed and surveyed the immediate area around him. It was frenetic. Somehow, a section of the combat engineers who had jumped with them had already laid their hands on a good-sized excavator and were in the process of tearing into the manicured lawn directly in front of the base's air traffic control tower.

Though the structure would stick out like a beacon for any artillery crew that got within ten kilometers of their position, the tactical advantages of the tower's elevation were undeniable, so he would take the risk of placing his command post in close proximity to the tall building.

Walking into the tower, Larocque hit the stairs at a jog and quickly ascended to the observation deck. The door to the tower's control room was open and without hesitation, he strode into the naturally lit room and took in a pair of young-looking soldiers wearing what he knew to be the uniforms of the US Air Force military police.

"Tiller One and Two, I presume?" Larocque asked.

"Yes, sir," the pair said in unison.

Larocque issued a grin in response to the simultaneous replies. "Well, let's play this by the book. At least for now. Give me your validation codes and then we'll see about putting you to work."

The female soldier went first. With sandy brown hair, hazel eyes, and an athletic frame, Larocque knew without a doubt that the young woman would have captured her fair share of attention, even without makeup and wearing the Army's entirely unflattering uniforms. Her code checked out.

He thrust out his hand at the woman. "Lieutenant Hall. A pleasure."

The male soldier had at least two inches on Larocque, which made him tall. He was lean to the point of being wiry and he too had the look of an athlete. Though where Hall was eye-catching, this young man's appearance was workman-like. Unremarkable was not exactly a bad look for a spy if that's what he was. His code checked out, so Larocque shook his hand as well.

"First off, you two have done a hell of a job here. I know Azim and the rest of the crew back at CANSOFCOM are thrilled with your contributions, and I am too," Larocque said. "And whether they know or not, the entire regiment owes you two big."

"It's all good, sir," Hall replied. "We're glad you made it and that you were able to take the base with only minimal resistance."

"Aces to that, Lieutenant, but things are only going to get tougher from this point onward. Listen, I wish I had more time, but there's a lot to be done before someone tries to take back this base. I can give you five minutes. Read me in on what you think I need to know and then we'll see if we can't put your unique skill set to work."

———

Outside Atlanta

Cameron's last words echoed in Spector's mind as he stared at the map on the large display embedded into the conference room's table. *"Mitch, for better or worse, our wagons are now hitched. We cannot lose the weapons on that base. If we do, everything, and I mean everything, gets harder for us. And remember, Missouri is not our people. Do what you need to do. If there are consequences that some may not like, it's that bastard governor who'll wear it – not you, and not me. I'm already taking steps to make sure of that."*

Spector had been given an order and a blank check. That the check had come from the devil himself, did not faze Spector in the least. He had known who the man actually was for many years now, and despite this, he had still thrown in with him.

Before becoming close with Cameron, Spector had first aligned himself with President Fitzgerald, the man who was the primary architect of his country's second civil war.

Spector had been present on the night when then-Senator Fitzgerald of Tennessee had proposed the course of action that led to the secession of the first tranche of Red states. As this plan had progressed, it had been Senator Cameron who had proposed adding agent provocateurs to the fateful 2nd Amendment march on Washington, and it had been Cameron who had proposed the use of paramilitaries to first harass and then burn down dozens of federally funded abortion clinics across the northeast.

Almost two years later and with the war raging on, providence had once again seen fit to put Spector in the same room as Fitzgerald and Cameron when they debated the Blue city nuclear strikes. By that point, Vice-President Cameron had his claws fully embedded in the older and rapidly declining Fitzgerald. It had been Cameron who convinced Fitzgerald that they shouldn't just strike military targets but to take the opportunity of a nuclear release to decapitate the most strident and unbending parts of the Blue states so that when the UCSA did win the war, their efforts to remake the country would be unopposed by the elites who 'infected' these irredeemable cities.

When word had gotten back to Fitzgerald that Cameron's people had been circulating rumors that Cameron had not been part of the discussions to incinerate the Blues and that the vice-president had gone on the record to voice his abhorrence of nuclear weapons, it was said that Fitzgerald had become white-hot with anger and had sworn to cut the Senator from North Carolina from his inner circle. Some five days later, Fitzgerald was found dead in his office. An already unwell man, the autopsy had been unable to confirm the cause of death as anything but natural causes.

The entire affair had been instructive to Spector. Cameron was as cunning as a fox and under no circumstances could the man be trusted. That was most clear. But it was also the case that the man had the political foresight and talent, never mind the balls, to pull off what was the greatest non-coup of the past one hundred years. It had been this masterful orchestration that had won Spector's support.

In the present, Cameron was the UCSA's best chance to win the war and fix everything that had been wrong with the United States prior to the civil war. If in the process of reaching that necessary end, he suffered the same fate as the Joint Chiefs or worse, Spector was old and wise enough to know that he could live with that. He now had five grandchildren and he would be damned if they had to make their way in a country that resembled the United States of the past ten years.

He lifted his head from the tactical display he had been studying and looked at the dozen or so officers with him in the spacious command bunker located in the hinterlands of Georgia.

"Alright, folks. We need to turn this clusterfuck around and on the double. I appreciate the briefings and recommendations you have sent me. I have given them my full consideration. As you are aware, the President has directed us to re-take Whiteman AFB. Above all else, this is our priority.

"Based on the intel that we have at this time, we do not think CANZUK and their Colorado allies are interested in holding onto the base for any length of time. Rather, we believe they are looking to remove the nuclear weapons and put them in the hands of Colorado. This cannot happen. Is this understood?"

Everyone in the room offered a quick verbal confirmation or a nod of their head to confirm they understood what needed to be done.

"Okay, as I understand things, the intelligence coming out of Colorado is the best we've got. The Colorado National Guard is pushing what sounds like an oversized but lightly armed brigade from the eastern part of that state across Kansas. If unopposed, they'll make it to the Missouri border this time tomorrow. Do I have this right?

"We think that's right, sir," answered one of the colonels who had been most engaged in fleshing out their strategy.

"Excellent, then I'm batting a thousand. Now, based on conversations with General Howe, it's Kansas where we will concentrate the bulk of our air assets, including the J-31s. If we concentrate our airpower, we think we can dominate this theatre. On the ground, the plan is for local militias to join what remains of the Kansas National Guard to identify and harass the Colorado force while a steady stream of air assets conducts round-the-clock search-and-destroy missions of these same forces."

"If we do this half as well as I think we can, what's coming out of Colorado shouldn't make it within a hundred miles of Kansas City before lead elements of the 3rd Cavalry Division out of Fort Hood begin to arrive. Whatever ground units the Air Force hasn't savaged up till this point, will then be engaged by 3rd Cavalry. Where we go from there, will depend on several things."

Spector looked at Howe who was standing across from him on the other side of the briefing table. "Anything to add, Steve?" he said to the recently promoted four-star general who was now managing the UCSA's air assets.

"I think we've got this right, Mitch. The wild card is where CANZUK's air assets will be operating from. We know that Colorado has a squadron of older F-16s and perhaps a few other birds. On its own, it's nothing we can't handle. But if CANZUK has added to Colorado's platforms, we'll be in tight. We'll be throwing the bulk of the J-31s into this part of the fight. If these fighters are as good as the Chinese think they are, they should allow us to carry the day in Kansas."

"Let us hope," Spector said. "Because we won't be getting any more of those planes any time soon. The moment the Chinese found out their planes would be going up against CANZUK, they vetoed our use of them. But as luck would have it, we were able to put a workaround in place. Let's hope these fancy platforms are worth whatever grief those CCP are going to send our way."

Spector moved his gaze back to the tactical display he had been studying moments before and gestured with a pointed finger in the direction of Missouri.

"Things north of Whiteman are less clear. Based on satellite images we do have and the limited local intelligence that has come in, we think that CANZUK could have as many as three full mechanized divisions pushing south from the Dakotas. Our strategy is simple. Nebraska and Iowa will do anything and everything they can to delay these forces' passage so that we can get our own forces from Kentucky to Whiteman first. It's a race, pure and simple."

Spector paused, leaned over the table, and with his finger, he pushed the digital map south and east so it showed the western part of Kentucky and most of Missouri. A red triangle with the designation of 'Fort Campbell', was at the west end of the map, while St. Louis and Whiteman AFB were north and east.

"As it stands, we have the 101st that has mustered at Fort Campbell. We know that CANZUK has leveled the two bridges at Lake City, Kentucky, but they've left the crossing where the Mississippi and Ohio intersect intact, no doubt because half of the bridge belongs to the Blues. A stupid and weak move, if you ask me.

"Now the Blues will go apoplectic, but we need that bridge to gain entry into Missouri proper, so that's the route we're going to take."

Spector again leaned forward and with both hands broadened the digital map so that Whiteman was at its center.

"People, this is our war zone for the next two days or so. Our troops on the ground and their proximity to the objective gives us an advantage. The wildcard is airpower. If we win or fight them to a draw in the skies over Kansas, our forces from Fort Campbell will be able to reach Whiteman before the CANZUK forces can make it there from the Dakotas. If we lose the fight over Kansas, then the highways across eastern Missouri are gonna be a turkey shoot and it will be our boys out of Kentucky who'll be doing most of the dying."

Spector once again looked at Howe. "It's not the kind of war you want to fight, General, but it's the war we need you and your pilots to win. You have to."

Howe locked eyes with Spector. "It's gonna be a close thing Mitch, but our pilots have years of fighting experience on their side. And if those J-31s can perform, we can win this fight. I'm confident of that."

"Good," Spector said. "Alright, everyone has the plan. I brought all of you together because I know you know how to fight a war. So do what each of you does best and let's get out orders so that we can hand it to these CANZUK sons of bitches."

————

Southern Iowa

For the first part of their drive south, Costen had elected to ride in the confines of the Boxer command and control vehicle. Eight-wheeled and well-armored, the newer machine had well-apportioned intelligence and surveillance capabilities. And if the truth was to be told, it was a much more comfortable ride than the upgraded Challenger 3 tanks he knew were rolling in and around his Boxer. If it came down to serious fighting, he would climb into his old girl and get his hands dirty like the tanker that he was.

For the time being, he and three officers from his ops team were sitting at the Boxer's workstations and were analyzing various types of intel as it streamed in.

"Sir, have a look at feed Echo," one of his junior intel officers said.

Costen toggled one of the two screens in front of him and brought up the image from the Australian-controlled Reaper drone. A good-sized number of military vehicles and civilian pick-up trucks were consolidating around what the display told him was Iowa Western Community College.

"What am I seeing?" Costen asked.

"Intel is telling us that the military vehicles are the best part of what's left of the Iowan National Guard, while the lorries are civilian. On the backs of the lorries, you can see they're loaded with men who are carrying weapons of all kinds. Signals has been monitoring local radio and cell transmissions. The Reds have put out calls for any able-bodied men to gather at several locations across the state. And if they have weapons, they're to bring them."

"So, this is our welcome party."

"One of several by the sounds of it, sir."

"Well, that's brilliant news, Captain. What's the count on this group?"

"At present, we're at twenty-two military vehicles of which only a handful are armored, but there are upwards of 120 lorries."

Costen whistled. "My Christ, that's a lot of wankers who have a death wish."

"It is. It's my guess they'll go for our fuel trucks and our other soft targets. Sir, without the diesel, we won't make it to Missouri. Not even close."

"Captain, get Ares on the BAM, and let's get a package going for this dodgy lot. And tell them, I don't give a toss if there are civilian trucks down there. They can see as well as you or me that every one of those daft bastards is carrying some type of weapon. Jesus, by the looks of it, some of the bastards even have fifty-cals."

"God bless the 2nd Amendment, sir," the intelligence officer offered.

"Bloody Americans and their bloody guns," Costen retorted.

Costen's eyes darted back to the other display at his station. Since kicking off at 0400 this morning they had made good time driving across South Dakota. State troopers had shut down State Highway 29 going south, allowing the massive convoy of British and Australian military vehicles to speed across the length of the state. That had been seven hours ago. Upon hitting the southern edge of South Dakota, the four battlegroups had separated, and each had made their own way south utilizing routes that used some combination of rural roadway and farmers' fields. Costen's formation had hugged the 29 on the Iowa side of the border and would continue to ride the motorway south for all they were worth.

Depending on when that growing mob at the uni got off the mark, one or more of the battlegroups would run into them this evening or first thing tomorrow morning. They wouldn't dare come at them in the night. In the end, the timing of the engagement wouldn't matter. It would be their first test and it was Costen's job to make sure his battlegroup was ready. They had a schedule to keep, and he'd be damned if this growing ramshackle of a force on his display would prevent him and his people from getting where they needed to be.

Chapter 18

Ottawa

On screen, standing behind a podium that bore the Canadian coat of arms, Bob MacDonald looked sober and resolute as he moved into the final section of his prepared remarks.

"And so, my fellow Canadians, it is the view of this government and that of the governments of the United Kingdom, Australia, and New Zealand that we had to act. The United Constitutional States of America has demonstrated time and again that its values are out of step with the traditions that underpin the CANZUK alliance, and we have seen that the leaders of the UCSA have no compunction when it comes to the use of nuclear weapons.

"We have seen the devastation on our screens, and we are now home to several million refugees, many of whom come from the UCSA itself.

"In sending the brave and dedicated soldiers of the Canadian Armed Forces into Missouri and in conducting targeted strikes across the controlled territories of the UCSA, as a country and as an alliance, we are choosing intervention at this time because this choice is still afforded to us. We are a sovereign country and to remain a sovereign country that makes its own choices, we must undertake the action I have just outlined to you.

"My friends, to those who will be upset with this monumental decision, Canada and our allies stand at a geopolitical crossroads. One path - the path we have taken, allows us to determine our own destiny, just as we always have. The other path that stands before us is one of hesitation and uncertainty. To do nothing in the face of the horrific actions we have witnessed in the past year is to place our fate in the hands of war criminals and tyrants who are not unlike the worst dictators of the twentieth century.

My fellow Canadians, the current death toll from UCSA strikes over the last year is now eleven million people. As your prime minister, I cannot and will not reconcile this number with anything but the greatest evil of our time.

"And while I fear for the lives of those men and women who are carrying out this policy of intervention in the State of Missouri, this monumental consideration aside, as a human being and as your prime minister, I will sleep well in the coming weeks, knowing this was the right decision for our country and the democratic and free world to which Canada is one of but a few remaining leaders.

"For the foreseeable future, a joint CANZUK briefing will be held daily at 3 p.m. eastern standard time. It is here that the press will be able to ask questions and receive updates about the alliance's efforts to secure the nuclear weapons at Whiteman Air Force Base for our allies in the Colorado Neutral Faction.

"This ends my statement."

———

Whiteman, AFB

From the observation deck of the air traffic control tower, Larocque surveyed Whiteman. Things were happening. The engineers and pioneers had purloined two more excavators from somewhere and were busy doing a quick repair on the airfield. On the tarmac, paratroopers aided military police in their efforts to organize the pilots and bomber crews that needed to be processed along with the base's other soldiers.

Looking out further, he could see each of the Airborne's four companies, digging in like badgers. The strategy drawn up to defend the base was straightforward. The base and the area around the property would be broken into quadrants, with each quadrant held with one of the Airborne's infantry companies.

As Kentucky had the largest and closest contingent of fighters, it was to the east of the base that his regiment would concentrate its defensive assets.

From the tower, Larocque could see the areas east were wide open fields with intermittent treelines for as far as the eye could see. It had been those same flat and recently tilled fields that he and his soldiers had jumped into almost two hours ago.

The lynchpin of their defense was the bunker system on the eastern side of the base where Whiteman stored its tactical nuclear weapons. Some forty bunkers in total, each storage unit was a low-slung, reinforced-concrete shell covered in tons of soil that had long ago been surfaced with grass. The redoubts and trenches they were now building amongst and on top of the bunkers, would serve as the Regiment's last stand position and the point from which all other defensive fortifications would emanate.

Though counter-intuitive at first blush, using the network of bunkers as a defensive pivot made sense once you came to realize that it was highly unlikely the Reds would use heavy weapons on that part of the base.

In the '80s, the US had upgraded all of its nuclear weapons so that they could not be detonated by secondary means. As Larocque understood it, you could place as many of Whiteman's bombs as you wanted into the world's largest bonfire or drop them off the world's tallest building and nothing would happen. At least nothing in the way of a nuclear explosion. But it was the case that these same weapons could be damaged to the point where they became unusable. It was this outcome he was betting the Reds would avoid at almost any cost.

As he continued to watch his soldiers busy themselves, Larocque heard what sounded like a small group of people walking up the stairs. Turning to the entrance of the observation deck, he saw a burly military policeman walk into the room. He was followed in by an American Air Force officer who held the rank of colonel.

"Sir, this is Colonel Havez," the MP said. "You had asked for him."

"I did," Larocque exclaimed. "Thanks for bringing him along so quickly. You can leave the colonel with me. If I need you to come back, I'll let you know."

Dismissed, the soldier turned back toward the large room's only entrance and began to clatter down the metal stairs.

Larocque waited several moments until the soldier was well out of earshot before he turned his attention to the waiting officer. He took a step toward Havez and thrust out his hand for a handshake.

"Colonel, it is a real pleasure to meet you. I am personally in your debt. What you've done in the past few days saved innumerable lives. Of my men and yours. I'm sorry we couldn't get you out of here as per the original plan, but I want you to know that we're prepared to do whatever it takes to put you where you want to be when this is all over. And that's straight from the top."

Releasing Larocque's hand, Havez turned and walked to the windows and looked out onto the airfield, taking in the scene of combat engineers and other soldiers busily making efforts to repair the car-sized craters that littered the runway.

Without looking at Larocque, Havez said, "It was the right thing to do, Colonel. I'm convinced of that. My country has seen enough death in the past three years. If I've helped in some small way to prevent another holocaust of my fellow citizens, what happens to me in the coming days and weeks is inconsequential."

Havez turned from the window to see Larocque's hand snap to his right ear. As the man's head cocked slightly, a look of concern emerged on the Canadian's face. Quickly, the paratrooper pivoted so that he was now looking to the southeast.

"Get the word out wide across the BAM Jen and fire up the klaxon."

Larocque turned back to face Havez.

"Trouble is on its way, Colonel. Helicopters – Apaches by the sounds of it are inbound. Follow me," Larocque said as he moved toward the stairs.

"My wife. She's at our house," Havez said, his voice filled with concern as he moved to follow the now quickly moving paratroop CO.

Larocque did not stop moving, but, over his shoulder, called back to the other officer, "She'll be fine. Hall and Wallace should be with her. As soon as they hear the air siren, they'll know what to do."

Larocque then paused his descent, turned, and again locked eyes with the other man. "Us on the other hand – it looks like we're going to get to see what war looks like up close and personal and sooner than I would have hoped."

———

As Brazeau was listening to the general message coming in about the inbound attack helicopters via his BAM earpiece, he heard the sound of the klaxon begin to go off. *Ha!* There it was. Just like the goddamned movies, he thought. For whatever reason Larocque had insisted they bring the screaming relic with them, and now he could see why. Unless you were full-on deaf, no one could say they didn't know trouble was coming.

As the air raid horn blared unceasingly, soldiers began to run to their assigned positions with purpose. As paratroopers, they had drilled for this scenario countless times.

He looked in the direction where Colonel Delgado had positioned his command. The 2IC had overall command of the Regiment's heavy weapons company. Delgado was no slouch, so

Brazeau had every confidence the man would have already deployed the Airborne's anti-aircraft weapons.

His own soldiers had dropped their entrenching tools and were taking up positions in the growing network of trenches and redoubts they were building on top and around the base's nuclear bunkers.

Relative to others, his company was in an enviable position. It was thought that the incoming attack helicopters would not use their rockets or missiles on this part of the base, lest they damage the precious munitions underneath and around them. He was less confident on the question of whether or not the Apaches would rake their position with their 30mm cannons.

"Where's the air support we were promised?" Brazeau said aloud to himself as he ripped a pair of binoculars out of his rucksack. Putting them to his eyes, he looked southeast and scanned low on the horizon. There they were – little black specks of death off in the distance.

As the klaxon ended and he continued to take in the scene of the approaching helicopters, his ears caught the distinctive scream of jet engines. Moving at an untold speed, objects flashed over the airfield in the direction of the incoming helicopters. Brazeau's naked eye made out the blur of the projectiles as they flew toward their targets. Air-to-air missiles, he thought. But from where?

Seconds later, he saw flashes bloom into full explosions as the projectiles found at least some of their targets. As the morning sky in the southeast lit up with several mini suns, soldiers pulled up from whatever they were doing and cheered. As they did so, two Canadian F-18 Super Hornets marked by their unique under-cockpit paint scheme screamed over their position. Flying at Mach-something, the concussive noise of their engines washed over Brazeau and the rest of his company as they raced toward the remaining Apaches.

Brazeau then watched as the two fighters banked sharply in op-posite directions as they simultaneously released a torrent of bright flares. No doubt the two Canadian pilots had just come into range of the Apaches' own air-to-air missiles and were themselves under-taking evasive maneuvers.

A voice popped into his earbud. He recognized the man's call sign as one of the officers who was leading up the Regiment's air de-fense platoon. The voice was nonplussed. "All units, all units, this is Mast Two. There are still seven targets bearing down on our posi-tion. As they enter range, they'll be engaged with our local assets. All heavy weapons are to concentrate on targets in their respec-tive zone of fire. All others are to keep their heads down. The hos-tiles will be engaging our position in under two minutes. Mast Two out."

Brazeau could see the helicopters clearly now. To his immediate right, he saw one of the Regiment's RZRs race forward to place one of the bunkers between itself and the incoming helicopters.

It was one of two RZRs the Airborne had with them that was equipped with the Swedish RBS-70 short-range air defense system. While each of the air defense RZRs had a pair of missiles each, Del-gado had another half dozen of the man-portable RBS-70 units po-sitioned elsewhere on the base. He heard a *crack* and *whoosh* as the first and then second missile ejected from the RZR's launch system and began to race toward their targets.

Taking his eyes off the missiles, Brazeau surveyed the scene around him. Everywhere, his paratroopers had stopped digging and were in their trenches waiting. They had two fifty cals and six C-6 machine guns in his company. He could see that all of these weapons were now facing in the direction of the approaching Apaches.

He activated his BAM. "Open channel, A Company," he said. "Channel open," the smooth, replicated female voice advised in his ear. "A Company, this is Brazeau. Steady-on everyone. This is the real deal, so stay tight and focused. Fifties, don't open up until these things are in range. When they are, talk it up and concentrate your fire on one at a time. You know the drill. Carl Gs - if these bastards are in range and hover – even for a second, take a shot. Everyone else – keep your heads down. 5.56 will be useless on these things, so save your ammo. It looks like you're gonna need it. Brazeau out."

Brazeau could now hear the ominous thumping of the killing machines' rotors. Five of the choppers were still bearing down on them. Three were coming at them straight on, while the two other birds were swinging west.

And then it started. On a knee and looking out from one of the shallow redoubts on top of a grassed bunker, Brazeau saw and then heard a pair of commandeered trucks explode several hundred meters to his front. Both vehicles jacked violently into the air and were quickly enveloped in a storm of dust and black smoke. Behind him, he heard more explosions as the Apaches' anti-armor missiles found other targets.

Seconds later, those paratroopers and combat engineers closest to the approaching helicopters received a salvo of rockets and multiple bursts of 30mm cannon fire. It was a maelstrom of violence that devastated and tore through the half-finished positions of Singh's company. Those few vehicles that had been set to the task of helping his friend build up his defensive area were efficiently torn to shreds.

In that same moment, one of the three Apaches exploded in a terrific ball of orange and black.

Not taking his eyes off the two remaining helicopters, Brazeau watched as the two machines continued to unleash their weapons. Anti-armor missiles – likely Hellfires, seared through the air to the right of Brazeau's position to find targets that were further back on the base. As the missiles found their targets, explosions rocked the air.

As he took in the full spectacle, he had not forgotten the two Apaches that had peeled away earlier. Turning his body west, he could see smoke billowing from the ground where one of the two attack helicopters had been shot down. The remaining pilot had gained altitude and as clear as day, Brazeau could see the pilot had lined up the bunker system and his men. "Tabernac," Brazeau said to no one in particular.

Outside of the range of his company's heavy weapons, the 30mm cannon slung at the front of the Apache began to flash. Instantly, the ground around Brazeau and his soldiers began to erupt as hundreds of the explosive shells began to tear through earth, sandbags, and flesh.

————

Larocque had a front-row seat as the pilfered excavator on the tarmac first exploded and then burned into a heap of slag. Other vehicles on the runway had shared the excavator's fate and were themselves inflamed piles of metal.

On the horizon, he saw the remaining Super Hornet make a lazy turn in the cloudless blue sky so that its pilot could once again bear down on the one remaining attack helicopter. The fighter pilot had to be down to his last few rounds as did the Apache.

The now-stationary Apache pilot, no doubt understanding how things would end up if he waited around for the faster fighter jet, banked south, drove himself to within one hundred feet of terra firma, and started a sprint in the opposite direction of the soon-to-be-charging Super Hornet.

"A total fucking shit show!" Larocque belted out.

Quickly, he looked at his BAM's wrist unit. Somewhere during the attack, he had brought up the casualty management app. The heart rates of thirteen soldiers were now off-line, including Delgado's and that of Captain Horth, his D Company commander. The data now coming in suggested an additional eleven soldiers were somehow at risk. 'Shit show' did not begin to cover what had just happened, he thought.

Activating his BAM, Larocque said, "Get me Rider Actual. Priority call Alpha Sierra."

"Channel open," said the replicated voice of the BAM's near-AI.

General Gagnon's voice then piped into his earbud, "This is Rider Actual. What's your status, Jack?"

"We've had better days, sir. How the hell did those things get within two hundred klicks of this base?" Larocque asked, his voice straining to maintain a level tone.

"I see your preliminary numbers coming in. If I were in your shoes, I'd be mad as hell and would be asking that same question. The short answer is that the Reds took out our on-station AWACS with one of those damned Chinese planes. The things are like ghosts. A British-operated Wedgetail was shot down. That's ten airmen and a critical piece of kit gone. By the time we got coverage back in place, those low-flying bastards were almost on you. I'm sorry, Jack."

"Well, I'm sorry too, General. I've lost some exceptional soldiers, including my number two."

"I see that. Delgado was a hell of a guy and the right 2IC for your outfit."

"A hard copy on that, sir. His men are going to take it hard. He was tough on them, but they loved that giant bastard," Larocque said.

"It's a terrible development, Jack. There's no getting around it, but we push on. You push on. This was never going to be easy," said Gagnon, the tone of his voice both firm and reassuring.

"Copy that, sir. We'll get it done," Larocque offered quickly.

"I know you will, Airborne," the general replied. "And since I've got you, I've got a few updates."

Having said his piece, Larocque resigned himself to move forward like the professional he was. Stalwart is what this situation called for – both for himself and for his men. "Read me in, sir. What's the latest?"

"The Reds have mobilized in Texas and Kentucky quicker than we anticipated and at the moment, they're giving us all we can handle in the skies over Kansas. The consequence of this means that the Colorado National Guard has been chewed up pretty bad, so we're diverting three of the Canadian battlegroups to central Kansas to help them out. Their mission is to now engage the forces coming out of Texas, so they can't hit you from the west. Once these three battlegroups get there, it's gonna be a real dog fight. That means Colorado force will not be linking up with you at the thirty-six-hour mark as per Plan Alpha."

Larocque exhaled loudly, issued a solitary expletive, and said, "Well it didn't take long for things to go off the rails. What about the Brits and Aussies?"

"Thankfully, things look better up north. Nebraska and Iowa are throwing everything they can at us to slow us down, but there's no question we'll get through. It's only a question of when. The Red Faction forces out of Kentucky are pushing hard and there are lots of them, but they only have so many routes to get to your location. As long as we dominate the air in that part of the fight, we can slow them up, if not stop them altogether. But there's a big but," Gagnon said.

"And that is?" Larocque asked promptly.

"Those J-31s are giving us fits. And the rest of the Reds' air force is fighting like demons. We're confident we can win, but it's likely to be touch and go for the next twenty-four hours in your area of operations. If I had to guess, some of what is coming out of

Fort Campbell is going to reach you. With our bases in the Dakotas, the pace of our air operations is going to leave gaps and that means that some of the Reds coming from Kentucky are going to get through to you."

"General, so long as you don't let any more of those flying tanks take potshots at my soldiers, we can hold this place. The ground is perfect for digging, so we're going to trench up the place like it was 1916. If they do come, we'll be burrowed in like ticks and we'll be looking for payback. So put your money on us."

"No questions there, Jack," the overall commander of the operation said. "There's one more thing, and it's a question. When do you think you might have that runway back up and running so that we could land a Herc?"

Larocque had continued to survey the smoking wreckage on the airfield while he had been talking to Gagnon. They had one excavator left somewhere on base, and as soon as he got off this call, he would be ordering the Airborne's reconnaissance company, the Pathfinders, to go off base to track down more of the things. "I think we'll have it ready to go in the next hour or two," he said.

"Good, there's a flight of Hercs ready in Edmonton. We'll be sending in additional air defense assets and we're going to reinforce you with two companies from the 2nd Commando along with its colonel. He'll take over for Delgado."

If more soldiers were needed to hold Whiteman, it was Larocque who had first suggested that 2nd Commando be the unit to reinforce the Airborne. In the weeks since the bruhaha between the two regiments, Larocque and their colonel had worked together to smooth out the relationship between the two hard-charging outfits. In the process, Larocque had gotten to know Corporal Dune and his company commander, Captain Chen, increasingly well. Dune was indeed a feisty character but as it turned out, the kid did have humility in him, while Chen was an all-around solid junior officer who carried himself with an easy confidence.

"The Aussies were always part of the plan. I take it Capt. Chen will be one of the two companies being sent in?"

"I'm told he'll be first off the first plane," Gagnon said.

"Good, because those cocksure Aussie bastards are exactly the type of soldiers we need right now."

"They'll be wheels up in thirty and if all goes well, they'll be touching down at your location in three hours. However you do it, Jack, get that runway in shape."

"As long as there are no more surprises, we'll get it done, sir" Larocque replied, the tone of his voice resolute.

"Okay, the final thing. I'm going to transfer you to the Minister. She has something urgent that she needs to brief you on. Initially, I pushed back on the idea that she should pass the intel along to you, but it's one of those safe versus sorry situations. You'll see what I mean when she gives you the update. The feed will switch over to her once I leave."

"General, I really don't have time for politicians at the moment. I've got at dead and wounded soldiers and a list of things to do that's as long as the Trans Canada."

"I know, but you'll want to hear her out. It may be bullshit, but it's best you get the info directly and make your own assessment. She knows you're pressed for time. Remember she was a cop for over twenty years, so she can cut to the chase when she needs to. And as best as I can tell, she's one of the good ones. She really is on our side."

Larocque thought back to his previous and only conversation with Merielle Martel. He still couldn't bring himself to believe that Brazeau would have intentionally sold them out. It had to be that Josee Labelle was the person feeding intel to the Reds, and if that was the case, it meant she had his soldiers' blood on her hands. He couldn't do anything about it now, but if that separatist witch had contributed in some way to the death of his people, he wanted to know.

"Alright, put her on the line and let's see what Madame Martel has to say."

———

Gatineau, east of Ottawa

Altov read the message on the screen of his laptop. "Mission to proceed. Complete in next forty-eight hours at your operational discretion. Remainder of contract executed."

He had to hand it to the French. They had just gone all-in here in North America. He knew the country had undertaken several risky operations in recent years that had advanced their national interest. In all cases, the pay-offs had been fruitful and apparent. He was less sure about his current mission. This CANZUK outfit was not some backward African shithole. But he had been paid and it had been a kingly sum, so he and his men would get on with their business. If the fallout of what he was about to do became a problem for France, that was not *his* problem.

He wasn't surprised by the timing of the encrypted message that came in ordering him to undertake the mission. Despite the Canadian prime minister's calm demeanor and sage words to his countrymen, Quebec and other parts of the country were in an uproar over the country's decision to intervene south of the border.

Within hours of MacDonald's address, cars had been turned over and were burning in several parts of Montreal, Quebec City and Toronto. Online and on television, the talking heads were in a full lather, and in Quebec, the separatists were apoplectic. To say the Canadian PM's decision was controversial would be an understatement.

Despite the developments, Altov had been both surprised and reassured by the fact that security at the prime minister's residence remained unchanged. Not for the first time, he marveled at this country's naivete. Here they were, plunging headlong into the most deadly of political waters and their national security forces were acting as though it was business as usual.

Or perhaps it was arrogance? Altov had worked all over the world and believed himself to be a keen student of politics and culture. Never had he encountered a country that loved itself as much as Canada did. In the weeks he had been in-country and had been studying the country's politics and media, he had come to realize it was Canada's dirty little secret.

For decades, this second-tier Western power had stoked its own fire while it hectored others from behind the security apparatus that was the American hegemony. And then, when they thought the Americans weren't looking or didn't care, they would flounce, even denigrate, the very entity that made it possible for Canada to toss its meager weight around. It was as comical as it was outrageous.

Whichever it was, it was as ungrateful and smug a country as he had ever been in, even if the current prime minister seemed to be moving in a new and daring direction. Even with this American adventure, Canada still had much to learn about its own hubris and the perilous world it lived in.

Pushing himself up from his desk, Altov looked at the time before closing his laptop. Sixteen hundred hours on the nose. It was more than enough time. They would make it happen tonight.

He walked into the room where the other members of his team were transfixed on a single television. He did not work with stupid men, so each would have come to understand how the stakes of what they were being paid to do had dramatically increased over the past twelve hours.

As one, they turned to look at Altov when he entered the room. Each face wore a mask of calm determination. It was the right crew for this job.

"The order is in, gentlemen. Tonight, we pour gasoline on the dumpster fire you see on the screen before you."

Chapter 19

Western Iowa

Lt. Colonel Jacob Bloor of the 2nd battalion, 134th Regiment watched as the feed from the battalion's last recce drone went offline.

"The signal's gone, Colonel. They got it," said the young captain who was manning the station he was half-standing behind in the cab of the Stryker command vehicle.

No doubt they had, he thought.

The Stryker was one of a small number of armored vehicles they'd managed to cobble together over the past twenty-four hours.

The bulk of the Nebraska National Guard's equipment was out east standing off against the Blues. Not that there was much of it left. As was the case with every Red state involved in the vicious two-year civil war, the sons and daughters of Nebraska had seen their share of fighting. The worst had been in Maryland and along the no man's land that rimmed the southern reaches of DC.

It was in the midst of that inhuman fighting that he had been promoted from captain to major and then to lieutenant colonel. His predecessors, all good men, had died fighting a war he had never been sure about. But out of respect to the officers who had come before him, he had kept those thoughts to himself, and instead of ruminating or griping as some other officers did, Bloor spent most of his time trying to keep the soldiers of his battalion alive.

It was many of those same men and some women who were now with him as he tried his best to stem the tide of mechanized infantry driving south across the states of Nebraska and Iowa.

When they put out the call to muster, he knew those enlisted men and women who were in the state on leave would come. What he didn't anticipate was the number of other Nebraskans and

Iowans that would rally. All in, something in excess of four hundred pick-ups had shown up and, to the last, each irregular fighter was toting some type of weapon. Had the trucks not been in such good shape and presented in such a range of colors, the collection of vehicles might have been a scene straight out of the Mad Max franchise.

The bottom line is that they would take all comers. It was a desperate move to throw civilians into the mix, but that's what the situation called for. The situation had also called for a hands-off strategy, as there was just no way to coordinate that many people and vehicles. As trucks arrived, Bloor and his soldiers had got the word out – harass from afar and if you can, go after their logistics vehicles, with the fuel tankers being public enemy number one. They would never defeat CANZUK's fighting vehicles, but they could run them out of diesel. With the few military fighting machines they did have, the plan was for both National Guard units to hold those few defensible tracts of land that did exist in this flat and mostly treeless part of Middle America.

That strategy, over the past ten hours or so, had not gone well. Yesterday, early in the fighting, several cavalcades of civilians had raced north along the two states' various highways and county roads only to be set upon by an unknown number of special operations soldiers who had been lying in wait.

Riding in their own armored vehicles, these highly trained soldiers had patiently waited and then engaged the testosterone-fueled and undisciplined convoys speeding northward. With their longer-range weapons and airpower to call upon, these small units had unleashed a storm of death, wiping out entire groups of the unprepared irregulars. It had been an appalling loss of life.

Being untrained and no doubt awed by the slaughter, dozens of Bloor's new citizen-soldiers had elected to post images of the carnage on social media. Of all the debacles, State Highway 59 just west of the town of Denison had been the most unsettling.

There, at dusk, a convoy of what must have been thirty pick-ups had been set upon by a CANZUK airstrike and then ambushed by a small force of what he now suspected were members of Britain's Special Air Service. The voyeur of death who had captured the scene had spared his audience none of the gruesome details.

Trucks and ruined bodies burned, while those fighters who had managed to get out of their vehicles lay strewn in all directions across the highway, their bodies broken and torn. The horrific video had been capped off with the morale-boosting videographer framing up a young woman who had been separated into two jagged pieces, at which point, the person doing the filming panned away to throw up the contents of his stomach. It had all been Pulitzer-worthy stuff.

After this initial baptism and with darkness coming on, those civie irregulars that had chosen to remain in the fight had wisely elected to switch their tactics, with most choosing to lay in wait for the steadily progressing enemy in and amongst the many farms and tiny towns sprinkled across this part of Iowa.

Of the two strategies, it had been the more successful by far. Melded into the civilian properties, CANZUK soldiers could not easily distinguish the irregular fighters, and as the tactic had worked in Vietnam, Iraq and Afghanistan, the civilian-attired and hyper-localized combatants began to have an effect. By the early morning, a number of soft targets including several fuel trucks had stopped moving or had been destroyed altogether.

Bloor had been thrilled by the development right up until the point the encroaching forces altered their tactics. Whatever nation's forces he was confronting, they knew their business. Due to the wide-open nature of this part of Iowa, the advancing CANZUK forces had taken to the practice of swinging wide around any and all farmsteads or towns leaving Bloor's lying-in-wait irregulars out of range and out of luck.

The word from on high was that he had to make a stand to once again slow down the invaders. Considering the cobbled-together outfit now under his command, this would be no easy task.

He had divided his under-strength mechanized company between the towns of Shenandoah and Clarinda. The plan was straightforward. Whichever of the CANZUK units came between the two municipalities, his divided force would set upon them from the west and east.

They would be supported by what remained of an artillery regiment that was part of Iowa's National Guard. Like Bloor's outfit, most of the unit's weapons and equipment were out east and as a result, they had only been able to mobilize a half battery of training howitzers, which they had dug in next to a local high school.

Across the gap between the two towns, he had positioned soldiers who would observe and report on the oncoming CANZUK forces. It was from one of those men that the first sighting came in.

"Sierra Actual, this is Charlie-Echo. I have a visual on the approaching bandits. I'm seeing what looks like half a dozen armored wheeled vehicles and three, no, make that four MBTs."

Bloor took up one of the command vehicle's mic sets. "Charlie-Echo, this is Foxtrot Actual. Good work. Stay alive and keep the reports coming. Fire support is on its way. Actual out."

Bloor turned to the soldier who was manning the command vehicles comms station. "Sargeant, give me the battalion-wide channel."

"It's open, sir."

"This is Sierra Actual. The enemy has been sighted. We are a go. Begin to advance on your vectors, fire for effect, and may God have mercy on us all."

———

It had been three long hours since Costen last had a tea. What he wouldn't do for a thermos of the stuff, right now. Murder he thought wasn't out of the question.

"Sir, Reaper Three has movement coming out of Shenandoah."

"Put it up on my screen," Costen said, quickly subduing any thoughts he had of asking one of his subordinates to stop what they were doing so they could start to work a kettle.

The image of the American town was on the left-hand display where he could clearly make out the moving images of what appeared to be about fifteen armored vehicles and a larger number of those cursed lorries the American civies had been throwing at them.

Moving his eyes, he then looked at the right-hand display, which had a tactical map set at a resolution that allowed him to see a thirty-kilometer area around the battlegroup.

"Wentworth, put one of our local drones on the town of Clarinda ASAP. You'll see it's due east of Shenandoah. Let's see if the Yanks send anything out from that location."

"On it," said one of the captains with him in the back of the Boxer.

"Vezina, tag the armored vehicles coming out of Shenandoah and have Ares put an air package on them. Tell them I don't want to see any of that armor making it within five kilometers of us. And remind them – nicely this time – that the irregulars are a secondary priority. Once the armor stops moving, they can start in on the flaming lorries."

"Very good, sir," the other captain said.

This was it then, Costen thought. The Nebraskans and Iowans had not been able to link up with Missouri. It was here in the southern reaches of Iowa that the combined forces of the two Red states would make their stand. He wondered what they'd throw at the other battlegroups if anything. More of those civie trucks, no doubt. The cursed things were like ants.

"Sir, drone number two has picked up military and civilian vehicles west of Clarinda."

"Right. Vezina, tag them too and update Ares. Let us hope there are enough assets in our part of the sky to handle the volume."

Costen activated his BAM. "Open channel, all commanders, Battlegroup Alpha."

"Channel open," the smooth, synthesized female voice instantly advised in his earbud.

"Okay, you lot, things are about to get dodgy, so have an ear. We have two enemy forces approaching us from the immediate west and east. Capt. Vezina will be sending along the tactical feed momentarily. Air assets are on their way and should engage anything heavy before they are in range, but should any make it through, designated teams will peel off to engage, while logistics keeps moving. Remember people – forward motion is our friend and we're behind schedule, so stay aggressive and push hard. Costen out."

"Sir, incoming artillery," the third and final soldier in the command vehicle said. A lieutenant fresh out of Sandhurst, the still-green officer's voice was level and matter of fact.

"Find it, Richards," Costen replied promptly.

Seconds later, he heard the thump of artillery shells as they began to impact in and around his vehicle.

After several moments, the lieutenant called out, "Got it. It's coming from the vicinity of the local high school."

Costen grunted and looked at the tactical map that showed Shenandoah and quickly found the high school in the town's southeast. Toggling the screen brought up the streamed image being provided by the battlegroup's assigned Reaper. He overrode the operator's control of the soaring unit and rotated the drone's high-def camera, quickly finding what he was looking for. Four guns lined up along one of the school's north-facing walls. "Very Saddam Hussein of them," Costen mused.

He took a hard look at the parking lot. Not a car in sight. He then scoped out the residential houses about seventy-five meters due west of the gun placement. The battlegroup had a pair of APCs that had been fitted with automatic-firing 120mm mortars. It would be tight, but it had been the Reds who had put the damned guns there in the first place. And by his count, they were now a full five hours behind their next objective. It would not do.

"Vezina, give the order to put the mortars on that position," Costen growled. "School or not, we're not wasting another minute playing around with these daft bastards."

———

Above Kansas

It was Lt. Colonel Chet 'Cheddar' Montrell's second sortie of the day in the skies over Kansas. Of their original twenty-six J-31s, they were now down to twenty three machines. This compared well with the twenty-six CANZUK fighters and two AWACS planes his squadron had shot down. Over Kansas at least, the UCSA Air Force had been doing its part to dominate the enemy.

The kill ratio had been a testament to the skills of his pilots but also the American ground crews now keeping his squadron's fighters operational. It had only been a few weeks since the Chinese technical team that had been servicing the planes had been wrangled up in the middle of the night and shipped somewhere off base never to be heard from again.

Apparently, a single Chinese technician had stayed on and had been helping the American ground crews navigate the inner workings of the complex machines. There was a story there, to be sure, but whatever the arrangement was, it had worked and had allowed

Montrell and his pilots to beat the odds against a formidable larger force.

The current sortie was of the search-and-destroy variety. The UCSA's few remaining command-and-control-capable planes and the ground-based mobile radars supporting the 3rd Cavalry Division on the ground in Kansas would identify less-advanced incoming CANZUK fighters and when they did, Montrell and the J-31s with him would intercept and destroy whatever planes they could. It was simple and thus far had produced outsized results.

Their continued success depended on one thing. That some kind of radar be available to identify and direct in-theatre interceptors so that the stealth planes could avoid enemy radar right up until the point where they engaged their targets. It was the J-31's exceptional stealth capabilities that made this tactic so effective. As long as there was some other asset that could identify targets, he and his pilots could loiter in-theatre unseen and then as needed, they could appear and savage whatever targets had been served up to them.

That CANZUK's losses were so high was a testament to the skill of his pilots and the technology of the planes they were now flying. But it had not been all roses. In the short time the two sides had been having at it, CANZUK had adjusted its tactics and in the process had achieved their first victories against the Montrell's squadron.

It was now up to Montrell and his pilots to make the next move. They had other tricks up their sleeve that they could bring to bear to keep the CANZUK air forces guessing.

"Raven One, this is Bronco Four, we have zeroed in four targets at bearing one-three-five. The data should be on your screen. You are free to engage," said the officer coordinating the data coming in from the various UCSA radar feeds.

Montrell looked at the appropriate cockpit display and saw the targeting data appear. Four Super Hornets at fifteen thousand feet and just under two hundred klicks away. A ground attack run to be sure. They would need to move quickly if they were to break up the attack before they got within range.

"Bronco, thanks for the pings. We'll take it from here. Raven One out."

Montrell quickly thought through their approach. No doubt the British had positioned their own 6th gen fighter somewhere above the approaching fighter-bombers. There would be up to four of them waiting for him and his pilots to reveal themselves, looking to do to them, what they were about to do to the flagged Super Hornets.

He opened up a channel to the other three pilots in the air with him.

"Casper and Waxer, you'll take the Hornets. Drop to their altitude and let'em have it at twenty klicks. Hugs, you're with me. We'll see what comes after Casper and Waxer let loose. Once the Tempests reveal themselves, we'll turn the tables on the RAF bastards. It's time to bag our own first 6th gen trophy. Cheddar out."

———

5th Army HQ, San Antonio

Spector looked at the tactical display now showing eastern Missouri and where the various units of the 101st Airborne Division were relative to their objective. There was no getting around it. It was a mess, though an intentional one.

From Fort Campbell in Kentucky, there were two ways to get to Whiteman AFB. After skirting the most southern edge of Illinois, you could follow the Mississippi River north along Highway 55 until you reached St. Louis, at which point you headed due west to the central part of the state. If you were driving your car and you weren't worried about fighter-bombers blowing you up, this was the most traveled and fastest route into central Missouri. Alternatively, if you wanted a more scenic route and one that offered ample coverage from prying and armed eyes in the sky, you would take one of the dozen or so winding and smaller roadways that cut through the vast swath of thick vegetation that was the Mark Twain National Forest. He had elected to do both.

While the UCSA's air force had achieved success in the skies above Kansas, they had had their asses handed to them over Missouri. The result was that the forces out of Kentucky were being mauled, and badly. They just didn't have the number of advanced fighters they needed to be competitive in both theatres, so Spector had prioritized Kansas in the hopes that a series of quick wins in the west would allow him to transfer assets that would then turn the tide in the east. That they were almost there was what was holding his people together.

The J-31s had made all the difference. Of course, the Chinese were beyond furious with them, but that couldn't be helped, and it was not his problem. His problem was beating the Canadians and their allies and not letting the nukes leave Whiteman. Everything else, including the Chinese and their sensibilities, was secondary. The Sinos would change their tune the moment this little fisticuff was done and they had managed to kick those duplicitous CANZUK sons of bitches back across the 49th parallel.

He looked up from the table-embedded tactical display and focused in on a wall-hanging monitor that featured a none-too-happy, middle-aged soldier.

"General, I appreciate that you are being chewed up on the 55, but you have to keep your men moving. The plan is working. The more CANZUK focuses on your soldiers driving north to St. Louis, the fewer resources they can dedicate to the groups traveling through Mark Twain. By my count, those teams will start to emerge from the forest in the next two hours and within six, we'll have enough to move on the base, and then you should see the pressure come off as they move their air assets to defend Whiteman."

On hearing Spector's update, the general's resting face of thunder did not change. "Then what about more air defense? You have to give us something, Mitch. It's a goddamned free-for-all out here. My men are getting chewed up and bad."

"Rick, we don't have any more assets to send you. I believe you are aware of the civil war our country has been fighting over the past three years. Things like air defense were never in great supply. This is the reality that we're all facing. You and your men need to buck up. This is the reality for the next six to eight hours. Get creative and stay alive as best you can. There's no sugar-coating it for you."

The man's jaw tightened as he stared back at Spector through the screen. "So your order is for us to be creative?"

Spector counted backward from five and held back from exploding. What the hell did this son of a bitch expect him to do? He knew as well as Spector did what the situation was. In war, it was always the case that you never had enough of what you wanted. That this fight had been thrust on them on short notice had only served to make this truism all the more apparent.

"You want my advice, Rick?

"I'm all ears, General," said the other man curtly.

"Where and when you can, saddle up tight with the civies. We wouldn't be in this position if Missouri hadn't been so damned obstinate. The fact is, the governor deserves a little blood on his hands, so as best you can manage, leapfrog from town to town until you reach St. Louis. Get in nice and tight and dare those bastards to hit you. A few dead kids in the news should take off some of the pressure until enough of your men get through Twain. That's the best I can offer."

On hearing explicit direction that he could begin to shelter his forces amongst civilian targets, the general's face softened, if only slightly. "It's not ideal, Mitch, but you play with the hand you're dealt."

"My friend, war is not pretty or fair. There's no magic to this stuff. You roll up your sleeves and you work harder and get dirtier than your opponent. That's how wars are won."

"And what does happen if we can't get those weapons back, Mitch? Are you just gonna let happen to you what happened to Evans and the rest of the Joint Chiefs? You know we'll support you, right? For Christ's sake man, he nuked American cities. That sly bastard is a cancer. You know it. Everyone knows it. It just takes the right man with the right set of balls."

He had been prepared for the question. A two-star general before the outbreak of the civil war, Spector knew how politics was played in the beltway and he had always been someone who knew how to play the long game. But more important than those assets, Mitchell Spector knew when to keep his mouth shut.

Through the display, Spector stared back at the other man and said, "We fight this war, Rick. We fight and we win. That is the task before us. There is nothing else."

———

Whiteman AFB

Larocque cut the connection with the minister and did his best to process what Martel had just told him. It was now conclusive – the Red's had had advance notice of their arrival courtesy of this Guy-Paul Geoffroy fellow in Brazeau's company. It had cost his regiment eighteen lives and counting.

And while the loss of that many of his soldiers was devastating unto itself, it was the broader tactical implications that were fueling his anger toward the separatists.

Intel coming in from Kansas was painting a dire picture. The Colorado forces had been required to hunker down in the small city of Salina awaiting the arrival of three Canadian battlegroups that would help them beat back the UCSA division that had stormed out of Fort Hood, Texas. It was now clear that the Colorado National Guard would not get close to Whiteman as had been the original plan.

The intel coming out of Kentucky was less dire but was more ominous by several factors. Despite heavy losses from a determined CANZUK air campaign, various chunks of the Kentucky-based 101st Airborne and several other units were now clawing their way through Missouri's Mark Twain Forest. This force would be on Whiteman's outskirts within a few hours, at which point he and the Airborne would be so far into the shit, their current losses would seem a distant memory. And then there was the larger UCSA force making its way to St. Louis. Two to three times the size of the force moving through Mark Twain, this more heavily armed collection of fighting units could be on them in less than twenty-four hours.

That Larocque and his soldiers had a pair of self-righteous, twenty-something separatists to thank for their predicament was beyond maddening. As best Martel had been able to tell, Josee Labelle and this Lieutenant Gauthier/Geoffroy had given the Reds several hours, if not a full day's notice that CANZUK was coming. And while Labelle was out of his hands, Gauthier was not.

He activated his BAM. "Give me Brazeau, priority call Oscar-Delta," he said.

"Channel open," the female near-AI voice advised.

"Marcel, how goes it?"

"We're holding it together, sir. Looks like we may have come off better than I first thought. My count is four dead and three wounded who are bad enough that they'll ship out on one of the Hercs bringing in the Aussies."

"That's good bad news," Larocque replied.

"Yeah, it could have been a lot worse had those Apaches got here earlier. In the remainder of my time with this outfit, I'd better not hear one negative word about digging trenches. As it stands, in ninety or so, we'll be done digging and then I'll turn the boys loose onto getting the nukes organized. The door codes you gave us are going to save us a ton of time. Where did those come from by the way?"

"It's a bit of a story. Remind me to tell you when we're on our way out of this place. Listen, Marcel, how well do you know your Lieutenant Gauthier?"

"Curtis? Well enough, I guess. We've had a few beers together. He's mostly the strong silent type, but he's a solid dude, so he's never needed much of my attention. He does what he's supposed to, does it well, and his men respect him. You can't really ask for more than that. What's up?

"It's complicated. I need you to grab a few of your men and bring him here to the command post ASAP. Whoever you take with you, make sure they're geared up."

"Sure thing, boss," Brazeau replied. "Is there anything I need to be worried about?"

"Just handle it like a pro. It could be Gauthier is into something he shouldn't be, and it might be that he doesn't have the Regiment's best interest top of mind. When you go to get him, just be careful is all I can say at the moment."

"Gotcha. I'll grab him now."

"Good. I'm sending over an RZR with the RSM. When you do have Gauthier, make sure he's unarmed when you turn him over to St. Pierre," Larocque said.

"Will do, boss."

Larocque had been relieved to no end when Minister Martel had pronounced to him that Brazeau had not been a willing accomplice to Labelle's dangerous game. Instinctively, he had known that all along, but it had been a relief, nonetheless, when the minister had confirmed CSIS's position on the captain. If Brazeau stayed in the Forces, he had no doubt the man could one day command the Airborne. He was exactly the type of leader this kind of unit needed.

"You're doing a hell of a job, Marcel. Keep it up and keep me posted on Gauthier. Larocque out."

———

Ottawa

Merielle had watched in horror as the live feeds had come in from Whiteman during and after the Red's Apache attack. As she watched the brutal images of destroyed bodies and wounded soldiers being unceremoniously carted back and forth across the base, she had said a silent prayer for their lives and thanked whatever higher power was listening that no media had been on the base to capture the terrible images she had witnessed.

She had watched the grim faces of the generals and other officers who occupied the large operational room in the depths of ND-HQ as they saw and listened to the mix of panicked, furious, and highly professional soldiers as they worked to cope with the unexpected onslaught. Two thousand kilometers away, the best they could do to help was to vector in already too late air support. That there had been only two Canadian Super Hornets in the vicinity of Whiteman would no doubt be a serious point of contention for the command team for days to come.

During that same terrible hour of frenetic activity, Merielle had received word from Stephane that the RCMP raid on Labelle's apartment in Montreal had come up empty. The RCMP had since brought in Quebec's provincial police, the *Surete du Quebec*, and together, the two police forces had commenced a province-wide search for the young woman. At Stephane's request, she had reached out to the PM and secured his go-ahead to have the RCMP approach Labelle's father.

Unsurprisingly, the leader of Quebec's national-level separatist party had not been helpful when the police had paid him a visit and asked for information about the whereabouts of his daughter. Most unhelpfully, within an hour of the visit, the selfish bastard had been on Radio Canada informing the publicly funded national radio outlet that the federal government was employing Gestapo-like tactics in an effort to silence his criticism of the war by going after his family.

All of it had served to bring Canada's simmering national political scene to a full-on boil.

Merielle looked at her watch. It had been thirty minutes since she had talked to Larocque and apprised him of the developments on the Labelle file.

The man's words that ended their call still echoed in her thoughts. Despite all he had just been through, Larocque's tone had been level and matter of fact.

"I'll spare you the video feed Minister, but right now I'm staring at some twenty body bags, each of which holds a son or daughter of one of your taxpayers. To the last, I can tell you they were exceptional, dedicated soldiers, who loved the country and the families they fought for."

After a pause where she got the impression the hardened paratroop commander was trying to suppress his emotions, the Airborne CO had gone on to say, "Find Josee Labelle, Minister. I don't give a damn what you have to do but find her. And when you do track her down, you make sure she pays the full cost of what she's done. And not some bullshit political compromise, like we did back in the '70s with those FLQ bastards. You make her pay the full butcher's bill, or I grab a few of my boys and we settle the account ourselves."

In that moment, Merielle did not feel it would have been welcomed or wise for her to offer her own feelings of outrage toward the traitorous Quebecer. As she had come to learn more about Josee Labelle, Merielle's surface-level annoyance toward the beautiful political scion had changed into something resembling a smoldering hatred.

The FLQ Crisis of the early 1970s had been an ugly thing. Bombings, kidnappings, manifestos - it had all been there. But in Merielle's mind, the most outrageous part of the entire affair had been the miscarriage of justice that the Canadian government had perpetrated once the crisis had come to an end. The bastards that had been the FLQ had almost brought the country to its knees and through it all, they had been unrepentant. And for all of Canada's troubles, what type of sanction did these political extremists receive? All but one was out of jail within three years. In almost any other country during that same period of history, those men would have served life sentences, had they not been shot.

In Merielle's mind, what the younger Labelle had done to her country was far worse than any crime the original FLQ had committed. The leader of Canada's new FLQ movement, if indeed that's who she was, had committed a worse crime. She had given information to the enemies of her country and that information had led not only to the deaths of Larocque's paratroopers but to the loss of almost thirty CANZUK fliers during the initial surge of the air campaign.

Long before talking to Larocque, Merielle had promised herself that Josee Labelle's actions would receive the punishment that was due. What it would be and how it might be meted out was something she hadn't yet worked out.

So when Larocque had delivered his ultimatum – that she deal with Labelle or the Airborne would in its own fashion, she had been able to make a genuine promise to the colonel that she would make it right. When she had asked what he was going to do about Geoffroy, his brief reply was only to say that he, too, would "handle it."

Under the circumstances, Merielle had been satisfied with the reply. Larocque did not need, nor would he appreciate, her interference on the question of this Gauthier/Geoffroy fellow. Having provided the colonel with the information that she thought he needed to keep his troops safe, they had agreed to end the call.

Upon collecting herself, Merielle concluded things were now such that she could quietly skip out from NDHQ, drive home, have a quick shower, and grab a couple of hours of sleep before she had to come back to the building for the 1500 hours daily briefing the PM had committed to. Setting aside the hour of sleep she had snatched much earlier this morning on an uncomfortable couch in some random office, she was well short of the amount of rest she normally got. A shower and a couple of hours of shut-eye would do her well if she was going to do a press conference where the entire country would be watching. Looking disheveled and exhausted would not inspire confidence in a general public keen to see steady and thoughtful leadership.

As she turned the corner of the last hallway in the massive building and saw the bank of glass doors that was the complex's main entrance, her phone went off.

Immediately, she pulled it out of her jacket. Few people had this number. With all that was going on, the call had to be important. She looked at the number and the name associated with it and came to an abrupt stop.

Though it was a Saturday, many soldiers and bureaucrats were occupying the space. Some were moving with purpose, while others had their heads together and were speaking in hushed tones. She was not an uncommon sight on the campus, but with Operation Vandal now in full swing, people couldn't help but cast looks in her direction. Canada was at war, and she was the country's minister of defence and deputy prime minister. How could people not stare?

As more eyes zeroed in on her, Merielle stood alone and ramrod straight in the middle of the entrance rotunda. Slowly, she brought her phone to her ear.

"Yes," Merielle said.

"Good morning, Minister," said a velvety voice that was some combination of Parisian and upper crust Quebecois. "I understand you're looking for me."

Chapter 20

"Our intel is improved," Spector said confidently. "We've had a number of overflights and have people on the ground watching the base. We're certain they have somewhere in the range of a thousand to twelve hundred soldiers at Whiteman."

"And you just advised me you have three thousand good fighting men who are in the process of assembling, where was it again?" Cameron asked.

"They're spread out around the town of Versailles about forty miles north of the Ozarks. It's as dense a forest as this country has and the locals have been helpful in finding places to tuck away our vehicles. CANZUK knows we're there, but if they can't get a clear visual of our vehicles, they can't take a chance trying to hit us. They could just as easily hit civilians and they're already up to their eyeballs in shit on that score."

"And how far is Versailles from Whiteman?"

"As the buzzard flies, it's about fifty miles."

"So, what's the problem, then?" Cameron asked. "As I see it, you've got three-to-one odds, you've chewed them up already, and you seem to think they're low on air defense. Let's rally those troops in...."

"Versailles," Spector offered.

"Yes, Versailles. Get those soldiers going and let's take back our base."

"As I said, Mr. President, the problem is too much of our air power is hung up over Kansas. If I give the order for that force to make the dash to Whiteman, they'll be screwed like a Vegas call girl on a Saturday night."

Through the video conference, Spector both saw and heard Cameron sighing. The man might not like the image, but this was a fighting war so Spector reserved the right to metaphorize however he pleased.

"Mitch, you know that I trust you, but in this case, you have to hear me out."

"The floor is yours, Mr. President."

"Very good. Now as I understand it, if you shift what remains of those Chinese fighters to Missouri, they can do for that theatre what they've done to CANZUK in the skies above Kansas. How many of them do we have left?"

"Fifteen, last I checked," Spector replied. "But CANZUK is adapting and there's intel coming out of the UK suggesting they're sending over more of their top-end fighters."

"All the more reason for us to move quickly, then," Cameron countered. "You've said it yourself. Kansas is now a knife fight. Let the boys out of Fort Hood sort it out on the ground with whatever air support you can leave them, but let's press our advantage in Missouri. With those J-31s flying cover and with those three thousand soldiers fifty miles away, we can have that base by this evening. And let me remind you that those soldiers sitting on our base have not seen a lick of real fighting outside of the trouncing you gave them earlier today. Your boys can do this, Mitch. I know they can."

Cameron stopped to give the proud, independently-minded general time to work through the argument on his own.

After a long pause, Spector said, "I know a little bit about the soldiers that are at Whiteman. They're Canadian paratroopers – they're a close cousin to the British Parachute Regiment, and those guys are some of the toughest soldiers on the planet. My guess is that the unit on that base is gonna fight for every goddamned inch of that place and by now they're dug in like a bunch of pissed-off badgers. Even if we keep their air power at bay, it's gonna be a close-in and bloody job."

"Well, it's a good thing your boys know what blood looks like," Cameron replied immediately. "And let's say we don't take the base this evening, the bulk of the 101st will hit them the next morning. These Canadians you seem to hold in such high regard will be beat up, tired, and low on supplies. As I see it, tomorrow stands to be a walk in the park."

Spector listened to the other man's words and took in the tactical display to the right of Cameron's expectant face. The immediate situation was clear. But it was not the immediate situation that gave him pause. In war, it was always the case that the none-too-distant future was murky and perilous. Many things could change over the course of a twelve-hour period.

If Montrell and the J-31s could be shifted to Missouri, they could make all the difference. They were exhausted and they were running low on missiles, but Spector had growing confidence that whatever air assets he left above Kansas would be able to hold off CANZUK, allowing the Chinese fighters to make the difference in the east.

As he saw it at this moment and as he felt it with his gut, it was the advancing British coming out of Iowa that was now the biggest threat. The Brits could make it to Whiteman before his forces in St. Louis if he played this too conservatively.

Spector liked to think that he knew war as well as anyone. He had fought in Afghanistan as a young officer and had participated in every major battle the Red Faction had fought during its two-year war with the Blues. In this lifetime of fighting, he knew that when things were opaque, you had to go with your gut.

His eyes met Cameron's. "I'll give the order to shift the J-31s and we'll assault Whiteman this evening with what we have at Versailles. If Montrell and his airmen do for us in Missouri what they've done for us in Kansas, our forces coming out of St. Louis should be able to take Whiteman tomorrow by noon if the Versailles force doesn't do the job this evening.

Cameron smiled. "Are you sure? Because when push comes to shove, this is your call."

"I'm sure," Spector said after a slight hesitation. "Based on everything I know, I would agree that speed in Missouri is our best friend."

Spector's eyes once again found Whiteman on the tactical display, and he thought about the defensive works he had seen on the various recon images that had come in over the past couple of hours. The Canadians had been digging in like men possessed.

The thought of his men trying to pry loose well-trained soldiers of the caliber he believed this Airborne outfit to be made his insides churn. But there was no help for it. The men he would send into battle were no less tough than their opponents, and unlike the Canadians, they were veterans of some of the worst fighting the world had seen in generations. They could win this fight. If they executed well and moved fast, and if they had just a bit of luck, this could all be over before the sunset. But if they didn't have all of those things, many good soldiers would die in this first battle for that damned base.

———

As soon as he got off the BAM call with Larocque, Brazeau had tried to pull up Lieutenant Gauthier's position on his BAM tactical app and came up with nothing.

If one of his soldiers was wearing their BAM wrist unit, Brazeau should be able to see their exact location. Gauthier and three other NCOs from his platoon were, as of that moment, officially unaccounted for.

He had then called the warrant officer of Gauthier's platoon and had been advised that the lieutenant and three other soldiers had headed to an adjacent platoon's position to get a first-hand look at their firing vectors. That had been about thirty minutes ago.

Not liking this development one bit, Brazeau called over the company's senior warrant officer, Henri Leclerc, and asked the man to grab six soldiers from their HQ and get them loaded up with their full kit.

Now the question was, where was Gauthier, or whoever this guy was?

He activated his BAM. "Give me Major Landry."

After a brief pause, the smooth female AI-replicated voice advised that a channel had been opened.

"Jen, it's Marcel," Brazeau said in French.

"Hey, Captain. What's up?" the Regiment's talented operations office replied in near-perfect French.

"You're not gonna believe this, but I've got a few soldiers that have gone MIA. Has anyone reported into you about Lieutenant Gauthier being somewhere he's not supposed to be, or have you seen anything unusual on our drones? Something like some of our men being where they shouldn't be. Sorry, this isn't very helpful, I don't know exactly what I'm looking for."

"Give me a minute," Landry advised quickly.

As he waited, Warrant Officer Leclerc and six fully armed soldiers turned the corner on one of the grass-covered bunkers and pulled up in front of Brazeau. With their weapons half-ported and with grenades and other battle accouterments hanging off them, they looked like the bad asses that they were.

Landry's voice popped into his earbud. "Marcel, you there?"

"Here," Brazeau replied.

"Look on your wrist unit. You should see a drone image."

Brazeau's wrist snapped up to his face.

"What am I looking at?"

"For whatever reason, there are two lone bunkers at the south end of the system. The two bunkers you're now looking at are actually the last two to be prepped according to the schedule, but as you can see, there's a truck there and I've seen soldiers – ours – going in and out of the bunker on the left. There's one of them now," Landry said.

"Can you zoom up on him?" Brazeau asked.

Instantly, the high-powered camera on the Regiment's surveillance drone zeroed in on the soldier who had stopped. The man raised his head to look in the direction of the hovering surveillance machine.

Brazeau could see the man's face as if he were standing in front of him. "That's my man."

"Who, Gauthier?" Landry asked. "I take it you didn't ask him to be where he's at?"

"No, I did not. You better let the boss know. I'm heading over there now. Brazeau out."

––––

Only Major Landry, the now-deceased Delgado, and the Airborne's Regimental Sergeant Major, St. Pierre, had been given the capability to interrupt any BAM conversation Larocque might be having, and in his time in the Airborne, Landry had only done this on a handful of occasions.

"Colonel," the major's no-nonsense voice cut into his earbud.

Without hesitation, Larocque hit a button on his wrist unit and dropped the conversation he'd been having. "What's up, Major?"

Upon hearing Landry's update, Larocque asked for her to bring up the drone's image on the oversized tactical tablet he had with him. As he waited for the video to stream, his eyes moved in the direction where the drone was hovering in the sky. Once again, back in the observation deck of the air traffic control tower, his eyes moved to the southeast and immediately picked up the drone. It was hovering at about a thousand feet.

Out of the corner of his eye, he caught movement on his tac pad. Looking down, Larocque watched as Brazeau and a handful of men walked in the direction of the two bunkers and then split into three groups.

From the air, the two southernmost bunkers looked like one rectangular structure. One team of three soldiers maneuvered around the bunkers' east side, while the other team was doing the same on the west. They were going to try and pinch Gauthier and whoever was with him from opposing sides. It was a dangerous move as it meant that each team could have the other in its direct path of fire when they turned the corner of the grass-covered structure. A final lone soldier was climbing the north-end slope of the bunker and was near the structure's apex. That was Brazeau to be sure.

Larocque watched as the two teams of soldiers advanced to the mid-way point of the bunker's length in a lined formation that was a common tactic in urban warfare. In that instant, there were a pair of flashes on the tac pad. Through the windows of the tower, he heard the muffled cracking sound as the pair of detonations reached him. Larocque stared at the stream in growing horror as the scene on the ground resolved itself on the drone's camera. On both sides of the complex, bodies of soldiers were laid out in various directions. At least two of them were writhing on the ground, no doubt in throes of terrible pain.

As the scene of mayhem registered with him fully, Larocque unloaded a quick expletive and barked, "Jen, get the medics over there now!"

———

Hall and Wallace had changed into their civie attire. The plan was now to fly out with Havez and his wife on the soon-to-be arriving reinforcement flights that were coming from Edmonton. Following their briefing to the Airborne CO, Larocque had suggested they revert back to the original ruse of engaged couple.

He had made the point that it might be best for all concerned if they didn't become known as the two unknown soldiers who had mysteriously been waiting for them. Yes, a few of Larocque's soldiers had seen them in the American uniforms they had been wearing when the Airborne took the base, but this was a small number and Larocque was confident they would keep their mouths shut.

So the two of them had been sent away, told to grab Ms. Havez and then return back to the air traffic control tower where they would be his 'guests'. With the exception of Larocque, no one knew the role that Havez had played in support of CANZUK's takeover of the base. As far as everyone else was concerned, the Airborne commander had been keeping Havez in close proximity to help him manage any personnel or security issues that came up. That Larocque had elected to keep the base commander's wife, niece and his niece's fiancé close by shouldn't raise too many eyebrows.

And so for the past three hours or so, Hall, Wallace, Havez, and his wife had been sitting in the observation area of the control tower listening to Larocque and several other officers coordinate activities as the Airborne worked feverishly to build up the base's defenses. Now and again, Larocque would call over to Havez to enquire about some part of Whiteman's infrastructure or some other matter, but during that same time, he had said not a word to either Hall or Wallace.

The experience of sitting there had been both fascinating and frustrating. Fascinating, in that as a young officer, Hall was seeing firsthand how a highly professional military outfit like the Airborne managed its business in an actual theatre of war.

Despite this front-row seat to history in the making, Hall's inability to make any meaningful contribution to the many endeavors swirling around her was maddening to the point of driving her insane. She felt beyond useless sitting in the corner saying nothing and for what must have been the tenth time, she was debating going up to Larocque to flat out ask him to let her and Wallace do something beyond sitting there like slack-jawed idiots.

Just as she was working out what she might say to the Airborne's CO to get him to rethink their current non-role, Hall heard and saw Larocque shout out a string of curses and begin to bark out orders to the soldiers and officers around him.

_____

As they walked the last fifty meters to the two side-by-side bunkers Landry had identified, Brazeau directed his men to break up into separate groups. On his word, the two teams would envelop the bunkers, with each group taking one of the concrete paths that led to the complex's entrances.

For his part, Brazeau would lead the way taking the high ground. The angle of the grassed bunkers was such that they could easily be scaled. As his men converged on Gauthier, he would have the tactical advantage of height, and would have several options to support his men should their unexpected visit become a throwdown.

"Stay here," Brazeau said quietly to the two groups of soldiers.

"Yes, sir," said Leclerc.

"I'll go ahead and see what's up. Advance on my command. Understood?"

Leclerc, the warrant officer and the master corporal leading the other team both nodded their heads in agreement.

On seeing their confirmation, Brazeau shouldered his weapon and advanced up the grassed incline of the structure.

Dead-center at the summit of the bunker, he shouldered his weapon and slowly maneuvered himself to the building's edge. There, he took in two pairs of soldiers that were gingerly carrying a cylinder the length of a small car across two lengths of black strapping. He couldn't see their faces, but could easily make out that they were straining with the weight of the object as they moved in the direction of a waiting truck.

He activated his BAM. "Leclerc and Moreau."

"Yes, sir," the senior men leading the two assault teams said jointly.

"Listen you two, there are four of these bastards and they're moving one of the nukes into a truck. Move on them now. You shoot to kill," Brazeau ordered.

"Shoot to kill, sir?" asked Leclerc.

"Yes, warrant, they're stealing a nuclear bomb. Drop them where they fucking stand. That's an order."

"Copy that, Captain. Moving out now."

Brazeau raised his carbine to its firing position and placed the reticle of his sight on the man he thought to be Gauthier. He could feel his heart hammering in his chest as he waited for his soldiers to turn the corner of the bunker and begin to lay into these traitorous bastards.

Boom!

As the sharp sound assaulted his ears, Brazeau felt a pair of simultaneous bursts of energy strike him from each side of the bunker. As the two explosions reverberated through his body, the sound of screaming voices began to penetrate his ringing ears.

"Leclerc!"

On instinct, he darted across the top of the structure. Reaching the point where the bunker's roof began to decline, Brazeau took in a terrible scene.

Leclerc and the two other men that were with him were sprawled on the pavement. Around the three men, pumping fluids had already formed into smeared pools of dark red blood. Leclerc, a tough-as-nails career soldier who hailed from the northern reaches of Quebec, was writhing in pain and screaming incoherently. The other two paratroopers – both hard men in their own right, were unmoving and soundless.

"*Tarbernac,*" Brazeau growled. He took a step toward his men but something in the recesses of his mind stayed his movement. The bomb. He had to stop Gauthier before he left.

With a colossal effort, Brazeau tore his eyes away from his dying men, turned, and strode in the direction of the bunker's edge. Filled with righteous fury, he shouldered his weapon only to find the four turncoats had finished pushing the bomb fully into the truck's capped flatbed. No longer in a tight group and aware that their trap had been set off, the foursome were alert to trouble. Though primed, none of the four were looking in Brazeau's direction atop of the bunker.

Thumbing his weapon to automatic, Brazeau sighted in the first man who appeared in his carbine's mounted sight. His heart was still jackhammering in his chest. He pulled in a long calming breath, held it, and then, just as he was about to pull the trigger, the man who was the subject of his bobbing reticle saw him.

Brazeau could see his face clearly now. It was not Gauthier, but one Corporal Beaumont. He unleashed his first burst of supersonic retribution and cut the man down where he stood. As he moved to find his next target, Brazeau perceived the sound of gunfire that was not his own. Unfazed by incoming rounds and standing tall, Brazeau moved forward to the edge of the bunker as though he were bulletproof.

———

Ottawa

"Indeed, we are looking for you, Ms. Labelle," Merielle said in as calm a tone as she could manage. "I have several colleagues who would like to speak with you about a number of important things. Where are you, young lady?"

She had been caught off guard that the other woman had her number and had thrown in the ageist dig in the off-chance Labelle would take exception to the slight and give Merielle the opportunity to take control of the conversation. She had no such luck.

"Minister Martel, I am calling you in your official capacity as the minister of defence and the deputy prime minister, but perhaps most importantly, because you are the prime minister's right hand. What I am about to tell you will exceed the importance of anything you are doing at this moment. For reasons I shall soon explain, you don't have a lot of time. So for your sake and the sake of the men and women you have so recklessly sacrificed, I implore you not to play games with the 'young lady' to whom you are now speaking."

As Merielle's feet remained fixed in the center of the sun-drenched rotunda, she thought it better not to retort that it was in fact Labelle who had the blood of CANZUK soldiers on her hands. She looked beyond the bank of doors and saw her black ministerial sedan waiting for her. Wherever this conversation was about to go, she couldn't leave the building. Best that she was close to the operations room, where she could provide updates and get advice as needed. Executing what she hoped was a casual one-eighty, Merielle started walking in the direction she had just come from.

"You have my full attention," said Merielle.

"Good. Look at the time on your watch, Minister," Labelle ordered. "Do you see the time?"

"Yes," Merielle replied.

"Starting now, you have the two hours to make the following happen:

"First, an order will go out to all CANZUK forces directing them to cease any and all hostilities against the state of Missouri and the United Constitutional States of America. Second, within twenty-four hours of this cessation, you will have removed all

Canadian soldiers from the Whiteman Air Force Base. Third and finally, upon publicly announcing the end of CANZUK hostilities to the Canadian public, the prime minister and his cabinet will resign, at which point an election is to be called."

Away from the eyes and ears that had been at the building's entrance, Merielle took up the discussion with the other woman.

"And who are you delivering these extraordinary demands on behalf of, Ms. Labelle? And just as importantly, why should I believe they have any credibility?"

"I will indulge a few of your questions, Madame Minister, only because it will help you to understand the gravity of the situation that you and your country now face."

"Your country," Merielle said. "The last I checked, you were a Canadian citizen. No doubt that will be made clear once we lay our hands on you and your little band of friends in the Airborne. No doubt there are others. We made an error in letting this little project of yours get as big as it has, but we're in the process of fixing that."

If Labelle was concerned by Merielle's implied threat, it was not obvious when she next replied.

"I will answer your second question first. Within the next ten minutes, you will find out just how credible we are. But in a spirit of goodwill and in recognition of the timeline that now confronts you, I will advise you of what has transpired.

"The men you refer to in the Airborne have successfully commandeered two nuclear weapons from the Whiteman stockpile. One weapon has been set to detonate in just under two hours. The second weapon has successfully left the American air base and is now on its way to Kansas City. It too is set to detonate in just under two hours.

"Regarding this particular set of facts, Minister, it is critical that you understand two things. First, that the two weapons are linked. Should anything untoward happen to either, the other weapon will detonate automatically. Second, should the programs we have inserted into these two weapons sense they are being tampered with in any way, they will both detonate."

Labelle paused, no doubt allowing Merielle to digest the monumental statements she had just heard.

"As I said, in the next few minutes you will receive information from your people that validates what I have just told you. They may not have the details on the timing and mechanisms that I have just shared with you, but they will validate that the one weapon on Whiteman has been prepared for detonation and the other weapon has left the base.

"When we receive word from the Canadian government that our first demand has been met, and all CANZUK hostilities have ceased, the bombs' timers will be re-set to twenty-four hours, which is the remaining time the Canadian government will have to extricate its soldiers from Missouri. It is only when these soldiers have left that state and are on their way home, that these two bombs will be neutralized."

Turning a final corner, Merielle stood in the hallway that led to the operations room. She could see several soldiers wearing a variety of different uniforms coming and going from the ops room and the other offices and meeting rooms that made up this area of the building. *Jesus on the cross,* she thought, the information she had just heard was going to set this place on fire, never mind what it was going to do to the Prime Minister's Office, the cabinet, and their allies.

"Now, as to the question of who I am speaking for, let me say that I am but one member of a group of young and very determined Quebecois who will do anything to remove our country from the failed political experiment that is Canada. We are not the new-FLQ, Minister, as much as you and the media might want to label us as such. We are not Marxists, we have no manifesto, and we are hardly amateurs who should be underestimated or dismissed.

"In terms of why we have acted as we have, the answer is both straightforward and complex. Quebec does not want your federalism. It does not want your immigrants. It is long done with your country's obsession with woke ideologies and cancellations. And, it certainly does not want any part of this insane war you and your Anglo prime minister have just started. It is all madness and Quebec wants no part of it. As of this moment Minister, we're done with Canada."

"And what makes you so certain that you speak for the people of Quebec?" Merielle interjected.

"There is a sea change coming, Ms. Martel. It will start with the resignation of the MacDonald government and will continue as Canadians and Quebecers are given the opportunity to better understand the debacle your government has set upon them.

"Though a Quebecer of the Quisling variety, you know full well that enough people in our province are sick and tired of the path Canada has been walking. For the past five years, Quebec has stood on the precipice of separation. All it needs is a push in the right direction. This war and your prime minister's hubris are that final push."

Merielle again interrupted the other woman. "Even if we were going to consider your demands, two hours is not nearly enough time for me to gather together the right people and talk this through. There are other countries involved. I need five hours minimum."

"You have two hours," snapped Labelle. "Actually, by my watch, you now have one hour and forty-nine minutes to save Canada from committing the world's latest nuclear tragedy. We will talk once more, but only ten minutes before the deadline that has been set. So my advice to you Minister is to keep your phone close."

And before Merielle could say anything or ask any more questions, the connection went dead.

As Merielle stared at the display on her phone and tried to make sense of what had just happened, her device rang once again. Activating it, she put the phone to her ear and heard the voice of General Gagnon.

"Minister, we have a situation that we need to apprise you of immediately. Where are you?"

Merielle didn't answer the man but rather walked the twenty or so paces to the door of the operations room, opened it, and walked in. Gagnon's eyes widened when he saw her, but before he could say anything, she held up her hand in the universal declaration of 'stop.' Her face and posture radiated an air command that had been earned from her years as a hard-charging police officer who had led teams of equally determined men.

"I'm now all too aware of what the problem is, General. I was just on the phone with the person who organized this growing disaster of ours. But we can get to that in a few minutes. My immediate question for you is how are we going to fix it?"

Chapter 21

As Landry and several other officers acted on his orders, Larocque's eyes went back to the tac pad. Steeling himself, he watched the lone soldier atop the bunker make his way to the building's edge, where he tore into one of the four traitorous soldiers who had just loaded the pickup with one of Whiteman's nuclear weapons. As the one targeted paratrooper was cut down, the remaining soldiers moved quickly to take up close-by weapons and return fire.

For several long seconds, a hail of bullets was exchanged and then the lone soldier on the top bunker stumbled backward and fell to the ground in a heap. Watching the drone feed, Larocque willed the man to get back up. When he did not rise, he then urged the soldier to show some sign of life, but as he watched and poured his will into the tac pad's screen, the figure remained motionless.

No longer under fire, the three remaining soldiers checked on the man who had been first targeted. Presumably dead, they left him on the blood-soaked pavement while one of the three struggled into the back of the pickup with the weapon. The final two jogged to the truck's cab, got in and in seconds they were on the move.

"Landry, don't let that truck out of your sight. Eventually, it's going to get out of the range of our drones. When it does, Ares needs to put eyes on it. Tell them this is the highest priority target in the theatre."

"Copy that, Colonel," the female officer replied instantly.

Larocque walked over to the corner of the observation deck where Hall, Wallace, and Colonel Havez were now standing. Picking up that something important had just happened, all three were looking at Larocque, their faces expectant.

"We have a problem, people," Larocque said, his tone matter of fact. "The situation requires us to drop this little game we've been playing. Colonel, you've done so much for us already, but I'm going to have to ask you to do more. I need you to come with me. I'll explain on the way."

He then looked at Hall and Wallace. "Do you two still have access to a vehicle?"

"We do," Hall replied immediately.

"And your kit?"

Wallace reached down and hoisted up a large duffle bag and said, "We're good to go."

"Good, because I need you to get on the road right now. There's a military pickup truck with three Canadian soldiers in it and they have a nuke with them. Get in that vehicle of yours, put your eyes on them, and wait for instructions. Landry will give you the coordinates on where you can find them, so get your BAMs up and running."

"And what should we do when we find them?" Hall asked.

"Don't do anything. I have not a clue what's going on, but I do know we're gonna need someone on the ground close to these bastards, and I can't send uniformed soldiers to Christ-knows-where-Missouri. Whether this is in your wheelhouse or not, you two are getting the call. Are you good to go?"

"We're good, sir," Hall said without hesitation. Wallace said nothing but positioned the equipment-laden duffle bag in such a way that said he too was ready to roll.

"Then haul ass and get on those bastards," Larocque said.

———

As base commander and an administrator who took pride in being on top of everything that transpired within his command, Havez had taken the time to get to know the bunker system and the weapons they stored.

The network was extensive with nearly forty separate units. Built back in the '70s, the bunkers had been fabricated by the Air Force to withstand an indirect nuclear strike or a direct hit from standard conventional weapons.

In total, the base held 198 B-61 gravity bombs of which there were several variants ranging from a 0.3-kiloton tactical weapon to the behemoth 340-kiloton version. The former could be used for any number of reasons on an active battlefield, while the latter had one purpose – to pulverize a mid-sized city. According to the manifest Havez had on his laptop, there were seven of the city-killing variants in the bunker in question.

Bunkers L-32 and 33 were unique in that they held one of the last remaining caches of the country's most destructive bomb, the B-83. In the years before the civil war, the US government had elected to retire the bulk of its inventory for this doomsday weapon, but of those remaining, twelve of them were here at Whiteman and were divided between the two bunkers he and Larocque had just arrived at. If the highest yield B-61 could level a city the size of Buffalo, the 2,400-lb, 1.5 megaton B-83 could easily vaporize a city the size of Tokyo or had it still been a city, New York. It was a colossal and devastating weapon of last resort.

As they traveled to the bunker in the rear two seats of one of the Canadian's RZRs, Havez listened as Larocque briefed him on what had just happened. As the story poured out of the man, he was aghast.

As their driver came to a stop in front of the raided bunker, Havez took in the sight of the one dead soldier Larocque's men had managed to kill. Havez had done his best to ignore the activity along the side of the dual storage units. Before averting his eyes, he had caught Canadian soldiers and medics working feverishly on one of the men who had been cut down. Despite his long career in the military, until this moment, he had not seen medics in action and had never seen a dead body outside of a funeral.

On their trip over, Larocque had mentioned that it was likely the Quebec-based soldiers had set up a pair of sensor-triggered claymore mines along the flanks of the bunkers and had set them off on the unsuspecting paratroopers as they walked into the weapons' field of fire. Filled with explosives and hundreds of steel ball bearings, the two groups of soldiers had been cut down instantly.

"Wait here," Larocque said and then walked to the left of the bunker where Havez had seen the medics working frantically. There was no noise or activity coming from the right side of the second bunker where the second team had been waylaid.

Moments later Larocque returned, the look on his face pure wretchedness.

"Follow me, Colonel. Let's go see what these bastards took from your base," Larocque said as he walked toward the still-open bunker door.

Havez moved to follow the other man and as he stepped across the reinforced threshold of the entrance, he reached to his right and flicked on the structure's lights. He pulled up beside Larocque and together they looked at the two hip-high racks that ran along the interior walls of the bunker.

Havez's eyes immediately found the empty cradle that the rogue soldiers had pulled the stolen weapon from. Walking over to it, he placed his laptop on the bomb to the immediate left of the empty location and proceeded to check the manifest.

"They grabbed one of the sixty-kiloton variants. Wherever they're headed, they've got enough firepower that they can level a fair-sized city. The big question now is, do they have the tools they would need to set it off."

"I think we might have the answer to that," Larocque said.

Havez turned and saw Larocque standing beside one of the much larger B-83s bombs. The access panel to the massive twenty-four-hundred-pound gravity bomb was open and atop the length of its body was a tactical pad that had a length of cable that traveled into the guts of the weapon.

Havez quickly walked across the length of the bunker to stand beside Larocque. The Canadian officer was reading the tac pad's display. In the top right, there was what appeared to be a count-down figure. It had just breached the one-hundred-and-forty-minute mark. On the rest of the screen were bullets of text, Havez wasn't close enough to make it out.

"Fuck me, Mary," he heard Larocque say quietly. "They're de-mands. It says if CANZUK hasn't announced an end to hostilities here in Missouri within two hours, this thing goes off. It also says they've taken that other bomb to Kansas City, where they'll light it off at the same time if CANZUK doesn't give into their demands."

Havez got closer to the bomb and ran through the info for himself, noting that it mentioned the two weapons were linked via the tac pad he was now looking at.

"The bombs are linked," Havez said. "If we do anything to ei-ther of them, it sounds like they'll both go off."

As he said the words, his mind began to whir. "How old is this tac pad?"

"I don't know. I think they got issued across the Canadian Army four or five years ago."

After a pause, Havez said, "I think I have might have a solution. This bomb's software is at least twenty years old. If I can get into it, I should be able to manipulate whatever program your Quebec friends have created. I'm willing to bet they didn't have access to the bomb's software in advance of this whole mess, so whatever they've designed should be simple enough that I can out-program it. And whatever near-AI version this tac pad has on it, there's no way it'll be a match for what I've got on my laptop."

Larocque gave Havez a hard look. "And you have the skills to make this happen?"

Havez didn't hesitate with his reply. "I have a grad degree in computer science from Florida State and I did front-line cyber warfare for over half my career. I wasn't the best programmer in the US military, but I was no slouch either. There's a better than good chance I can run circles around whatever software they've dropped into this unit," Havez said, as he pointed to the Canadian Army's standard-issue tactical pad lying atop the huge bomb.

"But, I'm going to need two things."

"Name them," Larocque replied immediately.

———

Over Missouri

Lt. Colonel Montrell was exhausted and he and each one of the men and women in his squadron had surpassed every safety regulation the Air Force had when it came to the number of sorties that could be flown over a twenty-four-hour period.

Despite their ragged state, every pilot had heartily agreed to take the stimulants they had been prescribed and had further agreed to fly missions at what was now a record-setting pace. Knowing that they were the difference between winning and losing against the more numerous CANZUK air forces had been no small factor in pushing what remained of his squadron. As a unit, they were making history, and he had said as much to his pilots.

Over Kansas, their opponents had done an admirable job of adapting to his squadron's tactics, so it had come as some relief that he had received the order to shift the entirety of the squadron to the Missouri theater. He had been briefed and understood that ground forces in and around the town of Versailles would begin a dash toward Whiteman in the next twenty minutes or so. While other parts of his squadron would be looking to harass and otherwise destroy CANZUK's on-station fighter-bombers, his mission and that of his wingman was to work with air and ground-based radar to identify and then eliminate any air assets that could hit the blitzing units that would soon be emerging from the expansive canopy that was the Mark Twain National Forest.

"Raven One, this is Bronco Three. We have designated a target for you. Please confirm."

"Copy that, Bronco Three, I have the data on my screen. Moving to engage now. Raven One out."

Montrell looked at the radar feed coming to him from an air defense battery that the army had managed to sneak into Kansas City. It had picked up what looked to be a CANZUK tier-one drone flying just west of Whiteman at ten thousand feet. He noted the location with interest. Why would they have a drone patrolling that area? The two battalions of the 101st that would be assaulting Whiteman in the next hour or so would be coming out of the southeast.

Whatever its purpose, the drone had been flagged and it was now his job to make sure the highly valuable surveillance machine was taken off the board.

After several minutes of acceleration, the drone was within range. Montrell promptly designated the target and then pressed the weapon release button on his flight stick. For a brief moment, he felt a vibration as one of the missile bays on the undercarriage of his J-31 opened allowing one of the older, but still highly effective, Chinese manufactured P-12s to drop, ignite, and then streak to its target.

Quickly losing his visual of the missile, Montrell followed the munition's flight path via the encrypted data feed from the air defense battery in KC. It took exactly twenty-three seconds for the P-12 to connect with its target. Seconds later, the drone's radar signature had disappeared from his tactical display allowing him to notched up his fifth kill of the day.

––––

West of Whiteman AFB

Hall looked at her speedometer as she raced west along Highway 50 toward Missouri's largest city. It had been hair-raising to get to this point. In all of the training she had received as a soldier, none of it had her behind the wheel of a car driving over one hundred and sixty kilometers per hour.

"There they are," Wallace said as he pointed out in front of their car. "Ease up, we don't want to come up on them too fast. They'll pick us up for sure."

His eyes went back to the tac pad that was simultaneously streaming the drone feed and a map that had designated the position of their vehicle and that of the fleeing soldiers out in front of them.

"Shit," Wallace said. "The feed's gone."

"What happened?"

"I don't know. I just dropped."

Seconds later, Major Landry's voice popped into Hall's earbud. "Listen up you two, the drone that's been riding shotgun with you was just shot down. You're now our only eyes on that truck. Have you caught up with it yet?"

"We're about half a klick behind it," Hall said.

"Good, stay on them, but don't get too close until you hear from the Colonel. He's dealing with a situation at the same hangar these clowns hit."

The near-AI replicated voice of her BAM interrupted her conversation with Landry. "Priority one call from Winch Actual pending," advised the replicated male voice Hall had designated for her BAM.

"Keep Winch Six on the call and bring in Winch Actual," Hall advised the near-AI comms software.

"Copy that order, Winch Actual added to call," the BAM advised with a baritone smoothness.

"Hall, this is Larocque. Where are you and do you have those bastards in your sights?"

"We just caught up with them, sir. We're about five hundred meters back but we're not advancing any closer."

"Sir, it's Landry here. I was on a call with Hall when you dropped in."

"Aces. Good to have you on the call, Major. I have an update for both of you. These guys have wired up one of the bombs here in the hangar. It's on a timer and it's set to detonate in just over ninety minutes. And if that wasn't bad enough, the three cement heads you're following, Hall, have their own weapon. It's set to detonate at the same time. Their plan is to have it go off in Kansas City."

"That's insane," Hall said.

"It is, and there's more to the story, but those details aren't important. The good news is, we think we have a way to neutralize the weapon here at Whiteman and once that's done, we can neutralize the one in the vehicle you're following. As I understand it, it doesn't matter what we hit that truck with, the bomb they're carrying won't go off unless it's purposely set off.

"Major, tell me that drone you've got shadowing these guys is armed?" Larocque asked.

"Shit news on that front, sir," Landry said. "The drone was shot down a few minutes ago and I've just received word that the air in and around Whiteman is hot. Multiple enemy fighters have engaged our assets throughout the theatre. As it stands right now, Hall and Wallace are the only eyes we have on Gauthier."

Larocque let loose with a vicious curse. "I hoped the Reds might wait until the morning before they came at us. No such luck

by the sounds of it. If our air support is being occupied it means the
Red forces massing in Mark Twain will be on us within the hour.
These separatist jerk-offs – their timing is just impeccable."

"Sir, as soon as I'm off this call, I'll get Ares on the horn,"
Landry advised quickly. "I'll prioritize a strike package for Gauthier
and in so long as Hall and Wallace can put a target on him, we
should be able to take him out," Landry advised.

The connection went quiet as Landry gave Larocque the time
she knew he needed to work the problem through.

"Okay, this is how we're gonna play things," said Larocque in a
steely tone. "Major, get that strike package arranged. That is your
number one priority.

"Yes, sir."

"Hall, stick with Gauthier. I don't care what you need to do but
stay with him. And while you're following him, you and Wallace
should talk through options of what you might do if you need to
take these guys down on your own. We can't assume the air force is
going to get us what we need. Is that understood?"

"Understood, sir."

"Good. I'll keep you posted on how we fare with the weapon
here at Whiteman. And Hall..."

"Yes, sir?"

"The bomb here at Whiteman is a monster. It's the biggest
thing the Americans have in their arsenal. If things don't go well
and you see a mushroom cloud in your rear-view mirror, you two
bust your ass and you take Gauthier down pronto-like. There are
five hundred thousand people in Kansas City. If we're off the table,
they become your priority. Gauthier cannot make it to that city, no
matter what. Got it?"

"Roger that, sir."

"Good stuff. Keep your BAM on and stay in touch. Larocque
out."

———

Ottawa, NDHQ

"The prime minister is on his way," Merielle announced to the room. "He'll be here in under thirty. In the meantime, he wants us to work on a solution. I'm also going to have to step out in fifteen to brief the CANZUK working group."

"We have Larocque," one of the officers said, his voice interrupting Merielle's update.

"Sorry, Minister," General Gagnon said on the more junior officer's behalf.

"No worries, General. We need to hear from him," Merielle replied, unperturbed by the interruption. Put him on."

"Jack, it's Gagnon here. I understand you've been dealing with the same mess we have."

"That's an affirmative, sir. I think we might have all the details or at least enough where we've started to take action," Larocque said. If the Airborne CO was worried, he didn't sound it.

"Alright, read us in quickly. The politics around this is pretty intense as you might have guessed. The PM is on his way over here now and will be in the room in thirty minutes. Minister Martel is with us now."

"Alright, here's the skinny. Regarding the bomb that's here on base, we believe that we have a workaround so that no one will know we've taken it off-line. If we can do that, it gives us a free hand to take a shot at the nuke that's on its way to Kansas City. You know those two kids you had here on base setting things up for us?"

"Two kids... you mean Azim's people. Yeah, what about them?"

"Well, I sent them after Gauthier. They're shadowing them on the highway as we speak. Seeing as you sent them here covertly, I assumed they would have the skills to problem-solve this gale-force shit storm we're now facing. If you can put an air asset on Gauthier's truck and Azim's agents can tag it, we can neutralize the threat.

If you can't get us air support, we'll have to turn it over to Azim's people and they'll try to take Gauthier down."

"Okay, great work, Jack. It's good to have options. Give us some more details. What are the risks?" Gagnon asked.

"Well, it's Colonel Havez who's helping us with the nuke here on Whiteman. We hunted down the best weapons tech on the base and together, they seem to think they can bypass the tech that Gauthier used to arm the bomb. On this front, I'm cautiously optimistic. I mean, the risks are huge, of course, but there's no way I'm giving up this base because a bunch of treasonous separatists told us to. I've lost way too many good people for things to go in that direction."

"And the other situation?" Gagnon prompted.

"There are several unknowns that we've identified. We don't know how Gauthier has armed his bomb. Is it only timed like the one here in Whiteman, or is he able to set it off manually? Maybe they've set up a kill switch – we take him out and as soon as his heart stops beating, the nuke goes off. We just don't know.

"The best option is to eviscerate that truck so that the bomb and whatever trigger is in play is destroyed, but only after we've disabled our nuke. As I understand it, it is almost impossible to set one of these things off by way of a secondary force. Whatever you send to take out Gauthier, it can't miss, and it has to be big enough that no one survives. And we can't give a shit about the resulting dirty bomb that would be created. We accept a bit of local fallout, or it's five hundred thousand people dead. That's no choice at all if you ask me."

"Okay," Gagnon said, "you've offered a workable solution, but there's a problem."

"And what would that be?" Larocque asked with a degree of heat in his voice.

"It's one hell of scrap in the air above you, Jack. The Reds have thrown everything they have at us to support the push that's coming out of Mark Twain. As things stand, we're just holding on. And I mean just. Anything that we might have been able to assign to Gauthier has already unloaded on the armor that's headed in your direction, or worse, it's no longer flying. We're getting more birds up to help you with what's coming your way, but none of it is going to be able to make it to Gauthier in time."

"So it's on Azim's people, then?"

"Don't sell them short, Jack. Azim briefed us on what these two are capable of. They were the best of their cohort. They're smart and are quick on their feet. They can pull this off," Gagnon advised.

"Let's hope so, General, because without them, we're screwed big time. Anything else?"

"Hold up, Jack. Minister Martel is here. I'd like her to have the opportunity to weigh in before you go. Tactically, you have my blessing, but as I said, the politics around this are ... well I'm sorry to say they're goddamned nuclear, so it's best she has a say in how this moves forward."

Gagnon looked at Merielle expectantly from across the conference table.

"Thank you, General. Colonel, I'm sorry that you're in such a tough spot. This whole affair is an intelligence failure of monumental proportions. We'll brief the PM when he gets here, but by then it will be too late for us to shift the course of events you are about to set in motion.

"As you've already said, there is no way we're giving in to the separatists' demands. Everyone in this room is behind you and your soldiers. Leave the politics to the PM and me. We'll deal with whatever comes. You do what you need to do to get those bombs back and to hold off the Reds. We need a win on both these issues. Nothing else matters, Colonel. So go do what you need to do and know we've got your back."

Chapter 22

Ottawa, RCMP HQ

"Listen, eh. Your guy Pettigrew told me to come speak to you. He said you'd understand and you'd smooth things over if that's what needed to be done. My people and I don't want no more heat than we already get. So, on this one, I'm gonna do you a favor and I'm hoping you'll do the same for me. If this guy is somehow involved in this war you've started, I don't want none of it, and my people don't want none of it."

Stephane watched the high-quality video of the group of men as they unloaded several heavy bags and large cases into the back of a cargo van.

He toggled his mouse and opened up the still image of a man who looked to be in his mid-forties. He was Eastern European by the looks of him. His hair was short, dark and you could see the beginnings of gray hair peeking out here and there. Merielle would have thought the man handsome to be sure. His wife not so much.

"And where did you get this image of the guy you said did all of the talking?" Stephane asked the tall First Nations man sitting across from him.

The smuggler gave Stephane a hard, unblinking glare that was made more intimidating by the fact the man's irises were of the darkest brown. It gave the Mohawk an inhuman feel. It was as though Stephane was looking into the eyes of some wanting vampire. Eventually, the man pronounced in his deep voice, "I haven't heard you say that this is not gonna come back on us there, chief."

"You've got my word, whatever that means to you and your people," Stephane said.

"It means shit white man, but I've got a history with Pettigrew. So if he says I can trust you, then we can do business. At least under the current circumstances."

"Glad to hear it," Stephane said. "Gaetan's a hell of a cop. You could do much worse in our organization."

"He's a pragmatist, and unlike most of the Mounties I know, he can think for himself. But to answer your question, eh, the video and still image are from the casino where we did the pick-up. I know a guy who knows a guy, who knows another guy who works there," the man said as the first grin of the conversation appeared on his face.

Stephane reciprocated the smile. "It's good to know people who know people."

Getting up from his chair, the RCMP Inspector continued. "Listen, you've been very helpful. I want to get this info off to the right people ASAP. Shit is going down, as you know."

Taking the hint the conversation was over, the tall First Nation man dropped his grin and with surprising speed, elevated his lanky frame up from the chair so that he was towering over Stephane.

"You know, I was born on the Canadian side of the border – not that we recognize there is such a thing as Canada, mind you. I normally don't give two shits what either government does, but in this case, I think your prime minister did the right thing, eh. I had more than a few friends die in New York when those Red bastards nuked it. Those guys on that video are some bad hombres. I'm the furthest thing from an elder but the juju rolling off these guys – well, shit, even a heathen like me could feel it."

The smuggler paused and gave Stephane another hard stare.

"You've got the info, Inspector, so whatever happens from this point forward, my conscience and that of my people is clear. We've done our bit in whatever mess your government has gotten itself into, and you and I Inspector – we have a deal."

"We have a deal and you have my thanks," Stephane offered.

The Mohawk said nothing more. Despite his size, the Indigenous man gracefully turned and with long strides left the office and disappeared down the corridor in the direction of his escort.

Five minutes later, Stephane had sent off an ultra-high priority email with attachments to all the right people in CSIS. You didn't need to be an intelligence expert to figure out that this group of hard-looking men and their heaps of equipment were a problem. They had black ops written all over them. Within the hour, they would know the identity of the person who had compelled one of North America's most prolific smugglers to sing to the RCMP.

———

Somewhere in northern Missouri

As the Boxer APC continued to jostle and sway as it pushed south, Colonel Costen looked at the display screen that held the three other battlegroup commanders and a fourth tile that held three generals sharing a conference room in Ottawa.

"Gentlemen, thanks for making the time for this conversation," General Gagnon said as he started the call. "As you all know, the Canadian battlegroups out west are tied up with the Reds out of Texas. There is no way they'll make it to the objective in time. That means your side of the ledger is now carrying the full weight of this mission."

A green dot showed up on the screen of the colonel leading the Aussie battlegroup.

"Question, Colonel Smythe?"

"Yes, sir. Where's the fourth Canadian battlegroup? I reckon only three of the four were sent to help out the Colorado force."

"They're continuing in the direction of Whiteman, but because they're only one formation, the civie irregulars have been able to concentrate their numbers, so that lone group is going nowhere fast. It's now up to you four."

Costen forwent the question feature of the meeting software and jumped into the conversation. "Right, so what does that mean for us? By my calculation, we're now six hours back from where we wanted to be at this time and we're trending in the wrong bloody direction. I trust, General, you're here to tell us we can finally take the gloves off against the Red civies giving us so much grief. It's bollocks that we can't reach out and touch these blokes when we know well and good they're in this fight. The idea that we have to wait for 'irrefutable' evidence that these lorries are combatants is the problem. You loosen up our rules of engagement and we'll get our respective trains back on schedule."

"This is the purpose of our call, gentlemen," Gagnon said. "Senior command has discussed the situation and we're prepared to give you orders to free up your rules of engagement. As of right now, anyone or anything that you think is a combatant is fair game. Get as aggressive as you need to be, so that you can get to that base before the Reds massing in St. Louis. This is your number one priority."

"And where are the politicians on this?" asked the Australian officer. "Because you know it won't be long before we hit the wrong bloke – some farmer who was too stupid to get out the way. They're everywhere down here and these Red irregulars are blending in like the Talibs back when I was a much younger man in Afghanistan. It's all but an impossible situation."

"Leave the politicians and blowback to us," Gagnon said. "The chief priority for each of you is to make it to that base before the Red's main force. Everything else is secondary. If there's shit to be caught for whatever you have to do to get there, then we're telling you that you do what you need to do and that we've got your backs. War has never been pretty or fair, gentlemen."

One of the other British battlegroup commanders jumped in. "So you're giving us permission to go all Mad Max and the like, for which the lads and I will be eternally grateful. But what about the notion of consolidating our forces? If we combine two each of the battlegroups, we can strengthen our offensive capabilities so that we can reach out and touch up more of these wankers as we roll forward. The only risk we see in this kind of move is that our logistics trains become a bigger target for the Red's air force. Just how are things up in the sky at the moment?

Gagnon's face took on a grimace. "We're on a knife-edge. Those Chinese J-31s are demons. When they're not in the air, we're dominating, but as soon as they appear, we're back on our heels. There's no getting around it – the closer each of you gets to that base, the greater the risk will be from the sky. We just don't have it as secure as we would like, and I don't think that's going to change in the coming hours."

In the weeks before the operation kicked off, Costen had grown close with Larocque and a few of his officers. The Airborne CO was a solid bloke, and from what he'd seen of the Regiment, Costen would put the Airborne in the same category as Britain's own legendary Parachute Regiment.

In fact, the Paras had not avoided this war. At the same moment, the Canadians had dropped onto Whiteman, 3rd battalion of the Paras had lobbed into the morning sky north of Whiteman to secure two bridges that crossed the Missouri River. Now hard-pressed, those five hundred soldiers were another reason the four battlegroups needed to make like hell. And just as he wouldn't let the Paras down, there was no way he wasn't going to do everything in his power to get to Larocque and his lads before the Reds did.

"Colonel Costen, you've got something on your mind. I can see it on your face," said Gagnon.

"Yes, sir. I do. There's no way any of us are leaving Larocque hanging, so if it means we have to take our licks from the air, so be it. Just make sure you bloody well have our backs when the time comes because from this conversation onwards, my lads and I are done massaging the backs of these Yank irregulars.

"For the next hundred kilometers, we going to send these sods packing and hard, so if you would be so kind General and let the nail-biting public affairs officers back home they can take whatever bad press is to come and shove it you know where."

———

Somewhere over Wisconsin

Major Jian Li looked west out the window of the People's Liberation Army Air Force Dassault Falcon 7X private jet, in which he was one of several passengers.

Their hurried flight out of Beijing had been followed by a quick stopover at a municipal airport just outside of Vancouver. According to the flight plan logged with the appropriate authorities, their trip was to end in Milwaukee, but the pilots of the French-made jet had no intention of landing in this Midwestern American city. As they approached the city's airport, the onboard electronic warfare officer engaged the jet's customized systems to suppress any instruments within a ten-kilometer radius that could track their highly modified plane. Minutes later, the pilot was circumventing the mid-size city to the east placing the now low flying jet atop the greenish-blue waters of Lake Huron.

As a veteran of the PLA's special forces, Li had had many interesting and oft-times harrowing experiences. The physical sensations he felt as the Falcon's pilot banked the jet meters above the lake's surface were on par with any of the experiences he had gained while fighting in Taiwan. This current mission felt as real and consequential as any wartime action.

The hundred or so kilometers from Milwaukee to Chicago's O'Hare had been covered in under fifteen minutes. With the plane leveled out and with this part of the world entering into the early phase of dusk, Li's eyes took in the ghostly-looking landscape that had once been one of the world's great cities. Out of his window, large swaths of what was once northern Chicago was now a wasteland of black and grey husks of shattered buildings and endless amounts of debris.

He marveled at the devastation. He'd seen pictures and videos of course, but as it was with most things, seeing something first-hand evoked thoughts and emotions that no image on a screen could. Not for the first time, Li asked himself how the Americans had done this to themselves. There were so many lessons to be learned from American hubris and greed.

As the plane's wheels touched down on the runway, Li took in the devastated airport. Most of O'Hare's buildings were intact, though facades everywhere had been scorched and the majority of each building's windows appeared to be shattered. On the runways, planes of all kinds lay strewn in every direction, their melted tires preventing the locals from being able to tow and better organize the ramshackle display.

His earbud pinged. Touching the appropriate icon on his watch, he opened the channel to the senior Chinese on-the-ground intelligence officer who was waiting for his team somewhere on the airport's expansive tarmac.

"Major Li, welcome to Chicago," said an elated voice.

"Comrade Ren," Li replied immediately. "Good to hear your voice. All is well, I trust?"

"All is well, sir. The local collective currently in control of this part of the city has been very accommodating. Capitalism and the almighty dollar still reign supreme in this part of the United States, even in the scorched hole that is this city," the Chinese intel officer said haughtily.

"Well don't get too enamored with it. As it turns out, too much capitalism is not a good thing. You've seen more of the city than I have, but from the air, it looks like a horror show."

"My friend, I can assure you from here on the ground, it is worse. Much worse. The locals are as bad or worse than anything Hollywood could have concocted."

Looking out the window, Li could now see a group of people waiting beside the runway they had landed on. There were maybe a dozen people and most of them appeared to be carrying a weapon of some kind.

"How are your new friends?" Li asked.

"As I said, they've been accommodating. A few million in Canadian dollars and Euros have had the desired effect. Once you get off, we'll put you and your men into two vans and our new well-paid associates will escort you to the outskirts of the city where you'll be passed onto one of the local militias. If all goes well, you should be driving into St. Louis in the early morning hours."

"Outstanding work, comrade. When I heard it was you on the ground, I knew we were in the best hands," Li said.

"You're too kind, Major. It's nothing. It's always a pleasure to do work for the brave men and women from the People's Liberation Army, and this time around, for a war hero, no less."

"No need to make mention of that. I was but one man who happened to be in the right place at the right time. I did my duty as anyone would have."

"Nevertheless, the honor is all mine, Major. But I must let you go. The local savages need my attention. They get jumpy if you don't soothe them often enough. We can talk more once you and your team have deplaned."

————

Whiteman AFB

Alone, Larocque knelt on one knee beside Brazeau's now pale and serene-looking face. The body bag that held the soldier was open so he could see the upper part of Brazeau's chest and face.

In the firefight with Gauthier, Brazeau had taken an unlucky round at the center of his throat. The 5.56 mm bullet had entered directly into his Adam's Apple, had torn through his throat, and destroyed the upper part of his spine. His friend's death would have been a quick one.

He reached out and placed his now filthy hand on Brazeau's chest, right above the younger man's heart. There was no movement, of course. Larocque's eyes began to well and as they did so, he forced himself to breathe deeply.

Leaving Brazeau, Larocque's eyes shifted to take up the other soldiers laid out on the tarmac. Twenty-eight men wearing the maroon beret would be going home with the Australians.

"We part ways, my young friend. I'm sorry we can't give you and the rest of the boys the ramp ceremony you deserve. I'll make it up to you when this is done." As he said the words, Larocque's voice cracked.

"I'm so sorry, Marcel. If it turns out that I make it through what's coming, I'll make things right with Ms. Labelle. Whatever your feelings toward her, you know what needs to be done."

As he contemplated the separatist problem and what might have to be done, he heard the deep thrum of turboprops in the distance.

To Larocque's tremendous relief, air command had finally agreed to allow two of the six inbound Royal Australian Air Force C130 Super Hercules to land. Over the BAM, he had heard the commander of the 2nd Commando Regiment, Colonel Rydell, argue, yell, and then finally plead to CANZUK's generals to let him and his soldiers make the run through the plane-infested air that surrounded Whiteman.

Larocque looked at Brazeau's face one last time and then moved to zip up the dark green bag that would transport the captain and the other soldiers of his regiment back to Edmonton. Getting to his feet, he looked to the north and with his naked eye saw the RAAF Hercs low on the horizon.

He glanced at his BAM wrist unit. And not a moment too soon, he thought of the approaching transports.

He had negotiated eighty minutes out of Gagnon and Minister Martel to allow Colonel Havez to neutralize the B-83 and for Hall and Wallace to somehow get in a position to take down the weapon on its way to Kansas City.

While this was being done, the generals and the politicians back in Ottawa would work through what to do if one or both of the bombs remained in play. If the nukes were still an issue and they were twenty minutes out from Labelle's two-hour deadline, they had agreed the situation would become an entirely political matter. The prime minister, who was now with the generals and Martel in Ottawa, had agreed to allow Larocque to sort this mess out, but if he couldn't get it done in the time allotted, he would need to pass the ball back to the politicians and take whatever decision they were forced to make.

Despite the time crunch and with all that was going on, Larocque made time to slip over to the base's now repaired airfield. He had needed to see Brazeau to say goodbye and make sure the rest of his soldiers got away on the incoming transports. It was not a good feeling when someone you cared for died and they couldn't be taken care of straight away. For those paratroopers who remained, the notion that their mates were on their way home and would be honored would be a massive comfort, allowing them to focus on what was to come.

This was a good thing. He and every soldier of the Airborne would need to muster every last bit of concentration and will to confront the challenge coming their way out of the southeast.

At least two battalions of the Reds were en route from their hiding place in the Mark Twain. They would outnumber

Larocque's soldiers and were certain to have more firepower. The Airborne was about to get another dose of hell for its troubles, but he was damned if the men and women of his regiment wouldn't be primed to pay it back to the Reds in this second go-around. Only this time, they knew the Americans were coming.

Chapter 23

Somewhere over southern Iowa

Flying his Tempest at an altitude of twenty-two thousand feet, Major Khan didn't know how low the two RAAF Hercs were flying. That the two surface-skimming planes had not shown up on any of the radars that CANZUK had in the area was an indication that the Australian pilots had thrown caution to the wind. And so they should. Were they to be identified, there was no shortage of UCSA fighters in the area who would be glad to shoot down the lumbering high-value targets.

So important was the Australian sprint to Whiteman that CANZUK air command had assigned no fewer than six fighters to screen the transport planes' approach. Via a feed from one of the assigned AWACS Wedgetails loitering over central Iowa, he could see the six Canadian Super Hornets flying in formation at an altitude of twenty thousand feet.

Brave souls, thought Khan. If nothing moved on the Hercs, the six-pack of Canadian fighters was to wait patiently in the hopes that one or more of the Red's J-31s would reveal itself, giving Kahn and his wingman their own opportunity to bring down another of the Chinese killing machines.

He had shot down one himself not three hours ago and it had not been easy. Over the past thirty years, the Chinese had both pilfered and learned from the Americans and Europeans, allowing them to produce what Khan was now willing to admit was the world's best fighter plane. There was no getting around it. The plane scored high marks in the areas of stealth, power, and offensive capability, but it was the jet's peerless electronic warfare suite that truly set it apart.

By now, the Red Faction pilots had become masterful in their utilization of the J-31s' EW capabilities and CANZUK had been largely helpless to stop them. Were it not for the fact the Americans only had a small number of planes, Khan had heard his superiors freely admit the air war would be the Reds' to win.

The tactic Khan had seen the Americans work so effectively saw the Reds use their own AWACS or ground-based radars to identify CANZUK's more conventional airframes, at which point loitering J-31s would get within range – usually within forty kilometers – and launch a missile strike. It was while these targeted fighters evaded and died that planes such as Khan's Tempest would race to the location where the missiles had been launched and with radars blazing they would look to find, and then take down as many of the elusive Chinese fighters they could.

And to be sure, they had found targets. Stealth wasn't some magical invisibility cloak. CANZUK's mix of Super Hornets, F-35s, Typhoons, and Khan's own squadron of Tempests, had some of the most sophisticated avionics in the world. The challenge, however, had been defeating the powerful electronic countermeasures the J-31 fielded. Of the nine missiles he had launched at the Chinese fighters, only one had managed to make a kill. On all other occasions, the latest generation Meteor missile used by the RAF had simply melted off its target or had fallen victim to some other countermeasure offered up by the American pilots.

Engineers from the Meteor's manufacturer, MDBA had been flown in from Europe in an effort to quick fix the issue but had yet to find any success with the missile's targeting software. As a result, Khan and those pilots flying the UK's in-theatre Tempests had taken to the tried-and-true tactic of getting up close and personal with the Americans.

The challenge there was that the Yanks were playing hard to get. The missiles carried by the J-31s had their own state-of-the-art onboard targeting system and once launched, the Red pilots were free to make themselves scarce. In doing so, they had frustrated Khan and his fellow pilots to no end. The Chinese had outdone themselves with the J-31 and it was CANZUK pilots who were paying the price.

As though on cue, one of the radar techs from an on-station AWACS urgently announced they had picked up a missile launch to the front of the Canadian Super Hornets. Within a couple of seconds, seven, no make that nine, missiles had reared themselves onto the main display at the center of his cockpit. Khan listened as the now harried Canadian pilots began to communicate amongst themselves in an effort to evade and counter the incoming projectiles.

Khan tuned them out. They had done their job in drawing out the American pilots and from what he had seen, the Canadian pilots knew their business. It was now his responsibility to find the on-loan Chinese fighters and even the score. Tapping the right part of his plane's combat display, Khan activated the Tempest's radar, while simultaneously nosing the fighter in the direction where missiles had first bloomed. There were now eleven of the missiles on-screen but beyond them, two new pings flashed into view.

"There you are, you cheeky bastards," Khan growled. He toggled on his mic. "We have contact, ladies and gentlemen. Downer, you're with me. Let's see if the new software does the trick. We unload at thirty klicks and then we press in hard. Gravy and Ginger, hold your position for five and then sweep in after us and see what else you can find. There are more of these cagey bastards out there. I can feel it."

———

San Antonio, 5th Army HQ

Spector had not needed to push the commanding officer of the 101st Airborne to order his two battalions at Versailles to push on to Whiteman. The bulk of the 101st was being badly mauled as two of its brigades made their way to St. Louis from their base in Kentucky. Moving UCSA air assets into the Missouri theatre had helped to reduce the CANZUK airborne threat, but it would be several more hours before Montrell and his J-31s could truly begin to turn the tide. They only had so many of the Chinese fighters and only so many pilots that were qualified to fly them.

It was Spector's hope, and that of the general commanding the 101st, that movement of the two battalions out of Versailles would give their main force the breathing room it needed to get to St. Louis and prepare for the larger two brigade assault the 101st would launch on Whiteman the following morning.

Which wasn't to say that the force now pushing out of the Mark Twain National Forest was without hope. Quite the opposite, it was a veteran force commanded by a pair of highly capable officers and if his pilots could continue to over-perform for the next few hours, it could be that the first battle for Whiteman would be the only one.

Once again he looked at the tactical display that had laid out the Canadians' defensive positions as best they could identify them. With the nuclear storage bunkers at the center point, Spector could see that the paratroopers had positioned themselves in such a way that any force coming west along Highway 50 would be funneled toward a series of defenses that included trenches and a variety of other emplacements. Assuming CANZUK airpower was in play to encourage the enemy force to go where the Canadians wanted, it was the correct strategy.

The key for the two battalions that would attack the Canadians this evening was to employ speed to avoid the funnel, to flank the defenders, and then hit them where they appeared the most vulnerable. For the force that they had, Spector had agreed that the stronger of the two battalions should swing well south of the base and drive north into the paratroopers dug in along the south end of Whiteman, while the other battalion made a hell-bent run into the maw of the main defense on the east side of the base. This battalion's sacrifice would be the other battalion's gain.

Even if lightly armored, if the southern attacking formation overwhelmed this section of the Canadians' defense and got in close with the defending paratroopers, the fight would become a close-quarters affair. And experience told him that those kinds of battles could go either way.

———

Whiteman AFB

Larocque pulled his eyes from the second Royal Australian Air Force Herc as it lumbered through the air toward the north end of Whiteman's runway.

Now on the tarmac, the first RAAF plane was in the process of disgorging its troops. At the fore of the plane, Larocque saw Chen and 2nd Commando's CO, Rydell empty out of the plane's starboard door. Walking up to them, Larocque thrust out his hand to the Australian colonel.

"Great to see you, Brian. And you too, Captain Chen. I'm only sorry the rest of your folks couldn't make the trip."

"You and me both, Jack. If the lads in the sky can somehow get the better of the Reds, we'll get the rest of us here. But for now, we're it," Rydell stated loudly over the drone of the transport plane's engines.

"And I'm thankful for it," said Larocque. "I heard you on the comm twisting arms to get permission to land these first two birds. We're in your debt, Brian. Me, the Regiment, hell, all of Canada owes you big time."

"Jack, if the shoe was on the other foot, I know you would have done the same thing. Now, how can we help?"

"You've been briefed on our little situation with the nukes?" Larocque asked.

"The Captain and I have, yes. It's quite wrinkle," the Aussie commander offered with a wry smile.

Larocque chortled. "We've got people working on the problem, Colonel."

"As for what 2nd Commando can bring to the table, I need you to get those anti-armor drones you've brought up and running. We have upwards of two battalions of mechanized infantry coming our way. We're gonna need those drones you've brought to help us shepherd the Reds where they don't want to go."

"The Wyverns are outstanding pieces of kit. German-made and crafty. Consider it done. What else?" said Rydell.

"If you're up for it, I'd like you to take command of the heavy weapons company. Delgado, my 2IC, was lost when the Apaches hit us. They're a solid group, but when things get hot, I'd like for them to have a senior hand to keep them steady. And our backup command post is tucked in with them, so when you put it all together, this outfit is critical to our success."

"Done and done. I'll have my people operate the Wyverns from that position," Rydell replied immediately.

Larocque then turned his attention to Chen. "I'm sorry to report that Captain Brazeau was cut down when the separatists pulled their bullshit.

"If Colonel Rydell is okay with it, I'd like it if you could take three-quarters of your men to reinforce A Company and take over Brazeau's command. It's Brazeau's location where we're going to drive the Reds, so you'll be at the tip of the spear. You up for the challenge Captain?"

Chen hesitated a moment before offering his reply. "If that's what you need, Colonel, I'm up for it. But isn't Brazeau's company

French-speaking? I reckon they'd be better off with one of the company's junior officers who spoke the language?"

"Maybe," Larocque responded. "But things are gonna be real hairy in that neck of the woods, and I need to make sure I've got someone who's got the company-level experience and the balls to make sure my boys stay ramrod. Enough of them know who you are and what 2nd Commando is about, and I don't want to shift out one of my other company commanders. You're here, so I'm going to make use of you. And Quebecers or no, the boys will follow you because they know you're going to help them survive what's coming."

Larocque looked at his wrist and checked the time. "Listen, I gotta go take care of that other problem. Are you game, Captain?"

Chen looked at Rydell. The CO of Australia's 2nd Commando Regiment nodded his head in the affirmative.

"Looks like I'm good to go, sir."

"Good," said Larocque. Sergeant Major St. Pierre will be here momentarily and will bring you over to your new company. The RSM will hang with you a while to make sure all goes well."

Larocque turned back again to Rydell. "Colonel, before you jump into action, why don't you come with me? I have a man I need to speak to about a nuclear bomb. You may want to hear what he has to say."

————

Highway 50, east of Kansas City

Hall watched as the truck in front of them signaled that it was going to get off the highway. "Are they stopping for gas?" she said in a voice that held a touch of disbelief.

"Maybe," Wallace replied. "Maybe they didn't bother to check the tank when they grabbed it."

As their own vehicle approached the turn-off, Hall signaled to follow.

"How far are we out from Kansas City?" Hall asked.

"We're just over halfway," said Wallace.

"Well, if it is the case they need gas, that's a break for us. If we're going to do something, best we do it here than somewhere on the highway."

In the forty or so minutes they had been driving, they had talked through several options about what to do about Gauthier, his men, and the now-confirmed sixty-kiloton nuclear bomb they were driving.

As Hall drove, Wallace had had an extended conversation with the bomb tech that Larocque had grabbed for Havez. The tech had been less helpful than they both would have hoped. To be sure, he knew the guts of the absconded bomb inside and out, but what he could not help with was the nature of the software Gauthier had used to arm the weapon. On that front, the only thing he could offer was that the safety features built into the bomb they were trailing were now twenty years old, and in fact, were no match for any near-AI system that had been produced in the last five years.

Based on the information they did have, they had worked out several things that would need to happen if the two of them were going to take the bomb by force. The most important of these was to neutralize the three soldiers in such a way that they could not get to the tac pad they assumed was linked to the bomb in the back of the separatists' truck. Not knowing if the rogue soldiers' BAM wrist units were linked to the tac pad, or that they didn't have some other kill switch, they would have to take down all three soldiers so that they didn't have the chance to manually set off the bomb. It was a hugely challenging task.

"Well, look at that," Hall uttered. "They do need gas." As she turned right, she could see the US Air Force-marked pickup truck begin to pull into a large ten-pump Citgo station. As she drove in the direction of the gas station, she activated her BAM in order to call Larocque. "Call Winch Actual, priority call Bravo-Lima."

"Channel open," the male voice of her BAM advised.

"Sir, it's Tiller One. The target's truck has pulled into a gas station to fuel up and we're just over halfway to KC. It might be now or never."

_____

Whiteman AFB

For what had to be the fiftieth time, Havez looked up from his laptop at the master sergeant who was standing beside the tactical pad wired into the B-83. "This code, Gibson. It's some of the nastiest stuff I've ever seen," Havez said.

As they'd worked to secure the base, the Canadians had taken steps to confine the pilots, ground crews, and techs who flew and serviced Whiteman's bombers and other planes, so Havez had been able to ask for one of the senior technicians who he knew was an expert on the arming mechanisms contained within each of the bombs.

Upon tracking down the senior master sergeant, the Canadian military policeman had the insight to let the airman grab his tools, several of which were highly specialized to each of the bomb variants in Whiteman's inventory. It was this soldier, Senior Master Sergeant Kendis 'Gibby' Gibson who had created an alternative pathway for Havez to get into the B-83's arming software.

Once connected to the weapon's hardware, Havez quickly navigated to its operating system. Connected, he'd had no problems getting past the outdated safeguards that had been developed by the contractors who last modernized the weapon. By today's standards, the software fail-safes were ineffective to the point of being a joke.

It was the software on the tac pad that was going to be the hard part. The challenge standing before him would be in trying to isolate and then somehow alter the arming software that the Separatists had left behind without giving that same program any indication it was being tinkered with. The instructions on the tac pad had been clear on that issue. If the near-AI running the arming software sensed that it was being probed, it would set off the B-83 and that would be that.

In order for a processing unit to be certified as a 'near-AI' product, academics and industry had come together and created a scale that told users what percentage of human-like functions a particular near-AI unit could do without sentient assistance. As a second-generation unit, the rogue soldiers' tac pad had a rating of 92.7 percent, while Havez's fourth-gen processor had a rating of 96.2. Though only a 3.5 percent difference, the rating scale was asymmetric and as a result, Havez's top-of-the-line machine had more computing firepower by far. Which was helpful because whoever had created the program that was the separatist's arming software had been one hell of a coder. In the last twenty minutes, Havez had tried every angle he could think of to silently overcome the arming software, but in all cases, he had come up short.

Outside of the bunker, he recognized the engine of one of the Canadian RZRs and glanced at his watch. Based on his last conversation with Larocque, he had just under twenty minutes to figure out how to neutralize the behemoth that stood in front of him. He looked over and saw the Canadian CO and another man of a similar age, but who was wearing a set of fatigues that were different in color and pattern from Larocque's.

"Colonel Havez, this is Colonel Rydell of the Australian Army. He and a few of his men and women have just landed and are going to help us as we look to welcome the Reds."

The Australian, outfitted in his country's full battle dress, stepped forward and shook Havez's hand.

"Good to meet you, Colonel. The good Colonel here has sung your praises. On behalf of Australia, you too have my thanks," offered Rydell.

"Kind of you to say so, but the two of you may not be thanking me so much when I tell you I haven't been able to figure out this flipping arming software as yet. As best I can tell, whoever developed the code is world-class."

"And who's this?" Larocque said, gesturing to the Air Force NCO standing behind Havez.

"Oh right, sorry. I had one of your MPs grab Master Sergeant Gibson from the aircrews you've held onto. Gibson here knows these weapons inside and out and showed me a secondary access point that I've used to get into the arming software, but as I've just told you, that's about as far as I've got."

In response to the update, Larocque's head and steel-grey eyes shifted downward while his hand came up in the universal sign for 'hold up'.

In the short time they had been in each other's presence, Havez had come to recognize when Larocque was taking a call from someone within his command. Havez listened intently as the paratroop commander walked away and said, "Where are you at, and what's the situation?"

As he watched the back of the Canadian officer move away from their small group, Havez heard another voice. "Ah, Colonel."

"Yes, Sargeant?" Havez said as he turned to face the short but thickly built man.

"I've been thinking sir that maybe there's another way to solve this problem we've been hav'n." From Kentucky, the man's words had a slight backcountry twang to them.

"I'm all ears," Havez said.

"You've been saying the two weapons are linked and if something happens to the one, well, the other is somehow messaged and this leads to one or both of the bombs being set off."

"It's something like that," replied Havez. "Though if we were to somehow manage to neutralize our bomb, or worse, if I was to set the thing off, I suspect the soldiers who are on their way to KC would be advised something had happened and that it would be left up to them to decide when to detonate their weapon."

"Okay, well instead of trying to get past whatever software you're hav'n trouble with, why don't you create some type of shadow program that tells the other bomb that this here weapon is good and then I disarm the thing manually."

"Can you do that? I mean, can you disarm this thing with just your hands?"

"With my hands and a few tools, yes, sir, I can. It'll be a bit of a hack job, but if I start now, I can get'er done in twenty minutes, or thereabouts."

"And what do you need from me?" asked Havez.

"The tac pad's software – as sure shit, it's watching to see if this here bad boy is being messed with. If you can somehow get the bomb's software to make it look like everything is proper-like while I rig up the physical workaround I'm thinking of, I think we might be okay."

Havez thought through the idea and put himself in the position of the near-AI program currently connected to the huge weapon in front of him. The program would have most certainly sent out electronic tendrils into the bomb's older software to prevent exactly what Gibson was suggesting, but it was within that same older software that Havez's programming skills and the near-AI of his own laptop should be able to implement the type of ruse the master sergeant was suggesting.

He would have to precisely duplicate the bomb's software and lay it over the original programming so that when Gibson started his work, the AI in the Separatists' tactical pad wouldn't be able to pick up the difference. It would be precise and delicate work.

Of course, that plan of action would do nothing to prevent the Kansas City-bound soldiers from setting off the B-83 in the time that it took Gibson to disarm the weapon, but unless they had a reason to set off the doomsday weapon in the next twenty minutes or so, it sounded as though they could make this work.

Havez hadn't heard Larocque's return, so when the Canadian CO asked, "Can you do it?" from behind him, Havez jumped like a twitchy cat.

Havez turned to face the other man and after taking a brief moment to collect his thoughts, he said, "I think we might be able to pull it off as Sergeant Gibson describes."

"Brilliant news," offered Larocque. "How much time do you need before you can set up the program that will allow Mr. Gibson to do his work?"

"At least twenty minutes. Twenty-five to be safe," Havez said

"You have ten. We've hit a bit of luck, Colonel. The separatists have pulled off to get gas if you can believe it. My people have a plan to take them down," said Larocque as he slapped his hand down on the nose of the 1.2-megaton weapon.

The Airborne commander continued, "They're halfway to KC and if they take them now and their weapon goes off, a few dozen are killed. If they wait and let those bastards get back on the road and they make it to Kansas City, we're talking tens of thousands, if not six figures. That's not on."

Havez looked at Larocque and took a deep, calming breath. "Ten minutes is just not enough – fifteen, maybe."

Larocque gave Havez a kind look and placed his hand on the other man's shoulder. "You can do this, Vic. We can't let that truck back on the road. You have ten minutes."

Once again, Larocque cocked his head, letting Havez know his focus had moved onto whichever person he was speaking with via the system he called the BAM. "Tiller One, you're a go but you can't hit the target for ten minutes. Confirm that order," Larocque said.

After a moment of listening, Larocque said, "Yes, I understand it doesn't take ten minutes to fill a gas tank, Lieutenant. Find a way to delay them and then hit them after the ten-minute mark. We need the time on our end. Improvise Lieutenant. It's what you were trained to do."

Larocque paused as he again listened to the junior officer. "Very good. Keep me posted as best you can and good luck. The two of you got this, Lieutenant. Larocque out."

The Airborne CO's eyes moved back to Havez. "There you go, Colonel. You heard it first-hand. My people will give you ten minutes to make this happen. Starting now."

Chapter 24

Highway 50 east of Kansas City

Hall watched the soldier identified as Gauthier exit the passenger side of the truck and walk toward the back of the vehicle. To Hall's surprise, he was now wearing the standard uniform of the American Army, though he wasn't wearing any of that service's armor or battle gear. He was also wearing a sidearm. One of the other two soldiers got out of the driver's side of the vehicle and headed to the gas pump. He too was wearing US Army fatigues.

"These guys were prepared," Hall said aloud.

"They're acting pretty nonchalant, considering they're carrying a weapon that can blow up an entire city," said Wallace.

"For sure. Which tells us they have no idea they're being followed. That's good for us. You ready?" asked Hall.

Wallace exhaled loudly and then said, "Ready as I'm ever going to be."

Hall looked at her watch. It was on a countdown from ten minutes, and they had just passed the nine-minute mark. This was gonna have to be one hell of a charade, she thought.

"Okay, let's do this just as we discussed. If things don't go as planned, we improvise and do what we need to do to get us to ten minutes."

Hall's hand moved to open her door, but before pulling on the handle, she turned her head back to Wallace and looked at the unassuming man she had come to consider a good friend. He could never be more than that. At least not now. His dark water-blue eyes – easily the best feature on an otherwise unremarkable face – looked back at her. As always, he was unreadable, but she had come to like that about him. The strong and silent type, she thought and not for the first time.

"Good luck, Max. If things go to shit, I just want you to know that it's been great working with you. It's been a hell of a ride and I'm glad I did it with you."

Hearing the words, Wallace offered a rare smile and a most uncharacteristic wink. "Right back at you, Lieutenant. You're one hell of a leader and when you put it all together, I think we've made a great team."

"The best team," said Hall.

"The best," repeated Wallace, a pleasant smile still locked on his face.

Hearing the words, she leaned over and gave Wallace a quick kiss on his cheek. The young man's eyes grew and his smile widened. Not surprisingly, he said nothing. Turning back to the door, Hall exited their vehicle and without looking back began walking in the direction of Lieutenant Curtis Gauthier and his band of traitorous soldiers.

———

Gauthier stood a dozen feet back from the truck. They had parked at the pump furthermost from the station's convenience store. From this vantage point, he could see in all directions for some distance.

It had been bad luck that they had lifted a truck running on near empty. He had ordered Jean-Luc to fill it up, not knowing whether they would need to move beyond their pre-determined position in Kansas City. Better to be prepared.

His eyes fell on the truck's covered flatbed. He had spoken briefly with the soldier in the back on first getting out of the cab. Corporal Villeneuve, the third and final man of their group couldn't leave the confines of the capped truck bed because his upper leg was saturated in now-dried blood.

In the gunfight with Brazeau, a round had caught Villeneuve on the outer part of his thigh opening up a deep gash inches long. The wound had gushed like a harpooned whale.

In their rush to get to the bunker and complete their mission, they had forgotten to bring along a trauma kit, so Villeneuve had been relegated to cutting up his discarded Canadian fatigues to staunch the wound. For the most part, the effort had been a success, but enough blood had continued to seep that the man's new uniform was unfit for public display.

Upon confirming Villeneuve was doing okay, Gauthier had taken the corporal's order of beef jerky and an energy drink and told him to sit tight. Once in KC, they could stop at a drug store and get what they needed to patch the man up properly.

The gas station was not busy. As soon as they had gotten a few miles out of Whiteman, they had flitted through several local radio stations to get a sense of what they might find as they made their way west. Their greatest fear had been that Missouri state police or the National Guard would shut down the roads in and around the base, making their journey to Kansas City more difficult than they needed it to be, but the stations they had listened to had only mentioned that resources were headed upstate and that the National Guard was actively engaged in the task of taking back two Missouri River bridge crossings that some yet-to-be-identified special forces had taken. That would be the British Paras, Gauthier thought.

Catching movement out of the corner of his eyes, he turned to take in a leggy, athletic-looking young woman wearing a pair of form-fitting athletic pants and a black hoodie that had a large golden tiger on it with the word 'Missou' printed underneath the logo. As their eyes met, she flashed a smile to show perfect white teeth that contrasted wonderfully with her olive skin.

The woman stopped several feet away from Gauthier and placed her hands on her hips. She was an athlete of some sort to be sure. Underneath the tight fabric of her leggings, he could see well-muscled thighs. Gauthier wasn't into the girl-next-door look so much, but if he had been, this pretty young thing standing in front of him would have been worth chasing after, even if she was American.

"So, y'all soldiers from the base?" the woman asked, her accent most definitely local.

The renegade soldiers had agreed in advance that should anyone need to do any talking, it would be him who would engage. He spoke the best English and, in recent months, had worked diligently to soften his accent to the point where on first blush it sounded like he could have been from anywhere.

"Yes, ma'am," said Gauthier, figuring to say as little as possible so that the woman might take a hint and move along.

"Cause my brother, he's like stationed at the base. Y'all might know him. He's an airman and works on the B-21s, or that's what I think they're called. I never really paid attention when Jimmy was talking about his work. James Smith is his name, but everyone calls him Little Jimmy. You heard of him?"

"I can't say I have," Gauthier replied his voice uninterested.

The woman had a pensive look to her. If she had a brother at Whiteman, she was likely to be concerned for his well-being. Gauthier could understand that.

"So, like, I heard some army has taken the base and that there's been shooting, and that people have died. Like, I don't want to pry, but no one knows anything, and my folks are worried sick about Jimmy. If there's anything you can tell me about what's happening, it sure would help my parents. I mean, like, has there been fighting? Has anyone died? I'm sorry, I know I shouldn't be bothering you with all this, but if I didn't try talking with you, my momma would kill me."

"Ma'am, I can't share any information with you. My suggestion is to keep listening to the radio and to tell your parents to keep their phone with them."

Gauthier's eyes left the local and took in a grey sedan pulling in for gas two bays over. He performed a quick assessment on the man who got out of the vehicle. Lanky and tall, he was wearing a well-worn pair of jeans, an untucked plaid shirt, and the classic green-and-yellow John Deer trucker hat. Another local, he thought.

Gauthier turned his attention back to the woman, but then he heard Jean-Luc say in heavily accented English that the truck's tank was full.

Hearing that they were ready to move, he said, "I'm sorry, ma'am. We're on a tight schedule." He grabbed and tipped down the brim of his standard-issue patrol cap and headed in the direction of the gas station's convenience store.

"I'll come with you. My friend's on the other side filling up. I only came over here to talk to you guys." She fell in beside Gauthier as he walked.

"So, where are you from?" she asked.

"Upstate Vermont, close to the Canadian border."

"Wow," she said. "Betcha, it's like, really cold up there in the winter. Whatcha doing all the way down here? I would have thought you would have gone home when the war started."

Gauthier didn't reply but opened the door to the good-sized mini-mart, walked in, and then began to scope out the various items he had committed to purchasing for himself and his accomplices. Except for the middle-aged clerk, no one else was in the store. He felt a gentle tug on the fabric that covered his upper arm. Stopping, he first looked at the woman's hand and then directed what he hoped was a pissed-off at her. "Ma'am?" Gauthier said, "I think I mentioned I'm in a bit of a rush, but to answer your question, I was stationed here when the war started and I never left. Why fight a war when you don't have to?"

"Huh, I guess I might have done the same," the woman said. "And no, you didn't mention that you were in a rush."

As the words came out of her mouth, Gauthier thought there was a hint of obstinance in her voice. Whatever, he thought. He didn't have time to deal with the local trash. Time to shut this sorority girl down, even if she was a looker in those leggings.

"Well, as it turns out, I am in a rush and I can't help you with your brother, so please leave me alone. "

"Sorry," she said in a voice that pitched up an octave, "but, I'm desperate here. My brother and I weren't super close – he's like five years older than me, but my parents... He's a son of a bitch if you ask me, but they love him to death. If there's anything at all you could, like, share with me, I'd be super grateful to you." The woman's large, hazel eyes had a pleading look to them.

She continued, "Listen, if I give you my number, when you get back to the base, maybe you can take a look around for him? He's in the 509th Bomber Group or something like that. I'm really sorry to ask this of you, but like I said, I'm a bit desperate."

When he next spoke, Gauthier put the edge of command into his voice. "Ma'am, we're not heading back to the base any time soon, so I can't help you. As I said, we're in a bit of a rush, so I'm going to grab a few things and then we're back on the road. I can't help you or your parents, so if you could go about your business that would make my day."

As Gauthier's response registered with her, the woman's face took on a hurt look. "Okay, sorry. I don't want to hold you up. I just thought that I'd take a chance was all. Seeing as you're a soldier, I thought maybe you might wanna help. But I guess not. Whatever."

Gauthier couldn't help but look at the woman with contempt. Were he not shuttling a stolen nuclear bomb across a foreign country, he wouldn't have let this bitch get away with the sass. Fucking women, he thought.

When this mission was done and he was back home, he would look forward to the day when the concept of distinctive gender roles was re-introduced into Quebec society. Finally, the annoying but pretty American dropped her eyes from his and she turned away.

A few minutes later he was standing in front of the cashier, having found most of what he needed. The young woman had remained in the store the whole time doing her own shopping. In the reflection of the ballistic glass wall that protected the dejected-looking store clerk, he took in the woman's reflection as she filed in behind him.

As Gauthier finished paying for their supplies with a pre-authorized card, he turned and saw the woman with the hoodie looking at him once again.

Now smiling, she lifted up her right hand so that it was level with her breasts and pulled back the sleeve of her sweater to check the time. His eyes widened as he saw the woman was wearing what was most certainly a BAM wrist unit. Quickly, she tapped its display and holding it just below her mouth, she said, "Ten minutes, go."

Alarm bells went off inside Gauthier's skull as he dropped the items he was carrying and reached for the pistol on his hip. As his hand wrapped around the grip of the weapon and began to pull it from its holster, he froze, staring at the barrel of a suppressed handgun pointed at the center of his chest.

No longer smiling, when the woman next spoke it was in Anglophone-accented French. "Allo, Lieutenant. Any chance you're going to tell me how to shut off that bomb in the back of your truck?"

It was now Gauthier who smiled. "Anglo bitch." Relieved that he no longer had to speak that other language, he said, "If you kill me, you set off the bomb in the truck and the one back at the base – then what happens to your shit country's little imperialist adventure?"

"Maybe. But I wouldn't be too sure. Let the record show, Lieutenant Gauthier that you declined my request for assistance," the woman said.

The young woman's lips tightened, and then, as if in slow motion, Gauthier watched the subtle motion of her hand as it tightened on the matte-black weapon.

———

Wallace heard Hall's voice through his earbud, "Ten minutes, go."

Since pulling into the gas stall two spots over from Gauthier and his men, he had busied himself with putting gas in their car and then performing several other tasks. Dropping the hood to the car, Wallace casually moved to the passenger side of the vehicle and grabbed the needed item he had left on his seat and then turned and walked in the direction of the Whiteman pickup.

Conveniently, the soldier who had pumped the gas had moved to the back of the truck and had opened the window of the truck cap and was talking to the third soldier riding in the back with the bomb.

Wearing an untucked shirt, Wallace's hand easily slid toward the custom holster strapped tightly around his midsection and placed his hand on the suppressed handgun riding on his lower back. Catching his arrival out of the corner of his eye, the standing soldier turned to face him, at which point Wallace's hand snapped

forward with his weapon and fired off three rounds point-blank into the man's chest.

As the soldier stumbled backward, surprise bloomed on the
man's face as his brain made a frantic effort to register what had just
happened.

Closing the distance between himself and the rear of the truck,
Wallace calmly brought forward the flash grenade he was carrying
in his left hand, pulled the pin and tossed it into the open flatbed.
Dropping to his haunches, he heard the third soldier scramble and
curse in French. Less than a second later, Wallace heard the deafen-
ing crack of the stun grenade going off.

Springing back to his feet, Wallace's left hand shot out and
grabbed the release for the tailgate and quickly slammed it down.
Lying on the floor of the flatbed, the third soldier was moaning
in pain. Setting his pistol on the tailgate, with both hands Wallace
grabbed the man's ankles and with every ounce of strength he could
muster out of his sinewy frame, he hauled the prone man out of
the truck, pulling him several feet in the air before his unprotected
head and the rest of his body crashed into the concrete surface of
the gas station.

Grabbing his pistol off the tailgate, Wallace turned his attention back to the first soldier he had shot. He was lying on his back.
Wallace could clearly see that the soldier's chest was heaving, but
more disconcertedly, the man's right hand was struggling to manipulate his wrist unit. Prowling forward, Wallace pointed his weapon
at the soldier's face with a two-handed grip and fired three rounds
in quick succession.

Pivoting away from the destroyed paratrooper, Wallace pointed his weapon at the side of the head of the stunned man he had
just yanked from the truck. The laid-out body was moaning. Without waiting, and at a range of perhaps ten feet, Wallace fired a
round into the side of the man's skull. Perfectly aimed, the round

punched a hole through bone causing a fountain of blood and brain matter to spray onto the grey concrete the man's head rested upon.

As they had conceived their plan only twenty minutes earlier, several online sources had advised Wallace that a body's heart could beat for several minutes after it had been subjected to some form of death-inducing trauma. If the nuke in the back of the truck did have a kill switch that was biometrically linked to Gauthier and his two accomplices via their BAMs, he and Hall needed to make sure each of the soldiers' wrist units still had a heart to monitor.

Standing above the first soldier he had killed, Wallace knelt down and quickly un-velcroed the man's BAM and placed it on his left wrist.

As he turned to the second soldier, he saw that Hall had taken a knee beside the body. Standing, she pulled back the sleeves of her hoodie and held up both of her arms to display three wrist units. She had a relieved look on her face.

"Well, we're still here," she said as her gaze fell toward the large grey cylinder in the back of the truck.

Wallace didn't reply, but followed her eyes. In his haste to take out the two men, he had forgotten about the nightmare of a weapon. As he now took it in, he saw the tactical pad and the cable connecting it to the seven-hundred-pound gravity bomb.

"What's our time like?" he asked.

"We're thirty-nine minutes until Labelle's deadline. Which is not enough time to get us back to Whiteman," Hall said.

"Tons of time," Wallace offered casually. "So, what's the plan?"

Hall looked at him, smiled, and said, "I have an idea. I'll drive the truck and you can follow me. While we drive, I'll get the colonel on the horn and we'll check in with the higher-ups - 'cause this thing," she said, pointing over her shoulder to the nuke, "is way, way above our pay grade."

———

Whiteman AFB

"Time?" Havez asked as he once again wiped his sweating brow.

"You're at nine minutes in four-three-two-one," Larocque said calmly.

"We're not going to make it," Havez responded.

"You're almost there. Don't focus on the time, focus on getting it done," said Larocque.

To his right, Gibson spoke up. "Almost there, sir. I have one last adjustment to make, and the bomb goes inert, but I can't make that move 'til your patch is in place."

Without taking his eyes off the screen of his laptop, Havez replied in a strained voice, "Just a few more seconds."

There was complete silence around him. Even the noise emanating from the rest of the base seemed to be muted.

As a grad student at university, he had organized several hackathons for his fellow students, and though it had been many years since he had been in the crucible that was inter-varsity competition, Havez was pleased by how readily his long-dormant programming skills had reappeared.

In truth, with the advent of near-AI, hacking and program development had become a less-specialized skill, where almost anyone with basic coding chops would have been able to outmatch the very best technology of just fifteen years ago. But it was still the case that the greatest achievements in the field of AI came about when a talented human worked in partnership with one of the close-to-sentient programs.

"Near-AI had been 'birthed' a few years his graduation from the University of Florida, but as a young officer in the United States' cyber defense corps, he had spent thousands of hours working with the first near-AI systems as he and the units he commanded faced off with the best cyber warriors that China, Russia, and other miscreant states could put into the field.

Larocque's voice, still calm, jarred the quiet. "Ten minutes in five seconds, Colonel."

Havez had identified the rogue tac pad's presence in the bomb's ancient detonating system. The challenge before him was reproducing a precise version of the bomb's software and then sliding his doppelganger between the bomb's existing software and the invading program so that the near-AI in the separatist's tac pad did not notice the overlay. It had been a delicate bit of coding and if he had not had access to the fourth-gen near-AI on his laptop, this would have been an impossible feat.

"Colonel, we're out of time," Larocque said. This time, his voice was infused with a well-practiced authority.

Havez took a deep breath and let himself lock in with the information scrolling in front of him. In the cyber warfare world, it was standard practice to triple-check your work before you unloaded whatever program you had created. Studies had shown that the triple-check was the sweet spot where you achieved the highest level of efficiency, along with the most acceptable error rate. Finishing only the second full check of his code, Havez turned his head to Gibson and said, "Do it."

Poised over the weapon's control panel, the master sergeant leaned forward with a strange-looking tool in his right hand. Havez watched as the man's forearm disappeared into the colossal ordinance. Gibson closed his eyes and then Havez watched as the muscles along the man's arm strained as he turned something deep inside the body of the weapon.

Gibson opened his eyes and turned his head to look at Havez. A smile erupted on the man's face, his pearl-white teeth contrasting brilliantly with his dark skin. "We're good to go."

"And we're still here," said Havez.

"Yes, sir, and we're still here."

_____

Larocque had been right. When Chen arrived, Brazeau's soldiers had been vacillating between mourning and fury as they tried to come to terms with what had happened to their well-liked commander. But when Chen opened his BAM and advised A Company that he would be taking command and that part of his own company would be joining them to help them give it back to the Yanks, the feedback from the French-speaking paratroopers had been wholly positive.

Several accented variations of, "Welcome aboard and let's fuck these guys up," had poured in, while still more comments had come in French. The BAM's universal translator had struggled to keep up with the volume of comments, but he had been assured by the Airborne's RSM that all of the chatter had been top-drawer stuff.

Chen had thought St. Pierre's take on the situation had been an interesting insight. At the time, the Airborne's Regimental Sergeant Major had offered, "They know what happened and they're pissed with the separatists, but they're also sore because one of their own let down the Regiment, never mind the whole country. Moving A Company under one of the English-speaking captains would not have been well received. It's a pride thing. As an Australian, you'll be seen as a neutral figure, and they know 2nd Commando is a first-rate unit. The Colonel knew full well what he was doing when he put you in charge of Brazeau's lot. Just make more right decisions than wrong and you'll get through this fine."

With the pep talk under his belt, Chen had moved to quickly review Brazeau's plan of defense and plugged himself into the conversation taking place in the BAM network that had been set up to coordinate the company's upcoming battle with the Red force that had originated out of Mark Twain and Versailles.

The key to victory in the coming fight was forcing the Yanks to come at Whiteman from the east and not from the south or southeast. These latter two vectors were harder to defend because they were wide open and because this section of the defense was not aligned with the base's nuclear bunkers. Without the bunkers immediately behind them, the southern sector of the defense would be subjected to any and all of the heavy weapons the Reds brought with them.

To discourage the approaching Red force from attacking the southern flank of the Airborne's defensive line, CANZUK's air command had brought in additional Super Hornets from Canada where they had been dedicated to monitoring the country's airspace. In pairs, the Canadian fighter jets were now doing their best to harass the southern-most Reds, while at the same time dodging attacks from the tenacious UCSA air force. Every soldier on the ground knew it was dangerous and brave work.

Australia too had been playing a role in this crucial part of the strategy. The second Hercules that landed at Whiteman had been carrying eight Wyvern tactical drones, which Colonel Rydell now had airborne. Armed with the latest extended range Spike anti-tank missile from Israel, most of the speedy anti-armor units had flown south of the base and were doing their best to pressure that part of the approaching Americans to go where they didn't want to go.

Major Landry's voice popped into Chen's BAM. At Larocque's direction, he'd assigned the Airborne's senior operations officer a one-way open channel so that she could update him at any time.

"Captain Chen, I've just sent an image series to you. Give it a look-see if you would."

"Thanks. What am I looking at?"

"Well, first off, I'm pleased to report we've hammered the Reds that were coming at us out of the south. What's left of that formation is still on its way, however. The colonel has pre-emptively moved part of the reaction force into that sector to beef up C Company.

"The Red force that swung north and is now moving to your sector remains in fighting form. They've taken some hits, but eighty percent of that outfit will hit your sector. It has a core of about fifteen Strykers of which several are of the anti-armor variety. Those units will be flagged by our drones as they come into range and our own anti-armor units will look to put them down."

"And their distance?" Chen asked.

"They're five klicks out. If you look on your tac map, they're in and around State Highway 127. The next wave of air support won't be on your position for another twenty minutes at least, so that force is going to come at you unopposed from the air. And they're moving fast."

"Copy that, Major. I reckon we'll be ready for them. The lads here have briefed me on the various trinkets you have set out for our visitors. The Reds will see it as a bit of a nasty surprise, I reckon. Fingers crossed these gadgets work as advertised."

"No need to cross your fingers, Captain. The units are solid German engineering. They'll work to their specs. Ain't no doubt about that."

"Well, a little crossing of the digits never hurt anyone, so if it's all the same to you, Major, I'll keep my fingers crossed and my ass puckered for the next little spell."

"If that's what you Aussies do, feel free to cross and pucker all you like and let me know if you need anything else in the meantime. Good luck, Captain. Landry out."

Chapter 25

East of Whiteman AFB

Lt. Colonel Sam Springer, Commanding Officer of 2nd Battalion of the 502nd Infantry Regiment of the 101st Airborne Division felt the road underneath his Stryker command vehicle buck slightly as it transitioned from the paved asphalt of Highway 50 to the uneven farmland that was the norm in this part of Missouri.

"Colonel, air tac is advising that the sky is clear for at least three hundred miles."

"Thanks, Jefferies," Springer said.

While he'd been a Lt. Colonel for six months now, he still got a charge when he heard one of his subordinates mention his rank.

Four years ago, it would have been a crazy proposition that a twenty-eight-year-old lieutenant colonel would be commanding an infantry battalion in the 101st Airborne, but that's exactly what he was doing.

He was an excellent field commander, and not just in his own mind. The testimonies of his commanding officers and his subordinates had been consistent and sterling. He was one of those rare soldiers who loved fighting and who was exceptionally good at it. So, when the call had come from the division for battalion commanders to volunteer to lead what could be the first and possibly only attack on the foreigners who had taken the nuke base in Missouri, Springer had leaped at the opportunity.

In the short time he had commanded the battalion, he had come to find that his strong opinions on politics were in good company. So it wasn't a surprise that he and his soldiers were united in outrage that their pissant neighbors to the north had seen fit to insert themselves into what was clearly an American domestic issue. To the last man, the battalion was itching to get the opportunity to pry loose the thousand or so Canadians who were now eight miles to their immediate west.

He tabbed his mic and opened a channel to the fifty-four vehicles that made up his force. "Alright, this is Jayhawk Actual. Listen up, people.

"As planned, we proceed west in four columns with designated Strykers in the lead. Everyone knows the plan. We move fast and stay in columns to reduce exposure on our front. We know they dug in some number of those self-firing guns. There are also tank traps galore, so drive smart. In five mikes, all EW units are to fire up. We hit the bastards with everything we've got, and we move fast. With enough static flowing off us, we should be able to confuse whatever toys they've set out for us. If auto units do open up, designated units will peel off and neutralize while the rest of us keep moving. We've done this before, people. Speed wins us this fight. We are mechanized, pissed off, and loaded to bear. They're infantry. It's a simple equation, so stay fast and get mean."

Springer paused. He had given considerable thought to his next words and until this moment, he hadn't been sure if he'd deliver them.

"A final thing. When we get in amongst them, no quarter is to be given. These Canadian jerk-offs are a stand-in for every other country that would like to take a shot at us while we're down. Over the next hour, we're gonna send a message – you mess with the UCSA on our turf, and you go home in a body bag. Lots of them. No mercy, people. Jayhawk Actual out."

———

Whiteman AFB

Larocque's conversations with Hall and the generals back in Ottawa had been brief. The prime minister had been with Gagnon and the other generals, and as a group, they expressed tremendous relief that they'd recovered the two weapons. He had not told them how close they had come to disaster.

As it turned out, when Hall and Wallace had made their move on Gauthier and his men, the third man – the injured one who had been in the back of the truck – had managed to trigger the software to detonate the massive bomb the separatists had wired on Whiteman. The mimicking software that Havez had installed on the hulking weapon had picked up the signal to detonate forty-two seconds after the base commander and the master sergeant had disabled the B-83.

Havez had informed Larocque of this news in an 'oh by the way' manner, but he was still trying to make sense of it all. That they had dodged death by nuclear incineration by less than a minute was something he would wrestle with for some time to come.

Larocque would also need to make sense of the conversation he had with the PM, Minister Martel, and the generals about the Hall and Wallace bomb. It had been short and had ended with Larocque informing the leader of his country and his commanding officer that he would not be changing his orders to the two young officers to dispose of the bomb. He made it clear that he was the commander on the scene and that Ottawa's time would best be used to figure out what the detonation would mean to the larger war effort.

During this conversation, his wrist unit had received a series of urgent pings from Major Landry. While he was speaking to the PM, he had temporarily disabled her ability to interject into his BAM conversations, and so she had sent him several text messages to the effect of: "URGENT – RED ATTACK STARTING SOUTH AND EAST!!"

It was shortly after that message he heard the first barrage of artillery strike the Airborne's defenses. As the exploding rounds reverberated inside his dug-in command post, Larocque politely thanked the prime minister and the generals for their support and then proceeded to advise them – as gently as he could manage - that he was letting them go. He had a battle to run.

With the bomb neutralized, he and Rydell had raced back to the Airborne's CP next to Whiteman's control tower to find Landry and several other officers calmly orchestrating several actions in front of tactical screens and tabletop maps.

The approaching Reds were now close enough that Landry had issued the order to employ the Airborne's own surveillance drones. Several were now in the air and were actively tracking the fast-moving Americans.

Larocque listened as C Company's Captain Geddes advised that the Reds' artillery had zeroed in on his company's positions along the southern end of the base and they were taking heavy fire.

Out of Halifax, Geddes was the greenest of Larocque's company commanders, having only been in the role for the past seven months. But across the BAM, the young Haligonian sounded like the professional soldier he was. Steady and determined, he worked the network pressing for a counter-fire mission from the Airborne's mortar teams.

The battalion coming out of the south had taken the brunt of CANZUK's airstrikes and attacks from the Australians' Wyverns. This element of the attacking force had steadfastly refused to veer off its chosen path. The reward for their determination was that this part of the Red onslaught had lost over half of its original strength.

Over Landry's shoulder, Larocque watched the screens that displayed the two approaching forces. To the Red's credit, they would hit the south and eastern sides of the base simultaneously. Both forces were now just two klicks out and were coming into range of the AI gun emplacements his engineers had feverishly dug in earlier in the day.

"Sir, radar has just picked up four incoming hostiles. F-16s at five thousand feet, twenty klicks out and they're coming in fast," Landry reported calmly.

"Here comes the cavalry," Larocque said nonchalantly. "Tell everyone out there to keep their heads down but to stay primed. The Reds are almost where we need them to be."

Larocque stood like a statue as he continued to peer intently at the tactical screens, watching the approaching forces move all too slowly into the preset kill zone.

"Sir, we have nine missiles inbound."

"Perfect timing. It's like these bastards have done this before. Confirm air defense is on them."

Larocque heard the crack and rumble of artillery rounds hitting somewhere close to his command bunker. Someone on the other side had an idea of where his headquarters was located, he surmised.

"Air defense has engaged," Landry said, and then without taking her eyes from the display, she added, "Seven hostiles are still incoming. Get ready in eight, seven, six..."

Larocque removed his eyes from the two tactical displays and moved deliberately to activate the BAM channel he had preset to kick off the Airborne's ambush.

As Landry calmly completed her countdown of the incoming air-to-ground missiles, Larocque gave the order for the eastern and southern sectors of their defense to unleash hell.

————

Due to a titan-like effort on the part of the Airborne's infantry and combat engineers, the Canadians had built a network of solidly built trenches, bunkers, and tank traps that extended as far as seven hundred meters out from the base's eastern perimeter. The result was a well-coordinated kill box that would allow Chen's company to efficiently maximize its firepower. Including the sixty Diggers he had brought with him, Brazeau's now-reinforced company had nearly three hundred soldiers.

The earthworks they occupied had been set out in a series of convex trenchworks so that the concealed paratroopers would be able to offer withering fire in broad arcs allowing each position to cover off the flanks of their mates in other trenches.

Should it become necessary, these same soldiers could retreat to a set of interim trenches that had been built between the outer ring of defenses and the Airborne's last stand position in and amongst the network of nuclear bunkers just east of Whiteman's airfield.

It was in one of these outermost trenches where Chen and Warrant Officer Kalina, his own company's senior NCO, were holed up with ten French Canadian paratroopers including the sergeant who had been acting as his liaison and translator. All had taken refuge under a sandbagged overhang so that no one would get clipped by the mortar and artillery rounds that had been peppering their positions for the past ten minutes.

Several drone streams were available and were tracking the two approaching enemy forces. On his own tac pad, Chen watched the larger of the two units as it bore down on his newly inherited company from the east. It had broken into four neat columns across a two-kilometer front. Looking at the leading edge of the most advanced column, he knew it wouldn't be long now.

And then the word came – from Larocque himself – "Execute, execute, execute" the colonel said in a clear, but urgent tone via BAM earbud in Chen's ear.

With a company-wide channel ready to go, Chen promptly reminded the men of his company to hold firm. The plan was to give the Airborne's anti-tank teams time to get out from undercover and fire their first salvo at the approaching enemy force. It was only after this delay that his men would reveal themselves and open up with their own collection of heavy weapons.

Like caged thoroughbreds in the moments before a race, the men in his trench sat tight as new sounds invaded the air around them. From the entrance of the overhang, Chen heard the sound of numerous sub-sonic engines of anti-tank weapons igniting to roar forward to designated targets.

Somewhere to the front of their position, he then heard the sharp staccato of large-caliber weapons as the Canadian's hidden self-firing gun emplacements opened up on the approaching vehicles. Finally, and superseding all other sounds, Chen heard a series of thunderclaps. The noise was god-like and amplified as the walls of his trench reverberated from the concussive force of the nearby blasts. Airstrikes, to be sure, he thought, but based on what Landry had advised moments ago, they weren't courtesy of any CANZUK fighter plane.

Chen glanced at his watch. Sixty seconds were up. It had seemed an eternity. Through his BAM, he gave the order for A Company to emerge from their positions and add their firepower to the maelstrom that had been set upon the approaching Red Faction battalion.

Chen watched as the determined-looking paratroopers in his trench bolted out from the safety of the overhang to position themselves and their weapons into the preset firing positions they had built on the lip of their trench. Following them out, he did not look west in the direction of the approaching enemy force but instead back toward the airbase where he had heard and felt the impact of the powerful explosions.

From his position, a thick line of trees intersected his sightline of Whiteman proper. Nevertheless, he took in multiple columns of grey and black smoke rising into the air. Scanning the horizon, his eyes snapped to that part of the base that had once held the air traffic control tower. Through the turned-up grit and haze, he could see that the structure was no longer standing. Chen knew Larocque wouldn't have been in the tower but wondered if the man's nearby command post wouldn't have been struck by at least some of the debris from the falling structure.

As he took in the troubling scene, he realized there was nothing to be done for it. His only concern for the moment was to guide the soldiers of A Company and their efforts to stop the approaching Americans.

Pivoting to the front of the trench, Chen took in what could only be described as a spectacular buffet of war. The Airborne's anti-tank weapons and hidden gun emplacements had wreaked havoc on the American battalion's fighting vehicles. As heavy-caliber rounds zipped and cracked in the air around him, he focused in on the half dozen or so burning vehicles that lay to the front of his company's line of defense.

His eyes were drawn to a single Stryker that had just started to cook off. Even with all of the gunfire, the vehicle was close enough that Chen could faintly hear the desperate screams of the soldiers who were trying to escape the steel hulk's smoking body.

As the surviving soldiers hurriedly extricated themselves from the rear of the armored machine, he watched as a nearby C-6 heavy machine gun began to tear into the exposed soldiers. It was a short and brutal affair as hundreds of 7.62mm rounds cut into the men.

Tearing his eyes away from the carnage, Chen launched himself into the task of coordinating his part of the battle. Leaping onto the BAM network he had set up for his company, he moved between the voices of various officers and senior NCOs and multiple drone streams on his tactical pad to orchestrate the further destruction of the faltering Red battalion.

————

East of Whiteman AFB

At some point in their mad dash toward the Canadian front lines, Lt. Colonel Springer had moved from his workstation in the belly of his Stryker to the top side hatch that had been set aside for him to observe the assault firsthand.

In one of the middle columns and several vehicles back from lead elements of the battalion's charge, Springer both watched and listened to his soldiers and their vehicles as they ground forward under a withering barrage of heavy-caliber machine gun fire and anti-armor strikes. Based on the latest sit-rep from one of his junior operations officers below, a third of the battalion's vehicles were no longer in the fight. But at less than one mile out, they were where they needed to be.

Directing his attention forward, Springer braced himself as his armored command vehicle bucked wildly as it negotiated an un-usually deep irrigation ditch. "For Christ's sake, Riley, slow us down a touch for the next one. Like hell are we going to miss this fight because of your shit driving."

Springer had yelled the order in the direction of the open hatch directly in front of him. Riley, a still-young corporal who had fought in countless battles against the Blues over the course of the civil war, thrust one of his gloved hands in the air and gave a thumbs up.

Just as the ample suspension of their Stryker began to smooth out their ride, he caught movement low on the horizon to the north. At two o'clock and at maybe two thousand meters out, he took in three objects hovering over a thick copse of trees. Springer toggled on his mic, "All units, I have three hostiles – tactical drones, forty-five degrees off our vector of attack. Column Delta, get on these bastards ASAP!"

Over the thumping of machine-gun fire and the strained whine of his vehicle's diesel engine, Springer took in the ejection of anti-armor missiles by the three floating platforms. As the missiles ignited, the three units dropped behind the trees.

"Incoming anti-armor," Springer growled into his mic. "Multiple hostiles coming at us from the northwest."

As he looked to gauge the trajectory of the subsonic munitions, he felt the APC jerk underneath him as the thirty-ton machine turned sharply to the right and picked up speed. "Riley, what the hell?"

Specialist Riley didn't give an answer. Ahead, at perhaps three hundred meters, Springer eyed a small creek that already had a pair of destroyed civilian trucks within it. The corporal, a wily driver who was well aware he was carrying the battalion's CO, hammered the eight-wheeled vehicle's accelerator and drove hell-bent toward the depression.

As his Stryker barrelled forward, Springer caught two of the sub-sonic objects knifing through the sky in his direction. Son of a bitch, he thought. There were twenty other vehicles in the general vicinity of his machine, yet here he was staring down two of the fast-moving projectiles. That was just dumb luck.

Pulling his eyes from the horizon, he looked in the direction of the coursing brown water of the creek and wondered if the difference in elevation would offer the protection that Specialist Riley thought it would. In the end, he would never get to find out. At twenty meters out from the creek's edge, the first of the drone-launched missiles lanced into the top of Springer's Stryker, punching a hole through the top of the vehicle's armor. In that instant, the still new CO of 2nd Battalion of the 502nd Infantry Regiment saw and felt the crimson terror of the anti-tank missile as it tore through him and the veteran soldiers that made up the core of his command team.

———

Ottawa, NDHQ

There were no words to describe the sense of relief that Merielle had felt when she had heard Larocque's words that the two bombs were in the Airborne's possession.

Despite protests from the generals, Larocque had brooked no arguments with the plan the two young Canadian officers had come up with to unload the weapon they had come to possess.

After the Airborne commander had dropped the call, the prime minister had taken charge of the conversation and had assured the military not to worry about the political impacts that would surely come when the weapon detonated. The PM had been right in his assessment. Whatever the consequences of one bomb going off in rural Missouri, this outcome paled to what could have happened if the separatists' plan had worked.

MacDonald had sent Merielle away to brief their CANZUK allies of the development in detail and to wait to see if Josee Labelle called back.

The separatist and now-terrorist had committed to calling Merielle ten minutes before her two-hour deadline. That time had arrived and so she had enclosed herself in an empty office down the hall from the boardroom where she would brief CANZUK's political working group on the latest surreal developments.

As though on cue, Merielle's phone rang. "Allo," she said.

"You were warned, Minister, not to try and tamper with the weapons. We made this so very clear to you in any number of ways. It is you and your government who will wear the disaster that is about to unfold. Quebecers will not stand for it," Labelle said. The woman's voice was like steel.

Merielle smiled triumphantly. The woman did not know.

She recalled from Larocque's update that the third treasonous Quebec soldier had managed to trigger the massive bomb they had wired and left at Whiteman, but that the detonation instruction had come late. Whatever software the separatists had been using, it had informed Labelle that the detonation order had been given, but without actually being in Missouri there would be no way for her to confirm the massive weapon had actually gone off.

This time, it was Merielle who would hold the advantage in the conversation.

"I am relieved to inform you, Ms. Labelle, that the weapon at Whiteman Air Force Base did not detonate. Canadian soldiers were able to disarm it and it is now harmless. I am also pleased to inform you that we eliminated the separatist cell that absconded with the second weapon but that we've not been able to disarm it. As we speak, we are looking to dispose of it as safely as can be managed."

Hearing only silence, Merielle continued.

"If you are wondering why you haven't heard from Lieutenant Gauthier, it is because he is dead, as are the other three soldiers who were in league with him.

"Ms. Labelle, it is now my turn to be very clear. You have one chance and one chance only to put yourself in a situation where you do not spend the rest of your life in jail."

After another brief pause, Merielle offered, "I implore you, Josee – listen to my proposal. I can help you if you let me."

Curtly, the other woman said, "I am tired of your government's lies. The people of Quebec are tired of being lied to, of being manipulated, and most of all, they are sick to death of sell-outs like you, Marielle Martel. Politicians who are willing to sell their soul and their country, for the trappings of power and the privilege of doing the bidding of their English-speaking masters. Can you not see that Quebec is dying, Minister?"

Raising her voice several decibels, Labelle continued. "No, I will not listen to any proposal you might have. What you have told me may be true, and if it is, I wish you luck as you try to explain to your allies and the rest of the world why the Canadian military is setting off nuclear weapons in the United States. We will use this to our advantage. We are many, Ms. Martel, and we are determined. I can tell you for certain that Quebec will not stand for what you have done. So take whatever your proposal is and shove it up your Anglo prime minister's ass."

"Josee, listen to me, please. If that weapon goes off, we will not let this go. We will hunt you down and every last person in your movement. We will ruin as many lives as it takes. But if you make the right choice now, I can promise you it doesn't have to be that way. Give me the code to neutralize that weapon and it gives the prime minister room to maneuver. You can still have a future if you help us. Please, Josee," Merielle pleaded.

The other woman's response was both immediate and righteous. "The separatist movement is bigger than me, Minister, and it always will be. I suffer terribly every day that Quebec ingratiates itself to the likes of you and the government you represent. Our movement is tired of it, as are Quebecers. What you think you might be able to do to me is no worse than the suffering I already endure. Do your worst."

The connection went dead.

Without a moment's hesitation, Merielle pulled her phone from her ear and proceeded to tap out a message to General Gagnon. "No deal. Dispose of the package."

———

Missouri, west of St. Louis

This President Cameron fellow had grossly miscalculated how the leaders of Major Li's country would react to the UCSA's misuse of China's premier fighter jet. The state-of-the-art machines had been provided as part of a secret deal.

The Chinese would provide the planes for the purpose of helping the Red Americans win their war against the Blues and for no other purpose. In return, China was to be given a free hand in the

Pacific to take the Philippines. The Americans, despite their costly and stupid war, still had a sizeable navy, and if the country reunited whatever its form, its carrier groups and submarines would make up the balance of power in the South China Sea. The fighter jet deal had negated this possibility.

As it had been described to him, it had been one thing for Cameron to use the J-31s to pressure Missouri, it had been another thing altogether to steal the fighters to take on CANZUK. The intelligence the Royal Air Force would glean from fighting the J-31s here in North America would be invaluable when China made its move in the Pacific.

Indeed, the Royal Navy wasn't the force it once was, but when you added its firepower to Britain's ability to lead whatever alliance would confront his country's ambitions, the UCSA leader had gone too far. Cameron had put China's long-term strategy at risk for his own short-term gain.

Worse still, the arrogant American had gravely insulted the senior leaders of the CCP. China's president had leveraged considerable political capital in sending the J-31s. That Cameron had so cavalierly dismissed the old man's personal entreaty to ground the 6th gen fighters was not something the CPP elite would ever forgive or forget.

And so, here he was in rural Missouri. In the 21st Century, China's reach could be immediate just as it could also be long. Very long.

The drive from Chicago to just west of St. Louis had been uneventful. During the early morning journey, China's intelligence service had acquitted itself brilliantly. They had encountered two checkpoints – one in Illinois and one in Missouri, and on both occasions, the two vans that made up Li's team had been waved forward following a short conversation between the intel officer, Ren and the individuals manning the checkpoints.

Once again money, this time in the form of untraceable cryptocurrency, had paved the way for them to reach their destination.

Li now watched as his men efficiently worked to set up their equipment. In the presence of a waning moon, the team undertook their tasks with the assistance of red headlamps.

South of Interstate 70 and about a hundred kilometers west of St. Louis, this remote part of Missouri was thick with old-growth forest and sparse of people. When dawn arrived in a few hours, Li was confident he would be treated to a spectacular display of greenery, but at the moment, all he could see was a multitude of dark spires that contrasted sharply with the star-filled mosaic that was the early morning sky.

As he took in the scene, his ears picked up the faint sound of what experience told him was a jet breaking the sound barrier. A good sign, he thought. They were close.

Reminded of why they were here, Li turned his eyes back to the two vans and the darting red lights bobbing to and fro in the Missouri darkness. In the short time that his men had to practice, their fastest time to set up the fifty-meter-tall apparatus had been twenty-seven minutes.

To consider the team's work a job well done, he would allow them an extra three minutes. As a pragmatist, Li understood that you did not fly from Beijing to the central United States in under twenty hours and then drive across hostile territory for another five without seeing some decline in performance.

So it would be in thirty or less minutes that Archie Cameron would find out just how poor a decision it was to disregard the wishes of his country.

The twenty-first century was and would continue to be China's century. Cameron and his hubris had chosen to ignore this reality at the expense of his pilots and perhaps this little war his country was fighting.

Chapter 26

Missouri, east of Kansas City

The faint sound of fighting coming from the direction of Whiteman had begun to die down. Hall pulled her eyes from the darkening sky that lay in that direction and looked at her BAM wrist unit. They had sixteen minutes. If they hadn't heard from Ottawa at the twelve-minute mark, they would move forward as planned.

She looked at Wallace casually leaning against the side of the truck that held the still-active nuclear weapon. He had on goggles and was using them to control their remaining surveillance drone as it kept an eye on the entrance to the quarry they had broken into. When they cut through the lock to get into the property, they hadn't noted any obvious security features, but that didn't mean they weren't there.

The near-AI voice in her earbud came alive. "Priority call from Rider Eight."

"Accept the call," said Hall.

Colonel Azim's voice spilled into her earbud. "Tiller One, you are a go. Dump the package and get the hell outta there double-time. Great work by the both of you. Everyone back here thinks so, too. From the big boss all the way down. Once you make the drop, make your way back to your starting point at best speed. I'll make sure our folks know you're coming. Move fast and be safe. Rider Eight out."

Hall pursed her lips and issued a sharp whistle in the direction of Wallace and in that instant, he pulled off the goggles and locked eyes with her.

"We're good to go," Hall said.

"Finally!"

Quickly, Wallace made his way to the truck's cab and hopped into the driver's seat. The truck was about forty meters back from the edge of the quarry pool. Putting the truck into drive, Wallace stepped on the accelerator. Ten meters out from the water, he opened the vehicle's door and at speed, leaped to the gravel-covered surface, rolled several times and stopped just a few feet away from the water's edge.

In the dim light of the evening, Hall watched the truck hit the orange-and-pink dappled surface of the pool and send up a plume of water. Within a minute, the pickup and its cargo had disappeared underneath the now-rippling water.

Seeing Wallace get up and begin to brush off his clothes, she turned and walked back to their car. They had fourteen minutes to put as much distance between themselves and the now sub-surface weapon that would devastate the land surrounding this part of the United States.

On Wallace's tac pad, they had consulted the available commercial imagery to get a feel for the area that would soon become ground zero. They had identified a farm operation about eight hundred meters northwest and a good-sized upscale neighborhood just under two klicks northeast. The depth of the pool was their best hope to dull the edge of what they had found out was a sixty-kiloton weapon. In all likelihood, dozens or perhaps a few hundred unsuspecting civilians would die. They agreed there was no help for it. War always had consequences you did not like. For Hall and Wallace both, it was just one more thing the separatists would have to pay for.

———

Whiteman AFB

Larocque was sitting at his kitchen table back in their modest home in Chalk River. His eyes drawn upwards, he was staring at the ceiling fan he had installed in the recent past. Rotating at its medium speed, he could feel the warm air as it swam over his upturned face. He recalled the thing had been a horrendous bitch to install.

"Jack," he heard a woman's voice. It was Madison. His wife's voice always sounded as though she was straining to speak. It gave the impression she was permanently two beats away from having a good cry.

"We're down here," she said.

Larocque's gaze left the ceiling and he looked straight ahead. He took in that his arms were outstretched at forty-five-degree angles and that each of his calloused hands was holding one of the smaller, softer hands of the two women sitting across from him.

Madison was to his left. To his great relief, she did not look worn. Instead, her brown eyes were warm and inviting and her Mediterranean skin glowed as though she had just spent the better part of summer sunning herself on some quiet beach.

"My love," said Larocque.

She smiled and not saying a word, her head turned slightly to her left to look at the third person sitting at the table. For an instant, Larocque resisted moving his eyes in that direction, but only for an instant.

The pain that lurked in that direction would not dissuade him. She was too important.

At sixteen, the young woman's bloom was well on its way to beautiful. She had the brown hair of her mother, but the cold-water blue eyes of her father. No one had been sure where the healthy dose of freckles had come from, but their presence allowed her face to take on elements of mystery and mischief.

"Baby," said Larocque as tears began to gather in his eyes. "I miss you so much. Your daddy loves you."

"I know you do, daddy. I love you too."

He squeezed both of their hands tightly, and for several minutes, no one said a word. The windows to the kitchen were open and together they listened to a robin trill over the gentle hum of the ceiling fan that hung above them.

Lauren broke the silence. "Daddy, I want you to know I'm proud of you. I know you can't go back in time to fix things, but I know that you tried your best. You always try your best. We love that about you. You might not have the words, but you never give up, no matter how bad things get. You need to wake up, Daddy. Your soldiers still need you."

"And what about you, baby? I can't fight for you anymore," whispered Larocque.

"I know it's hard." Her voice sounding more mature and woman-like than Larocque remembered. "There are some things we can't explain and some things we can't change. I need you to fight. The men and women who look up to you, need you to fight. Get up, daddy. Make us proud."

"I will, baby. I will for you and for your mother. God, I miss you two."

"I miss you too. We'll see each other soon. I love you..."

Larocque's eyes fluttered open. For a brief moment, everything was a haze. Something in his brain began to shout at him to breathe and then as if needing to consciously oversee the practice of taking oxygen into his lungs, he gasped desperately.

As seconds passed and he collected himself, he perceived a sharp pain on the right side of his chest that seemed to flare with intensity each time his chest expanded.

"Christ on a fucking cross," he groaned as he made to remove the oxygen mask covering his mouth.

After several unsuccessful attempts to breathe deeply, Larocque gingerly removed the army-green wool blanket that covered him, and then with an effort, he tightened his torso and slowly raised his shirtless upper body off the gym mat he had been lying on. As he looked around, his mind slowly recognized the one-doc field hospital they had set up in a small movie theatre a hundred meters or so from the Regiment's command post. A dozen feet away, he took in Major Kiraly, the surgeon who had jumped in with Airborne, and his small medical team as they worked frantically on a soldier who was lying atop a standard eight-foot banquet table that was now performing the role of surgical platform.

From the angle where he was sitting, Larocque could see the doctor's forearms were covered in fresh blood. That the surgical team was working in the middle of the stage and were bathed in the theatre's overhanging lights gave the scene an intense, dream-like quality that made him wonder if he had unknowingly transitioned into some other stream of unconsciousness.

"Sir..."

Larocque heard a male voice to his immediate right. With pain receptors firing on all cylinders, he forced himself to turn in the direction of the voice. He recognized the face as one of the Airborne's medics and visually registered the man's name from his uniform.

While Larocque was still sitting on the stage not far from the surgical team, the medic was standing below him on the theatre's floor. In seats behind him, there were several soldiers in the first two rows of reclining seats who were laid out. While most had their eyes closed, a few had picked up that Larocque was now in the seated position. As his eyes met theirs, smiles crept on to each of their exhausted and pained faces.

"Corporal Bedard, good to see you. Any chance you have a minute to read me into why I'm here and what the hell is going on?"

"Great to see you up and at it, sir," Bedard said. "Long story short, your CP was hit, as was the air traffic control tower. A part of the structure came down on your bunker."

"Shit," Larocque said. "A double whammy. What were the chances of that happening?"

"Slim to none I would guess, but that's what happened. A bad bit of luck, sir. Half of the command post collapsed, and you and several others were crushed under the debris. It took them almost forty minutes to dig you out. The doc says it's a miracle you were able to get enough air into your lungs to allow you to survive that long. When they got to you, your body was in the process of shutting down. Doc also says you have two broken ribs. If you did wake up - which you have - I'm supposed to wrap you. How are you feeling?"

"Like you'd expect. It hurts to breathe. Did the doc give me pain meds?

"He did," said the medic. "If you're feeling groggy, that would be one reason why. It's also one of the reasons you might have been out for so long. He dosed you pretty good."

Larocque's mind raced back to the moments before everything went black. "Major Landry. I was standing right behind her. Is she okay?"

Based on the look on the other man's face, Larocque knew the answer before he opened his mouth. "She's gone, sir," the corporal said quietly.

"How many others?" Larocque asked urgently.

"Including the Major, four in total. I'm sorry, Colonel."

For a moment, Larocque didn't say anything. His eyes stared past the medic.

The words 'fight' and 'proud' echoed somewhere in the far reaches of his mind. His eyes once again connected with the other man. "Who's in command?"

"Colonel Rydell. He gave the doc orders to ring him if you came to, but as you can see, he's kinda busy."

"Let's not bother the good doctor. Did they save any of my gear?"

"I think we'd better wait for Major Kiraly before you start moving around, sir. You took a pretty serious knock. He'll want to assess you to see what other injuries you might have. And there's also the concern of brain function. You went with a limited amount of oxygen for a long time. Chances are good you'll be foggy for the next several hours, if not days."

"That's a negative, Corporal. My brain and the rest of me feel fine. Let's get me wrapped and then I need to find some caffeine. Two or three back-to-back strong coffees is what I need now more than the say-so of the good doctor. He's busy enough."

Larocque edged his way to the end of the stage and then, as slowly as he could, lowered his legs to the ground. The movement brought with it an astonishing amount of pain in the right side of his diaphragm. He mumbled a string of curses through his clenched jaw as his feet hit the theatre's now-filthy floor. Standing, he took several deep breaths and then turned to face the medic.

"Show me to my gear and help me get these ribs wrapped. As long as I can stand and breathe, nothing and no one is keeping me out of this fight. And that's an order, Corporal."

———

Northern Missouri

The gun from Costen's Challenger 3 main battle tank barked for the fifth time in as many minutes. At nearly fifteen hundred meters downrange, one of the American's ancient Humvees momentarily disappeared in a sphere of black smoke and dust. As he took in the scene through the commander's sight, he could hear the air around him tear as bullets of various calibers thunked into and past his tank's turret.

Head exposed, Costen sat in the commander's position of the tank and watched the scene unfold on the north side of the bridge that was being held by a hard-pressed company of soldiers from the British Parachute Regiment. The remaining Paras still held the bridge, but just.

The Missouri National Guard and other paramilitary forces had poured out of Kansas City hours earlier and had laid into both sides of the span with everything in the State's limited arsenal.

With ammunition low and a growing number of dead and wounded, the Para's on-the-scene commander had advised Costen they would wait only until the arrival of darkness before making a mad dash across the two-hundred-meter span to consolidate his forces on the more defensible southern end of the structure.

On hearing that assessment, Costen had urged the Para CO to hold on. If the Para's did retreat and the Reds were allowed to assume their defensive positions, it was an absolute certainty his battlegroup wouldn't make it to make Whiteman in time.

Understanding what needed to be done, Costen himself had seconded two platoons of armor from his battlegroup and in a race against the setting sun had sprinted south only to find that the Missouri National Guard had heard of their coming and had shifted itself to welcome Costen's too-small force.

A short-twenty minutes later, Costen and his soldiers had given a clinic on what a well armored and tightly commanded force could achieve in the face of a larger less competent force.

To his left, he took in the three Challengers that had just joined his own tank to form the centerpiece of a larger line of attack that would allow them to launch what he hoped would be a final charge on the Missourians.

Costen keyed his tank's mic. "Right then. Best, we finish this before more of those bloody lorries show themselves. All units, advance on my pace. We'll move in two hundred meter blocks. All weapons are free. Engage at will and give'em hell. Costen out."

The moment he gave the order, his tank's operator, one Sergeant Simms, began to pour fire from the pintle mounted 7.62mm general purpose machine gun at his station in the turret.

The sun having just set, Costen watched as the GPMG's tracer rounds blazed red and orange as they struck or ricocheted off the Simms' intended targets. As the other Challengers, Ajax and Boxer armored fighting vehicles performed similar feats, the air in front of their line of advance seemed to come alive with a swarm of fast-moving demonic fairies. It was a fearsome and glorious sight.

As Costen shifted his position to look through the commander's targeting sight to flag another vehicle for destruction, he caught an intense flash out of the corner of his eye. Instantly, the landscape around them lit up as though it was mid-day. Quickly rising out of his seat, he rotated to better take in the glowing colossus that had erupted on the southern horizon.

"My Christ," Costen said aloud.

Without Costen's prompting, his tank's driver brought their vehicle to a halt just as Simms had unilaterally stopped firing rounds downrange. In fact, all firing had stopped. As one, Costen's vanguard of fighting vehicles and the soldiers they had been laying into, turned south to collectively take in the awesome scene. In all of its roiled crimson and orange glory, before them on the horizon stood a massive and still-growing mushroom cloud.

The name 'Whiteman' screamed somewhere in his sub-conscience. Snapping out of his trance, Costen quickly oriented his position with that of the explosion and where he thought the American airbase was located. With a huge sense of relief, he was able to assure himself that the explosion was some distance to the west of their ultimate destination.

In that same moment, he heard the crack and rumble of the nuclear explosion as it reached them. As he took in the ominous sound, a gentle rush of heated air washed over him. Quickly,

Costen did the math and estimated that the detonation was maybe forty klicks from their position. Fallout, he knew, would be a serious and immediate concern of his soldiers, but there was no sense getting worked up about it until they had received word from whatever meteorological services CANZUK put on the problem. No, their immediate problem was getting to the north side Paras and securing that bloody bridge. Radiation be damned at least for the moment.

Costen clicked his mic and opened a channel to the armored vehicles that had stopped and aligned themselves to his left and right. "Listen closely lads and ladies, I want all eyes front. The Toms still need us and nuclear explosions or not, we're securing that bridge on the double. That little campfire you're all watching is some distance west of where we need to be, so let's be the professionals we are and get a move on. We fight and we win right now people."

Costen waited a moment for some type of reply or protest, but no questions nor griping came through the static. That was satisfying. His soldiers were a tough lot and if they didn't understand the stakes before, they would now.

"Advance the remaining distance to the enemy's line of attack and engage all targets. Now's the time to give it to them - the Yanks will be thunderstruck, or you can call me a right bastard. Let's bloody move, people! Costen out."

He watched as Simms swiveled his machine gun, took aim, and opened up with a long burst of fire that tore through the surreal quiet that had enveloped the battlefield. As the other vehicles opened up, Costen's seventy-ton Challenger began to growl forward in the direction of their waiting enemy.

————

San Antonio, 5th Army HQ

Spector vigorously rubbed his face with his meaty hands. It was just after two in the morning, and he was well past the point of exhaustion. Had it not been for a steady stream of coffees, he would have been about as useful as a warmed-over corpse.

To his surprise or dismay – he hadn't been able to figure out which, the man on the display in front of him seemed as fresh as a daisy.

"Why don't we move onto the events that necessitated this call, General?" commanded the UCSA President. "As you can understand, I'm anxious to get news about the latest developments."

"What do you want first? The assault on the base or the detonation?" Spector asked.

"Why don't we start with the detonation, shall we? It's not every day a nuclear bomb goes off unexpectedly in your backyard."

"That's the truth of it," Spector said. "We don't have a lot of detail on the why or how. What we do know is what and where. In a remote area about forty miles west of Whiteman a sixty-kiloton nuke – likely a B-61 gravity bomb – was detonated.

"Based on the location, flyover images, and seismic data, someone, for some reason unknown to us, placed the bomb into a quarry pool that we estimate was about fifteen meters deep. Apparently, the pool served as a barrel of sorts and channeled more of the weapon's energy upwards into the atmosphere than would have otherwise been the case. The result was that the blast radius was reduced, while more debris was hurled skyward."

"Interesting," Cameron interjected. "And what does that mean for the good people of Missouri and the rest of the country?"

"Well, the subsurface nature of the detonation means that only those people within a seven-hundred-meter radius would have been hurt or killed. As I said, it was a pretty remote area, so it can't mean more than a few dozen people."

"Well, that's something," said Cameron.

"It is, but it's the fallout that's the bigger problem. At the time of the detonation, the wind was blowing west and north. So, parts of southern Kansas City have been hit and Topeka is in the direct path of the cloud. For both locations, it will be like a radioactive crop duster hit them. The southern part of KC and all of Topeka will need to be emptied out."

"So it's bedlam, then?" asked Cameron.

The question annoyed Spector, but the tired Texan didn't let it show. "Not quite bedlam, Mr. President. We're taking steps to get people moving in the right direction and with the appropriate amount of speed. Thankfully, we're only talking about a few hundred thousand people that need to move, not millions. Still, it's going to make our efforts to retake Whiteman more difficult than was already the case. But in a way, it also helps us."

"Oh, and how's that?" asked Cameron.

"The exodus of people leaving Kansas City is going to delay those CANZUK forces in Kansas still moving in the direction of the base. The roads out that way will be jammed up over the next twenty-four hours at least. Now these CANZUK bastards don't have to use the roads, but when they don't it slows them up considerably. And they'll have to deal with the fallout just as we will."

"And what does that mean for our forces coming out of St. Louis? I believe the understanding we had was that the base would be in our possession by sundown this evening at the latest. From where I stand, General, this nuke going off doesn't change a thing. In fact, I would suggest to you that it means we need to move faster."

Spector held up both of his hands in the universal sign for 'hold on.'

"Getting our forces from St. Louis to Whiteman won't be a problem. We've already put out the word on public radio and contacted the right people on the ground to advise anyone who's planning to leave KC to head in the direction of Wichita or Tulsa in the southwest. Our forces west of St. Louis will be ready to move come morning - that I can guarantee. And assuming we can continue to outperform in the air, our lead elements should reach Whiteman by noon."

Seemingly satisfied with Spector's reply, Cameron returned to the matter of the detonation. "So, what's your speculation as to why this thing was set off? The best my people can come up with is that it was a warning from the Canadians that we shouldn't try to take the base again. My understanding is that the weapon detonated about the same time our Versailles force was attacking. That's quite the coincidence, is it not?"

"That's as good a theory as I've heard, though I would add it's an unsatisfying one because we've not heard from CANZUK with any message or statement confirming that is, in fact, what happened. Why leave it to us to try and figure it out? I mean for Christ's sake, who purposely sets off a nuclear weapon and says nothing about it?"

"Indeed," said Cameron. "It was the best guess of half a dozen half-baked ideas that were put to me. Your people are stymied as well?"

"We haven't given it a lot of thought, actually. It happened and we've adjusted our plans accordingly. Our priority is getting to that base. In the absence of a message from CANZUK confirming what the hell is going on, I'm happy to let your people do all the thinking on this, Mr. President"

An annoyed look dropped onto Cameron's face. "Well, that's mighty pragmatic of you. As you continue to fight this little war of ours, should you come across any better reasons as to why nuclear weapons are being set off unexpectedly, be sure to pass that information along to *my people* and we'll see what we can do."

Spector ignored the man's sarcasm. Even tired, he had a well of patience when it came to the leader of the UCSA. For all of his faults, and there were many, he continued to think that Cameron remained useful to the overall war effort. "Perhaps we should discuss last night's assault on Whiteman?"

"Why don't we, General," said Cameron. "Rumor has it our boys were chewed up pretty bad. And, I understand that one of the units we sent forward was led by the son of Wally Springer, one of our more committed senators out of Georgia. I think you may know him."

"I do know the Senator. He's a good man."

"Wonderful. Then you'll be better able to help me explain why we thought it was a good idea to send the good Senator's son, of all people, to his death last night. It was not our best performance, or so I'm told. Did Lt. Colonel Springer even have a chance?"

It was an outrageous statement, Spector thought. If there was a living example of the idiom 'sly like a fox', it applied to the man he was looking at on the display in front of him. While he could ignore Cameron's prickliness, Spector wouldn't allow the man to get away with a re-casting of history. He was a patient man, not a spineless one.

"Mr. President, you'll recall from our most recent conversation that I had mentioned that the troops at Whiteman had dug in hard and had a certain pedigree. Well, as of last night, we found out just how tough this Airborne outfit is."

On the display, Cameron waved his hand dismissively. "Save it, Mitch. I remember our conversation, and I recall very specifically that it was you who made the final decision to send forward those troops. Those are the facts, but let's cut to the chase. Where do things stand at the moment?"

The two men held each other's gaze, but it was Spector who elected to break away from the stand-off. He had made his point.

"The bottom line is that while we lost eighty percent of two frontline battalions and the Senator's son, the fight was not in vain. In fact, the tragedy that is the Senator's loss is the reason I'm now confident about tomorrow.

"Is that so? I'm glad to hear that, General. Do tell me what has your confidence brimming, because after this most recent performance, I could use a bit of a pick-me-up," Cameron drolled.

"Based on the intelligence we were able to gain from last evening's attack, we now know precisely where the Canadians have positioned their defenses. Tomorrow, when our forces arrive, we know exactly what they're going up against, and knowing what I know of the two brigades that are forming up on the west side of St. Louis, well-trained paratroopers or not, the Canadians aren't going to be able to prevent us from rolling up onto that base. You can tell the good senator his son's sacrifice will have saved hundreds of lives tomorrow. As legacies go, that's not a bad one."

"And what about the CANZUK forces coming out of the north?" asked Cameron. "I'm told they're in possession of two bridges crossing the Missouri. By my calculation, they're one hundred miles out from Whiteman, while our forces in St. Louis are over two hundred. It would appear the math isn't in our favor."

Spector grimaced openly. That the two brigdes in question were not in their hands was no small problem. "The British battlegroups are strung out to the north. It's going to take them several more hours to consolidate enough firepower on the south side of those bridges. It'll be too little and too late. But just to be on the safe side, we'll be hitting those two spans in the next hour."

"So you're confident, then?" Cameron asked.

"Confident of what?"

"Oh, don't be a obtuse, man. Are you confident you're going to take the Whiteman or not?"

Though he had seen the question coming, Spector hesitated with his response. If they weren't successful tomorrow, it wouldn't matter what words came out of his mouth. Whatever he said in the next few seconds, Cameron would use his words however he pleased. His staff and commanders had done one hell of a job to put all of their forces in the right places. They should win, but war by its very nature was unpredictable.

Deep inside of Spector, the professional soldier was screaming at him to hedge his words, but as a Texan and a lifelong risk-taker, he knew the cards he now held were a winning hand. Exhausted or not, he had to continue to work the odds in their favor – both on the battlefield and off. Cameron was not the only wily person taking part in this conversation. The Joint Cheifs' fate had been instructive and had driven home for Spector that long-held plans to protect his interests and those of his new country would need to be accelerated.

"I'm confident, Mr. President. One way or the other, we're going to take back that base by the deadline we've discussed."

"I'm so glad to hear that," Cameron said after a brief pause. "Because if we don't take back that base by the end of the day today, it's not my leadership or legacy that will be questioned. This enterprise that we're both committed to needs me more than it does you, General. We both know that. I cannot and will not suffer from the taint of another failure. There is too much at stake. You understand that, don't you?"

Spector did not pause in offering his reply because to do so, would give the man on the screen in front of him reason to doubt him. Offering even a whiff of disloyalty at this critical moment would only lead to ruin for the UCSA, never mind what it would mean for himself.

"I understand perfectly, Mr. President. I am and will always be your man."

Chapter 27

Ottawa, Somewhere Downtown

Merielle had been barely able to keep her eyes open as she received her final briefing from the generals. To say that the events of that evening were tumultuous was an understatement that had no parallel in Canada's history.

Via drone footage, she had watched the detonation of the nuclear weapon the two Canadian agents had dumped in the quarry. In high-definition, she watched the instant creation of a fifty-thousand-foot-high mushroom cloud, the energy from its explosion lighting up the surrounding countryside as though it was high noon. In less than twenty minutes, footage of the explosion was playing out on the net. There would be no comment from the Canadian government and CANZUK on the blast until the morning.

Following the disaster of the nuke detonation had been the general's debrief of the assault on Whiteman. Using tactical displays to showcase the Reds' two-pronged attack and raw footage from various soldiers' body cams, Merielle had received both a strategic and up-close overview of the battle. She had preferred the former. The images of the burning vehicles and dead American soldiers had almost been too much for her. But she had pushed through, her many years as a police officer giving her access to a reserve of grit that most civilians did not have.

It was sometime after that briefing and with the assurance that nothing else was likely to happen until mid-morning that she had agreed to leave NDHQ. The moment she had sat in the back of her RCMP-chauffeured sedan, she had fallen asleep.

Upon reaching her apartment, she'd been roused by her driver, only for Merielle to tell him to let her sleep in the back of the car for another hour. As a minister of the crown, it was an inglorious

move, but she wasn't a great sleeper and she worried that the journey up to her apartment plus the short nap she'd just had might
make another bout of sleeping all but impossible. If her body was
prepared to drift off in the back of this car, she knew enough to take
advantage of that small mercy.

She again woke, but this time to the sound of her phone. She
had set the thing on its highest volume so that it was sure to wake
her. Groggily, she silenced the screaming ring and without looking
at who it was, hit speakerphone mode.

"Mer?"

"Stephane, yes, I'm here. What time is it?" Merielle said, her
voice sounding almost punch-drunk.

"It's just after midnight. Sorry to call so early. I thought about
waiting till the morning, but that nervous part of my brain
wouldn't let me wait."

Merielle put the phone down and then proceeded to rub her
face, hoping the effort would help to spark at least some of the
synapses in her brain.

"You still there, Mer?"

"Yes, yes, all is good. What's up?" Merielle said as she picked up
the phone and placed it to her ear.

"First off and just so you know, I've already passed this intel
along to the right people at CSIS, so they're working on it."

"Appreciate that. That's one less thing I'll be asked to resign
over."

"Listen, it may be something or nothing, but with everything
that's happening, I thought you'd want to know ASAP.

"This afternoon, I interviewed this Mohawk fella from Akwe-
sasne. He's a big-time smuggler, who moves everything and anything across the border, mostly in our direction. Recently, he
moved what he thought was a team of mercs from upstate New
York into Quebec. He said they had a lot of gear with them, though

it was bundled up. With everything kicking off down south, he thought it might be in his long-term best interest to let us know these guys had crossed."

Nearly out of her dazed state, Merielle replied, "He's an astute businessman, then."

"Yeah, he's that and several other things. In any event, he was able to provide some images of these fellows, and CSIS, MI6, and the Aussies' SIS took a look-see, and once they did, all three agencies proceeded to catch fire."

"Hold up, Steph," Merielle said. She looked in the vehicle's rearview mirror and caught her driver's eyes. "Ty, get us over to the Timmies on Cumberland. It looks like I'm gonna need a coffee on the double."

"Done," the officer replied while starting the car.

"Sorry, Steph. Keep going."

"No worries," her ex said. "With what comes next though, you may not need the caffeine.

"Like I said, CSIS and the other agencies were pretty hot on these guys and the leader in particular. As bad actors go, apparently the guy running this crew is the closest thing the world has to a real-life Bond villain."

"Well, that's just what we need," said Merielle, her voice offering a hint of exasperation.

"Wait for it, Mer. His nom de guerre is 'The Machete', but intel out of Russia suggests his real name is Vadim Altov. Of Spetsnaz origin, Altov has spent the better part of twenty years doing various high-end dirty jobs for dictators and corporate actors who want to influence events in some of the world's less civilized backwaters. Apparently, over the course of this illustrious career, Mr. Altov has manufactured not one, but two successful coups. And would you like to know how he became known as *The Machete*?"

As Merielle's sedan pulled in front of the Tim Horton's and her RCMP driver opened his door to grab her coffee, she lowered her tinted window to breathe in the humid night air common to Ottawa at this time of year.

"No, I wouldn't like to know, but you should probably tell me anyway since this sick bastard is running around our country somewhere."

"He cut his teeth with Russian special forces in Syria, and it's said the unit he was attached to had taken to the nasty habit of hacking off the heads of any Syrian rebel leaders they managed to get their hands on. Headless corpses are now considered a surefire sign by Western intelligence that Altov is operating in one particular country or another. His latest known adventure was in Venezuela two years ago, where it's believed he was hired by the Perez government to assassinate the leader of the country's largest opposition movement."

"And where do we think he is now?" asked Merielle.

"Our Mohawk friend said he had five other men with him and that they had a car and van waiting for them on the Quebec side when they got across the river, but from there he has no idea where they might have gone. That was weeks ago. They could be anywhere."

"What do the intelligence services think?"

"No one thinks the timing of Altov's arrival is a coincidence with what's going on down south, so as of about an hour ago, we put out a nationwide alert on Altov and the two vehicles they were seen leaving in."

"Good. That's what I would have done. Okay, so here's the million-dollar question. What the hell do we think he's doing here?"

As Merielle asked the question, she heard what sounded like the detonation of fireworks in the distance. As the sound reverberated amongst the buildings surrounding her, another series of booms invaded the night sky.

Grabbing her phone, she exited her car and stood on the road. There, she could see none of the telltale signs of an after-hours fireworks show. She looked at her watch. It was 0047 hours, so it was well past the city's noise curfew. Two more deep-sounding eruptions washed over her and as they did so, she did her best to triangulate where the noise was coming from.

She cocked her head in the direction of Rockcliffe Park, that old monied part of Ottawa that was home to a good part of the city's societal upper crust and several ambassadorial residences. There was another boom. Explosions, she thought. Two more of them sounded off, loud and menacing. She heard sirens begin to wail.

"Stephane, can you hear what I'm hearing?"

"Yeah. Late for fireworks, isn't it?"

Merielle didn't answer. Out of the corner of her eye, she saw her driver, Corporal Tyson Anderson, one of several officers the RCMP's VIP protection division had assigned to her. Holding two coffees, he too was looking in the direction of Rockcliffe Park.

"Steph, I've gotta go. Love you."

Cutting the connection, she walked to Anderson, grabbed the two coffees, and then walked to the front passenger side of the VIP version of their Audi A7.

Her voice firm, Merielle said, "Get in the car, Corporal, and take us to 24 Sussex as fast as you can drive this thing."

————

Whiteman AFB

His torso tightly wrapped and with whatever painkillers he could take that wouldn't dull his wits, Larocque carefully eased himself out the open doorway of the RZR and reached out to take the hand of Colonel Rydell.

"Great seeing you, Jack," the Australian 2nd Commando CO said.

"Great being here. Thanks for holding down the fort, Brian. I understand we took it to the Reds pretty good."

"Your lads gave 'em a hell of a go. Why don't we get you below? We'll walk you through what happened. Coffee's on the brew and should be waiting for us."

"A million thanks, my friend," said Larocque. "But it wasn't just my folks. I understand your men were in the thick of the shit too. You did a hell of a job stepping in once my location got hit. A hell of a job."

"Think nothing of it, Colonel. The truth of it is mate, I hardly had to do anything. Your junior officers performed magnificently. I daresay they didn't miss a beat. They either don't need a commanding officer, or I reckon they're one well-trained bunch."

Now three hours past midnight, the two colonels left the near-moonless Missouri night and walked down a set of stairs into the secondary command bunker that Delgado had carved deep into Whiteman's soil.

As Larocque's eyes adjusted to the light, his nose immediately picked up on the smell of freshly brewed coffee and saw a corporal walking toward him. With a smile, the man handed him his own travel mug. Blessedly, some kind soul had salvaged it from his now-destroyed HQ. His wife had given it to him as a gift ages ago. He returned the soldier's smile and brought the sacred vessel to his lips. Two sugars and one cream. For a second or two, the pain in his body subsided as he relished the coffee's smooth taste and the influx of caffeine. Manna straight from heaven, the neurons in his brain broadcasted to the rest of his body.

Three-quarters of his HQ team had survived the airstrike that had scored direct hits on the Airborne's main command hub and the four-story-high air traffic control tower. The felling of the tower had been a devastating one-two punch. That the tower had collapsed in the direction of his HQ had been a stroke of terrible luck. Bad luck was one thing. Stupid and arrogant mistakes were something else altogether and, in this instance, his decision had cost him four excellent officers, including the incomparable Major Landry. Jesus, she had two kids under ten.

Larocque brutally suppressed that line of thinking. If they got off this base, there would be time enough for rumination and recriminations. In the present, however, he had to set the conditions so that the remainder of his regiment and the Australians won this fight and got to go home.

In the center of the bunker there were two side-by-side folding tables and on top was a large, printed map of Whiteman and the surrounding area.

Larocque set down his mug and looked at Rydell and the handful of other officers and NCOs standing around the well-marked display. "Folks, I'm banged up pretty bad, but I can still lead this fight. Is everyone good with that?"

Without hesitation, everyone in the bunker gave some indication of assent, with some of the junior officers and NCOs sounding off with a 'for sure' or 'hell yeah'.

For his part, the Australian colonel gave Larocque a vigorous thumbs up and offered, "Banged up or not Airborne, you're our man. Let's give these Yanks a real go."

"Good to hear. From all of you. Because come what may, there's no damned way I'm prepared to let a single American come onto this base unless its to die," Larocque said, his voice brimming with determination.

"Now, read me into what I missed and where are things at?

———

Northern Missouri

Major Harry Khan once again checked the radar feed coming in from the Wedgetail AWACS loitering above his flight of RAF Tempests.

On the radar and above the small Missourian cities of Lexington and Waverly, Khan noted no less than nine CANZUK fighters. Off radar, he knew another six planes were being held in reserve. Considering their losses over the past twenty-four hours and the many other fighting priorities that the alliance had at the moment, it was a massive commitment.

Their mission was singular. Keep their radars on and actively probe and defend the two bridges on the ground below them. If one of the two bridges fell, it was quietly being acknowledged by the officers running the war that a CANZUK victory would become unlikely. If both bridges were destroyed, Whiteman would fall, and CANZUK would be faced with a political disaster on par with the likes of Dunkirk and the fall of Afghanistan.

The long and short of the air war was that CANZUK had been bested and this shortcoming was quickly turning the odds of winning the fight in the direction of the Reds. Whether it was poor intelligence or Western hubris, CANZUK's military planners had greatly overestimated their ability to take on the UCSA's J-31s. Though it was only one squadron, the planes had wreaked havoc well beyond their numbers, with the outcome being that CANZUK's combined air forces had not been able to dominate the sky over Missouri.

At best, they were now standing even with the Reds. No matter how you looked at it, their forces on the ground were having a tougher go than should have been the case, and this would continue until Khan and his fellow pilots figured out a way to do better against the Chinese fighters.

Time, however, was not on their side, which is why the generals running the air campaign had elected to assign so many fighters to the task of defending the two bridges. Despite flying some of the most expensive and modern flying machines ever devised, CANZUK's military planners had been relegated to employing the ancient tactic of numbers and brute force in the hopes of holding off the Americans.

"Knife One, this is Ares Three, we have four hostiles on an approach vector to your position, their radars are active. They're three hundred and twenty klicks out and we have them at twenty-six thousand feet. The data coming in confirms that all four are Js."

Khan toggled open his comms channel. "Roger that, Ares. I've got them on screen. Permission to engage?"

"Permission granted. We'll keep streaming the data as it comes. Ares Three out."

He looked at the large display at the front and center of his plane's cockpit and took in the four data points that were American aircraft. What the hell were the Yanks on about now? he thought. In all of the fighting they had done to this point, they had yet to see the Chinese fighters allow themselves to be identified in advance of an attack. And that they would do so at such a distance was stupid beyond measure. He'd wager a month's pay they were up to something, the crafty bastards.

Khan toggled open his comms channel to the flight under his command. "Ginger, you're with me. The rest of you hang tight. Whatever the Reds are on about, it can't be good, so stay vigilant. Pony out."

Manipulating the appropriate controls, Khan barrel-rolled his aircraft, dropping it several hundred feet, and then punched up the plane's speed and began to race in the direction of the four radar-glowing Chinese fighters.

Moving at over five hundred knots, Khan and his wingmate closed the distance with the four J-31s in minutes.

In the short time it had taken Khan's plane to reach its optimum firing range, he had stopped trying to understand why the American pilots were presenting themselves as they were. If there was some type of chicanery afoot, he couldn't conceive of it.

After a series of quick commands, Khan designated his targets. He would launch all four of his plane's internally stowed beyond-visual-range Meteor missiles and would let the missiles' own onboard radar system find their targets.

Once launched, he and his wingman would then storm toward the Americans with their shorter-range air-to-air armaments at the ready. If he needed to get into a knife fight to bring down these Chinese killing machines, that is exactly what he and his pilots were going to do.

Heart thumping and adrenaline coursing through his veins, Khan toggled open the comms channel to his wingman, or in this case, wingwoman. "Lady Ginger, I see that you've acquired your targets. You may have the honors."

"Roger that, Pony," replied the female pilot. "Payback is launching in 3, 2, 1."

———

Colonel Montrell watched in growing horror as the eight missiles bloomed on his plane's tactical display. For the past ten minutes, he had struggled to make sense of the impossible. This, his eighth sortie of the war had started like all others. Accompanied by three other J-31s, his flight had taken off from Altus Air Force Base in Oklahoma with the intent of launching a crucial air-to-ground attack on the two Missouri River bridges CANZUK paratroopers had secured in the first hours of the war.

Though rushed, their pre-flight had gone off without a hitch as had the rest of the mission. Until it didn't.

They had just flown into the range of whichever country's AWACS plane had been loitering over central Missouri when, as if by the hand of God, his plane had become unresponsive. That had been ten minutes ago, and, in that time, Montrell had tried everything he could think of to get the plane to do his bidding. The flight stick was inert. The plane's comms were inoperable. The fighter's powerful radar had been turned on and would not shut down. He had even tried to get the landing gear to deploy, but this, too, was ineffectual.

As he watched the incoming missiles race closer on the main tactical display, Montrell desperately toggled through the plane's powerful suite of electronic warfare countermeasures, but none of it would respond.

With various warnings firing off in his helmet and throughout the cockpit, Montrell finally reached underneath his seat and grasped the ejection handle. Gritting his teeth and closing his eyes, he pulled. Nothing happened. He pulled again, this time with every ounce of strength he could bring to bear. Again, nothing happened.

His eyes opened, and he looked into the ink-black darkness of the night sky that surrounded him. Rationally, he knew he wouldn't be able to see the supersonic missiles homing in on him. It was too dark, and they were moving too fast.

As images of his wife and children rushed into his mind, he finally saw a bright flash, and then for a too-long moment, panic raced through him as he saw and felt the metal and glass around him begin to disintegrate. As Montrell left the world, his dying thoughts were not of his family, but of China and how those double-crossing bastards may have just changed the arc of history in North America.

Chapter 28

Ottawa

With it being after midnight, Merielle's driver expertly raced around the light traffic on the short drive to 24 Sussex.

The car's wheels squealed as Corporal Anderson turned the corner onto Sussex Drive. Punching the accelerator, the car sprinted across the bridge that crossed the Rideau River.

Her window still open, she could clearly hear the pop of gunfire over the growling of her car's powerful engine. As they left the bridge and began to take in the scene that had consumed this quiet and regal-looking part of the city, Anderson had begun to slow down their vehicle.

"Jesus. It's a war zone," Merielle uttered as they took in the scene before them.

Blue and red lights from half a dozen police cruisers – both RCMP and Ottawa police – blazed, their primary colors saturating the street's many trees, making their foliage an ugly purple.

Stopping fifty meters back from the initial tranche of vehicles, Merielle saw the bodies of two unmoving officers laid out on the street, while several others were huddled behind patrol cars. Randomly, one or more of the officers would quickly rise, assume a firing position, and open up with a burst of fire from whatever weapon they were armed with. As Merielle took in the surreal state of affairs and listened to the cacophony of gunfire and screaming voices, she shifted in her seat and moved to open the door.

As her hand moved forward to pull the door's handle, she saw and then felt Anderson's hand shoot across her body and latch onto her forearm. Though not a large man, the RCMP officer's grip was vice-like.

"You can't go out there," he said, his voice incredulous. "You're a cabinet minister. You're not a cop anymore. As it is, we're way too close to whatever the hell this is."

Merielle locked eyes with the younger man. "Corporal, look with your eyes at what's going on out there? That's the prime minister's residence for Christ's sake. There's no goddamned way I'm sitting here. You can stay here and say you told me so, or you can haul ass with me and see what we can do to help. But what you're not going to do is stop me from getting out of this car, so take your hand off me right now. Right fucking now, Corporal."

As they stared each other down, Merielle heard a distinctive *thunk* of a sound and then heard and felt a detonation in the direction where the police were hunkered down. As she felt Anderson's grip leave her arm, she turned her head and saw that one of the three cruisers in front of them now had shattered windows that were issuing tendrils of greasy grey smoke. A third police officer was now lying down on the street, writhing in pain.

Merielle's eyes turned back to her driver. "You can stay or come. It's up to you."

Anderson snarled a reply. "Piss on it. Fine, we'll go. But come with me for one second."

Free from the policeman's grip, Merielle quickly got out of the car and saw that Anderson was already at the rear of the vehicle and had popped the trunk. As the snap of gunfire continued, she darted toward him.

"Take this," he said while handing her his standard-issue Smith & Wesson pistol and a ballistic vest that he had pulled from the trunk. "Put this on, or I manhandle you back into this car and we high-tail it from whatever disaster this is."

As she took the vest and weapon, Anderson reached down and pulled out a matte-black 12-gauge shotgun and a second ballistics vest, which he quickly put on.

He pumped a shell into the gun's breech, looked at Merielle, and said loudly over the fighting, "As we move, stay behind me."

"Got it," Merielle said.

Without another word, Anderson moved from behind the cover of their vehicle and began to jog forward to the police cruisers positioned in front of them.

On their arrival, the officers crouching behind the vehicles did a double take as they turned from the battle to see who had joined them.

Taking a knee behind the engine block of a petrol-driven Ottawa Police Service patrol car, Merielle ignored their stares. After a moment to catch her breath, she rose to her feet and took in the scene. Erect, she saw what could have been the set from a hyper-realistic Hollywood action movie. More police vehicles and still more bodies of officers – these in tactical gear – lay strewn everywhere, their uniformed corpses resting in pools of what could only be blood.

Some thirty meters away, at the southern entrance to the property, a nondescript dark blue van was parked askew, its rear doors flung open. Beyond the vehicle, Merielle could see that the sturdy steel gates that had once controlled access to the three-story neo-gothic residence had been shorn from the granite pillars they had been attached to.

She felt someone grab her left hand and firmly pull her down, but she resisted as her eyes caught the movement of something in between the van and the gate. Jerking her hand away, Merielle watched as a four-legged menace slowly prowled into her vision.

Though its walk was more akin to that of a spider, the machine's robotic architecture was most certainly modeled on that of a canine. Charcoal black and sporting plates of what was most certainly armor, Merielle focused on the sleek-looking two-barrel turret that sat squarely on the robot's back.

Without turning its body, the turret silently swiveled in Merielle's direction, and without warning, it leveled a green targeting laser dead center on her chest.

When asked weeks later about what she had been thinking at that moment, Merielle had no words to describe what she had felt. The one thing she could say unequivocally was that she had not frozen. Whatever ball of sentiments had been roiling through her, she had stood tall and had waited to feel the impact of the killbot's high-caliber rounds. But instead of feeling bullets, Merielle heard a series of loud metallic clicks and watched as the turret disengaged from her person. Then, slowly, the autonomous machine lowered itself to its haunches, where at the terminus of its descent, it released a loud sigh of hydraulic gases.

To her right, someone said, "It's out of ammo." Another voice bellowed for someone to call forward emergency services. Merielle felt a hand on her shoulder and turned to see Anderson standing beside her with a concerned look on his face.

"You okay?"

"Yeah, I'm good."

"There's another one of those things still guarding at the north entrance, but it looks like the sergeant on this end is going to try and move forward with the officers she has left. I take it you would like us to tag along?"

"Definitely," Merielle said.

In less than a minute, six officers, plus Anderson and Merielle, were advancing to the front entrance of the residence. Here, too, the bodies of law enforcement officers - some uniformed, some plain-clothed - lay on the ground.

As they advanced slowly, with each of their weapons pointing in a different direction, Merielle's eyes took in what she knew to be part of the prime minister's motorcade. Two police-modified black SUVs sat in front and behind the PM's own armored Suburban. Lit up as well as the property was, Merielle could see that something had penetrated the top of the PM's SUV and had exploded within the vehicle's cab. Though it had held in place, the reinforced bullet-proof window at the front of the unit was a white shattered mess. As she passed within a few feet of the vehicle, she saw a body spattered with blood slumped over the steering wheel.

As a unit, they kept moving in the direction of the three-story, 18th-Century mansion. Upon arriving at the singular front entrance to the residence, Merielle could see the building's sturdy door had been blown inwards, the force of the blast ripping out large chunks of wood and concrete where the door's hinges had once been affixed to the bones of the residence.

In the RCMP, she'd gained years of experience in the art of house clearing, so when the sergeant leading the eight-person team gave the order for them to change their formation, she did so without thinking. She was now last in the line with Anderson and his shotgun steps in front of her.

One by one, their weapons at the ready, the officers stepped across the rubble-strewn threshold and entered the house.

As a senior minister within cabinet and one of the prime minister's most trusted colleagues, she had been in 24 Sussex many times. Though it was no palace, it was also not small, and the floorplan offered any number of nooks and crannies where someone who knew their business could lie in wait. Silently, she said a word of thanks that the lighting in the home remained operational.

As she advanced through the small entrance and into a larger room that held several connections leading to other parts of the home, she saw that the officers had formed a semi-circle and were covering off each of the conduits. Merielle and Anderson flowed to their left and took up positions at an entrance that led into a good-sized study with floor-to-ceiling bookshelves.

As she looked ahead into the stately Victorian-era room before her, she listened intently. While there was still an orchestra of violent noise coming into the home from outside, the inside of the residence was hauntingly quiet.

"Minister," a hushed voice called to her. Turning, she saw the female RCMP sergeant who had been leading them was now standing at the center of the room and motioning for her to come over. As quietly as she could, Merielle walked over to the other woman and then by some combination of instinct and training, they leaned their heads into one another.

"How do we want to play this?" asked the sergeant in a whisper.

"I'm not an Inspector anymore. You're in command, so it's your call."

"Bullshit," the sergeant scoffed. "This whole situation left crazy town a long time ago. Like hell am I going to make this call. Not with you here. I'll tell you what I think we should do and then it's on you, retired or not."

Now that they were in the house, Merielle's anxiety to find the PM and his wife was increasing. With only eight of them and with a building so large, they would have to make some tough choices. There was no doubt the policewoman in front of her could decide how to proceed, but if the roles were reversed, there was no question Merielle would have deferred.

"Okay, what's your plan?" Merielle asked.

"We need to find the PM ASAP. I know there's a safe room upstairs. Standard operating procedure is to clear this floor before we go upstairs, but there's no way I'm prepared to wait that long. I say we split. You and the Corporal can go up with two of my guys and we'll stay here and clear the main floor. The other killbot just shut down, so we'll have more bodies in here in a few moments. As more of us arrive, we'll join you upstairs."

The relief that Merielle felt when the sergeant had suggested she be the one to head upstairs had been monumental. Something terrible had happened to her friend and mentor. She needed to be the first up those stairs. Hardening her voice, Merielle said, "I agree. The PM is the priority. Give me your two people and let's get this done."

Without saying a word, the sergeant turned away from her and spoke with two of the other officers, both from the RCMP. They both nodded their heads in agreement.

Merielle moved toward Anderson, tapped him on the shoulder, and motioned for him to follow her. Pivoting, and with her weapon once again in the ready position, she moved in the direction of the home's grand foyer, which held a curved staircase that led to the second floor.

The foyer, with its vaulted ceiling and burnished parquet floor, was empty. With all of her senses keenly attuned to the space around her, Merielle led her small team up the stairs. At the three-quarter mark of their climb, her eyes picked up the first indications of violence from within the building. At the stairs' upper termination point, some type of explosion had ripped several of the ornate oak spindles from their moorings along the balustrade.

Merielle quickly scanned those parts of the second floor that were visible. Across the distance of the open space, she saw the body of what looked to be a plain-clothed police officer lying in a heap in front of a pair of double doors she knew to be the master bedroom.

In pairs and moving quickly, they leapfrogged forward, clearing the rooms that lay between the stairs and the prime minister's sleeping quarters.

As a team, they arrived at the doors of the bedroom. Merielle took in the police officer. Around the body were dozens of shell casings suggesting that a determined last stand had taken place. The man had several entry wounds on his body, but the killing blow had been the one that had entered into his skull via his right eye. Merielle recognized the man as one of the senior RCMP officers who ran the PM's security detail.

Her eyes left the body and took in the double doors in front of her. Over the pounding in her chest and ears, Merielle could hear no sound coming from the room. Through the crack of the doors, she could see that the room was lit. Reaching forward, she placed her hand on the left door, while Anderson's raised shotgun was held an inch back from the door on the right.

In a whisper, she started the countdown, "In one, two, three, go!"

Together, Merielle and Anderson pushed the two doors inwards and with the two officers behind them, they pressed forward.

Merielle swung whip-like to the left to take in that part of the room where the bed was located.

As she took in the display, she stopped moving and lowered her pistol as her eyes and brain tried to work together to make sense of the appalling scene laid out before her.

"Oh, my God," Anderson said softly from behind her.

Merielle could say nothing. Despite her time as a police officer and seeing violence of all kinds, what was before her was beyond words.

———

Altov calmly walked out the door that faced the Ottawa River and then turned in the direction of the cliff face where the other four members of his team were waiting for him. They had already staked in the climbing gear that would allow them to rappel down to the water and reach the fast-moving boat in which Heng was waiting.

As the distance between him and the residence increased, Altov picked up the sounds of fighting coming from the front of the property.

Their execution had been flawless. Their laser-guided mortars had flown true, the prime minister's security detail had responded as predicted, and from what he understood from Heng, the two Chinese-built Hyena X2 kill-bots they'd left to welcome the police reinforcements had exceeded all expectations. The expensive and hard-to-get pieces of kit had more than justified the effort and money needed to obtain them.

Clipped onto the rappelling line that had been set out for him, he took one final look at the pleasant-looking residence. Having worked in both Africa and South and Central America, he'd seen his share of gaudy and overdone presidential compounds. He had appreciated the modest grandeur of the building's interior and felt as though the bureaucrats who were responsible for maintaining the property had done their jobs well. Nothing was brash. Rather, the motif had been both steady and modest.

As Heng piloted the boat away from the cliff face and they sped through the dark water in the direction of Montreal, his thoughts drifted to the too-brief conversation he'd had with the Canadian prime minister. The man had been both respectful and stalwart and as a result, Altov had elected to reward the man with the small mercy of putting a bullet into his wife's skull and then his own.

What he had done after that had not been necessary or asked for by his employers. He did not question his compulsions, just as he did not question why he was so good at the career he'd fallen into. Some things just were. He'd done what he'd been paid to do. If there were unexpected consequences for his proclivities, the French would have to deal with it. That was not his concern.

Some thirty minutes later, still under the same starry sky, Heng carefully piloted the boat toward the marina they had pre-selected. With the same efficiency they had operated with all night, Altov and the rest of the team unloaded the remainder of the equipment and walked to a pair of waiting cars they had dropped off hours earlier.

As he fell into the passenger seat and the car began to move, he turned to Heng, who was behind the wheel. He put out his fist, and the other mercenary bumped it.

"That was some fine work back there," the Chinese operator said.

After a moment's pause, Altov responded, "My friend, it was some of our very best."

———

San Antonio, 5th Army HQ

Spector gave a hard stare in the direction of the man standing across from him. "So, you're telling me your people still don't have any idea what happened?"

"That's not what I said, Mitch," replied the tall and increasingly agitated three-star general. "I said it could be a few things, but we can't say for certain and until we get this figured out, it's my strong recommendation we pause all further missions. Our pilots won't be able to do their jobs like they need to if one part of their brain is worried their plane is going to go rogue on them."

"That is a negative," retorted Spector. "If you're telling me that the only machines that seem to have caught this bug are the J-31s, then you can keep them on the ground. But you will keep your other planes flying and they will continue to fight like hell."

Spector leaned his robust upper frame over the conference table and placed both his hands on its surface, continuing to stare at the other man.

"Is my position understood, General Howe?"

"You're putting our pilots at risk unnecessarily, but your position is understood."

With a rapidity that belied his size, Spector came up from the table and exploded at the other man. "You're damn right my position is understood. What part of we need to win this war do you not understand?

"No, don't answer the question, it was rhetorical for Christ's sake. If your pilots are not contesting the sky above that base as our soldiers make west from St. Louis, we don't stand a chance. So, whatever you have to do to motivate your pilots to get back into this fight, you better do it. I need every last pilot you've got in the sky above Missouri, and I need them fighting like the devils they are."

As Spector's eyes remained locked with the other man's glare, he made an intentional effort to moderate his tone. "Listen, Ken, I feel for you and your pilots. I do. I get it. But I know you and I know you're a fighter. As of this moment, we're officially up to our necks in shit. All of us. We need to win this battle. This is no time for ifs, buts, or I think so. You have to be with me all the way, or all of us are screwed. Are you with me, General?"

Howe took a deep breath, tightened his lips, exhaled, and then said, "I'm with you."

"Good man," said Spector as he turned his attention to one of the other officers in the room.

"And what's the current count of our citizen-soldier army? I trust the sons and daughters of Missouri have continued to rise to the occasion."

"They have, sir. The last estimate I have is somewhere in the range of twelve hundred to sixteen hundred trucks evenly split between Kansas City and St. Louis. We're estimating four bodies per truck, so there could be just over six thousand irregulars heading in the direction of Whiteman as we speak."

"Well, that makes my heart sing. They're brave souls each and every one of them. Thank God our country stood up for the Second Amendment. If there was ever a justification for the blood we've shed with the Blues, let this scrap with these CANZUK bastards show we were right to stand up for our rights."

Spector looked around the conference room and made eye contact with each of the officers who would play a key role in the hours to come.

"Gentlemen, given the circumstances that confront us, it is my opinion that we have a winning plan despite the loss of the J-31s. The numbers on the ground make victory inevitable. We'll saturate the sons of bitches with every God-loving man and woman in this part of the country that can shoot a rifle. And as these brave patriots give their lives, it is our job to push forward with those fighting forces we've positioned west of St. Louis. Numbers and brute force. It's as timeless a strategy as it is straightforward. Are there any questions about what we must do?"

None of the officers in the conference room said a word.

"Good. Then let's make this happen, people. In under six hours, Whiteman AFB is ours."

Chapter 29

An hour earlier, Chen had been gathered in the Airborne's new HQ with the other fighting captains, where a wincing Larocque had walked them through the latest intel and their strategy for the coming battle.

The Airborne CO had given the attending officers a short history on both American civil wars. In both conflicts, he reminded them that it had not been uncommon for one or both sides of a particular battle to incur hundreds, if not thousands of casualties. Larocque had followed this daunting tidbit with an update that CANZUK intelligence was suggesting that something like five thousand Red Faction irregulars had amassed around Whiteman and that this force would be first to assault their positions.

As Chen rehashed the conversation in his mind, he took in a long calming breath. Despite what was to come, the crisp morning air was refreshing to the point where he could almost make himself believe he wasn't sitting in a hole in front of the gates of hell.

There was no help for it of course. He was a Digger and like the men of Gallipoli and all the soldiers that followed, you made your peace with what was to come, and then you got on with it. It's what the Aussie fighting man had always done.

Exhaling, Chen took up his tac pad and manipulated the screen to bring up the real-time video from the tactical drone the Airborne had assigned to his sector. Hovering at four thousand feet, the drone's thermal camera was tracking the movement of nearly a hundred civilian trucks as they slowly moved in a wide arc across the endless soybean fields that spanned the full length of his company's defensive line.

On the display, his finger quickly dabbed the rearguard of the approaching force, designating a dozen or so of the civilian trucks as targets for the Airborne's waiting mortar teams. As he touched each vehicle, a yellow icon was attached to the plodding gaggle of trucks.

The desired targets designated, Chen activated his BAM. "Open a channel for A Company, all soldiers."

"Channel open," the smooth, synthesized female voice advised.

He said nothing, but watched the tac pad's screen and took in the blazing white thermal images of the approaching vehicles and walking figures, as the first part of the irregular force moved past a virtual marker he'd set three hundred meters out from his company's outermost trenches. Each entrenchment was expertly camouflaged and held ten to twenty determined soldiers from both Canada and Australia. Looking up from his device, the swath of light from the emerging sun allowed him to easily make out the silhouetted trucks with the naked eye. The Yanks were where they needed to be.

Dropping his eyes back to his tac pad, Chen quickly drew a circle around the trucks he had designated moments before and double-tapped the grouping. As their icons turned red, he stopped breathing and listened. To his rear, he heard several 'thunks' as the first of the Canadians' 81mm mortar rounds leaped into the early morning sky. The designated BAM channel for the company still open, Chen said calmly, "A Company, all heavy weapons, open fire."

As the order left Chen's mouth, a storm of fire erupted from all around him. All at once, snipers, high explosive rounds from his company's six Carl Gustafs, heavy machine guns, and his own light mortars roared, cracked, and chattered, as they began to tear into the wholly inadequate sacrificial force before them.

For this first battle of the day, Chen had placed himself in one of the trenches that lay between his company's outermost positions and the heavily fortified last stand amongst the nukes. Standing on top of a block one of his soldiers had built for his diminutive stature, he took in the initial barrage of their assault and bore witness to the savagery of war.

Well behind the leading elements of the irregular attack, rounds from the Airborne's heavier mortars exploded above and around the vehicles Chen had designated moments before. He watched in some combination of horror and fascination as the mortar teams expertly walked their fire in the direction of his company's lines, creating a wave of panic in the rear echelons of the Americans just as the lead elements of the attack were being torn apart by his soldiers.

Here and there, Chen saw a Ford or Chevy explode in a burst of fire and dust as it took a shot from one of the company's short-range anti-armor weapons. When struck, men on the back of the trucks were ejected from their positions like leaves on a windy fall day. Those irregulars who failed to find some type of cover were cut down by torrents of machine-gun fire courtesy of the company's C-6s. The first minutes of the battle had been an appalling, and one-sided affair.

But as Chen's eyes evaluated this first bout of carnage, he noted that more of the irregular trucks were moving in the distance. Many more vehicles, in fact, with more irregular soldiers on foot among them.

In putting down this first wave of attackers, the American militiamen had forced the Airborne to reveal their positions and the many tank traps his men had feverishly dug over the course of the night. The Red Faction officers who were running this war weren't stupid men, Chen reminded himself. They knew exactly what they were doing, even if that made them callous bastards for doing it.

As the next wave of irregulars began to enter his company's kill zone, Chen set aside whatever empathy he might have for the imperiled men to his front. At some point in the coming hours, he

knew full well the Yanks would get to level the score, and when
they did, he knew they would employ the same savagery his own
men were doling out. This was war and this is what soldiers had
done for millennia.

Forcing his eyes from the spectacle, he suppressed whatever humanity was bubbling inside of him and like a maestro of violence
he now was, Chen orchestrated the men of his company to kill with
as much efficiency and brutality as they could muster.

———

Larocque watched the display intently. It was divided into
quadrants with each square streaming a different drone.

The Red irregulars were pushing from all sides, though the
presence of Knob Noster State Park, which ran along the western
side of the base, made that direction impassable to vehicles.

On another monitor, he saw the growing queue for the Airborne's heavy mortar teams. The Regiment had eight remaining
mortar tubes, which they had dug in at two different locations. Via
the entrance to his command bunker, Larocque could hear the re-
peating 'thunks' of the weapons closest to his position. Colonel Rydell would once again oversee the mortars and the Regiment's remaining drones, both tactical and surveillance.

The Red's strategy had been predictable and necessarily simple.
For this first part of the fight, numbers and the local geography
were the advantages they would play to. The farmland to the east
and south of Whiteman was mostly open and flat. With enough attackers coming from those two directions, the Airborne and their
Aussie allies would be hard-pressed to hold their lines.

"Colonel, you may want to come and take a look at this," said
the captain who had assumed Landry's role as the Regiment's lead
battlefield coordinator.

Larocque gingerly shifted to that part of the bunker and took in the screen in front of the twenty-something officer. "What am I looking at?" Larocque asked.

"This is Highway 50 about twenty klicks east of us. It's a convoy of twenty military vehicles with another sixty or so civie trucks."

The captain zoomed in with the drone's powerful camera. It was well south of the formation it was observing, so the image it was streaming was a high-def side profile of the fast-moving convoy. The camera panned from one vehicle to the next. While there were a variety of models, all of the military vehicles were four-wheeled, up-armored, and had some type of turreted weapon. Heavy machine guns, 40mm grenade launchers and Javelin anti-tank missiles were all present.

"It's a bit early for the cavalry, isn't it? Where the hell did these guys come from?" Larocque asked.

"Out of Sedalia, sir. They must have slipped in with the civies sometime in the night."

On one of the captain's other tactical displays, he could see the small city, which was twenty-five klicks due east of Whiteman. "Put an airstrike on it. Priority one," Larocque ordered.

"I already have, sir, but the coordinator has denied it. They've directed all available assets to help out the Brit battlegroups to the north and any planes that remain above us are being held in reserve to deter any Red airstrikes against our positions. The word I've been given is that for the time being, we're on our own for anything that comes at us on the ground."

Larocque grunted but said nothing.

"Get those feeds to Singh and Chen, and work with Rydell to prioritize that convoy for the mortar teams. As soon as that convoy hits three klicks out, have the 81s start to harass them."

Larocque activated his BAM. "Give me Singh and Chen, priority one call, Hotel-Charlie."

"Channel open," said the AI-manufactured voice in his earbud.

Larocque moved to another station within the bunker, where another officer had already placed the northeast quadrant of the base on full screen. They were only forty-five minutes into the battle and the area in view was already littered with burning trucks and pockets of irregular soldiers who were working in small groups to direct fire at the Airborne's dug-in positions.

You didn't need to be a tactical genius to see what the Reds were trying to do. As the number of pick-ups grew, each company's zone of fire was getting clogged, making it increasingly difficult for his soldiers to employ their longer-range weapons.

The enroute convoy of military vehicles would be a trial run to see how the Airborne would manage to fight through the growing detritus. Without doubt, those pick-ups that were with the convoy would hit Singh and Chen's lines first and then the armored trucks would dodge and weave forward past the wall of sacrificed irregulars.

Even now, less than an hour into the morning's fighting, he was overhearing conversations on the BAM that soldiers were finding it difficult to get a clear line of sight on approaching targets.

A voice piped into Larocque's earbud. "Singh here. Sorry for the delay, boss. The shit is flying in my neck of the woods."

A second voice came through, this time Chen. "Same here. Nothing serious, but there's no shortage of blokes who have a death wish. You got to give it these Yanks – they're bloody hardcore."

"Yeah, well keep both of your heads on a swivel, cause more of these irregular bastards are coming your way, along with what looks like a company of reg force armor who are armed to the teeth. We've sent the data to your BAMs.

"I have a sense of how they're going to hit your positions, and for the time being we're without air support, so here's what I need you to do."

———

Somewhere in Paris

Besson was once again sitting across the table from the second most powerful politician in France. This time, the courtyard that lay outside the window they shared was in full bloom. Fresh tendrils of green Creeping Charlie was doing its best to soften the grey stonework of the imposing 19th-Century building.

"I'm to meet with the President within the hour, so our conversation will need to be efficient. I trust this will be acceptable Monsieur Besson?"

"Entirely acceptable, Minister. Where would you like to start?"

"The detonation," Charron said immediately.

"Well, we can't talk about the bomb without first talking about Ms. Labelle. We have spoken with her, and I believe we now have the full story of what transpired."

"Excellent. Do tell."

"Well, as it turns out, Ms. Labelle is both a talented and highly ambitious person. In addition to acting as our informant, we now understand that she was quite active in the Quebec separatist movement. While she would feed us first-rate intelligence on a range of issues, she was simultaneously readying at least four different cells of Quebecois to agitate the Canadian political system at a time of her choosing. These efforts were separate and apart from anything her father might have been doing through legitimate political means."

"Most interesting and entrepreneurial of her."

"As I said Minister, this woman is a talent and a rare one at that."

"And we had no idea what she was up to?"

"None. We should have known to be sure. We're looking into this misstep closely."

For a moment, the politician said nothing allowing the word *misstep* to ferment in the air between the two men. His eyes narrowed in on Besson and then he casually offered, "The youth of today, Monsieur Besson - they are nothing if not ambitious. You throw in some talent and it would appear the sky is the limit. In the figurative and literal sense, it would seem."

"The detonation of the weapon works in our favor. Admittedly, we didn't anticipate the audacity of Labelle's plan, but who could have? It was outrageous in every way. Even now, I find it hard to believe."

"The President said the same to me not thirty minutes ago, Monsieur Besson. We are both fortunate that she is such a forgiving woman."

As was always the case, Charron's face was unreadable. For another long moment, the politician again said nothing. Finally, crossing his arms languidly, he said, "Fortunately, I too know that your organization is not prescient. Tell me the rest of the story about this Quebecois woman we are now attached to."

The reprieve delivered, Besson was flooded with relief. Had he wanted to, Charron could have ended his career with but a word. However annoyed he might be about the unexpected developments in the United States, it would seem the little man still had a use for Besson and so the intelligence officer pushed on.

"As you will recall, it was Labelle who was able to provide the final piece of the puzzle that allowed us to anticipate CANZUK's move on Whiteman."

"I have a recollection of that, yes. What of it?"

"Well, on realizing what CANZUK was up to, she saw a once-in-a-lifetime opportunity to advance the Quebec separatist movement in one daring fell swoop. Making use of the cell she had developed within the paratroop unit that was to take the American base, she came up with the plan to arm two nuclear weapons and then use them to gain concessions from the Canadian government."

"And she pulled this together over what period of time?"

"Less than two weeks. As I said, she's quite talented and perceived rightly that the dated software contained within the Americans' bombs could be circumvented with the latest near-AI tech."

"With events that have transpired, I take it her plans didn't go as she hoped."

"They did not, Minister."

"Then what *did* happen?"

"She doesn't know precisely. She knows the Canadians somehow managed to wrest control of both weapons, but for one of them, they could not stop its countdown. Hence the detonation in the remote location."

"Quite the story. And Ms. Labelle, where is she now?"

"Her ingenuity persists, Minister. She flew into St. Pierre and Miquelon early this morning. She is now asking for our assistance."

"*Incroyable*," Charron said the word as though he did not think the development was incredible at all.

"And what does the DGSE think should be done with her?"

Besson exhaled more deeply than he intended. The last twenty-four hours had been stressful beyond measure. Events in North America were moving at a clip far in excess of any file he had managed in the past. And complex did not begin to describe the calculations that needed to be made before France made its next move.

"It is an entangled situation as you well know. On the one hand, Labelle is a liability for us. Canada and her allies know what she has done, and they'll want to get their hands on her. And desperately so. If we harbor her, whether here in France or somewhere friendly to us, we'll be seen as complicit and this will bring consequences, some of which we cannot foresee."

"Fair enough," said Charron. "What's in the other hand?"

"When we sat in these same chairs weeks ago and we discussed the prospect of chaos, I'll confess I did not anticipate, Ms. Labelle would serve us so admirably.

"She informs us there are inactive cells she can trigger, even from a remote location. We'll discuss the evolving political situation in Canada in a moment, but suffice it to say there's still more this Labelle woman could do to help us further destabilize North America."

"So she might still have value to us?"

"She may."

"But what happens when the Canadians find out her location and ask for her? By any definition, she's now a terrorist and the first non-government entity in history to have set off a nuclear weapon. This is no small thing."

"A bold accusation to be sure," Besson said quickly, having anticipated this line of thinking. "In fact, the whole situation is so bold and so outrageous, it's our view that the Canadians will look to keep the matter quiet."

"Certainly, we would," Charron offered plainly. "Let us say for the moment that we did take on Ms. Labelle - might the Canadians not try to deal with the problem informally? They have that capacity now, do they not?"

"It is an interesting question, Minister. It's true that in recent years the Canadians have become more involved in foreign intelligence operations. But our current sense is that they lack the inherent realpolitik that is required to undertake such actions. They are still new to this game and the grief they endured in the aftermath of their Haiti adventure a few years back will also serve to give them pause."

"And what of MI6? Certainly, the British have no such compunctions. And one might suggest the two countries have never been so close as they are now. Perhaps the British will take on the Canadian's problem?"

"We don't think that will be the case, Minister. As you are more aware than I, our relationship with the British is fragile and in light of the upcoming Franco-German alliance discussion, we don't think they'll risk rocking the continental boat. Their hands are full with this North American adventure they've committed to, never mind what's brewing in the Pacific. You will have seen the latest briefings coming out of China."

"Indeed I have. Very good Monsieur Besson," said Charron in a tone that suggested this part of the conversation was at an end. "I'll chew on this and will discuss it with the president. I'll get back to you before the end of the day about what we'll do with Ms. Labelle. For the time being, she can stew where she's at."

The politician's eyes moved to his wristwatch.

"We have ten minutes. Tell me what you can about this most unfortunate turn of events in Ottawa? The news reports I've been listening to have been circumspect, to say the least."

"At 1100 hours, eastern standard time, Canada will be advised it has a new prime minister."

"This is the Martel woman, I presume?"

"Yes, Minister, that's our understanding."

"What do we know of her?"

"Well, we know that she was perceived as one of MacDonald's most relied-upon acolytes and that she was being groomed as a possible heir. We've sent your office a full briefing on her, but the long and short of it is that we think she's a lightweight and that without MacDonald's support, she's likely to be ineffective.

"There will be some in her party who will think that as well, so if it's her intention to remain prime minister, she'll not only have to manage this war with the Americans but also fend off those in her party who don't think she's up for the job. Which is to say nothing of what the Quebec separatists might do."

"So, you don't think she's up for it?"

"Minister, until a few years ago, Merielle Martel was a mid-ranking police officer, who by all accounts was decent at her job. I've seen far worse pedigrees, but as you'll see in the detailed analysis we've shared with you, we have it on good authority this woman is in over her head and by some measure."

"So you say. And with *authority* no less."

"Yes, sir. Our intel is solid. I'm entirely confident of our assessment," Besson said confidently.

"We shall see Monsieur Besson. My sense is that you also had a firm handle on this Lebelle woman."

From behind Besson, someone walked into the room. "Minister, your next appointment awaits. One minute, sir."

Without looking in the direction of his bureaucrat handler, Chasson acknowledged the reminder.

"Our time is up, Director. Despite the trouble you have allowed this Labelle woman to cause, I have not forgotten that I had asked you and your people to create chaos in North America. And as I have thought through what lies before the government I represent, I am reminded that by definition chaos is an unpredictable phenomenon."

Besson made no reply to the acknowledgment.

"Stay close to your phone, Pierre Besson. I'll call you after my meeting with the president. I suspect there is still more for you and your people to do."

Chapter 30

Larocque's plan was both crafty and highly dangerous, so Chen and Singh had agreed that any of the Canadian paratroopers or Aussie commandos who took on the assignment would need to be volunteers.

When the call went out through Chen and Singh's companies, they easily hit their number. Within minutes of the notice going out on the BAM, they had received three times the number of soldiers needed to make the plan happen.

As the Airborne's mortars and other heavy weapons worked to silence what remained of the morning's first onslaught, the fifty men who volunteered had been pulled back from their positions and briefed among the last stand thicket that was the nuclear bunker complex.

Chen had watched a battered Larocque explain to the volunteers what needed to be done. The soldiers present had been delighted to see their CO, his head sporting the Airborne Regiment's maroon beret.

When the control tower had come down and comms had ceased to come from the Airborne's HQ, everyone had feared the worst. It was a true credit to the Canadians' toughness and training that they'd continued to fight as they had.

Having traveled back to his trench in the intermediary line of defense, Chen watched as the volunteers from both the Airborne and 2nd Commando moved forward from various positions into the smokescreen that the Canadian mortars had dropped to his company's front.

Chen turned his eyes away from the scene of disappearing volunteers and looked at Warrant Officer Karlina, his company's senior NCO. He had pulled the man into his trench as two of the soldiers that had been with him during the morning's first attack had volunteered for Larocque's plan. Karlina returned his gaze with keen dark eyes.

"This Larocque fellow is one reckless bloke," said the older man. "The odds facing those lads out there are steep. I reckon it's near suicide."

"This whole mission was suicide from the get-go, Warrant. I think the Canadians knew what they were doing when they chose the good colonel for this mission."

After a pause, Chen said, "Fortis fortuna adiuvat."

Karlina gave the younger man one of the patented looks that senior NCOs bring to bear when a junior officer says or does something stupid. "Are you seriously quoting Latin to me?"

Chen smiled at the other man. "It's from John Wick. It's a tattoo he wears."

"So you think this Larocque fellow fancies himself as a bit of a hero, do you there Captain? Well, I'm not sure my confidence is inspired by that sort of fellow if you don't mind me saying, sir. I thought the man a bit queer for getting in the ring with Dune, though I'll admit the kid had it coming."

"No doubt the colonel is prideful, but he's got two things in short supply in today's world: a big heart and a huge set of balls. Considering our situation, I'll take whatever Larocque is selling. The moment we start to get weak in the knees or predictable, we lose this fight." As Chen said the words, his eyes move back in the direction of the wall of smoke the volunteer soldiers had just disappeared into.

"So what's it mean then?" asked the warrant officer.

"What does what mean?"

"Oi, the Latin."

Chen grinned at the other man. "Fortune favors the brave, Warrant."

Karlina harrumphed loudly and then said, "Yeah, well I reckon the lads out there in the smoke we'll get to test that mantra sooner rather than later. I just hope some of them survive to tell us the tale is all."

"Me too, Warrant. Me too."

———

Fate was a funny thing, Larocque had thought as he watched Lance Corporal Dune walk up to Master Corporal Kettle and ask the other soldier to join him on the ambush Larocque had just run through with the volunteer soldiers. He had watched them laugh at some joke and then shake hands. Both men had grenade launchers underslung on their rifles and both carried two each of the latest version of the single-use M-72 anti-armor rocket that both Canada and Australia carried in their inventories.

Despite the pain and everything else that was going on, Larocque had smiled as the two men walked away together. There went two fine young men of the Commonwealth, he thought. One each of Canada and Australia's most valuable products going forward to do what their countries had asked them to do.

Twenty minutes later and back inside his command post, Larocque watched on screen as the next wave of pick-up trucks approached the Airborne's outermost defensive lines.

He had been receiving updates from Ottawa that the situation in the air had improved markedly in the last couple of hours. For reasons that remained unclear, CANZUK's combined air forces had finally overcome the Reds' Chinese fighters and in doing so, they were approaching the level of air superiority and operational pace that Vandal's mission planners had first envisioned.

Though the combined air forces of Australia, Canada, and the UK had suffered significant losses in the hours since the war had started, it was now the case that a steady streams of attack sorties were being undertaken to properly savage the Red Faction ground forces delaying CANZUK's battlegroups to the north. Getting the Brits and Aussies to Whiteman ASAP was now air command's leading priority.

In speaking with General Gagnon back in Ottawa, Larocque had been advised that support for their position from the air would continue to be spotty, with the thought being that Larocque and his soldiers could hold against the numerous, but lightly armed irregular units that had been hitting them since first light.

Whether he agreed with it or not, the generals had made their decision and it was now Larocque's job to make the situation work.

Not surprisingly, the next wave of approaching irregulars had altered their tactics after what had been a costly morning for the Americans. While another huge number of pickups were moving toward the base from the east and south, an on-station AWACS had been using its highly sensitive ground radar to precisely track a pack of armored vehicles at the center of the approaching irregular cavalcade. This armored and quick-moving force was now just one kilometer back from A Company's outermost lines.

Larocque moved his eyes to another data point - this one showed the live stream of a drone that was much closer to the action. It had zeroed its high-def camera in on a group of the approaching pickups. In all of the trucks, he could see that the flatbeds were now stacked with sandbags.

Moving to another display, he took in the vanguard of the force as it approached the thick cloud of smoke the Airborne's mortar teams had laid down. Switching the drone's feed to thermal, he watched the first of the trucks and dozens of on-foot combatants begin to slowly weave in amongst the ruined trucks from the morning's earlier battle.

It was in moments like these that commanding officers earned their pay. Throughout the bunker, he could feel the tension of the other officers and NCOs as the Red Faction irregulars slowly moved closer to the frontlines of A Company.

"Wait for it people. We're almost there," Larocque said aloud in an effort to steady the officers manning the half-dozen tactical stations in the bunker.

More time passed. The lead elements of the irregulars were now less than fifty meters from Chen's front.

It was at that moment that enough of the American fighting armor got to where they needed to be.

Larocque activated his BAM. "Open preset channel Romeo-Zulu."

"Channel open," replied the AI-generated voice.

"All bandits, execute, execute, execute."

———

Dune and his best mate, Lance Corporal Mark Crandell, sat statue-still in the cab of a shredded silver Ford F-250. In the passenger seat, his head lolled in the direction of the shattered passenger window while his mate, Cranny, was slumped against the steering wheel. The inside of the truck was a wreck. The windshield featured countless holes and random splashes of dried blood, while the roof of the vehicle had multiple gashes where shrapnel from mortar fire had torn through the pickup's unarmoured skin.

They had needed to drag out a still-warm body that had been slouched in the driver's seat when they first come across the devastated truck. Though the man's blood had stopped flowing, he hadn't bled out entirely, so in the act of grabbing the fellow and hoisting him, Dune had managed to cover much of his dusty brown fatigues in fresh blood.

As he undertook the effort of moving the dead Yank, it occurred to Dune that if Larocque's ruse was going to work, more of the dead man's fluid would be needed, as would some of the irregular fighter's clothing. As he had wiped the corpse's blood onto his face and put on the man's jacket and ball cap, Crandell and the two Canadians they'd teamed up with looked at him with disgust. To their credit, the penny quickly dropped for three men and they moved to join him in the macabre act.

Their gory disguises in place, Dune and Crandell took up residence in the truck's cab, while the two Canadians, Corporals Kettle and Stockton, laid askew in the vehicle's flatbed.

Some twenty minutes later, all four soldiers listened to the Red Faction irregulars' trucks as they slowly moved past them, their petrol and diesel engines growling as they rolled through a sea of green calf-high soybeans.

Being the only one of the four who was upright, Dune cracked one of his eyes open and took in several of the slow-moving trucks. There was an assortment of American-brand petrol and electric pick-ups in a variety of colors. In each, there was a gang of mostly male fighters carrying every make and model of weapon you could find at Joe Blow's gun shop. More than a few of the passersby had looked in Dune's direction, but when their eyes fell across his blood-caked face and unblinking eyes, they would quickly look away.

After several more minutes and as the smoke from the Canadian mortars began to dissipate, he heard the rumble of a larger, more powerful engine. Without moving so much as a centimeter and through fake dead eyes, Dune took in the sight of one of the few military vehicles the Reds still seemed to have in large numbers.

This variant of the Oshkosh Light Armoured Tactical Vehicle or LATV had an open-air turret that sported a fifty cal and an operator who was looking intently to the front of his vehicle. Further out, another LATV rolled past.

Larocque's mission briefing to Dune and the fifty other volunteers explained that the bulk of the civie trucks would pass them by, and then a smaller contingent of armored vehicles would roll through. It was when this secondary force arrived that the volunteer and inert Canadian paratroopers and Aussie Commandos would be set loose.

During their briefing for the crazed mission, Larocque had impressed three key instructions on his soldiers. Get in and hide amongst the vehicles furthest out from their lines, do not engage with the approaching vehicles until he provided the word. And when the shit did start to fly, they were to prioritize whatever armored vehicles they could get to.

As a third LATV slowly rumbled past their position, Dune heard the now-familiar voice of the Airborne CO pipe into his earbud, "All bandits, execute, execute, execute."

Instantly, Dune moved. In less than five seconds, he was out of the truck and had extended the firing tube of the M-72 anti-armor rocket he'd pulled from the floor of the truck. Getting down on one knee, he put the weapon on his shoulder and tilted his head so he could see through its optical sight. As his finger was about to depress the weapon's firing mechanism, he heard the *whoosh* of an M-72 that wasn't his. He watched the high explosive projectile streak through his field of vision and hammer into the back end of the LATV he had been targeting. At this distance, he took in the flash and boom of the explosion simultaneously and then heard one of the two Canadian soldiers belt out a celebratory curse.

As the haze of the rocket strike cleared, Dune saw that the soldier in the turret of the LATV had survived and was in the process of rotating his heavy machine gun in their direction. Still in his firing position, he lined up the vehicle for a second time and quickly depressed the M-72's firing button.

Instinctively, his eyes closed as the rocket's engine ignited and jetted out to its target. He was so close to the wounded vehicle that he heard a thunderous boom before he had a chance to open his eyes.

Taking in the scene, Dune saw that the high explosive round had fully penetrated the backside of the vehicle's hull and that thick black smoke was pouring out of the machine's blown-out windows. As he watched, the driver-side rear door of the LATV opened and a soldier stumbled outwards. On fire, the man shambled a dozen feet in Dune's direction and then collapsed to the ground, screaming.

He forced himself to take his eyes off the horrific display and take in the broader scene around him. Instantly, he perceived the sound of close-by automatic gunfire and supersonic rounds tearing through the air all around him. Just as he was about to get himself lower to the ground, Dune heard a voice scream from behind him, "Back here, Duney!"

Turning, he saw Kettle making a waving motion. Like a shot, he moved to the truck's cab where he grabbed a second M-72 and his F-88. Weapons in hand, he darted to the back of their truck where the other three soldiers were waiting.

"Oi, that was a hell of shot, mate," Crandell said.

"Aces for sure, man," Kettle said, echoing the compliment. "Right in the belly of the beast."

As the senior ranking man of the four, it had been agreed in advance that Kettle would guide their efforts after their initial attack.

"This is gonna be a hot mess, right from the get-go." Kettle was yelling to be heard over the torrent of gunfire. "We're gonna leapfrog from LATV to LATV until we run out of the M-72s, at which point we'll move onto the pickups. We move in pairs and fast. Sound like a plan?"

"Good a plan as any, mate," Dune offered quickly.

"Good. Then let's go and get ourselves some more Yankee red-necks."

————

Unlike the first American assault hours earlier, Chen and his company would not be able to rely on the use of the Airborne's mortars to help suppress the approaching fighters. The Red armor that was in amongst the militia had brought their own mortars and the two light artillery forces were now dueling in an effort to distract or outright destroy each other. And where the Airborne's mortar teams were well dug-in and protected, the Reds had more of the weapons. As a result, this next engagement would be an affair dominated by direct exchanges of fire.

Looking over the lip of his trench and keeping a close eye on the tactical drone image on the tac pad in front of him, Chen could see that the Red force had already progressed beyond the attack line of the morning's earlier assault.

The American irregulars were making good use of the de-stroyed trucks as cover from his soldiers' heavy weapons, and in al-most all cases, the approaching civilian vehicles had received some type of rudimentary modification increasing their survivability. They looked ramshackle, but there was no doubt that each one of the pickup trucks had become harder to kill.

As planned, Chen's company had waited for Larocque's order before opening up. It had been an unnerving delay, but when the order came, every weapon in his company's arsenal had reached out to the slow-moving militia, and do-it-yourself armor or no, the out-going fusillade was devastation personified.

As his soldiers unleashed their barrage, Chen did his best to shepherd the fight. Through his BAM, he was in constant contact with his junior officers and senior NCOs across the company's de-fensive line.

As he engaged in the most recent of these conversations, he heard the *crack* of his trench's Carl Gustaf as it sent forward yet another high explosive 84mm round into one of the approaching pickups. The two Canadians working the anti-armor weapon were sure-fire pros and had rarely missed a mark in the time he'd been with them.

At a mere one hundred and fifty meters out, the truck in question jacked backward and up as the Gustaf's round tore into its engine block. As the vehicle bucked, several of the men who had been firing from atop the flatbed cartwheeled into the air.

Pausing the conversation he was having with one of his inherited sergeants via his BAM, Chen shouldered his F-88 and through the rifle's scope, aimed and then unloaded separate bursts at two men who had survived their ejection and who were now trying to get to their feet. Chen watched as one man pirouetted and fell to the ground while the other scampered to safety behind another destroyed vehicle.

As Chen stood higher in their trench, he took in his first direct sighting of one of the Red Faction's armored fighting vehicles as it stormed past the pickup his trench had just eviscerated. The fast-moving hulk was the six-wheeled version of the US Army's Cougar Mine Resistant Ambush Protection, MRAP vehicle.

As the heavily armored war machine began to draw an increased response from Chen's soldiers, more of the irregular pickups hit their accelerators and raced forward to flank the Cougar and its crew. Less than a hundred meters from his outer lines, the huge vehicle hammered its brakes. Soldiers atop the vehicle poured withering amounts of fire back in the direction of A Company's trenches and were soon joined by a half-dozen pickups, each with their own complement of fighting men.

As he took in the scene, Chen knew that the commander of the attacking American force would be giving orders for another set of vehicles to leapfrog ahead of the now-stationary Cougar, putting this next set of vehicles virtually on top of his outermost trenches.

As bullets snapped around him, he calmly looked down at his tac pad on the lip of his trench and quickly designated the MRAP and several of the adjacent pickup trucks using the targeting laser on surveillance drone that remained high above their position.

Over the roar of the fighting, Chen activated his BAM.

"Open channel to Mast Seven."

Larocque had dedicated two of the Airborne's Spike anti-armor missile teams to his company. Back amongst the Regiment's last stand position and behind a long treeline just behind his own trench, the soldiers operating the two Spike LR units had been waiting patiently on a fire mission.

"Channel open," the voice of his BAM announced clearly in his earbud.

"Mast Seven, this is Winch Nine. Targets have been designated in grid Alpha Niner. Light'em up."

"Solid copy, Winch Nine. Here they come."

Seconds later, Chen heard a deep *whoomph* and then a sharp *crack* as the heavily armored Cougar and one of the civilian trucks were simultaneously struck.

While the fourteen-ton fighting vehicle seemed not to move an inch, the gunner who had been sitting protected in the fighting machine's turret ejected into the air as the vehicle's thick armor chimneyed the missile's energy through its top-side aperture. The explosion of the one civilian truck that had been hit offered its own spectacular result. The missile shredded the vehicle front to back and in the process set off the machine's gas tank. In conjunction with a deep boom, a spectacular orange-and-crimson fireball billowed high into the air.

As black smoke from the explosion poisoned the clear blue sky, another pair of civilian trucks were hammered by anti-armor missiles creating a second round of fierce explosions. With four vehicles cooking off, the rate of fire coming in from attacking irregulars began to slacken, if only slightly.

Consulting the drone stream on his tac pad, Chen could see that more civie trucks and a smaller number of LATVs were moving up to reinforce those vehicles they had just obliterated. Working the tac pad's display, he canceled the Spike teams' current fire mission and re-designated this next set of attackers.

The voice of Chen's BAM advised him he had a priority call, which he immediately authorized.

"Chen, it's Larocque."

"Hearing you loud and clear, sir. What's up?"

"Top notch work holding your line, Captain. Your boys are fighting like lions."

"They're first-rate, sir. A real credit to Brazeau."

"A hundred percent," said Larocque, "Marcel would be proud as hell, but it's time for your lot to pull back. The air force has been giving the approaching Reds a real pounding, but that larger force out of St. Louis has made great time and they're not going to quit. We don't have enough assets in the air to stop them all. They'll be on us within less than an hour and they'll have 155s with them. My guess is that those guns will start to pound your lines in the next twenty mikes or so."

"What do you need me to do?" Chen asked.

"I want a third of your company to fall back to my position in the thicket, while the remaining two-thirds will move to the intermediate line of defense where you are now. With that treeline and subdivision at your backs, you'll have cover when you need to bolt back to the base proper. I'll be giving the same order to the other companies as soon as I'm done with you. We're just too thin based on our current footprint."

"Copy that, sir. It's getting tight out here, for sure. As soon as I've received word that the surviving volunteers have made it back to our lines, I'll give the order to move."

There was a quick pause over the connection.

"Don't wait all day for them," Larocque said in a firm voice. "Give 'em ten more minutes, and then I want your men on the move from the outermost lines. Those who haven't made it by then aren't coming."

Chen ducked instinctively, as a burst of high-caliber rounds tore through the air around his head. A scream of pain issued to his right and one of the men in his trench slumped hard to the ground as blood began to pump liberally from a chest wound that cut through the paratrooper's body armor.

"You still there, Captain?" said Larocque, his tone still on the level.

The Aussie officer ripped his eyes from the futile effort. "Yes, sir. The lads in the outermost lines move in ten."

"Good, we'll make this next stand with lots of on-station air support and because of that, the Reds are gonna come at us hard and fast. You have a handful of guys still in the fight who are certi-fied for forward air control, so make sure they're distributed evenly along your lines. I've sent you a file with their names. All of them know what to do. Ares will manage their requests as they come in."

"And what's the latest on the cavalry, sir? Someone has gotta be close," Chen said.

"It's down to the Brits coming out of the north," advised Larocque. "The Canadian battlegroups in the west are out of the picture entirely. The Brits are close but not as close as we need them to be, so no matter how you look at it, we're gonna be on our own when the main force hits us. It'll be knife's edge stuff. Are you up for it, Captain?"

Chen reply was instant. "Solid copy on that, sir. We fight like hell until our mates get here."

"That's right Captain, you give'em hell until I tell you otherwise. Larocque out."

Chapter 31

The Atlantic Ocean, off the coast of South Carolina

Following the grounding of the UCSA's remaining J-31s, the most noteworthy development in the air war in the past four hours had been the sudden appearance of the British aircraft carrier, the *HMS Prince of Wales* and her escorts off the coast of South Carolina.

At the kick-off of Vandal, the UK's only other aircraft carrier, the *HMS Queen Elizabeth*, had steamed up from the Caribbean to launch dozens of sorties with the twenty-six F-35s on its deck. The result had been the hammering of military targets across the American Southeast. Following these attacks, the *Elizabeth* and her support ships had made speed back into the Atlantic, drawing a sizable UCSA flotilla with her in hot pursuit.

Cruising somewhere in the mid-Atlantic, the *Prince of Wales* had sprinted south and upon coming into range of the same geography as its sister ship, the Royal Navy's second aircraft carrier, along with her Tomahawk-armed escorts, launched a series of devastating airstrikes on a host of targets that were feeding into the conflict taking place in Missouri.

But unlike the *Elizabeth*, the *PoW* had been given orders to hold fast off the American Southeast and to deliver and take as much punishment as it could.

The situation at the center of the country had officially become desperate. For the Canadians to hold, and for CANZUK to win, the British admiralty needed to do what the Royal Navy had done so many times before. Like the ships of the line from a different and glorious era, Great Britain resolved itself to once again dominate the Atlantic Ocean, if only for the next few hours.

———

Above Missouri

Major Khan pushed on his flight stick hard, forcing his plane into a steep dive. One of the tactical displays in front of him was flashing urgently, while his plane's near-AI was telling him for the umpteenth time in an infuriatingly calm voice that a pair of missiles were on his six.

"I know, I know," Khan said through clenched teeth. "I'm working on it, now just keep quiet for a bloody moment while I get things sorted, you gobby cow."

At five thousand feet, Khan pulled back savagely on the flight stick to level off, while at the same time toggling a button to release a stream of chaff from the underbelly of his fighter.

Immediately, he juked into another dive – this one shallower and within moments his Tempest was screaming hundreds of feet above the surface of rural Missouri. He released another salvo of chaff and then banked his fighter hard to the left.

As his body compressed under hundreds of pounds of gravitational pressure and as he flexed the right muscles to ensure enough blood got to his brain, his plane's near-AI advised in a tone of complete detachment, "Missiles have disengaged."

"About bloody time!" Khan howled back at the sterile voice. "You know, it might not be a bad idea for you to offer just a touch of urgency when we're in the thick of things. Your ass is on the line as much as mine."

"Command not understood," the voice calmly advised.

"Oh bollocks! You just wait until this war is over."

"Command not understood," the plane's onboard near-AI repeated.

"Oh, go shove off."

Khan pulled back on his flight stick and felt the nose of his aircraft elevate. As the altimeter data on the oversized center display screen began to roll upward, a voice jumped into his helmet. "Knife One, this is Ares Three, do you copy?"

"Ares, hearing you loud and clear. Go ahead."

"Knife One, you and the rest of your flight are to break off from your current action and make your way back to FOB Lima-Zulu ASAP. There is a high-priority action in the hopper that needs your attention."

"Copy that, Ares. It looks like we're done with this lot for the moment, anyway. Knife One out."

Khan again looked at the display that held details on their current mission. They had lost Downer, the fourth pilot from his squadron. Someone needed to tell the Yanks they had lost this part of the war, he thought bitterly.

Toggling open the comms channel that would connect him with the pilots that remained from the current mission, Khan said, "Alright everyone, you heard Ares, stop whatever you're doing and head back to Lima-Zulu on the double. Let's form up and get to where we need to be. It might be that we have some payback waiting for Downer when we touch down. Pony out."

————

Ottawa

The past eight hours had been a blur. The sudden and horrific death of the prime minister and his wife, and the unprecedented changes that followed, had come at Merielle in a torrent.

As she had taken in the scene of the PM's destroyed body, additional police officers had arrived and cleared the rest of the residence. The perpetrators – Altov and perhaps four other men – had rappelled down the cliff at the back of the property and fled along the Ottawa River. As neither the Ottawa Police nor the RCMP had a helicopter in the region, there was no hope that the assassins would be tracked down quickly.

From 24 Sussex, she had gone to Parliament Hill, the Canadian government's center of power, where her fellow cabinet ministers had been asked to gather by no later than 0600 hours. At that time,

Merielle, the head of the RCMP, CSIS, and a small group of the country's most senior bureaucrats, briefed her colleagues on what had happened.

Merielle had been surprised by the range of emotions that had been on display during the briefing by her fellow cabinet ministers.

For her and the rest of the cabinet, the past thirty-six hours had been a roller coaster of emotions. Members of Parliament had been inundated with a deluge of emails and social media by Canadians who were against the CANZUK action, while two constituency offices – one in Montreal and one in Vancouver – had been firebombed. Layered over these, no fewer than a dozen large-scale protests had erupted in cities across the country, and in a few cases, they had turned violent.

When you put it all together, it was a recipe for frayed nerves and second thoughts. But when the crying and shouting had ended, Merielle, with the help of the prime minister's staunchest allies, had wrangled the twenty-six cabinet-level politicians into line. Canada would see out the course of action now underway in Missouri and Merielle would be sworn in as Canada's twenty-ninth prime minister sometime in the afternoon at an undisclosed location.

But before that could happen, her colleagues had demanded that she address the country to clarify the many inaccurate news reports that were consuming the Canadian and international news media about what had happened to the PM, and that she reaffirm with certitude the necessity of the intervention into Missouri. To this, an exhausted Merielle had agreed.

"My fellow Canadians. I speak to you this morning as the bearer of terrible news.

"In the earliest hours of this morning, a terrorist cell of unknown origin or affiliation stormed the prime minister's residence at 24 Sussex Drive and assassinated my colleague, dear friend, and our country's twenty-eighth prime minister, the Honorable Robert C. MacDonald. Also killed were the prime minister's wife, and eight members of his security detail, along with another six police officers who bravely raced to the scene.

"At this time, we know the identity of some of the attackers, but we lack details on the motives behind their horrendous crime. Also, we have yet to confirm satisfactory details regarding the organization or country behind this act of terror. The RCMP and other agencies are working in partnership with our allies to piece together these details. Rest assured, Canadians will be apprised of more information as it becomes available.

"I want to address the rumors that are circulating that the assassination of Prime Minister MacDonald and his wife was somehow linked with the ongoing CANZUK operation taking place in Missouri. The Government of Canada has no information confirming that the terrorist operation that took place has any connection with the government of the United Constitutional States of America.

"However, in stating this, I have been asked by cabinet colleagues to make two critical points. First, Canada, acting in conjunction and full cooperation with its CANZUK allies will not be dissuaded from the mission it has undertaken to remove the nuclear weapons located at Whiteman Air Force Base. It remains the view of the Canadian government that the UCSA cannot once again become a nuclear power. Second, to the organization or country that undertook this horrific act, know that the full weight of the Canadian government in collaboration with our friends and allies will identify, seek out, and punish those who perpetrated this abominable crime.

"My fellow Canadians, I understand recent events have no precedent in our history. But it is also the case that Canada is a member of the global community and more specifically, we are an intimate partner on the North American continent. The mass destruction of cities and the slaughter of millions of people is not something Canadians can afford to take lightly.

"To this end, the policies of the MacDonald government will continue. This morning at exactly 6:34 a.m., eastern standard time, my cabinet colleagues voted unanimously in support of my becoming Canada's next prime minister. In honor of my friend Bob MacDonald, out of respect for my colleagues, and in solidarity with the men and women of the Canadian Armed Forces who are currently fighting to defend our country's interests and our way of life, I have accepted this nomination.

"I will be sworn in by the Governor General in an undisclosed location this afternoon, at which point I will make further remarks about ongoing developments concerning our actions in Missouri and the investigation concerning the prime minister's death.

"Until then, regardless of your political persuasion, I would ask that you send your thoughts and prayers in support of the MacDonald family, the valiant police officers who gave their lives in defense of our democracy, and our valiant soldiers who have laid down their lives for the security of our great nation. Today, as much as any other day in the past five generations, we are all Canadians. As a people, we must be united and show our support for those who have made the ultimate sacrifice.

"As you contemplate what has transpired in the past twenty-four hours, remember that democracy and freedom is not free. There has always been a cost to the fundamental freedoms that we hold dear. We have paid these costs with the sacrifice of lives in the past and we must do this again if we are to maintain who we are as a nation and a people. This is our policy. This will remain our policy.

"Thank you."

———

San Antonio, 5th Army HQ

"No, Mr. President, I am not transferring fighters from the Missouri theatre to the East Coast. You and that part of the country are going to have to make do with the resources that you have to fend off the British. Every plane I move away from this fight is one less fighter I have to take back Whiteman. Whiteman is the priority. Those were your words, your sentiments, Mr. President, and I'll be damned if I don't give the men and women under my command the support they need to achieve the mission we've assigned to them."

As Spector put the final touches on his defiance, the tinge of Cameron's face grew redder by the second. And then the explosion came.

"How dare you. How dare you?!" On the high-def screen in front of him, Spector could see spittle eject from Cameron's mouth. "After all that I have done for you, you have the audacity to sit here in front of me and deny to me what is mine by rights. I am Commander-In-Chief, General – not you. And it is I who has the final say on how we deploy our forces in times of peace and war. Not you. I would have thought that was made clear to you when you saw what happened to General Evans and the others."

Spector had known all along they would arrive at this juncture. That it had come so quickly was the only thing that was a surprise. Nevertheless, he had made the appropriate preparations, and while not all of his plans were fully set, enough were in place that he could put things into motion with confidence.

Spector gave the agitated man on his display a hard stare. "Mr. President, you may be the Commander-In-Chief, but you are just a man. A man I once felt was the best person to bring our country back together. I now wonder if this is the case. Per your orders, I have a base to retake and a war to win. Whatever it is you think you need to do to me, then my suggestion is for you to go ahead and do it. War is bigger than any one man. Goodbye, Mr. President."

"You son of a bitch, don't you dare disconnect from me..."

Spector fingered the button to cut his connection with Cameron and then let out a huge gust of air from his oversized upper frame. After a moment's pause, he pulled a phone from his pocket. Activating it, he brought up the desired number.

"I'm here," a male voice said.

"We're a go, Colonel," said Spector.

"Yes, sir. Confirming that we are a go."

———

Whiteman AFB

Through the entrance to the command bunker, Larocque listened to the latest salvo of artillery shells explode as they hit somewhere close by and then said loudly, "Listen, I'm telling you, if you don't find a way to put down that incoming fire they're feeding us, we won't hold this base more than fifteen minutes once they start their push. You put whatever resources you need on finding those batteries and take them offline and pronto. I'm telling you from here on the ground and in no uncertain terms, this needs to be your top Goddamned priority."

The Airborne CO paused, signaling he was listening. After a brief spell of silence, he said, "I don't care what you need to do, just make it happen. Winch One out."

"Ares?" asked Rydell.

"The one and only," said Larocque. "It would seem the Air Force doesn't have a good appreciation for how difficult it is to defend a position on the ground when your soldiers can't raise their heads out of their trenches."

"Sir," interjected an officer manning one of the tactical management stations.

Larocque turned away from the Australian colonel and cast a hard stare at the junior officer, "Yes, Captain?"

"We've just lost video from drones four and five."

"Perfect timing. Here they come. And faster than I would have thought possible," said Larocque. "What do we have left in the air?"

"We still have ground radar from the AWACS and two tactical drones still flying over the northern and southern sectors."

"How high can we get those things?"

"The tac drones have a ceiling of six thousand feet, sir."

"Get them both to four thousand feet and shift the drone in the north to the eastern sector over A Company and Chen. As best you can, keep feeding the right people what's coming their way."

Larocque turned to Rydell. "You still have some of those drones you brought with you?"

"There's a pair of them left and they're ready to go."

"Now's the time to get them going. We're weakest to the south, for sure, so send them that way. Have your operators hit their heavier stuff as best they can. There'll be lots to choose from, by the sounds of it."

"Copy that. They'll be on the hunt in moments," said Rydell in an entirely business-like tone.

Larocque's eyes locked onto the Australian and after a brief pause, he said, "Brian, I need you to stay here to manage things."

"Where? Here? In the CP?" Rydell said while hefting his thumb in the direction of the bunker's reinforced ceiling. "Listen, mate, I know you want to go be with your lads, but I've watched you try and move around all day - you'll be next to useless out there. Best you stay here and let me handle it. With the drones and me feeding you, you can do the work right here."

A smile touched Larocque's lips. "You're a prince of a guy to offer, Brian, but I can't let that happen. I know we're a team and I'll be forever in your debt for what you and your regiment have done since arriving, but those are my boys out there, and broken or not, they need to see me fighting alongside them. And besides, if they break through, they're going to go straight for the nukes. Somebody's gotta be there to make the call to throw in the towel if it comes to that. It's us who dragged you into this little war, so if a call needs to be made to pack it in, it's gotta be with me and with my own eyes. You know what's on the line if we don't pull this off."

Rydell took a step closer to Larocque and lowering his voice, said, "You think Colorado will incinerate this place if we don't hold?"

"They've done it before," Larocque offered soberly. "As I understand it, this Anders is one tough lady. In the grand scheme, our units are insignificant pieces. Hell, even our countries are pawns in comparison to what's at stake here in the US. As soon as that woman gets word the base has fallen, we'll have less than an hour. That's my guess. She won't risk the chance of one weapon getting off this base. Intel is certain of that. I know if I were in her position I wouldn't wait even that long."

Larocque paused, waiting for the Australian colonel to offer a counter-argument or some rationale to convince him that the Governor of Colorado wouldn't follow through on her threat, but the man offered nothing.

Larocque stuck out his hand. Rydell stared at it for a brief moment and then took it up and pumped it. "It's been one hell of a privilege working alongside the men and women of Australia's 2nd Commando, Colonel Rydell. A braver and tougher lot I couldn't have asked for." Larocque said the words so that the whole of the bunker could once again hear the exchange.

"Steady on, mate," Rydell said. "I think you're a touch gone to go out there, but I can understand why. Truth of it is, I'm glad it's on you to make the call if it's needed. It'll be a hell of a burden to bear if it comes to that."

Hearing the Australian's words, Larocque grimaced and said, "Duty, it's a hell of a thing sometimes, but as it turns out, I'm pretty good at carrying a burden."

For the briefest moment, Rydell allowed a look of sympathy to cross his face. "Bottom line, Airborne, is that between the two of us and our people, we do what needs to be done so that we don't have to make that call in the first place. I reckon that's the best plan."

Knowing that the soldiers in the command post could hear their conversation, Larocque held the other man's gaze, smiled, and offered his reply. "Our two countries don't like to lose, Colonel. Not ever. Today and together, we fight to win."

Chapter 32

Missouri, somewhere north of Whiteman AFB

Costen watched the sky as three Super Hornets approached the length of forest that stood in front of his vanguard of Challengers and Boxer armored vehicles.

Flying parallel to a long chain of trees that stood between his battlegroup and their final dash to Whiteman, the three pilots were angled on a gradual descent. At perhaps two kilometers out, the three fighter-bombers unleashed twelve fully loaded pods of their Canadian-manufactured CRV7 rockets on that part of the forest that surrounded the now-destroyed bridge that Costen's battlegroup needed to cross.

In grey puffs of smoke, the unguided rockets ejected from the fighters' wings and screamed through the air toward the ground. After a momentary flight, the individual projectiles created a choppy, thunderous clap of a sound as they struck the heavily treed ground that surrounded the road leading to the collapsed span.

Moments earlier, watching via one of the battlegroup's remaining drones, Costen had been helpless to stop the Red soldiers who had blown the short concrete bridge that crossed the meandering creek which now confronted his exhausted soldiers. As the bridge-crashers completed their work, dozens of Red Faction irregulars had moved into the dense foliage to lay in wait on the south side of the slow-moving brown water.

"Units four through ten, advance. Move down to the bank and draw fire from whoever's on the other side," Costen said into his headset. Thirty meters in front of his tank, he saw six Boxer infantry fighting vehicles start to move forward, their diesel engines roaring to life. Each vehicle was armed with a remote-operated heavy machine gun that would spew 30mm rounds and was carrying ten infanteers all armed with their own accouterments of war.

As the Boxers came within two hundred meters of the creek's edge, Costen heard the eruption of gunfire from the forest. In turn, each of the Boxers' top-side machine guns opened up. Over the crackle of exchanging fire, Costen heard the explosion of the IEDs the Reds had buried in the ground around the road leading to the now-collapsed bridge.

Courtesy of a high-flying Reaper that had been shadowing his battlegroup's advance, the drivers of the Boxers had driven their machines in such a way they avoided the worst effects of the detonations. Skirting by the worst of the massive explosion, Costen watched the Boxers stop within fifty meters of the water and begin to disgorge their soldiers, who in short order began to advance in leapfrogging section movements to the edge of the creek.

He toggled on his headset. "Bridging team, you're up. Straight through, no delays. Get that bloody span down chop-chop like and then get out of the way."

Ahead of him, one of the British Army's Titan bridge layers, a support vehicle carrying a bundle of aluminum stanchions, and four more Boxers, roared to life and began to move in the direction of the fallen bridge.

An ugly thing, the Titan was a Challenger chassis that had the wholly unsexy, but critical responsibility of lugging around a massive twenty-six-meter bridging span atop its steel spine. Costen smiled like a proud father as the ungainly thing lurched forward with increasing speed.

That the bridge layer was here at all was a small miracle. From the moment the Red irregulars started to attack the non-fighting components of his battlegroup, they had taken countless shots at the Titans. Recognizing their peril, the officer leading the battlegroup's combat engineers had given the order to strap down sandbags atop each vehicle's folded bridge. Having done this, that same officer had put in for whatever light and heavy machine guns the battlegroup could afford to put on loan and turned the two ungainly vehicles into mobile redoubts of death.

With his own eyes and via the on-station drone, Costen watched the four Boxers and the two sapper vehicles roll up to the severed concrete structure. While two of the Boxers planted themselves to the right and left of the shattered bridge, the other two APCs drove to the bank of the creek and proceeded to slowly cross the ten-meter-wide waterway. The creek could be forded by the battlegroup's fighting machines but not its many logistics vehicles.

As the two armored machines crested the lip of the opposite embankment, Costen picked up movement on the drone further down the forested roadway that lay ahead of them.

Before any warning could be given, he saw a flash and then the lead Boxer exploded in a spectacular shower of fire and debris.

Costen cocked his head and bellowed at the exposed head of his tank's driver. "Timmy, get us moving to that bridge, now!"

Immediately, the idling engine of the seventy-ton Challenger 3 tank roared to life and shot forward as Cpl. Timothy Brown engaged the tank's drive system.

In seconds, the tank was at speed and Costen's gunner, a reliable man out of Bath, had already shouldered the tank's pintle-mounted heavy machine gun and was looking downrange at the chaos that had erupted on the far side of the bridge. Costen toggled the tank's internal comms system. "Timmy, go to the left of the bridge and put us up through that bloody water. When we come up on the other side, pull us out in front of our lads. As we get there, anything and everything in front of us gets a round straight up the arse. Understood?"

All three of his crew members belted out a simultaneous, "aye."

As they approached the bridge Costen took in what had become a desperate scene. The heavy weapons of the bridging team's three remaining Boxers were chattering in the direction of four ar mored and fast-moving vehicles that had sprung out from the tree-line up the road. As his tank sped forward, Costen did his best to line up one of the vehicles but for all of his tank's jostling and with the Boxers and the bridging vehicles in the way, he couldn't risk taking the shot. Slowing down, but just slightly, Cpl. Brown expertly muscled their tank down the creek's embankment and as the machine hit the water, a burst of brown and white froth erupted over the prow of the tank.

Accelerating, the Challenger crested to the left of the broken bridge and without hesitation, pushed past the now-burning APC.

Perhaps two hundred meters behind the closest Red Faction armored truck, Costen zeroed his tank's sighting optics on the American-made LATV that was armed with a single-tube, reloadable Javelin anti-tank missile. Atop the vehicle, a pair of soldiers were struggling to reload a missile into the rooftop weapon. As the tank's targeting software flashed that it had a lock, Costen triggered the Challenger's 120mm cannon to reach out and touch his target. Instantly, all of Costen's senses took in the satisfying sound, smell, and feel of his tank's main gun as it bellowed. Ahead, the LATV and the men within it were shredded into a grey-and-black mess.

Just as the round connected, Costen heard the tank's loader, one Private Gillespie, bellow, "Loading," as he hefted another high-explosive round into the breech of the tank's main gun. Seconds later, the young man from Manchester hollered, "Ready!"

Having already lined up another of the LATVs, Costen again made his tank reach out to tag the now outgunned Americans.

As he eviscerated a second vehicle at close range, he noted with relief that the two remaining lorries had begun to reverse in the direction they had come, their drivers expertly juking, making it all but impossible to land a third kill shot. Costen made the call to let them go.

As he took his eyes off the fleeing vehicles, his BAM wrist unit vibrated, signaling that it held a high-priority message. He looked down and after reading the short note, he belted out a vicious curse.

He toggled his tank's comms unit to re-connect him with the bridging team.

"Lieutenant Hawthorne, if you haven't started putting down that bridge of yours, you best be on it now. First across are the medics and then the rest of you lot start coming across as planned. From there, the designated teams push through to points Delta, Echo, and Foxtrot, and we do so with all the speed we can muster without cocking up the process. We need to be on point, people. I just got word from Whiteman. The Yanks out of St. Louis have just set upon the Canucks. We are officially out of time."

———

Whiteman AFB

Chen had ordered a fallback of what remained of his company. Per Larocque's orders, one-third had moved to the last stand position in and amongst Whiteman's bunkers, while the remainder of his soldiers had hunkered down in the interim trench system where he was now located.

Due east of Whiteman, there was a good-sized span of trees and a subdivision that held maybe one hundred or so family-sized dwellings. The trees and the solidly built homes together with his well-dug-in soldiers would be a tough nut to crack, so the assumption was that the Reds would look to drive the bulk of their attacking force north of where Chen's company linked up with Singh's B Company.

If you looked at Whiteman from the air, his company's area of defense was where the north end of the base's runway terminated. But for a few thin bands of trees that signaled the property lines of local farmers and the base's outermost chain-link fence, the area in front of their trenches was green, flat, and wide open. It was on this canvas that his inherited company would meet the oncoming wave of Red Faction fighting steel.

As tough as the Canadians and his Diggers were, and for all the tank traps and other obstacles the Airborne's engineers had feverishly built in the past twenty-four hours, Chen knew it would not be enough, but for the CANZUK fighter-bombers finally in the sky above the base. Though there weren't many, if they were going to repel the surging Americans, it would be because they made full and effective use of the waiting Super Hornets and Typhoons over this part of Missouri.

As Chen heard the deep thump of an airstrike in the not-too-far distance, he forced himself to draw in a series of calming breaths. The fighting to this point had been difficult and vicious, but for all intents and purposes, it had been one-sided. That was about to change. Until this moment, the Americans had experienced the equivalent of a bloodied nose. Their mates slaughtered and their ample pride bruised, the Yank regulars were coming, and they would be rightly pissed. Chen reminded himself that the same units now charging toward his lines had participated in some of the most savage bloodletting in the American civil war. On that charge, he had no illusions of what would happen if things went poorly for them.

The concussive force of another airstrike reverberated the trench. This one was closer. Ahead, maybe two kilometers away, his eyes took in a growing plume of roiling blackness. Not long now, he thought. This final battle for Whiteman would be a brutal, touch-and-go affair. A last stand for the ages.

In the pantheon of war, perhaps Whiteman would rest beside the likes of Thermopylae or the Alamo. Not a bad place to be if you were into the notion of a glorious death.

"Piss on it," Chen said aloud.

"Eh? Piss on what, exactly?" said Karlina in response to the outburst. The Aussie warrant officer had been Chen's shadow for the past two hours.

"Piss on the Yanks. We're gonna hold this base and we're gonna send these bogans packing. History can go wank itself."

One of Karlina's eyebrows raised. "Stumbled onto some more Latin, did you, professor?"

Chen looked at the older sganoldier and offered up a tired-looking smile. "Not Latin my good Warrant. Just the realization that history ain't worth shit to a man in a trench."

"Amen to that Captain. Amen to that."

———

Whiteman AFB

Somehow, Kettle and Dune had both managed to survive the batshit crazy jaunt Larocque had sent them out on earlier in the morning. It had been a hell of a ride and when their little rampage was over, their team of four had taken out two of the Americans' LATVs and half a dozen civie trucks along with quite a few of the rednecks riding in them. It had been savage but entirely satisfying work.

On making it back to the outer line of trenches the Airborne now occupied, the foursome had agreed to stay together, and along with two other Canadian paratroopers who were operating a C-6 heavy machine gun, Kettle, Stockton, and their two new Aussie friends were as ready as they could be.

Over the past twenty minutes, Kettle had both seen and heard multiple airstrikes, as pairs of CANZUK fighter-bombers streaked and looped across the clear blue sky in an effort to hunt down the approaching 101st Airborne. The last strike couldn't have been more than two kilometers away.

"Straight ahead," he heard one of the machine gunners say.

Kettle shifted his gaze and saw the movement at the edge of a far-off tree line. Two, three, and then five hulking vehicles emerged to their front. They were maybe one klick out from their position. Two Stryker APCs and two LATVs each flanked one of the Americans' iconic Abrams main battle tanks. At the center of the rolling formation, the MBT dominated the scene, its turret and gun muzzle pointed in the general direction of the Canadian defenders.

"Look at that pig," Kettle said aloud.

He felt a slap on his shoulder and looked to his right to take in Dune.

"Now ain't that a thing of beauty, eh, mate? A real American hero that there tank is."

Kettle laughed. "You're fucked, Duney."

"Oi!" cried Dune. "Why in Christ's name do you Canucks insist on throwing a 'Y' onto everyone's name anyway?"

"Don't ask me," said Kettle. "You play hockey and whoever has a last name where a 'y' fits, that's what's you're called. And don't think for one second you can tell people you don't want your new name. It's your new name. End of story."

"And what about your name, mate? Why are you 'Kets' instead of 'Ketty?'"

"Dude, do I look like the expert on how people get their names? You get the name you get from some guy on your team and that's how it goes. It's not a science, man. It's art, and you can't explain art. Or that's what my last old lady told me."

"Fair enough, I reckon. Kets you shall remain," Dune said as he casually moved to grab up one of the half-dozen M-72s they had leaned up against the wall of their trench.

The paratroopers operating to Kettle's left opened up with their C-6. This close, the report of the machine gun was ear-splitting thunder. In that same moment, Kettle felt and saw the five approaching vehicles open up with their own weapons. The Abrams' main gun roared. Instantly, Kettle heard an explosion somewhere behind him. As the maelstrom of violence kicked off fully, he caught the scream of incoming mortars and bellowed, "Incoming!"

Somewhere close, an anti-personnel mortar shell exploded high in the air peppering the ground with a burst of shrapnel. He heard more whistling and in the seconds that followed more kernels of red-hot steel began to shower the immediate area.

As the unfazed men in the trench continued pouring out rounds in the direction of the approaching enemy, Kettle heard a detonation that overwhelmed all other sounds. To their front, one of the two Strykers exploded in a spectacular burst of orange and black. To the destroyed machine's right, the Abrams' gun thundered again and without losing any speed, the tank rolled through and over the steel link fence that was the outermost perimeter of the American airbase. As it did so, the fast-moving seventy-ton machine ripped a huge gap in the fifteen-foot-high fence, clearing a path for the vehicles that were a part of its formation.

Now less than four hundred meters from their position, the American behemoth came to a stop and began to aim its main gun in the direction of their trench.

With the C-6 heavy machine gun to his left still blazing away, Kettle heard Dune scream, "Get down!"

In that same moment, a bright flash erupted on the right side of the tank. The Abrams bucked so violently that the machine's right track cleared the ground. Its muzzle now unmoving, black smoke began to seep out of the tank at various points signaling that the insides of the venerable fighting machine and its crew had been incinerated by some type of anti-armor munition.

As the tank undertook the beginnings of a full burn, the remaining vehicles from the attacking formation overtook the Abrams and formed a new line of attack.

As each of the Red Faction vehicles continued to lay down suppressive fire on the trenches in front of them, handfuls of the irregular pickups began to filter forward to take up positions to the left and right of the reg force armor. Soon, as many as two dozen pickups of various makes and colors had joined the fighting, adding their own collection of personal weapons to the growing onslaught.

With bullets whizzing over his head and the sound of mortars still erupting, Kettle grabbed an M-72 and quickly extended the anti-armor weapon. Placing it on his shoulder he aimed the rocket-carrying cylinder at a bright red Ford dually next to one of the Reds' LATVs and fired. Hearing the now-familiar *whoosh* of the weapon, Kettle saw the front end of the truck jack violently and burst into a black mess of superheated gases and fire.

"Oi, you don't miss with these things, do you?" said Dune to his right.

Reaching down, Kettle took up another of the one-shot rockets and extended it. Taking in Dune, Kettle saw that the Aussie commando had also taken up his second M-72.

"Four for five. We're all tied up, Kets," Dune yelled over the sound of the nearby chattering C-6. "Looks like we have six of these bad boys left. Interested in a bit of a wager?"

"With you – anything," Kettle said.

"Man with the most kills has to buy the other man a slab. And quality stuff mind you. None of this cheap piss you Canadian cunts are so fond of drinking."

"If by slab, you mean a two-four, then you're on. And the bet is for a case of Moosehead, Canada's best beer, bar none."

"Ah, there's a good lad. A deal it is."

Without another word, Kettle watched Dune step onto the firing step of the trench and in less than five seconds, the Aussie commando unleashed his weapon. Looking downrange, Kettle saw the backend of a gray pickup flash and then explode as the vehicle's gas tank ignited.

As the explosion of a full tank of petrol rolled over them, Dune casually turned back to Kettle with a huge grin on his face. "Five for six, mate. I can taste those coldies already."

Whiteman AFB

Looking south, Larocque lay prone in one of the small redoubts his troops had built on top of some of the nuclear bunkers. Rounds of various calibers zipped and snapped by him on a near-continuous basis, while the sound of explosions and jet engines tore through the air with a busy ebb and flow.

"C Company, pull back to Point Lima now. I repeat, C Company, pull back. I'm calling in a strike to cover your retreat. Air assets will hit the positions you now hold and everything that is south of you, so put down smoke and get on your horses and move to Lima now," Larocque barked into his BAM.

He manipulated the back of his mouthguard, signaling to the comms system that he wanted to open a new channel. "Get me Ares Three, priority Mike-Papa-Niner."

"Channel open," the BAM synthesized voice advised in his earbud.

"Ares Three, this is Winch Actual, do you copy?" barked Larocque.

"Ares Three here," said the female voice he had been speaking to on the regular over the past hour.

"Ares, we've been overwhelmed in the southern sector. The place is crawling with the enemy. They're everywhere. Abrams and other nasty shit. Whatever you have left up there, hit our trenches in the south end and everything beyond them for five hundred meters. And no, I don't give a fiddler's goddam if there's still some of my men in that mess. They've been told to high-tail it and that's what they're gonna do. When your pilots see smoke, that box will be free and clear, so hit it hard with everything you can throw at it. Do you copy?"

"Solid copy, Winch Actual. We have a package on standby. It will hit the designated area in under five. They'll start with the smoke and go five hundred meters beyond. Confirm that order?"

"Confirmed, Ares. Give 'em hell. Winch Actual out."

His BAM wrist unit vibrated in a pattern that advised him he had one or more priority calls waiting. "How many priority calls?" he asked.

"Two are waiting," said the velveteen voice that he had designated for the comms software.

"Put through the call that's been waiting longest," Larocque said.

"First caller is being put through. Channel open," the BAM advised.

"Jack, it's Rydell," said the 2nd Commando CO. As had been the case since his arrival, the man's voice was steady.

"You're still with me, eh? What's the story, my friend?"

"Just thought you should know we've got large numbers of irregulars coming through Knob Noster forest on our western flank. Dozens, if not hundreds of them are pouring into the base and laying into us from the cover of several buildings. It's like bloody Stalingrad over here. I've pulled us back and given the order to consolidate around the HQ and the medic station. I'm not sure how long we'll be able to hold out, Jack."

Larocque's reply was instantaneous. "You gotta hold them, Brian. Except the doc and whatever medics he needs, put everyone on your lines and give 'em hell for as long as you can. I don't care who you have to put back into play – if the near-dead can hold and shoot a rifle, put them in the fight. You got that, Colonel?"

"Copy that, Jack. The walking dead and all others. We'll make it happen."

"Aces. Give him hell, 2nd Commando. Larocque out."

"Give me the second priority call," Larocque directed the comms software.

"Second priority being put through. Channel open."

"Sir, it's Chen. We need to pull back. They're on top of Singh and me, and all of our heavy weapons are offline. We're taking a shit-kicking."

"Captain, I need you and Singh to hold for another ten. Find a way, soldier. We've just lost the south and have asked Ares to lay into that sector pronto. As soon as we're done with that area, we'll see what she can do to help in your sector, and then we'll get you and your boys moving back. I'll send two Carl G teams your way in the meantime. Can you give me ten?"

After a pause, the Australian commando's voice piped into Larocque's earbud and said, "We'll make it work, sir, but any longer and we're done. There are just too many of those bloody civie trucks. They're like goddamned ants."

"Keep giving 'em hell, Chen. We're almost there. Give me ten. That's all I need. Larocque out."

———

Hall had lost count of the number of bodies she and Wallace had moved from the theatre to the grass that surrounded the east side of the converted surgical station. The Regiment had run out of body bags sometime before their arrival back onto the base. They had reported into Larocque and after making a couple of quick remarks about the success of their mission, he had sent them off to support the medical team in whatever way they needed.

When they arrived, they had found an overwhelmed team of medics and the Airborne's one and only surgeon working feverishly on a pair of soldiers laid out on makeshift surgical tables.

In the rows closest to the stage, badly wounded soldiers or bodies were propped into theatre seats. Between the still-living men
and one female patient, and the now-dead bodies, enough fluid had
been produced that pools of dark red blood had begun to gather
underneath and beyond the first row of seating. In the initial moments of walking into that scene, Hall couldn't decide if it was the
dreadful images or the horrific smells that had brought her to the
cusp of retching.

While she was getting herself together, Wallace managed to ac-
cost a harried medic and after informing the soldier that they'd
been told to come here to help, they had been directed to start
moving bodies from the theatre to the grass outside the building.

As they got to work on their dreadful task, they had stumbled
into Havez and his wife who had been off in a darkened corner of
the theatre providing comfort to a pair of dying Canadian paratroopers.

With the sadness of the dying all around them, the four of
them had refrained from any type of warm reunion. Looking exhausted and wearing clothes that were covered in blood, Mrs.
Havez told them how glad she was to see both of them alive.

The colonel, now in civilian clothes, had a sad look on his face,
but when his eyes met theirs, he offered the two young officers a
warm smile. "It's good to see you two again," was all that he had
been able to say. As quickly as they had connected, the American
base commander and his life partner moved on, presumably to find
another dying soldier to whom they could speak.

As Hall held the front end of their blood-soaked stretcher and
exited the front of the building with yet another body, she took in
the sound of heavy fighting all around them. Hearing a roar immediately above their position, she stopped moving and looked upward to see three fast-moving RAF Typhoons flying low in the sky
on a north-to-south trajectory. She watched as bright flashes and

wisps of white smoke appeared from underneath each of the three planes' wings. Streaks of what must have been rockets *whooshed* as they raced forward to whatever targets the three pilots had set upon. The rockets released, her ears then caught the rolling chatter of the planes' opening up with their cannons.

As the three fighters pulled out of their descents and broke in different directions, each plane released a parade of flares creating a Hollywood-esque spectacle across the early afternoon sky.

To cap off the dazzling display, a series of massive explosions erupted from the same area the Typhoons had just exited. In an instant, her eyes took in half a dozen huge black clouds where another set of fighters at a higher altitude must have dropped a separate salvo of laser-guided ordinance. As Hall took in the remarkable visual, the ground beneath her feet rumbled as the concussive wave from the massive explosions rolled over them.

Behind her, she heard Wallace whistle. "Where's that been all day?" he muttered.

Hall offered no reply. She was too spent. Taking her eyes off the scene, she pulled forward with her part of the stretcher, and together, they moved to add another body to the growing cord of death they had been stacking in neat rows next to the theatre where still more CANZUK soldiers were taking their last breaths.

Chapter 33

Whiteman AFB

They would not make it ten minutes and Chen knew it. There was just no way. To the front of his company's position, there was a pair of wounded, but still moving Abrams tanks, another half-dozen armored vehicles, and interspersed among these platforms were some number of the irregulars scurrying to and fro in their cursed trucks. It was chaos personified shitstorm and was about to overwhelm his lads.

On their side, they had been joined by the two Carl Gustaf anti-armor teams that Larocque but this had been a drop in the bucket in the face of a storm surge.

In those trenches where men continued to fight, they were now down to personal weapons, a dwindling number of M-72s, and a handful of unused claymore anti-personnel mines. Had it not been for the engineering magic of the Airborne's sappers and their numerous tank traps, ditches, and well-constructed trenches, Chen's company would have been washed over long ago.

He triggered his BAM. "Give me Singh," Chen shouted over the din of the fighting.

"Captain Singh's vitals are off-line," advised the comms software.

Chen belted out a savage curse.

"That command is not understood," the near-AI voice said calmly in his earbud.

Chen resisted the urge to let loose another profane tirade.

"Open a channel for A Company and B Company, authorization, Romeo-Victor-Seven."

"Authorization approved. Channel open."

"A Company and B Company, this is Captain Chen. I am assuming command of B Company. We are pulling back to the last stand position. Everyone is to blow smoke and then make their way back to their designated positions in the thicket. I repeat A and B Companies, blow smoke and move to your designated fallback positions in Position Delta. Execute, execute, execute. Chen out."

Chen looked at his wrist unit. Eight minutes. It would have to do.

"Give me Larocque, priority Mike-Niner."

"Channel open," advised his BAM.

"Sir, Singh is offline. I've taken command of his company. I've ordered us back to Position Delta per the plan. We're done if we don't move now. You should see smoke going up any second. Any help you could give us would be greatly appreciated."

"I see Singh is down. Good move on pulling the two units together. You're doing a hell of a job, Captain. I have eyes on your position now and see the smoke. Tell your men to keep their heads down as they move, and we'll open up with what we have here in the thicket. I just got off the horn with Ares. Something big is coming our way, so get your asses in tight with us ASAP. Keep holding your soldiers together, Chen. They need you now more than ever. Larocque out."

Of the original six soldiers in the trench, four remained. Two Canadians, one of the C-6 machine gunners and Stockton, Kettle's mate from Saskatchewan, both lay dead on the floor of the trench. The nature of their injuries had been such that they could not be saved. With only a few words, the surviving soldiers rejected any notion of trying to evacuate the two bodies. Dune and the rest of them knew full well that the pair of dead paratroopers would not be the first or last Commonwealth soldiers to lie dead at the bottom of a trench while their mates kept on with the fight.

As Chen's message to set down smoke and retreat piped into his earbud, Dune watched as Kettle aimed and then fired their last

M-72. Not missing a beat, the Canadian reached for one of the two smoke grenades affixed to his body armor, and then on pulling the pin, tossed the munition in the direction of the approaching Red Faction vehicles. Dune and the others followed suit and soon the space in front of their trench was filled with thick white haze.

"Move!" Kettle bellowed and as though he was a big cat, in two quick motions he climbed out of the trench and was running.

Dune moved but stumbled as he tripped on one of the two bodies lying on the trench floor. Recovering, he launched himself up and out of the trench, and in seconds he was sprinting in a straight line to the bunkers where the Canadians had built up their final sector of defense.

His legs pumping and eyes looking ahead, Dune saw Kettle stumble and career forward to the ground. He was on the man in an instant, and as he took a knee beside the Canadian, he could see an entry wound the size of an Aussie fifty-cent piece at the center of the man's back. Grabbing at his friend's body armor, Dune uncere-moniously rolled Kettle over.

The paratrooper's eyes and mouth were wide open, the ex-pression resting on his face some combination of pain and shock. As Dune's eyes moved down to the area where he knew the exit wound would be found, his brain worked to somehow stave off the firestorm of war that raged around him.

The wound was grievous in every way. A hole the size of a man's fist had been punched through the center of Kettle's chest, having torn through the area that would have held the Canadian's heart. Bright red blood was pouring out of the wound like a fountain. Mercifully, Dune realized that Kettle would have been dead before hitting the ground.

With his free hand, he closed the paratrooper's eyes and then pressed his open hand on the man's chest.

"Rest easy, mate. We'll have to finish that little wager when I meet you on the other side."

A close-by explosion buffeted him and snapped his attention back to the melee all around him. Without looking back, Dune got up from his knee and began to sprint in the direction of the grassed mounds that represented the last stand position being held by the Canadian Airborne and what remained of 2nd Commando.

As bullets zipped around him, he took in a pair of soldiers waving frantically, urging him to come in their direction. Reaching the men's position, Dune screamed something unintelligible and jumped into the relative safety of the trench only to have his knees buckle when they hit the dirt-packed floor.

One of the Canadian paratroopers was standing over him and thrust out a hand. Taking hold of it, the exhausted-looking soldier pulled Dune to his feet.

"Welcome to this next stage of hell, Captain. By the looks of what you brought with you, the best part of this shindig is yet to come."

———

When Larocque had first heard General Gagnon's voice pipe into his earbud, he had thought the three-star general in charge of overall mission was calling in to give him an order to surrender. As things had grown more desperate, he had been girding for this development. He had been ready to tell the Ottawa-based general to take a walk. This was his fight and he'd make the damned call. But surrender had not been why the general had called.

Months ago, back in Edmonton as the now quaint final touches were being put on their plan take Whiteman, Larocque, Gagnon and several other high-ranking officers from each of the CANZUK nations had war-gamed under which conditions they might choose to employ Great Britain's inventory of hypersonic missiles, the Perseus.

Like no other weapon in RAF's arsenal, the speed and resulting
hitting power of the Perseus cruise missile meant that the targeting
data being used to guide the weapon needed to be precise in every
way.

Speaking in the now, Gagnon had assured Larocque they had
real-time targeting data that was needed and that the missiles
would fly true if they were used, but they would only be employed
with Larocque's on-the-ground authorization. It was his call.

He didn't hesitate. "You have my authorization, sir. Drop the
hammer. We're screwed otherwise."

Before cutting the feed, Larocque had heard Gagnon speak to
someone offline to give the order to launch four of the hypersonic missiles. Traveling at just over five thousand kilometers per hour,
the general had advised that the projectiles would hit their targets
north and south of the base in under two minutes.

———

Over Missouri

Capt. Harry Khan along with three other Tempest pilots waited anxiously as a pair of Australian F-35s over Whiteman collected
data via the targeting pods each plane carried underneath its fuselage.

The Aussie pilots' mission had not been an easy one. To the
benefit of the Royal Navy sailing off the American eastern
seaboard, the Reds had pulled in another batch of fighters from
bases in Florida and Alabama to support their final push on Whiteman. As a result, fighter planes from all three CANZUK nations
were in one final slugfest in the air over central Missouri.

In the midst of it all, the two RAAF F-35s had skillfully slipped
from an extreme height to their current altitude and, using their
targeting pods, were in the process of taking an accurate accounting
of the vehicles massing to the south and north of the Canadian-
held base.

The Perseus missiles that Khan and his fellow pilots were carrying along the length of their own fuselages needed accurate, real-time targeting data so that the Mach 5 hypersonic missiles could precisely triangulate themselves to hit the designated enemy targets and not the paratroopers or the nuclear bunkers that the Canucks had desperately bound themselves to. In Khan's estimation, 'threading the needle' was an entirely insufficient metaphor for what was about to happen.

The tactical display interfaced with the Aussie F-35s' targeting system flashed green.

At just under two hundred kilometers west of Whiteman, Khan couldn't help but smile as he chalked up a first for the history books. His index finger triggered the launch of what was arguably the world's most powerful conventional weapon. Feeling the airframe of his Tempest shudder as the lone Perseus separated from the centreline of his plane, Khan watched as the GPS-guided weapon ignited and instantly tore through the dazzling afternoon sky.

Missouri, north of Whiteman AFB

The sixty armored fighting vehicles Costen had pulled from his battlegroup had lost any and all notion of trying to coordinate itself as one cohesive unit. Desperation trumped good tactical sense. Now working in teams of eight to twelve vehicles, each unit was independently fighting like hell as they took multiple routes in the direction of the airbase.

At some point, he had patched into the Airborne's BAM feed and could hear the officers and soldiers' conversations as they fought to hold off the encroaching Reds. Larocque, cursing with reckless abandon, had urged his men on in general terms, all the while barking out specific orders to all fronts. From everything

Costen had heard, the man's performance under fire was magnificent.

Costen himself had stopped consulting his tac pad to see where
he and his small team of vehicles were relative to their destination.
It was no longer necessary. Moving south down a tree-enclosed
strip of state highway, he could see nearby pillars of dark smoke just
over the treetops and could easily hear explosions over the rumble
of his tank's growling engine. Whiteman was bloody close.

As his own team of vehicles sped forward and turned around
the forested corner of a three-way stop, he took in what had to
be fourscore of the irregular lorries that had been his battlegroup's
nightmare for the past twenty-four hours.

Staggered in a line that bunched up several hundred meters
down a forest-enclosed roadway, the vehicles and the men standing
on them were facing away from Costen's formation intently watching whatever was on display where the greenery opened up.

"Jesus. Not a single bloke looking this way." Costen muttered
aloud. "Cold-blooded murder is what this is gonna be."

"Timmy, come to a stop," Costen ordered his tank's driver.

"Sergeant Simms, back on the GPMG if you would be so kind.
I'll take the main gun," Costen said.

Costen toggled open the radio frequency to the collection of
vehicles making up his small formation.

"Taskforce Foxtrot, here are your orders. Tank main guns are
to target the front of this rabble, while cannons and machine guns
work from back to the front. Find your targets promptly, people.
We tear into these poor sods in thirty. After the initial barrage and
on my mark, we move forward to where the tree line ends and we
see what there is to see.

"Questions?"

Only silence pervaded the frequency. When his count from
thirty got to five seconds, Costen spoke into his mic, "In five, four,

three, two." On one, he triggered his tank's main gun and heard a gratifying thunderous *boom*.

Through its optical sight, he saw his target, a filthy white Ford with four men on its flatbed, devolve into a gritty black explosion that ejected bodies in every direction. As he moved to target another of the irregular trucks, Costen took in the sound of the brass shell casings cascading across the steel of his tank as Sargeant Simms ripped into the closest of the panicked American fighters with his machine gun.

As Costen waited for his loader, Gillespie, to confirm he had another round breeched, he worked to find his tank's next victim. Finding it, he watched intently as men on the back of a bright green lorry riding atop a set of huge, gnarled tires began to fire a variety of long guns in his tank's general direction.

"Ready," announced Gillespie.

Absent mercy or hesitation, Costen sent another 120mm high explosive round downrange immolating the Chevy and the men who had been on it. The hint of a smile came to his face as one of the truck's huge tires was shorn from its axle and bounded into the nearby forest.

Pulling his eyes away from the wrecked vehicle, Costen toggled open his mic. "Team Foxtrot, all units advance in single file along the right side of the Yank column. Rake them as we go. Stay on my pace and don't get closer than thirty meters. We do not have time to dally with this rabble, so keep moving."

Toggling his mic to his tank's stand-alone frequency, he said, "Timmy, get us up to twenty klicks. I want to get to the end of this column and see what this lot found so interesting."

As his tank began to move forward, Costen stood and took in the chaotic scene of irregular fighters as his small contingent of professional warriors worked to put down as many of the American irregulars as they could. It was carnage of the highest order.

As Costen's Challenger passed the leading part of the frazzled column and drove beyond the trees that flanked this stretch of rural highway, his tank barreled into a wide-open farmer's field that had been torn to shreds by the tracks and wheels of dozens of heavy vehicles. As he took in this wider field of vision and everything contained within it, his brain made several quick calculations.

"Timmy, advance another one hundred meters and hold up," he said loudly into the guts of his tank.

"Aye, Colonel," the young man called back.

To his front and across what was perhaps a kilometer of open field, Costen took in with his own eyes what historians would call the 'Battle of Whiteman'.

He toggled opened his tank's radio. "Right. Here we are then. Form a firing line on my position people. With the first salvo, the Abrams are the priority. After that, we concentrate on whatever's closest to the Canadians' front lines. And mind the bunkers you lot. Any bloke who tags one of those things will have hell to pay. We let loose on my mark."

As he finished with his instructions, Costen's BAM earbud pinged with a high-pitch operation-wide notice, the first he had heard since Vandal had kicked off nearly two days ago. There was no option not to hear the message. That meant the notice was of the highest importance and going out to every soldier and officer in the field.

As the tone finished, it dawned on him what the message might be about. Don't you dare shut this down, Jack you bastard, he thought in an instant of panic. They were so damned close!

"All units, all units at Whiteman AFB, this is Ares Three. Daggers are incoming. I repeat, Daggers are incoming in sixty seconds. This is not a drill. All units in the vicinity of Whiteman take cover. Repeat. All units take cover. Ares Three out."

Upon hearing the message, Costen's mind raced. Lowering his chin, he again yelled into the interior of his Challenger. "Daggers, people. Remind me what the hell that is?"

Gillespie called back immediately. "It's that hypersonic missile the RAF brought into service a few years back. Right nasty things they are, Colonel. Each unit flies at Mach 5 and releases the equivalent of three MOABs when they hit their target."

"Jesus to hell, man, could you speak the King's English – what's a bloody MOAB?"

"Mother of All Bombs, sir. The Yanks developed them to blow up mountain bunkers and the like in Afghanistan, back in the day. Mini-nukes, some people call them."

Costen stood higher in the turret and looked out to the scene in front of him, estimating they were perhaps six hundred meters away from the closest American vehicle. "Bloody RAF and their bloody toys."

He clicked on his mic to give the order to reverse his formation out of what he suspected was the designated kill zone, but before he could begin to get the words out of his mouth, the ground in front of him simultaneously flashed and erupted as though it had been struck by the hammer of some wrathful god. As he felt his tank buck wildly, Costen's legs strained mightily to hold him in his position. As the pressure wave from the blast rolled through him and his body began to register pain, his only thought was that was the shortest sixty seconds he'd ever experienced in his whole bloody life.

———

Side-by-side, a smoking Abrams tank and a burning Stryker APC sat forty meters in front of the large slit trench that Chen and twenty other fighting soldiers occupied. Spread out behind the two armored behemoths were still more tanks that had taken to the task of skillfully firing their main guns to shear off the firing position the Airborne had built on top of the nuclear storage bunkers behind him. Because of the Yanks' careful aim, Chen had heard a decreasing number of the Airborne's heavy weapons firing from within the fenced-in final stand position.

Just past the two wounded vehicles to their front, he watched as a pair of Stryker armored personnel carriers rolled forward and began to disgorge soldiers. Hitting the ground in front of his trench, the American army regulars began to unload with their individual weapons. At just forty meters apart, it was a riot of screaming and death.

Having lost his BAM earbud in the mad dash retreat from their last position, Chen was relegated to bellowing his orders and relying on the men and women in each individual trench to decide on how best to repel their attackers. This was war as it had always been fought.

"Fix bayonets! Fix bayonets!" he screamed. Hearing the order, soldiers left and right began to affix their respective armies' six-inch blades to the end of their rifles.

Turning back to the front of the trench, Chen elevated himself onto the firing step, and shouldering his weapon, waited for the still-prone infantry to start their charge. As rounds zipped past his helmeted head, he heard Dune's screaming voice to his right.

Turning to the noise, he saw paratroopers and Diggers along the length of the trench had squatted down well underneath the lip of the emplacement. Several of the lads had fingers or hands pressed onto ears.

"Oi!" Chen shouted. "What are you lot up to?"

Finally, he caught the sight of Dune and, over the cacophony of incoming fire made an effort to make out what the other man was saying.

As he made out the words "get down", his attention was overtaken by a collection of guttural screams. The Yanks were coming.

"What the bloody hell?" Chen screamed at the men along the floor of the trench. "On the line! On the line, you bludgers!"

While several of the closest soldiers looked in his direction, none made to move. He was out of time. Pivoting, he drew up his rifle and aimed at one of the charging soldiers, letting loose with a short burst of fire. At twenty meters away, his target stumbled and fell to the ground. Moving to the next soldier, he unleashed another barrage but in one of the many miracles of war, not a single round connected, and, at ten meters out, the enraged American beelined for Chen, his own weapon churning out high-velocity lead.

As both men issued war cries, the horizon behind the soldier turned a bright white. Instantly, Chen's exposed upper body was struck by an incomparable force of energy that sucked the air out of his lungs and hammered his eardrums as though he was caught in the wake of a jet fighter's sonic boom. Eyes dazzled, he somehow registered he was careening through the air. An instant later, his body had been driven into the chain-link fence surrounding the bunker system.

For the briefest period, he was pinned high in the air against the barrier as though some supernatural force had him in an ethereal grasp. And then as quickly as it came, the force was gone. He fell, hit the ground hard, and perceived something in his upper body snap. Unable to breathe and with his brain registering untold levels of pain, Chen's body did what any person's body would have done under similar conditions. It began to shut down.

Chapter 34

Whiteman AFB

Lying prone between a pair of soldiers sniping from one of the northernmost bunkers of their last stand position, Larocque took in the two dozen or so Red Faction fighting vehicles methodically pressing forward against the Airborne's buckling defensive front.

Several armored personnel carriers had dodged forward at various points along the line and had begun to unload the infantry who would begin the process of trying to pry his paratroopers and the Aussie commandos from their positions. In many places, it would come down to hand-to-hand fighting.

Larocque heard the now-familiar, patrician voice of the British officer operating as the Ares coordinator for all airstrikes, issuing the BAM-wide notice to every fighting soldier in the war what was about to hit this part of Missouri.

As soon as the warning had been given, Larocque instructed his BAM to open a regiment-wide channel, and in the time left before the missiles arrived, he issued orders for the remaining heavy weapons on the inner ring of their defense to open up full bore, giving the soldiers in the outermost trenches the opportunity to go to ground. Broken ribs or no, Larocque grabbed one of the snipers' carbines and poured a full magazine at a clutch of American soldiers who were preparing to assault one of the trenches a hundred meters to his front.

And then the strike came. Without any prelude and well in advance of the advertised sixty-second warning, four missiles, two north and two south of Whiteman's only runway, thunder-clapped into their designated coordinates, their solid tungsten cores driving deep into the earth at hypersonic speeds, creating four massive eruptions and one fantastic pressure wave that ravaged everything in its furious path.

The shockwave from the strike was earth-shattering and magnitudes beyond anything Larocque had felt over the past twenty-four hours. Lying flat, he felt his entire body rise inches off the ground and contract as the air around him instantly thickened, as though he had been magically transported to the world's hottest jungle. As gravity reasserted itself, his body and broken ribs slammed back to the ground forcing him to howl in pain.

The soldiers beside him issued their own cries of terror along with a selection of well-practiced profanities. For his part, Larocque was speechless. Resting on his stomach, he fought to ride out the pain racking his broken body. As the noise from the explosions fell away, he slowly raised his head and propped his upper body over the edge of the scrape he had been operating out of for the past twenty minutes.

The scene in front of him was one of utter devastation. At maybe four and then six hundred meters out from his position, two now fully developed gray mushroom clouds stood tall in the sky.

Near each strike, the vehicles that had been badgering the Airborne's trenches moments before were now askew or overturned. In more than a few cases, parts of vehicles were burning. It was as though a giant child had descended onto that part of the battlefield and in a temper tantrum of titan-like proportions had let loose on his toy things. As best Larocque could tell, among those vehicles closest to the strikes, there was no movement of any kind.

Gingerly, he got up on one knee and surveyed those trenches closest to the missile impacts. Some fifty meters out from his current position, Larocque could see that in at least one of the trenchworks, a large portion of its north-facing wall had collapsed in on itself and a handful of soldiers were working frantically to dig out their trapped comrades. In other trenches, soldiers appeared to be standing dumbfounded as they took in the apocalyptic scene that lay before them.

It was not far beyond these trenches that Larocque noted the closest collection of American vehicles – the ones that had just unloaded their infantry. While the attacking armored personnel carriers remained in place, those soldiers who had left their APCs to carry out their attack were nowhere to be seen.

In that same moment and through the dusty pall that had taken hold of the battlefield, Larocque heard the distinctive sound of chunky disel engines beginning to rev. Peering into the haze, he could vaguely make out that many vehicles had not been unaffected by the strike. For a too-long moment, Larocque marveled at the American soldier's perseverance. The bastards were going to keep fighting.

As the attacking force began to organize itself in the distance, he reminded himself that the soldiers and officers they were fighting were products of the greatest fighting force the world had ever known and that most had spent the better part of two years fighting a vicious war against the Blues. In battle, when setbacks happened, it was always the veteran soldier who was best placed to endure and overcome.

As though the attacking soldiers had been able to hear his thoughts, the closest moving vehicles suddenly opened up with their weapons, raking them across the trenches where many of the Airborne's gobsmacked soldiers had been taking in the scene.

Ahead and to his left, Larocque watched as two of his paratroopers were horrifically cut down by large-caliber cannon fire. Parts of their bodies exploded and flew through the air as rounds designed to punch reinforced steel instead connected with flesh.

Larocque keyed his BAM. "Open a regiment-wide channel".

"Channel open," the near-AI comms system voiced instantly.

"Colonel Larocque here. Listen Airborne and 2nd Commando, it's now or never for the Reds. If they don't take us now, they know

they are not going to take us at all, so all of you need to dust yourselves off and get back into this fight.

"Every APC that has soldiers in the back of it is going to come
our way. They're done waiting for us to die from afar or run out of
ammo. They're gonna ride up on us hard and tight and when they
stop you know what's coming out of the back of those steel bastards. Be patient, and when you see a body, you let'em have it. We
fight until I say we don't. We are close, people. Help is on its way, so
chins up and give 'em hell. Larocque out."

_____

"Here they come!" someone yelled further down the trench.
Dune stopped giving CPR to Chen's unbreathing body, stood up
and glanced to the front of their trench. Straining to see through
the curtain of dust caused by the earth-shattering missile strikes,
he took in a foursome of Strykers rushing in a line to assault the
trenches that made up this part of the Canadian defense. Each
vehicle was armed with a remote-operated automatic cannon and
each weapon was belching out short bursts of fire at the defending
soldiers.

As the hulking vehicles' brakes engaged and they skidded to a
halt, Dune watched a small horde of Red Faction infantry begin to
disgorge from the back of each machine. As the soldiers assumed
prone firing positions, light machine gun and rifle fire took over
from the Strykers' 30mm cannons.

In the mad scramble to find Chen and then drag him back into
the trench, Dune had left behind his F-88. Without his rifle, he
watched helplessly as Canadian paratroopers and the few remaining Aussie Diggers traded point-blank fire with the approaching
American infantry. It was a furious action.

"Grenade!" came a cry to Dune's right. Snapping his head in
the direction of the voice, he saw a Canadian soldier quickly bend
over and wrap his hand around an object on the trench floor. Hav-

ing no sooner picked up the object, the munition exploded into the doubled-over paratrooper, the bulk of the grenade's energy cutting into the man's body.

As there were more cries of "grenade," this time to his left, Dune's gaze remained fixed on the assaulting Reds. In textbook fashion, several of the Yank soldiers jumped to their feet while others continued to lay prone so as to fire a stream of lead at the heads of the entrenched CANZUK soldiers.

As the Americans dashed forward, one half of the charging group was cut down by the defenders while the other half hit the threshold of the trench, their weapons firing. In ones and twos, enemy soldiers leaped to the dirt floor and went at the Canadian and Aussie soldiers like men possessed.

Too close to reload magazines, brutal hand-to-hand fighting ensued. Weaponless, Dune's eyes darted to the trench wall and he grabbed up one of the standard-issue entrenching tools ubiquitous among the Canuck paratroopers. Serrated spade in hand, Dune moved in the direction of a Canadian and American soldier who were locked in a mortal struggle to control the Canadian's bayoneted rifle. As the larger of the two, the American had forced the Canadian against the trench wall and was using his leverage and strength to line up the paratrooper's bayonet underneath his own chin.

Arriving at the struggling pair, Dune issued an inhuman scream and swung the head of the shovel at the back of the American's exposed neck. Connecting, he heard a sickening crack as the hard steel of the implement drove deep into flesh and bone. With a terrified yelp, the American jolted upright, and then, just as quickly, dropped in a heap to the trench floor. The Canadian, back in control of his rifle, unhesitatingly loaded a fresh magazine, pointed the weapon at the terrified Red soldier and pulled the trigger. Turning his eyes away from the terrible scene, Dune sprung forward and headed to another pair of grappling men.

On the trench floor, an American was on top of another Canadian. Dune could see the hands of the two men struggling for control of a nasty-looking knife that the Red soldier had in his right hand.

Arriving at their position, Dune, with the practiced skill of a first-rate batsman swung the serrated edge of the digging tool into the American's left hamstring. Again, the blade hacked deep into flesh, causing the soldier to flail and issue a howl of pain as he rolled off the paratrooper.

As he stared at the screaming man, Dune caught the movement of the soldier he had just saved step past him. His weapon shouldered, he leveled its muzzle at the brutalized American soldier and pulled the trigger. The rifle spat out a burst of 5.56mm rounds that caught the man dead center in the face, eviscerating the man's humanity.

Breathing heavily and looking down the rest of the trench, Dune could see no other fighting. By way of some miracle, of those soldiers who had survived the assault, half a dozen were back on the trench's firing step and were putting rounds down range or were throwing their own grenades in the direction of the Red infantry who hadn't taken part in the first charge.

The first Canadian he saved reached down and helped his mate off the ground. Together, they turned to face him.

"Look at you, you sweet Aussie bastard. You're a medieval savage with that shovel of yours. That guy just about had me," the first soldier Dune had saved yelled over the still incoming gunfire.

The other Canadian, helmetless and bearing a wan face that looked like he had just cheated death, placed his hand on Dune's shoulder. But just as the man was going to say something, he looked past Dune and said, "Well, would ya look at that? Now that there's one hell of a tough officer. You Aussies, eh – tough as nails and balls the size of fucking moose."

Dune turned and saw Chen slowly shambling in their direction. A huge smile lit up his face. "Oi, there you are! Up and about, eh, Captain? Fucking invincible you are, mate."

Arriving at their location, Chen reached out a hand and steadied himself on the wall of the trench. Wearing a grimace and with blood trickling out of his nose and ears, the Aussie officer gathered himself and raised his scratchy voice over the still-raging battle. "I can't hear a thing, so whatever smart-ass comment you just made, Corporal, you can stuff it, find your weapon and get back on the line and start giving it back to the Yanks." Chen's eyes moved to the two Canadians. "Same for you two. Break time is over. This is still our fight to lose."

The closest of the two missiles to strike the north end of the base had impacted the ground some four hundred meters to the front of Costen's tank. Standing high in the turret, the combined explosion and pressure wave had crashed into him like a near-boiling tidal wave. His face, the only part of his skin exposed to the six-thousand-degree kinetic strike, had suffered a painful burn, while his back had been wrenched terribly. Despite the pain, he had seated himself properly and after several minutes of allowing his eyes to recover from the flash of the detonation, he deemed that he was once again in fighting order.

"Gillespie, be a good lad and grab me two Percocets, won't you?"

"On it," said the tank's loader.

As he waited for the painkillers, he looked through his optical sight, and through its thermal lens, he was treated to a black-and-white hellscape. The closest of the two missiles had struck the north end of Whiteman's only runway. There, he took in what looked like a fifty-meter-wide cauldron of white-hot energy. Emanating from the epicenter, armored vehicles of all kinds sat askew in every direction. Those few bodies that he could see were burning.

Beyond this initial circle of destruction, Costen could see that many of the American armored vehicles that appeared to be unaffected were unmoving, just as he was.

As his loader handed him the painkillers, he toggled open the frequency that would connect him with the other vehicles in his formation and undertook a roll call.

"Right then, sounds like we're ready to go. Let's get on the move and take advantage of what those overzealous bastards in the sky have given to us. Timmy, get us moving. Captains Tinker and Reeder, put your machines on my flanks and have your gunners target any Red vehicle that's within a hundred meters of the Canadian's outer lines. Abrams are the first to go. The rest of you, mind our flanks and suppress any gobs that so much as look in our direction. Once the Yanks understand we've joined this party, things are gonna get real hairy, real fast. And mind that we're low on ammo. We need to be efficient, people. Questions?"

"Yes, sir," said Reeder, a Londoner who was in command of one of the formation's other two Challengers.

"Let's hear it," said Costen.

"How will the Canadians know not to unload on us? It'll be chaos in that there blight, Colonel."

Costen painfully stood up and looked past his tank's high-tech sight and into the wall of dust the hypersonic missiles had kicked up. "Fair question, Captain," said Costen, "For whatever reason, I've not been able to reach anyone from the Airborne in the past hour. As best I can figure, we fight our way in and figure it out when we get there. That's been our policy since we crossed that bridge, and look at us now. This was never going to be pretty."

"Sir, perhaps now might be the time for us to fly some colors?" offered Reeder.

Costen brightened. "A keen suggestion, Captain. All units, you have two minutes to make it so."

————

As the Americans started to re-engage, Larocque dashed back to the center of the Airborne's defenses and again placed himself atop one of the bunkers.

Minutes earlier, he opened a regiment-wide channel with his BAM and ordered a general retreat of all soldiers to the last stand position within the actual bunker complex. As the Americans organized themselves, the time had come to consolidate what was left of those soldiers still fighting.

The bunker system that stored Whiteman's nuclear weapon cache was surrounded by a twelve-foot-high chain-link fence topped off with concertina wire. Outside the fencing, and on the north and south ends of the complex, the Airborne's sappers and pioneers had dug a series of slit trenches and tank ditches. It was from these positions that the bulk of his remaining soldiers were now retreating via a series of holes that had been cut in the compound's chain-link barrier.

Inside the fence was another series of trenches and tank ditches, backed by half-a-dozen sandbagged hardpoints. The arrangement was a tightly packed defense that had a number of overlapping kill zones that held what remained of the Airborne's heavy weapons. Larocque wasn't sure who had coined this final defense "the thicket," but the person deserved credit because the label was apt.

With the mushroom clouds from the two Perseus strikes towering in the background, Larocque looked to the northern section of their defense and took in what was most likely the end of his regiment.

Through the dust, a pair of still-operating Abrams, along with a handful of other armored vehicles, formed into a rolling steel line one hundred meters long from end to end. With their top-mounted weapons blazing, the armored cavalcade rolled over the Airborne's now-unoccupied slit trenches and, as one combined wave, smashed into and over the length of fence that had been the bunker system's outer perimeter.

In seconds, the charging vehicles arrived at the line of northern-most storage bunkers and the Regiment's last line of defense. At point-blank range, CANZUK soldiers on top of each mound fired their remaining M-72s or retreated further in the direction of the thicket's center.

Around the western edge of the line of grassed bunkers emerged one of the Abrams. It was quickly followed by a Stryker, its autocannon pouring high caliber rounds in the direction of the central thicket's sandbagged hardpoints. Soon the two machines were joined by a third vehicle which added another autocannon to the hell storm. The combined firepower was breathtaking in its ferocity.

As Larocque listened to the screams of dying soldiers, he watched in growing panic as the Abrams main gun swiveled to line up one of the hardpoints closest to him. The tank's main gun recoiled and obliterated the position that held the Airborne's last 40mm automatic grenade launcher.

This was it. They were done. He had to make the call. Brazeau, Landry, his country, his soldiers, his family – they would all have to understand. For whatever time he had left on this world, Larocque knew he would hate himself for what he was about to do.

He gave the order to his BAM to open the Regiment-wide channel.

"Channel open," the near-AI voice advised in the same calm, velveteen voice it had been speaking to him in all morning.

"Airborne and 2nd Commando, this is Colonel Larocque. It's time to..."

His words ended abruptly as the Abrams that had just shattered the grenade launcher bucked forward and in a flash of violence that somehow managed to shuck the tank's turret from its lower body. An instant later, one of the marauding Strykers suffered a similar fate as it exploded in a crimson storm of shredded steel and oily black smoke.

Larocque took a moment to consider the scene. Those weren't airstrikes. Someone close by was putting rounds downrange. The Regiment-wide BAM channel still open, he bellowed, "Airborne, keep fighting! Reinforcements have arrived. I repeat, reinforcements have arrived. Keep fighting you glorious bastards, you hear me. Keep fighting!"

_____

The amount of supersonic lead hitting his tank's hull was intense. Small and heavier caliber rounds were impacting his Challenger's thick steel skin from all angles creating a furious sound. The Americans had caught on to his formation's arrival and by all accounts were determined to do something about it.

As they churned forward across the scarred field of soybeans, three of his formations' eight-wheeled Boxers and one of his Challengers had been immobilized. Though unmoving, each vehicle remained operational and was doing its best to tear into the Reds around them.

Captain Reeder's Challenger, his own tank, and the remaining Boxers of his small task force continued to roll forward apace. Sitting low in his own tank's turret, Costen watched disconcertedly as a wave of Abrams and other armored vehicles trampled into and over the northwest portion of the chain-link fence surrounding the bunker complex. Larocque and whatever soldiers he had left had just run out of time.

"Captain Reeder, if you please, take the Abrams on the east end of those bunkers and then move on to the APCs. Don't stop until you run out of rounds, or I say so," Costen said calmly over the radio.

"Copy that, sir. Executing now."

"Sergeant Simms, I trust you have that other Abrams in your sights?" Costen said to his own tank's operator, who was once again manning the Challenger's main gun.

"Aye, sir, I do. We're primed."

"Then fire."

———

Down on one knee atop his bunker, Larocque took in the full vista of the battlefield. Through the dusty haze that still dominated the air, he eyed the pair of tanks and several APCs slow-rolling across the northern end of Whiteman's runway. The turrets of the two British Challengers were pointed in the direction of the thicket.

As he surveyed the scene, one of the tanks jerked as it fired its main gun. Some fifty or so meters away, another of the American armored vehicles – this time an LATV – crumpled as the tank's penetrator round easily ripped into the vehicle's steel hide, shredding its guts.

As he watched black smoke begin to pour out of the mortally wounded vehicle, the voice of his BAM advised him that a priority call from outside the Regiment was pending.

"Accept it," Larocque said immediately.

A familiar, accented voice piped into his earbud. "Colonel Larocque, so kind of you to make the time to take my call. I've been trying to get you on the BAM for the past thirty minutes. I take it you've been busy?"

Hearing the other man's voice, Larocque brightened, "Colonel, it's great to hear from you, my friend. Sorry about putting you off.

My hands were kinda full. Is that you on the runway?" As he asked the question, Larocque fired his arm into the air and proceeded to wave in the direction of the British flagged tanks.

"Yes, that's me, you daft bastard. Keep your bloody head down. There's no sense in dying at this stage in the game," Costen growled over the connection.

"How many of you are there?" Larocque asked.

"My full battlegroup is maybe two klicks away, but there's something like thirty fighting vehicles that will be on our position in the next ten minutes or so. What do you need us to do?"

"Are the rest of your folks coming from the north?"

"We are."

"Then have them move north to south along the runway. Anything along that corridor is Red Faction and needs to be put down."

"We can do that. What else?" the Welshman asked.

"I've still got people on the base proper. Our field hospital, my original HQ, and my Pathfinder company. The last I heard from them, Red irregulars were pressing them hard out of the Knob Noster Forest in the east. See if you can't get a couple of your vehicles into that mess double-time."

"We'll make that happen," Costen confirmed quickly. "What else?"

"Just lay into these bastards as they stand before now and get the rest of your people here ASAP. We're razor-thin here."

Larocque paused, and when he next spoke his voice began to crack. "Jesus Christ, Simon, I was just about to call this thing. What a waste this all would have been. So many of my people are gone. What a goddamn mess."

"Steady on there, Airborne," Costen offered kindly. "You and your lads have done a hell of a thing holding out as you have. No one is going to dispute that. Whatever the brass has to say about how we got here is for later. Right now, we're still up to our necks in it, so my advice is to get that chiseled gob of yours back in the dirt and help your lads stay alive."

The line stayed quiet for a moment and when Costen next heard Larocque, the man's voice had firmed back into steel. "Copy that, Colonel. Let's finish the delivery of this bloody miracle of ours. I'll see you in the flesh soon enough. Airborne out."

———

A runner had burst into the theatre and relayed orders for all soldiers, excluding the doc and the two medics that had been acting as surgical assistants, to muster in the lobby immediately.

Hearing the order, Hall and Wallace, several medics and a handful of badly wounded soldiers rallied to the building's entrance where they found Colonel Rydell.

The Australian officer advised that the encroaching Red Faction force had just severed the field of battle between the Airborne's last stand position amongst the bunkers and the field hospital on the base proper.

'The Yanks', Rydell had said, were pushing their armor in the direction of Larocque and the bunkers, but more and more irregulars were pouring into the base through the densely wooded Knob Noster State Park, and these fighters had managed to push back the soldiers holding this part of the Canadian defense.

Rydell and what remained of the Airborne's heavy weapons company, military police, and a few other ancillary units, had fallen back from their own positions to the theater and added their strength to the Airborne recon soldiers defending that part of the base.

Like Larocque and his soldiers at the bunkers, Rydell announced that every man and woman that could fight would help to defend the makeshift field hospital. They would make their own last stand and they'd fight until Larocque gave the word, or they were overrun.

As they listened to the briefing, Hall had helped herself to a dead officer's carbine and his body armor. With windows shattering and bullets thwacking into the brick façade of the old theatre, Hall, Wallace and a handful of other soldiers were loaded up with additional ammunition and ordered to reinforce the paratroopers on the north side of the structure.

Once loaded up, eight of them stormed out of the theatre's front entrance, took a quick left, and then moved along the length of the Reel Time Theater to the section of defense they had been assigned. This was the same length of the building in which Hall and Wallace had spent the better part of the last hour organizing dead soldiers. Knowing the bodies would be there, Hall had been able to ignore the heart-wrenching scene, while others of their newly formed group slowed down or stopped to take in the stretch of their dead comrades.

As Hall moved past the stunned soldiers, the group's most senior NCO, a sergeant, ferociously snapped at the gawkers. "You three retards. We're not at the fucking zoo. Get your asses in gear. Payback's just around the corner. C'mon, move!"

With one final glance, the soldiers tore their eyes away from the bodies and doubled-timed to where Hall and the rest of the group had huddled at the northeast corner of the building.

Around the corner, Hall could hear torrents of gunfire and the voices of soldiers calling out enemy positions. The same sergeant who had just ripped into his gobsmacked fellows leaned out from the building and then quickly jumped back undercover as several rounds tore into the theatre's brickwork.

"Good times await, people," the big man growled. "Our redneck friends are everywhere." He pointed to two military police officers that were a part of their group. "There's a trench just around the corner. It's about twenty meters long. You two hit the far end on the right. Go!"

Without hesitation, the two MPs, loaded down with their weapons and extra ammo, galloped forward.

The sergeant next looked at Hall and Wallace. "I'm told you two are officers. What's with the civie gear?"

"It's a long story," said Hall.

"Yeah, well, maybe I'll get to hear all about it when this shit-show is over and done with, eh? As it is, you two can join the left side of the trench. Ready?"

"Ready," Hall and Wallace said in unison.

The sergeant smiled at their joint reply. "What are you, brother and sister? No, never fucking mind. Go!"

With that, Hall drove herself forward and flew around the corner. Quickly taking in the scene, she darted in the direction of the left side of the trench. As multiple rounds snapped past her unhelmeted head, she lowered her profile, scampered, and then upon reaching the trench, jumped downwards. Hitting the earthen floor, her legs gave out and she crashed into the packed ground in an unceremonious heap.

Wallace was standing above her in an instant. "You okay?"

Issuing a sheepish grin, she said nothing, but reached up with her hand and let him help her get to her feet.

Erect, Hall surveyed their part of the trench. The entire fortification was perhaps the length of a school bus and on their end of it, three soldiers were on a firing step, while a fourth and fifth soldier were propped up in the trench's terminus, unmoving. One of the fighting soldiers cocked her head in their direction and bellowed for them to get on the firing line.

"Here they come!" the female master corporal yelled.

Hall didn't hesitate. She moved to the female paratrooper, stepped onto the firing shelf, shouldered her carbine, and started to look for targets.

In front of them was a wide-open, well-manicured area of grass framed in by several buildings. Where the open space ended about one hundred meters out, she could see a dozen pickup trucks with men standing in their flatbeds, firing an assortment of hunting rifles and military-grade weapons in their direction. From behind these unmoving trucks, she saw another half dozen or so pickups of various makes and colors advancing. Up-armored with steel plates over their engine blocks and piled high with sandbags, each of the trucks was bristling with men shooting a variety of weapons.

As she flipped her carbine to full auto and took aim at an oncoming Ford, she heard the thunk of multiple grenade launchers firing on her left and right. As the explosive rounds landed, the approaching pickups began to weave wildly. As they did so, the vehicle Hall had been tracking exposed its broadside. Making sure to lead the truck's flatbed, Hall squeezed her weapon's trigger and peppered the length of her target. A pair of men jerked and fell to the ground, but the truck kept moving.

In a wild movement that resulted in another of its passengers careening through the air, the rust spotted white F-150 was now approaching her head-on. Having inserted a new magazine into her carbine, Hall unloaded on the truck on full auto. Working from bottom to top, she saw the truck's right front tire explode. As her fire worked over the cab, the head of a man standing low in the flatbed detonated into an ugly red spray just as his body fell out of sight.

Out of rounds, Hall pulled back from her rifle's scope and took in the truck with her naked eye. Though herky-jerky, the bullet-saturated vehicle was still moving forward. Across her broader field of vision, she caught the movement of other fast-approaching vehicles of various colors. As bullets zipped all around her, the female paratrooper beside her yelped in pain. Hall ignored the urgent-sounding cry.

At twenty meters to their front, the wounded Ford came to a shuddering halt. In the vehicle's back-end were a half-dozen irregulars. All were huddled behind sandbags and were alternating between firing their weapons and hurling any number of vicious, curse-filled threats in the direction of their trench.

Beside her, Wallace lobbed a grenade at the wounded pickup. As she changed out her magazine, she heard the munition explode. Shouldering her weapon, Hall leaned against the trench wall to look for targets, but no sooner had she found one, her body executed an involuntary pirouette so that she was facing in the opposite direction of the fighting.

Managing to stay on her feet, she struggled to make sense of the horrendous pain now radiating from an area just above her left breast. It was as though someone had just driven a railway spike into that part of her body. And not once, but several times.

As her eyes began to well from the pain, she struggled desperately to draw air into her lungs. On instinct, her hand reached to the area of pain and upon pulling away, she was relieved to see that her fingers were bloodless. Whatever caliber bullet had struck her body armor, it had not penetrated its anti-ballistic material.

As she struggled to regain her breath, she saw that her rifle had managed to land outside the trench and was lying on the grass. As oxygen began to re-enter her lungs, she pulled herself upwards and over the lip of the trench to grab the butt of her weapon.

As her hand made contact with the carbine, she looked east in the direction of the base's airfield. There, and to her sudden alarm, she could see the front-end of a monstrous black-and-green armored vehicle bouncing toward her at high speed.

Struggling to get air into her lungs so she could scream a warning that they were being attacked from behind, Hall watched helplessly as the top-side cannon of the fast-moving fighting vehicle erupted. She flinched as she both heard and felt the concussive force of dozens of 30mm rounds scream like banshees as they passed over her.

With as much gusto as she could muster, Hall bellowed for her fellow defenders to get down, and just as the words left her mouth, she squatted and watched the undercarriage of the eight-wheeled, thirty-ton vehicle as it thundered directly over her position.

Back on her feet, she watched as the behemoth of a vehicle rammed the back end of the same white Ford she had been targeting moments before. At contact, the much lighter vehicle was jacked into a violent spin sending several of the men in the flatbed flying through the air.

Springing from hatches from the top of the armored hulk, soldiers with light machine guns and automatic rifles began firing in all directions at the astonished Americans irregulars. As she took in the scene, she caught the glimpse of a second armored fighting vehicle rolling headlong into another part of the fighting to her right. It was then that she saw the glorious, red, white and blue of the Union Jack sailing above the APC's hull.

She whooped with delight and then yelled, "The goddamned Brits, and none too soon, eh. Jesus, it's about time. Max, can you believe it?"

On hearing no reply, Hall's eyes snapped to where she had last laid eyes on Wallace.

Strewn on the floor of the trench, she took in her friend's long body lying on his back, his plain but kind face looking straight up into the clear afternoon sky.

In an instant, she was beside him and in that same moment could see why he had not acknowledged her. The left side of her friend's neck had been shredded, his carotid artery laid bare and pulpy. Underneath Wallace's pale face and broad shoulders, the brown soil of the trench floor was saturated with dark red blood.

As she felt for a pulse on the other side of his neck, Hall looked into Wallace's pale blue eyes and saw that they were lifeless.

Tired and sore beyond imagination, Hall forced herself to rip her eyes from Wallace's dead form. In a cold fury, she grabbed up the rifle that lay beside her friend. Changing out its magazine, she stalked like a lioness back onto the firing step of the trench. Shouldering the weapon, she took in the scene.

There were still dozens of American irregulars on the field concentrating their fire on the newly arrived pair of British vehicles. Lowering her eye to the weapon's scope, Hall took a deep, calming breath and drew down on the back of a man who was perhaps sixty meters away, perched on the back of yet another American pickup. Pulling the trigger, Hall watched her target jerk violently and then slump forward.

In the minutes that followed, she pulled the trigger of her weapon again and again. It was both terrible and satisfying work where men screamed, bled, and died. At no point did she hesitate.

As another pair of British fighting vehicles dashed onto the scene, she felt a firm hand on her shoulder. She stopped firing and looked to her right where she took in the face of the grizzled sergeant who had ordered her and Wallace into the trench.

"Ease up there, ma'am. They're on the run. Both here and at the runway. You've done enough for today." The man's face had a sad and knowing look to it.

She stared back at the sergeant and without saying a word she released the rifle from her shoulder and exhaled heavily.

Slowly, she forced herself to look past the NCO to again take up Wallace. Though smeared in drying blood, his face had a noble look to it. Her thoughts then turned to the parade of dead paratroopers and commandos that they had disposed of not a hundred feet away. Madness and waste.

It didn't have to be this way, she thought. This new FLQ or whatever it was, and anyone that had helped them, would need to pay for what they had done. And though she was but a fresh-faced officer, she would be damned if she wasn't part of whatever was to be done to make things right.

In the harsh reality that now pervaded the world, she understood now more than ever that there were times when bad people needed to go away, or in the case of the separatists, there was a political cancer that needed to be removed.

Whatever was to be done, she would be a part of it and she would do what needed to be done. She would make the right people pay for what they had done to her, to Wallace, and to her country. Without remorse and with the greatest satisfaction.

———

As Larocque watched the last of the heavy logistics vehicles roll past Whiteman AFB's Welcome Center, he felt at least part of the weight of the world leave his shoulders.

Two hundred and eighteen nuclear weapons were now on the road to Colorado. Just enough trucks had made it to Whiteman in the mad dash from the Dakotas. In all, about half of the vehicles from the eight battlegroups had made it to this part of Missouri.

As the last bomb-laden truck turned north onto State Highway 23, Larocque's attention was overtaken by the sound of someone bellowing, "Airborne!"

He turned his head in the direction of the sound and took in a soldier who was riding atop a green and brown-hued Canadian LAV. The young man's fist was thrust in the air and on his face was a wide and approving grin.

Wearing his maroon beret, Larocque waved back in acknowledgment from atop his own idling vehicle. For the first part of their trip west, he would bring up the rear of the convoy. His LAV would be the last vehicle to leave what had become Canada's most significant dying ground in generations.

They had done it. Within minutes of Costen's arrival, dozens and then hundreds of British and Australian war machines had poured into Whiteman. With the Chinese fighters no longer in play, CANZUK's combined air forces joined their brothers and sisters-in-arms on the ground to blunt and then decimate what remained of the Red Faction attacking force.

Whatever resistance waited for them as they moved across the western part of Missouri and then all of Kansas, it would not be enough.

He keyed the right place on his mouthguard to activate his BAM and said, " Personal call. Authorization, Mike-Lima-Three"

"Authorization approved," said the smooth near-AI replica voice that had been his constant companion for the past forty hours.

"Call Madison Larocque."

"Call being made. Please hold."

Seconds later, a familiar voice joined the call. "Hello. Jack... Jack, is that you?"

"It's me, my love. I'm here."

Epilogue

Houston, Texas

It was the height of summer and had they not been close to the ocean, Charron, wouldn't have been able to bear the heat, even at this early hour.

As it was, a breeze that held the slightest hint of air from the Gulf of Mexico wafted through the veranda where he and the rest of the French delegation were seated.

Four men and one woman sat comfortably at an elongated and beautifully set table, while a pair of servers moved deftly from person to person offering coffee and reconfirming the meal order that each official's staff had relayed the evening before.

As the service staff spoke with the last of his colleagues, the spectacled Frenchman watched as the broad-chested American with graying hair leaned forward in his seat and placed a massive pair of elbows on the table in front of him.

"Friends, welcome to Texas and the United Constitutional States of America. I'm thankful and humbled that you are here."

While Charron offered a forced smile to the brute of a man, it was the sole female at the table who spoke.

"Thank you, Mr. President. It is we who are humbled by your offer to have us here to meet with you. Our governments are living through extraordinary times, so I for one appreciate the importance of you taking the time to meet with us personally."

"Well then, we're both humbled, Madame President," said the American. "That can't be a bad thing when it comes to international diplomacy, can it?

"In my experience, it never hurts," the leader of France replied.

"Well, since we've started off on the right foot, why don't we just jump into things? There's no sense pussyfooting around. We both know why we're here. Now, I'm gonna guess you huddled up together last night and went through our proposal? Well, what's the verdict then?"

The President of France accepted the American's brash entreaty with the same grace and warmth she had been projecting from the moment of her arrival in this broken and brash land.

"We may be from two different countries and have two very different backgrounds, but we both know a great deal about being direct and efficient. It bodes well for our relationship."

"Efficient and direct have served me well my entire life Madame President. As I sit here now, I can't see a reason that needs to change."

"Then we should proceed as you suggest, Mr. President."

"Then my question stands."

France's first female president and the leader of France's largest and most ardent national party, seldom allowed another person to manage a political discussion. On this occasion, she calculated she would make an exception for the American barbarian who sat across from her.

To be sure, the man was a physical caricature with his ample girth, his too broad shoulders, and what was a decidedly an over-done and ridiculous-looking mustache. Despite appearances, she would not permit herself to underestimate the man. Archie Cameron had done that and had found himself dead and hanging upside down from a rope in the DC demilitarized zone for two weeks during one of the hottest summers on record. Bloated and picked over by a murder of unrelenting crows, it had not been a pretty end for the most recent UCSA president.

"Indeed, we did spend the evening reviewing your proposal, Mr. President."

"And?"

"And, while we are hesitant in the extreme to involve France directly in your country's civil war, it is also the case that we cannot

abide while other countries make efforts to impact the internal affairs of the former United States. To this end, and on conditions
that will be determined after this morning's conversations, the
Government of France is prepared to approve your government's
request for military aid."

If her words registered with the American, the man failed to
evince any outward indication of it. Instead, the bull of a man
pressed, "And what of our other request, Madame President?"

France's President had to check herself. That the man would
not take but a moment to acknowledge the monumental commitment that had just been made was maddening in the extreme. But
in a testament to her patience and innate ability to see the bigger
picture, she ruthlessly strangled her affront. She needed this man
to achieve what her country had achieved in Europe. The future of
her movement depended on it.

"Mr. President," she said smoothly. "I believe you understand
that France is a nationalist country with nationalist policies. I also
believe, just as my colleagues do, that France is a country best
served by a world that is nationalist in its orientation. Having said
this, I would like to confirm directly that under your leadership, the
enterprise that is UCSA will remain a nationalist enterprise?"

"Madame President, if by nationalism, you mean things like
less damn immigrants, no more outsourcing, and no more of this
progressive horseshit that you hear on the news every day, then yes,
the UCSA will be a nationalist enterprise. From hooves to horns.
And so will a re-constituted United States of America when we win
this war we're fighting."

"Your words please me, Mr. President." As the words left her
mouth, she leaned into the table and clasp her elegantly manicured
hands in front of her. "But perhaps more importantly, I *believe* you
when I hear you say these words. It is for this reason that my government and I are prepared to issue orders that will see the French

Air Force and various units from our special operations command begin to arrive in your country. We are ready to help you counter the liberal threat that lies to your north. France and her armed forces are prepared to help you purge this insidious disease that has infected far too much of our world."

On hearing the woman's pronouncement, Mitchell Spector's massive shoulders released the tension they had been carrying. He did not exhale in relief, however. He knew enough about diplomacy that he could get away with uttering crass words like 'horseshit' and playing the rube, but the card he could not play was that of weakness. To physically exhibit the relief that was now coursing through his body would have been to show how desperate he was to get the French to throw in with him.

Despite the odds, he had done it. He had deposed of that sly son of bitch Cameron, he had ruthlessly consolidated power, and now he had won over the French. That the UCSA would grow stronger again was now inevitable as was its victory over the Blues.

And when Blues had been put in their place and the United States of America once again dominated the continent, he would turn his attention to the little outfit that was CANZUK and he would make that gang of middling and meddling countries pay for what they had done.

Perhaps if they said the right things and made the right commitments, the UK, Australia and the New Zealanders could be let off with a milder form of retribution. Those countries could still have useful roles in the new world order that was to come.

The Canadians on the other hand - their role would be to become an example for the rest of the world. Someone had to be made to suffer for his country's humiliation. Someone had to demonstrate what the cost was for crossing the United Constitutional States of America. Canada would pay for what it had done. It would pay dearly.

_____

Cayenne, French Guiana

The café, which was on the edge of the city's unremarkable downtown, had a European feel to it and received a steady stream of wealthy locals and mostly white French-speaking tourists. When it became busy and the collection of people and voices began to feel cosmopolitan, it almost felt like she could be in a café in the south of France or even old Montreal. It was in this milieu that Josee would tuck herself into a corner and alternate between people-watching and writing notes to the movement that she was still helping to guide.

Though the developments that had taken place months before had been a setback for her personally, it had always been the case that others in the movement could lead. From here, or from wherever the DGSE wanted to put her, she could continue to contribute to the philosophies and overall strategy of the movement that had become her life's work.

And who knew? Her father and the mainstream separatist movement he led had at least as much political support to break up Canada as the separatists had back in '95. With time and perseverance, perhaps Josee could once again set foot in her country and breathe in the cool, rich air of her home.

Her reminiscing came to a regretful end as someone interrupted the mid-morning sunshine streaming underneath the lip of the café's cabana overhang. Looking up, she looked into the face of one of the establishment's servers.

It was Nadine. Tall and athletically built, the woman's light brown hair matched the hue of her sun-kissed skin perfectly. Josee had spoken with the young woman briefly on a few occasions and had come to learn that she was a university dropout who had arrived from Toulon only a few weeks before Josee had been spirited here by France's intelligence service.

The city was crawling with young people like the svelte nymph standing in front of her. They were cut from one of two different pieces of cloth. They were trying to find themselves or, as Josee suspected in the case of Nadine, they were running from something or someone.

"Hi, Simone," said the younger woman in a dialect that confirmed she was most certainly from the south of France.

As part of the agreement to let her come to this establishment, Josee had promised the head of her local security detail that she would not talk to anyone, but with Nadine and a few of the other ex-pat staff, she had broken this promise. She could see no harm in it.

"A good morning to you, Nadine. Working again, I see," Josee said.

"You know how it is. Bills to pay and all that," the younger woman said as she folded her arms across her chest. "Hey, do you have a second?"

"It depends. Some things I'm prepared to discuss and others not," Josee said with a friendly smile that signaled the other woman could proceed.

"It's about a boy," Nadine said quickly as though she had been waiting some time to get the words out into the open.

"Ah, men. Then, yes, that's an area to which I would be willing to listen. Have a seat," Josee said, gesturing to the seat across from her.

"Thanks a bunch. I've talked to all my girlfriends, but they're back home and they just don't understand what it's like over here. You live here and, if I had to guess, you have more life experience than all of my friends put together, so I thought you might be able to help."

"Wait, did you just call me old?" Josee said in a tone of faux sternness.

The waitress's face took on a look of panic. "Wait. No! That's not what I meant. I mean, yes, I think you're a bit older than me, but the way you carry yourself. The way you take in the room, there's something deep going on behind those amazing green eyes of yours."

Josee's face softened. "Okay, that sounds much better than being old. How can I help?"

Hearing the offer of assistance, the younger woman's face beamed. "That's great. Give me a second. I have to let my manager know I'm taking my break."

With that, the young woman bounced to her feet, and Josee watched her as she headed back to the coffee bar and had a quick word with an older black woman that Josee had seen in the café on all of her previous visits.

When Nadine came back to the table, she was carrying something wrapped in white serving linen. Still wearing a smile, the server sat down and gently placed the wrapped object on the table.

One of Josee's eyebrows rose questioningly as she looked at whatever the other woman had placed in front of her.

"Not to worry," the server said, pointing to the covered item. "It's the crux of my problem. Would you like me to show you what it is?"

As she listened to the words coming out of the younger woman's mouth, an alarm in Josee's brain went off like a cannon.

"What happened to your accent?" said Josee with a hint of urgency in her voice.

Nadine, the fetching young woman from the south of France, stopped smiling. Casually, she reached forward and placed her right hand underneath the linen, while her opposite hand adjusted the fabric so that Josee could see the first inch of what looked to be a jet-black cylinder.

"Josee Labelle," the waitress said, "the Airborne Regiment and Canada send their regards."

She did not hear any of the bullets that entered her chest. But she felt them. Unimaginable pain radiated through her body as bullets from the hidden weapon tore into her. As her heart pounded and she struggled desperately to draw air into her lungs, Josee watched the sandy-haired woman casually stand up. Nadine, or whoever the woman was, silently turned and walked in the direction of the kitchen.

As the assassin disappeared from Josee's field of vision, the café manager arrived at her table with a confused look on her face. On seeing her condition, the woman's confusion instantly flipped to panic. As her vision began to darken, Josee did not make any attempt to try and communicate with the now hysterical woman. Instead, in the time she had, her thoughts turned to Quebec, its wonderful people, its sacred language, its endless beauty. That she would never get to see her home again, nor help in its efforts to achieve freedom filled her with a sadness that easily overwhelmed the pain.

As blackness began to overtake her, she took solace in the notion that her efforts had given birth to something important. Something bigger than her. Something that would carry on and grow even in her absence. Some day, she knew her beloved Quebec would be free. Those who remained, those true patriots who loved their country as much as she did. They would not be denied.

———

Ottawa

As the convoy of vehicles drove along Ottawa's Rideau Canal on another spectacular mid-summer day, Merielle silently stared out the window, watching people of all kinds walk, run, and bike along the UNESCO-designated world heritage site. It was as comforting a sight as one could imagine.

Her phone vibrated. Looking at the display, she recognized the number. With her chief of staff the only other person in the black armored SUV, she took the call and placed the phone to her ear.

"It's been done," said a male voice.

"Good. And our asset?"

"She's safe and on her way home."

"Also, good."

"Will follow up Colonel Larocque and let him know?"

"I will."

"And what of our other project in France?" Merielle asked.

"We continue to make progress," said the voice.

"I'm glad to hear that. Thank you for the call, General Azim."

"My pleasure, Madame Prime Minister."

The End.

Afterword

Dear Reader,

A million thanks to you for reading *Take Whiteman*. It is my first full-length novel and I hope you enjoyed it. Doing anything for the first time is hard and it took me the better part of sixteen months to write and publish this novel. I'm proud of it.

One thing that is critical to authors are reviews and this is perhaps more true for new authors. I would love for you to leave a review of my story where ever you purchased my book. All feedback is welcome and greatly appreciated. If you don't want to leave a review but still want to provide feedback, write to me at: raf@raflannagan.ca

Again, thank you for reading my story. The second installment of the CANZUK at War series, Red Blue Storm was released July 2023. It can be found on Amazon.

Want more of Ryan Flannagan's Writing?

Following the well-trodden path of authors who've come before me, I have a few ways you can stay in touch with me so you can be the first to hear about upcoming writing projects.

- **Option One:** Sign up for my newsletter directly. My newsletter will go out every six to eight weeks and will feature news and events that inform/inspire my writing, my own blogging insights, and of course updates on my writing.

- **Option Two:** Visit my website at: http://raflannagan.ca. On my author page, you'll find info on my other books, blog posts and previous editions of my newsletters. If you peruse what's there, you'll find out what I'm working on and you'll get a good feel of who I am.

Want to connect with Ryan directly?

Don't want to join my newsletter but would still like to connect with me? As a budding author, I would love to hear from you regardless of the reasons. Rest assured, should you write, you will hear back from me directly. I can be reached at: raf@raflannagan.ca

Copyright

Cover design by Ares Jun: aresjun@gmail.com

Special thanks to my editor: Stephen England

Special thanks to my beta readers: Bob Flannagan, Karen Flannagan, Craig Flannagan, Tara Richmyre, Lyndsey Ellis-Holloway.

---

1. https://en.wikipedia.org/wiki/October_Crisis

Other Works

Caribbean Payback, the *CANZUK at War* series, Book 0.5

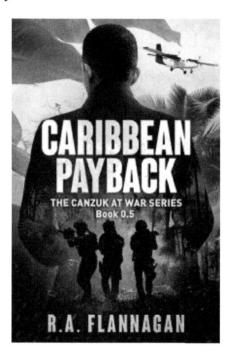

A UN peacekeeping mission has turned into tragedy. Peacekeepers are dead, a soldier is now a hostage, and a country is looking for answers.

Special forces and intelligence operatives are given the task of settling the score in a country where corruption and chaos are a way of life. The best of Canada's military and intelligence services converge in a race against time and hidden agendas to save one of their own and to repair a country's honor.

Politics, espionage, and military action drive this standalone story, which sets the stage for the CANZUK at War universe and the action-packed near future full-length novel, Take Whiteman.

Fans of Clancy's Red Storm Rising, Bond's Red Phoenix or Vortex, Lunnon-Wood's Long Reach, or Greaney's Red Metal will enjoy this fast-paced, action-packed short story.

Notes/Explanations For Readers

List of Faction States – US Civil War II

UCSA – The Red Faction	FAS – The Blue Faction	The Neutrals
- Alabama		
- Alaska		
- Arkansas		
- Arizona	- Connecticut	
- Florida	- Delaware	
- Georgia	- Illinois	
- Idaho	- Maryland	- California
- Indiana	- Mass.	- Colorado
- Iowa	- Michigan	- Missouri
- Kansas	- Minnesota	- Montana
- Kentucky	- New Hamp.	- New Mex.
- Louisiana	- New Jersey	- Nevada
- Maine	- New York	- North Dakota
- Mississippi	- Ohio	- South Dakota
- Nebraska	- Oregon	- Wyoming
- North Car.	- Penn.	- Hawaii
- Oklahoma	- Rhode Is.	- Wash, D.C.
- South Car.	- Washington	
- Tennessee	- Wisconsin	
- Texas	- Vermont	
- West Virg.		
- Virginia		
- Utah		

Battlefield Asset Management system or BAM: This is a critical piece of command and control kit used by CANZUK forces. It includes an earbud, a wrist unit (think an oversized Apple Watch), body and helmet cams, and a mouthguard. Pressing specific parts of the mouthguard enables the user to issue verbal commands to a near-AI system that seamlessly connects soldiers with other individual soldiers or units (e.g., a platoon, company).

Printed in Great Britain
by Amazon

28265996R00260